T0131655

The
Wish
Child

ALSO BY CATHERINE CHIDGEY

In a Fishbone Church
The Strength of the Sun
The Transformation

The
Wish
Child

A Novel

Catherine Chidgey

COUNTERPOINT
California

The Wish Child

Library of Congress Cataloging-in-Publication Data
Names: Chidgey, Catherine, 1970– author.
Title: The wish child / by Catherine Chidgey.
Description: First Counterpoint hardcover edition. | Berkeley,
California : Counterpoint, 2018. | Includes bibliographical references.
Identifiers: LCCN 2018023438 | ISBN 9781640090972
Subjects: LCSH: World War, 1939–1945—Children—Germany—
Berlin—Fiction. | New Zealand fiction—21st century.
Classification: LCC PR9639.3.C535 W57 2018 | DDC 823.2
LC record available at https://lccn.loc.gov/2018023438

Paperback ISBN: 978-1-64009-267-9

Jacket design by Donna Cheng

COUNTERPOINT
Los Angeles and San Francisco, CA
www.counterpointpress.com

Printed in the United States of America

to Tracey Slaughter

. . . everything created
Deserves to be annihilated;
Better, then, if nothing began.
—Mephistopheles, Part I Scene III, Goethe's *Faust*

Contents

Puzzles

Let me say that I was not in the world long enough to understand it well, so can give you only impressions, like the shapes left in rock by long-decayed leaves, or the pencil rubbings of doves and skulls that are but flimsy memories of stone. Just these little smudges, these traces of light and shadow, these breaths in and out. They feel like mine.

1995
Near Nuremberg

Sieglinde is shuffling and turning the pieces of paper, releasing the scent of old typewriter ribbons and pencil sharpenings, rubber stamps and vinyl chairs, ink pads, carbon paper. There are shelves of destroyed documents, rooms of them, ripped apart in the last frantic days of the GDR and crammed into sacks. Some are simple to reconstruct, torn only in two or four, and you can read whole sentences, even paragraphs – but others are in pieces no bigger than postage stamps and bear mere fragments of words. There is no telling what will emerge from the sacks; no way of predicting whose life she will pull out in tatters. One day it's a university student who told a joke about Honecker; the next it's a housewife whose parcels sent from friends in the West betrayed clear capitalist leanings: aluminium foil, instant pudding. There's a train driver who refused to let a camera be pointed from his apartment towards his neighbour's, and so was monitored for years himself. A mother who let her son grow his hair long and wear jeans to school. A teenager who covered her bedroom walls with pictures of Michael Jackson. The intercepted letters are the easiest to put back together, the phrases well-worn, expected: *I miss you. I love you. I wish I could see you.* Sieglinde spends a week reconstructing a drawing of someone's apartment – it's a detailed floor plan, viewed as if from above, as if the roof has been cut away to let you see into every room at once. It shows all the furniture down to the last footstool, and all the electrical fittings, and the measurements of every wall. There is even a newspaper on a coffee table and a cat asleep on an armchair; everything is there but the people. She finds photographs in the sacks, too: Polaroids of rumpled sheets, books in a bookcase, dishes left to soak in a kitchen sink – a record of the ordinary, so that after a search it could all be put back in the right place and nobody would notice a thing. Sometimes she pauses over these small domestic scenes, tracing with a finger the crinkles in lace curtains tied into bunches, the eddy of an unmade bed.

She has developed her own system, as all the puzzlers have. She lifts the scraps from the bags as gently as possible to preserve the original strata, sorting them according to size, paper colour, texture, weight, as well as typeface or handwriting, before fitting ragged edge to ragged edge to restore the destroyed file. It can take days to complete a single page, and always there are pieces she cannot home, holes she cannot fill. Sixteen thousand sacks, six hundred million scraps of paper – it will take centuries to finish – but she trains herself to focus only on the snippets in front of her, to find the patterns, the matches. She knows she is running out of time; soon she will retire, and she will return to her old life in Berlin, give notice to the student who is subletting her apartment. She pushes herself to work as quickly as possible, restoring the stories of ordinary people, watching the puzzles decipher themselves beneath her hands. And always, in the back of her mind, the puzzle that has never left her: Erich Kröning. She searches for him in every file, her heart turning over when she thinks she sees his name – though it is never the right Erich, never her Erich; of course not. I'm not telling that sort of story; I can't put everything back together.

But I am getting ahead of myself.

Strength Through Joy

I don't know whether the little bones,
Rinsed by the sea, will tangle together,
Or whether, wrapped in clouds,
They will reach for music and   .

I know that   without fragrance,
Like   fingers stiff in the joints,
Offer no   magic
For which the living call in sleep.

July 1939
Near Leipzig

The Krönings rose earlier than usual, though everything was already in order: the pathways were swept, flowers cut and arranged, windows polished until the glass all but disappeared. In the fields the wheat grew straight and golden and in the orchard the bees were waking in their hives. The living-room curtains shifted a little of their own accord – was a window loose? Was there a draught? Emilie and her husband Christoph sat in each chair in turn and pretended to be guests, looking at their home through outside eyes. The sun was not yet up, the rooster only just beginning to crow, but they suspected it would be a stifling day. It was sensible to be prepared for the visit, to allow themselves time to check that nothing was out of place. Perhaps they had not noticed that the fringe of a carpet was tangled, or that the blessing hung askew; perhaps a clock needed winding or a cushion punching back into shape – but no, all was correct: flowers in the vases, wheat in the fields, bees in the hives and *Mein Kampf* on the shelf.

When they were satisfied with the house, the Krönings began to prepare themselves. Emilie sat at her mirror and parted and braided her pale blond hair, pinning it into place so it would not move. She could feel her scalp and the fine skin at her temples pulling, but the sensation was quite bearable. She was proud of her hair; it hung to the small of her back when she brushed it out, and the strands of her braids were as thick as thumbs.

'I'll give you my skin if you give me your hair,' her sister Uschi used to say when they shared a bedroom.

'I'll give you my eyes if you give me your ankles,' Emilie would reply.

She pinched a little blood into her cheeks now and smoothed her church dress over her slim hips. You really could not tell she was a mother. 'Thank you for coming,' she said to her reflection. 'Thank you for considering our case.' *You-you, you,* the turtle dove called from the forest. *You-you, you.* The sound drifted to Emilie's window and seemed to float there in the indistinct early morning. The day had not yet decided what it would become.

She watched Christoph splash his razor in the water. He paused to wipe steam from the mirror – he kept disappearing – and then he held taut the skin of his throat. He was a tall, sinewy man; he had to crouch to see himself. He frowned away a lock of sandy hair that fell forward into his eyes, giving Emilie a small smile when he noticed her looking at him. The sound of the blade against his flesh called to Emilie's mind the first rasp of fire burning off a spent crop. In a way she regretted those blazes – a certain melancholy rose in her as she watched the remains of a harvest begin to crumple and vanish – but unless you cleared away waste matter there could be no new growth, and any small sentiment always passed once the flames had burst and spread. Christoph smoothed his hair down with water, flattening the curls at his brow. The little scar above his eye was pale in the early light, almost invisible, though as summer wore on and his skin turned browner it would show itself more. His father had been teaching him how to use the scythe and Christoph had stepped too close. His mother still fussed over it: if it had been half a centimetre lower . . . Sometimes Emilie touched it with her long, cool fingers and said the same thing.

At breakfast the Krönings sliced open their rolls and spread them with butter and jam while their wedding clock tutted at them from the far wall. Today the little woman had swung out from the clock's insides to tell them that rain was on the way, but it didn't feel like it. The oilcloth table-cover caught the pale light from the window to the north and lay cool beneath their wrists. They took measured bites, neither hurrying nor dawdling. The guest was not getting into Leipzig until after ten. There was plenty of time.

'Is this the last of Uschi's jam?' said Christoph.

'Of the cherry, yes,' said Emilie. 'There's one more apricot.'

'The apricot is very good too,' said Christoph. 'Though I prefer the cherry.'

The guest arrives just as the wedding clock strikes eleven: a tall, well-groomed man with dark hair and a calm voice. He looks like the kind of man who always knows what to say. He looks like the kind of man who would take your hand if you were lost and make sure you got home safely. He wears an expensive black suit instead of a uniform, but his Party badge glitters on his lapel. Christoph conducts him to the chair they have deemed the most suitable and Emilie lifts the cover from the bee-sting cake.

'I'm afraid I have very little time,' the guest begins, but Emilie is already reaching for the knife.

'It's made with our own honey,' she says. 'My husband will show you the hives later. His father carved them himself

– they're the traditional kind, in the shape of people.' She hands him a plate and an embroidered serviette. 'And you must see our copse of larches – Christoph planted them in 1933, to celebrate the election. In autumn they're quite something.'

They pause to eat their slices of cake, and for a moment it seems the guest might choke on a sliver of almond – but he gives a little cough and everything is fine.

'We can, of course, show you the nursery,' says Emilie. 'If you think it would help.'

'Thank you,' says the guest. 'That won't be necessary.'

'Yes, of course,' says Emilie.

'We'd like the matter dealt with swiftly,' says Christoph. 'To prevent further suffering.'

The guest nods – he is a kind man, a fair man.

'Thank you for coming,' says Emilie as they see him off. 'Thank you for considering our case.'

Yes, he is kind and fair; after he has gone, the Krönings agree that this is so. And then they return to their work.

September 1939
Berlin

But this is where I'll start: some weeks later, when the absurd man with the absurd moustache calls off the Peace Rally so he can send his troops into Poland.

The war begins punctually and according to plan. Sieglinde Heilmann, six years of age, sits with her parents and brothers and listens as the voice from the radio crackles through their Berlin apartment, a fire taking hold of its fuel.

I see her father Gottlieb pinching the antenna between his thumb and forefinger and hunting the signal: reception can be poor in their living room, which seems unjust, he says, given that they are in Charlottenburg, which is a respectable part of town, and on the uppermost storey, what's more – but no matter, no matter, one mustn't make a fuss. When he thinks he catches the broadcast he freezes, though he looks so uncomfortable, his narrow frame all angles and corners, even his long face motionless. Sieglinde's mother Brigitte points to the right, but he moves too far over and loses the signal again.

'Back a bit, Vati!' Sieglinde tells him, and with a little perseverance he manages to tune in, moving the wire through the air until the Führer reaches them undistorted.

Jürgen, who is almost five, is building houses with his wooden blocks. Before they can fall he knocks them down and they clatter against the parquet – 'On the carpet, Jürgen! The neighbours!' – and Kurt, who is just a baby, murmurs in his cradle.

Sieglinde looks out the window and says, 'But where is the enemy?'

Above the sofa the Führer stares out from his portrait, frowning a little, straining to make sense of himself. Vati repositions a leg.

'Mutti, where are they?' says Sieglinde.

My whole life has been nothing but one long struggle for my people, says the radio. *Just as I myself stand ever ready to lay down my liver for my people and for Germany – anyone can take it from me – so I demand the same of everyone else . . .*

'His liver?' says Mutti. 'Our livers?'

'His life,' hisses Vati, who has heard the speech earlier that day, on the loudspeakers at work.

'That must be it. Life. It did sound like liver, though. But why would the Führer want us to lay down our livers?'

Jürgen builds and destroys another house, and another, and Sieglinde comes away from the window and settles back on the sofa with Mutti, and the baby sighs and sleeps, and Vati stands motionless, thin hands raised like a holy man, fingers alive with blessings, and I watch them, these ordinary people, the Führer's face above them and his voice off to one side, quite the ventriloquist, and if I could have spoken I suspect they would have heard only static, rain, tumbling blocks, the sound of blank air. And when there is an air-raid alarm that same evening they file down to their cellar, though nobody really knows why: there are no planes to be seen or heard. When they emerge, everything is just as it was.

★

15

She is right, though, the little girl: if Germany is at war with Poland, where are the Polish? And then, where are the French and the English? Not on the trams or buses, not reclining in wicker beach chairs at the Müggelsee, not in the cinemas or the vaudeville halls. Day after day Berliners watch the sky and wait for the war to show itself, and night after night they observe the blackout rules. Even the famous neon signs are snuffed out: the fizzing glass of Deinhard Sekt; the Sarotti chocolate Moor in his little turban. And yet – people go sailing on the Wannsee, and picnic in the Tiergarten, and sunbathe on the lawns at Friedrichshain. Trains run, and clocks strike, and dogs cock their legs. Men drink beer and women try on gloves and children visit the zoo and hear the monkeys screeching, and watch the elephants plucking up hay with their trunks, and pet the lion cubs and feed the bear cubs, who drink milk from bottles, just like proper babies, and the orangutan reaches his arms through his cage, wanting something, and looks for all the world like the drawings of greedy men in the children's schoolbooks. And yes, the schools open again, and the children learn to sit, be silent, obey; they learn to copy and repeat, to divide and subtract, to calculate solutions. There is nothing to fear. The sandbags stacked against the cellar windows are just a precaution. The sky is quite empty.

'All is well,' Vati tells Sieglinde, pointing to the newspaper headlines that turn the fingertips black, every day a plague of good news. 'You see? We are happy and secure. There is plenty of food. We cannot be bombed.'

A crow watches from the window ledge as Sieglinde helps Mutti put the kitchen to rights. She does not like its black stare, the way it runs its eye up and down the glass as if searching for a way in. She opens the window and the bird vanishes into the courtyard; the dark, empty space at the heart of their building and every building like it in Berlin. She does not linger at the ledge. There is a house rule – Sieglinde knows it is recorded in the caretaker's register, along with the rules about swearing and spitting, and the conducting of loud conversations in the stairwell – that forbids anybody from staring into anybody else's apartment. Everyone pretends that everyone else's business – and therefore their own – is private.

Sometimes, as a treat, Vati takes Sieglinde out on her own for cake. (Is this a father? Is this, is this? I know nothing of such things.) They go to Café Kranzler on the Ku'damm, where they sit beneath the striped awning and watch the ladies pass by in their smart hats, or to Haus Vaterland on Potsdamer Platz, with its silver palm fronds in the ballroom and its thunderstorms that strike on the hour. Vati lets her try his coffee and she takes a sip as if she were a grown-up, even though she does not like the taste and has to make it go away with a big bite of Sachertorte. Vati smiles at her then from behind his little round spectacles, and his grey eyes make her feel quiet inside. He is kinder than any of her friends' fathers, and has fine brown hair that is never untidy, unlike her own, and clever hands that can cut from paper any shape you can imagine. As they make their way home he points out interesting things to her: the Prometheus fountain on Hardenbergstrasse; the Palace balcony – which is looking rather shabby – where the Kaiser said *Today we are all German brothers, and only German brothers*. When they come to their building in Kantstrasse he holds the street door open for her like a gentleman, and then he takes her arm and leads her back into their courtyard, and no matter how fine the day it is always a cave, a well, a place of shadows too deep for the sun, where in winter the snow does not melt. Her good shoes click against the chill flagstones, and banks of unlit windows rise up around her. They pass the screens that hide the dustbins, and the rails where carpets are hung and beaten, and the sandpit with its falling castles. Last spring Sieglinde planted marigolds in the marshy soil by the entrance to their wing, but they never took.

The Heilmanns are lucky, says Vati, to live up on the fourth floor, where there is plenty of air and light, and nobody above to disturb their quiet household. It is true that the marble stairs stop at the first floor, giving way to wood, and it is true that the building has no elevator, but the Heilmanns value their distance from the pushy street, from the stubbed-out cigarettes and the jangling bicycles and the news vendors who yell as you walk by, the spiky umbrellas and the little dogs underfoot, the boys selling badges you must be seen to wear, the amputees from the last war with their pinned-up trouser legs and their empty sleeves. And the marching! says Mutti. One group or another is always trooping past, which rattles her nerves: the National Socialist League of German Switchboard Operators; the Reich Association of German Rabbit Breeders. There's nothing wrong with being proud of your job, says Vati, but he does agree they are fortunate to be living well above eye level. They must refrain from remarking on their good fortune to their neighbours, however – it would be a sign of very poor breeding – and they must be mindful of the family one storey beneath them, taking care to wear their house-shoes and to tread softly, to lift their dining chairs rather than dragging them, which is better for the parquet and the carpets, after all, and never to be so thoughtless as to drop a knife, a jar of peas, a weighty book – the Bible; *Mein Kampf.* A cautious life, says Vati: that is the thing.

I see them visiting the Schuttmanns (second floor, front building) one Sunday afternoon. The Heilmanns have become friendly with them over recent months; Herr Schuttmann is also a Party member and wields some local influence, it is believed.

'But more than that,' says Vati, 'they're just our sort of people.'

And so they are. They have three young children and are expecting a fourth; they make a point of using the proper German greeting rather than a lazy *good day*; and they even took the same cruise to Madeira and Italy the previous year. Sieglinde wishes she could have gone – she and Jürgen stayed behind with their aunt – but Mutti sent her postcards, and Vati brought her back a bracelet with the name of the ship spelled out in naval flags, and a little swastika one at the end.

'How pleasant it would have been had we known you better then,' says Frau Schuttmann. 'We could have shared a table, and played quoits.'

'We did see you on board, of course,' says Vati, 'but one doesn't like to intrude.'

'No, quite right,' says Herr Schuttmann. 'We saw you too, but as you point out . . .'

There is a pause in the conversation, and above them the ceiling lamp trembles. The Schuttmanns do not seem to register the movement, nor the sound of footsteps overhead, but Mutti stares up at the swaying globe for a good long minute – thinking of their cruise, perhaps; of the motion of the ship as they sailed through the English Channel. She told Sieglinde that it flickered by night with luminous dust, as if all the stars had fallen.

'Anyway, all that is over – the cruise liners are to be hospital ships,' says Herr Schuttmann. 'Which is just as it should be, given that we are at war,' he adds, in case anyone should take his comment and make it into something else.

'Yes of course,' says Mutti, but when they return home and Sieglinde asks her if it's true, that the cruise liners are to be used for sick people, she says that Herr Schuttmann must be mistaken. Their ship, she says, their beautiful ship, surrendered to the wounded and the diseased? She remembers stepping on board in Hamburg beneath all the banners strung up as if for a party, and there was a band playing marching songs, the trumpets and trombones flashing in the sun, and the passengers were calling and waving to their friends and family on the dock. When they were about to set sail they threw streamers that spiralled through the air, reaching all the way to the people left behind, and for a moment that was all that held the ship to the land, these flimsy strips of paper. A hospital ship? She had danced on its decks in her green silk as the lifeboats hung high above, and Vati had held a handkerchief in his right hand so as not to spoil her dress; she had bathed in the swimming pool beneath the mural of Neptune in his chariot, and on the dining tables the starched serviettes sailed across the dinner plates, ships of cloth on a clean white sea, and she had eaten black swordfish with fried bananas when they stopped in Madeira, and it did not matter that after a bite or two she decided to wait for the evening meal back on board, which was rissoles with mashed potatoes; the fact remained that she had tried black swordfish in Madeira.

Mutti had never been on an ocean liner before, and it took her some time to adjust to the motion. It was a strange feeling – the sense that the ground was not stable beneath her, that she needed to correct her gait in order to retain her footing when the waves were high. To begin with she wondered whether she had made a mistake, whether she would ever adapt to this new way of moving, in which she had to take so much care not to harm herself. She did not mention it to Vati – the cruise had been his idea, his surprise – but there were moments out on the deck, she tells Sieglinde, when she could see no land in any direction and knew that they were nowhere, that she feared where they were going and where they would end up. She remembers the gulls crying and crying, circling the ship. Some of the passengers fed them, throwing crusts of bread and morsels of cake, even scraps of meat, but Vati said such creatures should not be encouraged, and feeding them upset the natural order of things – before you knew it they would take over, clawing food from the plates, from the very mouths of the passengers – and this was sensible advice, and he was a sensible man, and she trusted that soon they would see land. And she looked about her at the other couples laughing and enjoying themselves, taking photographs of each other smiling so they could remember that they were happy, and she watched them drinking coffee and eating cake in the sun, and filling their mouths with great fresh gusts of air, and bathing in the pool beneath the Neptune mural, and applauding the fireworks that spun and burst and fell into the sea, and she thought: I can do that. I can be like that.

Each morning began with the trumpet call and the flag ceremony, and then there were so many programmed activities that there was no time for idleness or uncertainty. She and Vati rose early for calisthenics on the sports deck, and attended concerts and talks, and listened to a German author reading from her novel – *He had never been able to* stand the chosen sons of Israel. He hardly knew why; it must have lain in his blood – and at German folk music evenings they sang Praise the Rhine, the proud river resting in the lap of vines, and they sang There stands a man, a man as steadfast as an oak, and they sang Be always true and honest till you're in your cold grave.

And when they disembarked at Naples and the beggars thrust out their hands, they said to each other how lucky they were to live in Germany, where everyone was equal, and where everyone had a job, and a home, and the right to a subsidised cruise to places where you could try black swordfish with fried bananas, even if you preferred proper German food. Mutti says she would have liked to dock in England, to see Buckingham Palace and to hear Big Ben telling a different time, to drink tea with a slice of lemon and to marvel at the wax people who looked so real they might begin to speak, but England would not permit their ship entry because then the English would see how well Germany treated her workers. They would hear the enthusiastic German songs, and smell the rissoles, and see the Germans busy with their leisure on the large and sunny decks, and they would realise how poorly off they were to live in a country where people queued without question and you could not buy proper bread.

And if she is not mistaken, she says – no, she is not mistaken – Kurt was made at sea, their little sailor, their stowaway; conjured up in their narrow cabin with its fitted cupboards and its tiny wash-basin, its built-in sofa and its tethered beds, everything just so, everything in its proper place, not a centimetre squandered, and the porthole a blue sun above them.

★

Every few weeks Sieglinde's class visited a factory to learn about all the clever and marvellous things Germany made. The children looked forward to these outings; no sooner had they returned from one than they were asking Fräulein Althaus about the next, but she never told them where it would be.

'It's a surprise, children,' she would say, smiling as she stood in front of the blackboard, the perfect alphabet suspended above her, too high to smudge.

Perhaps they would visit a toy factory, the children said to one another, and they would see boxes of eyes and hands and hair, and stacks of unstuffed skins, and stringless yoyos yet to whirl until they knotted and choked, and puzzles before they were cut apart, and unpainted soldiers missing their medals and their faces. Or maybe they would visit the factory where the special badges and buckles and daggers were made, all the glinting rewards they could earn one day when they were big enough, and they would be allowed to touch them and hold them and maybe even try them on, and pretend they were older children, so long as they gave them back before they returned to school, because things went very badly indeed for liars and thieves. Or perhaps they would visit a stamp factory, where giant sheets of gum-backed paper waited to receive the image of the Führer repeated countless times over, and then a machine full of needles would punch all the holes in between the countless Führers so they could be torn off and stuck to letters. Some of the children thought this would not be a very interesting outing, to see all the Führers printed and punctured, but they did not say so, because everybody knew you did not say such things, not even when you were quite alone.

Their own school was a factory of sorts, too: every day they picked mulberry leaves for the silkworms that filled the classrooms, stripping the bushes bare to feed the white larvae stacked in their shallow trays beneath the windows. The creatures were ravenous, never satisfied, fattening overnight, it seemed, their chewing a rainstorm that accompanied each lesson. When the caterpillars began spinning their white cocoons, the children knew it would not be long before they were taken away and made into parachutes. The teachers told them how important it was to care for the silkworms, making sure that their trays were clean and that they had plenty to eat. This might save a pilot's life, the teachers said.

'Can we visit a parachute factory?' Sieglinde asked Fräulein Althaus, but Fräulein Althaus said such places were not for children, and that they were going to visit a biscuit factory instead, which was a lovely surprise indeed, because biscuits were in short supply these days, and how wonderful to think of a whole factory full of them.

It was just a short ride on the U-Bahn, and they didn't even have to change trains, but when they emerged into daylight again none of the children recognised where they were. It was a different neighbourhood, not their own; a new and different part of town where people made biscuits and toys and daggers. They walked from the station two by two, listening to Fräulein Althaus as they marched along.

'Our biscuits contain only the purest ingredients, children,' she said. 'They are free from any trace of inferior cinnamon or low-grade sugar. Who can tell me what inferior means? Yes, Gisela, that's quite correct, thank you. Now everybody remember the word *inferior*, because it is a useful word. The butter for our biscuits comes from healthy German cows, tended by healthy German farmers. The English eat biscuits made from flour and water, children. Flour and water!

'Here we are. Do you see the factory behind the tall gates, with its tall chimneys? This is where the biscuits are made. Here is Frau Miller to let us in, we cannot glimpse more than her face because the people who make the biscuits must cover themselves up, all except their faces. They cannot allow so much as a single hair to fall into the mixture, a single hair is not very big but imagine if you found one in a biscuit, that would be very disgusting and unacceptable. Perhaps such a thing would be acceptable to the English. Frau Miller is shutting the gates behind us, because not everybody is allowed to come and look at the biscuit factory, that would not be sanitary, so let us say thank you. Thank you, madam, Heil Hitler and good morning, and yes, please do count us as we file past. Now wait here, children, because we must listen to the rules before we can go into the main part of the factory, where the biscuits come from. Do we all hear and understand what is being said? We must put on our special white hats, and the special covers for our shoes that make us look as if we are walking on little clouds. Now we are all alike. We must not touch anything. We must not eat anything. If we need to use the lavatory we must do so now, although we must remove our special hats and our special shoe-covers to do so. Under no circumstances are we to leave the group to explore on our own. I heard someone cough. There is to be no coughing. And I heard someone sneeze. There is to be no sneezing. No touching, no eating, no leaving, no coughing and no sneezing. Heil Hitler!

'Come through, come through. Now I will have to shout, children, because we are in the main part of the factory, where the biscuits come from, and it is very noisy. Normally a woman would not shout. A man who shouts is not a handsome sight, but a shouting woman is even worse.

Her voice grows shrill, and she starts to claw at people, or stab at them with hairpins – but this is different. This is an exception. Can you all hear me? It may be wise to hold the hand of a friend, for safety reasons. There are many pieces of machinery and equipment, as you can see – vats of flour and sugar, mixing bowls as big as bathtubs, blades that cut the butter, iron arms that hook and scrape – and I imagine it would be quite easy for a child to become caught up in this machinery and turned into biscuits. Therefore we must remember the rules. A stray braid, a flapping cardigan, a finger snatching a taste – you can appreciate where all this leads. Look at the workers in their clean white uniforms. They make thousands of biscuits per day here, children, isn't that wonderful? We are standing in one of the world's foremost biscuit factories. What does foremost mean? Foremost? Well done, Hannes, thank you, yes. We must learn the word *foremost* because it is an important word. We can be very proud of our biscuits, children, all our biscuit makers are the same and so are all the biscuits, each one just as it should be, except for the broken ones that cannot be sold, because even if they taste like the others, they are defective. It is said that the Führer enjoys a Butterkeks with his evening cup of tea – the Führer does not take any alcohol – and so every year, on his birthday, the factory sends him a one-kilo assortment, which he enjoys very much, and finds most fortifying, and in this way our biscuits are helping us to defeat the English, who have never produced a biscuit of note.'

October 1940
Near Leipzig

Erich Kröning was a quiet child, hiding behind his mother if strangers came to the farm trying to buy fruit or eggs or honey, and hiding from her sometimes, too: she would find him under his bed, drawing shapes in the dust and talking to himself in his own language, or out in the stable, murmuring to their horse Ronja. If she asked whether he was hungry, he would nod or shake his head; if she asked whether he was tired, he would simply continue playing, or lie down on the sofa and close his eyes. He was as pretty as a doll, with a cloud of downy yellow hair, and when Emilie took him into the village in the wagon he watched the sky passing above him, his blue eyes moving over its blueness as if searching for something.

At the market other mothers stopped to admire him. 'Is he your first?' they asked. 'The first is always special.' They gave him plump cherries and slices of cheese to eat, stroked his cheeks and his hair as he shied from their touch.

When his grandmother visited on Sundays after church, though, he was a different boy. My heart is clear and pure, she told him. I sing and cannot cry. Oma Kröning was a small, soft woman who dressed in black and wore her dove-grey hair in a knot at the nape of her neck. She gathered him onto her lap and taught him old songs about mermen who took human brides, and roses that fell from the sky like snow and wine that fell like rain, and nightingales and crows that spoke as clearly as you or I, and wanderers far from home. At first he tried to sing along with his wrong words, but soon he learned the proper ones, and if Oma Kröning stopped in the middle of a line and looked at him, her eyebrows raised, he would complete it, putting birds in their trees and fish in their streams, roses in their valleys and wanderers in their forests.

'He is a perfect child,' she said. 'Just perfect. Will there be, one day, perhaps, a second, or . . . ?'

Nobody completed that line.

On his birthday, Emilie woke Erich at seven o'clock. His face was still dull with sleep as she lifted him from his bed, and he stared at her as if he knew neither her name nor his own. She caught the odour of urine rising from the boy and found herself wishing – as she wished every day – that time would quicken, that soon he would be able to control himself overnight. Still, she reminded herself, it could be worse. It could be far, far worse. *You-you, you,* called the dove from the forest.

Erich was turning five – the age when colours and sensations, aromas and tastes and sounds begin to knot into permanent memories: the sour fur of a chewed and eyeless toy, or the patter from a watering can on fusty soil, or the hardness of a little wooden stool in a white and clattering room. And who can tell why certain episodes take hold while others are lost to the sky as smoke? And why some are retained only in part; fragmentary joys, half-formed horrors?

'Slowly, Schatz,' said Emilie over breakfast – Erich always bolted his food, which was dreadful for the digestion.

He pushed his new wooden snake across the table, its joints clicking as it curled its way about the milk jug.

'What does the snake say?' asked Emilie.

'Hissssssssssssss,' said Erich and Christoph.

After breakfast Emilie washed Erich's face and combed his hair flat with water. He was her summer boy, as blond as wheat, sky-eyed. You couldn't deny that the race was getting better looking; you had only to look at the children. He slipped his little warm hand into hers, and with the other he trailed the wooden snake across the floor. Click. Click.

He was tired by mid-afternoon, and when Tante Uschi and Oma Kröning arrived he would not stop crying. He kicked his feet, knocked over his milk. They wondered if he ever would settle; he gazed at them as if he saw monsters.

'What's wrong with him?' said Emilie.

'What did the nurse say?' said Oma Kröning.

'To give it time,' said Emilie.

'There's nothing wrong with him,' said her sister, who was not married and had no children and could not know. 'They cry from time to time, and sometimes for no good reason. It's quite normal.'

'You're right,' Emilie agreed, and they pulled faces at him, and shook a bear at him, and spoke made-up words that had no meaning. Look, she said, look at Mama, trying to distract him from his sorrow the way that mothers do, changing her voice so that it was no longer her own, making spiders and wolves of her hands. *Bumpety bump, rider*, she sang as he struggled on her lap. *If he falls, he cries out*. She gave him one of her Leipzig larks to eat, which were not birds but little bird-sized cakes filled with jam to suggest plump hearts. Then, after she had mopped up the milk and wiped clean the gift from Tante Uschi – a book of animals – she hugged him close and whispered, 'You are the gift. You, you.' But those who whisper tell lies.

I watch Erich with his new book, each page cut into three. He makes a bear with a lion's body and the legs of a dog; he joins an elephant's head to a duck with goat's hooves. It seems there are endless combinations, a whole menagerie of the fake, all those turned away from the ark and left to face the flood. It is troubling to me, this severing and grafting. I do not blame the boy because he does not understand that the creatures are impossible, and that even if such a specimen were to be produced it could not survive; it would be too deformed, too far from normal. The adults, though, watch him turning the pages with his little fingers, and they watch him smiling because they smile, and laughing because they laugh, and nobody finds the book – nor even the idea of the book – in the least bit troublesome.

Later Emilie takes Erich to his bedroom and tucks him in, perhaps a little too tightly; he struggles, but she strokes his head and tells him to sleep, and pulls up the green satin quilt that is cool to the touch and swishes like Christoph's scythe cutting the wheat. She repeats his name to him – *Erich, Erich* – and his blue eyes watch and watch her, and do not close. She switches on the lamp beside his bed; its transparent shade is patterned with birds, and after a moment, when the bulb is hot, it starts to turn.

I watch the shadow birds stealing around the walls, wavy when they pass over the curtains, bent in two at the corners of the room.

'Shh,' says Emilie, 'shhhhh,' her voice as soft as the wind in the pines.

Outside the bees grumble in their hives; something has changed.

November 1940
Berlin

At the theatre there is standing room only for the Führer's speech. The women hand over their furs to the coat-check girl, who cannot, it seems, trouble herself to smile, and may not even be German. They find their seats, which are ten rows back from the stage and afford an acceptable view of the lectern, until a vast individual with blond braids piled high on her head takes her place in front of them. It is difficult to see past the bulging hair, which the women agree must be false. Such persons need to acquaint themselves with mirrors, they remark, but they refuse to let her ruin their evening. Through their opera glasses they take in the one-man show, the feverish aria tumbling from the stage: swords and blood, blood and earth, betrayal and sacrifice, disguise, salvation: all the traditional and tragic themes. And how the women applaud! How they cheer.

FRAU MILLER: Look at his words – they're caught in the lights; they're falling like rain.

FRAU MÜLLER: If we were further forward they'd be falling on us.

FRAU MILLER: I secured the best seats I could, Frau Müller. We're lucky to be here at all. You didn't see the queue.

FRAU MÜLLER: Still, if you'd gone a little earlier . . .
FRAU MILLER: As I have explained, Gabi was sitting for
                her portrait that morning. You cannot
                dance at two weddings, you know.
FRAU MÜLLER: Of course not, of course not. How did it
                come out?
FRAU MILLER: As a portrait, it's excellent – you can make
                out every whisker, and she's holding
                her tail just so – but unfortunately he
                couldn't capture her saluting.
FRAU MÜLLER: Oh that is a shame. And after all your
                training . . .
FRAU MILLER: I know. I kept saying Heil Hitler, and he
                kept clicking, but every time she raised
                her paw it was either too early or too
                late.

Führer Weather

When I was still a child I took up the lyre –
For early I forgot my childhood games;
I   only in the silent land of the   ,
            from the raucous throng of sisters.
And even if my song clanged shrill and off-key
As a   that had split in two,
Thudding dully, sounding its discordant chime:
Still I knew what   of   meant.

December 1940
Berlin

Time spins blue and gold, blue and green; it is spring and autumn; it is morning and dusk; it is then and it is now and it happens over and again and all at once.

'Can you breathe?' says Vati, tightening the strap.

We are elephants, we are aardvarks, we are glass-eyed flies. Our hands we clasp, our heads we sink, and of Adolf Hitler we think.

'Yes,' nods Sieglinde.

At night her mask waits at the foot of her bed, and she listens for the siren and thinks of a golden comb slipping through lengths of golden hair. The poem comes to her as she lies listening – but it is not a poem, Fräulein Althaus has told them, it is a folk song, a traditional old German song written by nobody. Still, the children do not sing it, this old siren song, but recite the lines in unison, and at night they come to Sieglinde as she waits for the bombs to flash above her, jewels glimpsed from a little boat at the river's deadly bend. O, dark water.

'As soon as we hear the siren, we must wake up straight away,' says Vati. 'We must jump from our beds and grab our masks and our suitcases and hurry – calmly hurry – to the cellar.'

I cannot determine the reason that I am so sad at heart.

They do jump from their beds. They do grab their masks, and their little cases that stand packed and ready as if for a holiday, and they do hurry down to the cellar. On the second floor the Metzgers are just emerging from their apartment, Herr Metzger in his thick black coat that smells of camphor, and his wife in all her furs, sable, chinchilla, mink, three pelts thick about her shoulders. Jewels adorn her wrists and fingers, earlobes and throat – does she sleep in them? Do they dig into her dreams? Herr Metzger helps her descend the stairs, slowing everybody down, and Herr Schneck, the caretaker and house warden, shouts, 'Quickly, please! This is not a drill! Masks on! One two, zackzack!'

Down they go, down and down, and it is even colder than in their cold apartments. Beneath the earth they feel the bombs: a monster in the distance, stamping its feet.

'Please keep in mind that all talking is forbidden,' says Schneck.

'How long must we stay here?' asks Frau Metzger.

'No talking,' says Schneck.

'Only my arthritis . . .'

'Silence!' says Schneck.

'But Mutti, *he's* talking,' says Sieglinde.

Schneck turns to her. 'I have to talk in order to tell everyone else not to talk,' he says.

'Quite right,' whispers Herr Schuttmann.

'Shh!' says Schneck.

'I wasn't talking, I was whispering,' says Herr Schutt-mann.

'And now you're talking!'

'I am merely trying to explain, Herr Schneck,' he whispers, 'that your reprimand was unfounded, as I was not talking but whispering.'

'Whispering still depletes the shelter of oxygen. We all have an allotted amount, and you are taking more than your share.'

'So now the air's rationed,' someone says, and laughter glances off the cellar walls.

'Who said that?' yells Schneck.

Silence.

'And speaking of not talking,' says Schneck, 'I must ask you to refrain from scaring your children with stories about bombs. There is simply no need for such stories.'

Sieglinde wants to ask him if it's true that the English coat their planes with invisible paint, and if that's why the searchlights hardly ever catch one – but she doesn't dare. After a time Kurt begins to wail, and he wakes another baby, who wakes another baby, who wakes yet another, and the cellar fills with their high cries.

'Ladies, ladies!' shouts Schneck. 'Control your infants!'

'They are so small,' says Vati. 'Their lungs do not use much oxygen, even when crying.'

Schneck scrutinises Kurt and the Schuttmann baby. 'This may be true,' he says. 'This is a logical line of thought.'

'Thank you,' says Vati.

'Be quiet,' says Schneck.

'Shhhh,' say the mothers to the babies, 'shh-shhh.' Little waves on dark water.

It is only after an official notice from the Reichsmarschall that Schneck relaxes the rules.

'There is no scientific evidence for the oxygen-depletion theory,' he announces. 'A shelter would have to be airtight for this to be an issue. Sealed completely shut. Of course such chambers do not exist, and therefore we are quite safe. The person who made this ludicrous recommendation was mistaken – he will have been dealt with accordingly – and it is fortunate that Herr Göring has brought the truth to our attention and assured us that we may speak freely.'

Silence.

★

Brigitte Heilmann has always been a light sleeper, awake long after the rest of the building is dreaming, when even Schneck is off duty. She is familiar with the noises of the night – the S-Bahn pulling into the station at Savignyplatz, wheels scoring the darkness; the ticking of the roof as the pitch cools beneath the tiles; the drumming of Fräulein Glöckner's dancing shoes on the stairs when, despite the rules, she returns home well after midnight: twelve steps and a landing, twelve steps and a landing. And the smaller, closer sounds: the intermittent murmurings of Jürgen and Sieglinde; the baby's sighs and whimpers; the grandfather clock from the Heilmann family villa chiming the hour. And closer still: her husband's breaths as he sleeps; the way the air catches in his throat again and again, as if he keeps taking fright in some looping dream, as if his fear keeps meeting its own beginning. Tonight, though, she hears a new noise – or, at least, she thinks she does. The prising open of a stuck door; a low, off-key note; the dragging of heavy furniture across a wooden floor, leaving a mark that will never come out.

'Gottlieb,' she whispers, touching her husband's shoulder. 'Gottlieb, did you hear something?'

He growls and turns away from her, and she withdraws her hand. She can hardly make out a thing as she feels her way to the door of their blacked-out bedroom; she looks for herself in the mirror but all she sees is a shadow in a patch of black ice. And is that her own hand reaching out in front of her, or the hand-shaped vase that sits on the dressing table at the centre of a crocheted mat? It was one of the first presents Gottlieb ever gave her, as slender and white as the hands that advertise soap, wristwatches, scented lotion, *nourish your skin, steel your nerves, the mirror does not lie, your hands reveal all. You are as old as your arteries, but you look as old as your skin.* To begin with she filled it with flowers, but she soon discovered it was not very stable, and had a tendency to fall over if she so much as closed the dressing-table drawers too roughly. Gottlieb has glued the base back on twice, as well as one of the fingers, and even though you can hardly see the joins, it no longer holds water and is only for show. When Sieglinde was little Gottlieb told her that there was a lady trapped inside the dressing table who was waving for help, and that at night you could hear her knocking on the mahogany, calling for someone to come and let her out. Sieglinde refused to go anywhere near the vase after that, until Brigitte picked it up and showed her that it wasn't attached to anything, and certainly not to a trapped lady.

In the hallway she hears the noise again – a shifting, a rupturing. Gottlieb sighs in his sleep.

★

Most Saturdays, when school was over for the day, Mutti took Sieglinde and her brothers to visit Tante Hannelore in Dahlem. Her building was much grander than theirs; stone boys and girls flanked the windows of the façade, arms raised, holding up the lintels, and the entranceway glittered with chandeliers and mirrors and brass fittings polished to gold. Tante Hannelore was tall and elegant with deep-set green eyes and glossy brown hair and you could tell she came from money; she knew how to select crystal and how to make conversation, and she had a way of speaking to shopkeepers and market vendors that won her the freshest fish, the largest eggs. She lived on the ground floor, her large apartment giving onto a tree-filled courtyard of chestnuts and oaks. In summer they cast their green shade across her rooms, and in winter the bare branches let in the light. Her carpets were genuine Persian and her photograph frames solid silver. Some of the residents in her building even had maids, though Tante Hannelore had let hers go when her husband died and she found herself in a difficult position for a time. Twelve years older than her brother Gottlieb, she had four sons, all in the Wehrmacht, and one of them already a senior lance corporal; she wore her Mother's Cross every day.

'Come in, come in,' she said, ushering the Heilmanns through the entranceway, past the oak settle carved with dancing bears that Sieglinde longed to sit on, and into the parlour with its damask chairs and its painted bamboo screen in the Japanese style. The samovar was simmering – don't touch, children – and on a blue china plate lay Jürgen's favourite Spekulatius biscuits, thin and crisp and smelling of spices, though where the ingredients had come from Sieglinde did not know. Mutti said it was impossible to find such things nowadays, but Tante Hannelore always made the special biscuits for Jürgen, even when it wasn't Christmas, and she let him nibble around their edges, right up to the outlines of the windmills and mermaids and castles and ships, rather than taking polite bites. Mutti thought this rather indulgent, though she only ever said so at home. She never said a word, either, when Tante Hannelore dressed Sieglinde up, arranging her hair in styles that were far too old for her, whisking a powder puff over her cheeks and nose and dabbing lipstick on her mouth, draping her in her own expensive clothes; Sieglinde was forever losing her hands beneath trailing sleeves and trying not to step out of shoes, trip over hems.

'Oh, I would have loved a little girl like you,' Tante Hannelore said now, smoothing down the sailor collar on Sieglinde's dress. 'Brigitte, you're so fortunate to have a daughter. Little boys fall in love with their mothers, but daughters look after them later on.'

Most of the jewels belonging to Oma Heilmann had been lost in the Depression, but Tante Hannelore retained the Berlin iron pieces passed down from her great-grandmother – a pair of wide black bracelets as fine as lace, and a ring that read *Gold I Gave For Iron*. This was not a private message scored inside the band like the one on Mutti's wedding ring (*To my treasure 13.6.33*); the words ran around the outside, designed to be seen. Tante Hannelore wore the ring in place of a wedding band, just as her great-grandmother had, and on special occasions such as Heldengedenktag and the Führer's birthday she put on the black bracelets, and people on the street stopped her to commend her excellent lineage, and to remark on her family's sacrifice.

'Your great-great-grandmother gave up her jewels for the war,' she told Sieglinde. 'Not this war, of course, a different one – she surrendered them all, even her wedding ring, and received these in return.' She showed her the iron band, turning it on her finger so Sieglinde could read the message; she took the iron bracelets from their box lined with sky-blue silk and fastened them about Sieglinde's wrists. 'Never mind,' she said when they slipped off. 'You'll grow into them.'

Mutti owned just one piece of Heilmann family jewellery, given to her by Vati on their wedding day – a sprig of gold with green enamel leaves and white flowers. They looked like pearls, but really they were teeth: Vati's baby teeth. Oma Heilmann had it made when he was still a boy. Mutti said it was not to her taste, but sometimes she let Sieglinde borrow it for a special treat, and when they came home from Tante Hannelore's that afternoon, Sieglinde asked if she could wear it.

'Is it edelweiss? Snowdrops?' she said, running her finger over the tiny stem, smoothing out the safety chain that was so fine you could barely feel it. Mutti said she didn't know; she thought there was no such plant, and no such flower, but that only made it more special to Sieglinde. 'Was Vati really as small as Kurt once?' she said, and Mutti said yes, Vati was once a baby, and here was the proof, his little teeth, right here in her hand.

'Did you have a nice time?' said Vati, who liked to stay at home by himself on Saturday afternoons and work on his silhouette pictures.

'I tried on her bracelets,' said Sieglinde. 'They used to be gold, but now they're iron.'

'We had a lovely time,' said Mutti. 'The apartment is so immaculate; I really don't know how Hannelore does it. Especially given how large it is.'

Vati laughed and said women have a special skill that men lack: they can kiss a friend and at the same time stick a needle into her.

★

Brigitte heard the noise again that night, and again she rose from her bed to see if she could identify its source. She pulled up the blackout blind and peered through the bedroom window, but all was quiet down on Kantstrasse.

She listened. The noise seemed to be coming from the living room, and indeed, when she turned on the light the space did seem different – had something been added, something taken away? The gramophone stood between the windows; the radio and the blue lamp rested on the end table; the sofa and chairs occupied their usual positions, the antimacassars shielding the upholstery from heads and hands, and the portrait of the Führer hung above them, a wall to himself. There was the piano, its stool pushed in just as was proper when the instrument was not in use, the songs shut away beneath the needlepoint lid, and in the corner the tiled stove crouched, still warm. Twists of newspaper lay piled next to it, ready for the morning, now and then fluttering their inked wings of their own accord. *Think of Victory Day and Night. Dutch Island of Tholen Capitulates. 13 English Fighter Planes Shot Down by 6 Messerschmitts.* The tassels all lay straight on the Persian carpet – not genuine Persian, but so close to it that only a Persian himself could tell the difference, and as the likeable young man at Wertheim's had asked, how many Persians came to visit? He and Brigitte had laughed at the thought – a Persian gentleman, with his billowing trousers and his funny little curl-toed slippers, calling on the Heilmanns of Charlottenburg, Berlin! And there in the corner sat the cherrywood sideboard, a remnant from another time, too large for the apartment, in truth, but along with the grandfather clock one of the few pieces remaining from Gottlieb's family villa in Grunewald. It always looked as if it were about to topple forward, pinning beneath it anyone who happened to be passing; Brigitte would have preferred the oak settle carved with bears, but that had gone to Hannelore. Here in the dim light she caught sight of her reflection in the polished veneer, an indistinct figure, out of place too. But no, she told herself – the room was the same as ever. It was the same room in the same apartment in the same building. All was as it should be.

★

'Gather round, children, gather round; I have no intention of raising my voice today. Now, do you see the rows of beautiful new radios? At the moment they are quite empty, of course. They all start out like that, in much the same way humans do, but by the time they have made their way along the production line they will be fully functional. Functional, children – a useful word – who can give me another word for functional? Excellent, Sieglinde. Add *functional* to your list of useful words, everybody – just in your head for now, but when we're back at school we can write it in our vocabulary notebooks so that we will learn it. Now, here we can see the workers fitting all the different parts together that will make the radios go. Remember, if you have an intelligent question, you may ask it. So many separate pieces, children, aren't there? And if just one of them is left out, or fitted incorrectly, the radio will be defective and therefore useless. Defective, children? Defective? Another one for the list. You can see what complicated machines these are, and yet they are also affordable machines, because in this country we believe that every family should have its own radio, and this is why we call them our Volksempfänger, our People's Receivers, and so we shall pause for a moment and say thank you to our Führer Herr Hitler and thank you to our Gauleiter Dr Goebbels, even though they are not here in person.

'And do you know what makes our radios so special? They are very particular about the company they keep.

What am I getting at here, children? What is my meaning? Well, in addition to being affordable and beautiful – and yes, Jutta, I suppose they do look like little churches, churches for dolls and mice – they will pick up only German stations. Our Volksempfänger simply refuse to listen to transmissions from anywhere else. English and American radios, on the other hand, do not discriminate, and will blurt all kinds of dangerous and disgusting stories that have no place in a decent home. They catch whatever is floating around and they pass it on. But look how particular our workers are – how clean and exact. These radios are built to house the Führer's voice, and the Gauleiter's voice, and the stories that describe our latest victories, and Beethoven and Bach. They do not stuff themselves with gossip and slander and weird syncopations. No, they bring us the Request Concert that unites us with our brave soldiers who are listening at the front, and together we can hear "Good Night, Mother" and "Three Lilies" and the amusing "Nothing Can Shake a Sailor", and we can hear the names of newborn babies whose fathers are away at war and may not yet know that they are fathers. And look, the last man on the production line – what is his job? Once the insides are where they should be and the back is screwed down? What is he doing, children? We can't ask him because he doesn't appear to speak any German, but we can see that he is the man who attaches the warnings, the little signs that tell us how to behave, because we must not mistreat our Volksempfänger and we must not try to listen to enemy broadcasts, and it is sensible and proper to remind ourselves of this.'

★

At home, only Vati was allowed to handle the radio. It occupied a small table at the far end of the sofa, a dark block sitting with its back to the wall, watching the family, working up a temperature. *Being a prophet is a thankless business*, it said. *We National Socialists seldom make prophecies, but we never make false ones.* When the signal faltered, when ghostly voices talked over the broadcast, Vati knew how to fix it; he took the wire and cut through the ghosts until the proper words became clear, until they buzzed through him like blood. He did not listen to Sieglinde when it was talking. If she opened her mouth to ask him something, he held up a hand and she knew she had to wait. What if Germany won the war, but missed the announcement?

In the evenings, Vati liked to sit with a tray on his lap and cut out his silhouettes, and Sieglinde sat beside him, watching the shapes emerge from the black paper: cathedrals and mountains, fir trees and foxes, night birds that dipped their wings above dark houses. The light from the ceiling lamp struck Vati's spectacles, and sometimes, from certain angles, Sieglinde could not see his eyes at all, just the glare of the glass. She knew that other girls sat on their fathers' laps and listened to stories – but the silhouettes were Vati's stories, and she did not mind that it was these he held instead of her. She studied his wristwatch as he worked, cupping her palms around it to see its lopsided arms shining pale green and poisonous; little arrows pointing now at her mother, now at herself, now at the black paper falling like leaves, now at Vati's own heart. Gently he pulled his hand away and continued with his cutting, making not just a bird but a bird-shaped hole; not just a house but the space a house once filled. When he removed the watch each evening, Sieglinde knew, it left behind a pale patch on his wrist, a memory of itself, so that he would not forget to put it on again in the morning when he was getting ready for work. He had an important job, and could not be late, and never was.

Vati timed himself with the watch when he cleaned his teeth at night – one minute for the upper row and one minute for the lower – and then he placed it next to his bed, where it carried on ticking even when he was asleep, the hands meeting once every hour, a pair of scissors snipping away at the night. If Sieglinde crept into her parents' room after one of her bad dreams she could see the hands glimmering from Vati's bedside cabinet, moving too slowly for her to catch. She wanted to witness time passing, to know that morning would come, and she tried fooling the hands, pretending she was not looking, watching them from the corner of her eye. And there on the dressing table was the hand-shaped vase, as white as the moon – was it also moving? Its fingers trembling at the sound of distant planes? On these nights, when the planes were almost too remote to hear, Sieglinde wished she could climb into her parents' bed. But this was not a gypsy camp; this was not a den of dogs.

★

Brigitte scanned the meagre contents of the pantry and frowned. She looked in kitchen cupboards and drawers; she looked on bookshelves and in the sideboard in the living room where she kept the good tablecloths and the little green demitasse cups. She opened the medicine cabinet and the wardrobes, the hatboxes and the cake tins. If something terrible happened – there had not been many bombs, not so far, but everyone whispered that more would come, and she could not rest, she could not sleep. And if she had no proof of what she owned – if there were no records – then where and who would she be? It was curious, she thought, how an object embedded itself into a person's life; how it disguised itself in familiar surroundings. The person might touch it every day without giving it a second thought – a particular coffee pot used each morning, or a ring with an inscription rubbed almost smooth, from a time when pet names still applied. But if that object were suddenly destroyed, could the person describe it beyond its most superficial qualities? *White with blue trim. Rose gold with a milled edge.* Brigitte recalled a stage act she had seen at the Wintergarten with Gottlieb in the early days, shortly after they met: the performer asked the audience to make up a story, calling out lines to him, the more complicated the better, and then he relayed them back to the delighted crowd word for word. She had glanced at Gottlieb as they clapped and cheered with everyone else, trying to imagine a future time when she would have committed to heart the line of his jaw, the reach of his long fine fingers, the secret swirl of his ear. What was the trick? Across what instrument are we stretched taut?

She unwrapped the ledger. She had chosen it for its thick spine and marbled cover, its calm weight a wonder to her restless hands. The latticed pages, ruled up in columns and rows of red and blue, held no surprises, no shocks, each one the same as the last. She began to count.

★

When Sieglinde and Jürgen returned home at lunchtime Mutti had all the crockery stacked on the kitchen table and was going over it piece by piece, her fingernail a bird's beak tapping at the plates and cups and bowls, checking each pile not once but several times before making a note of it in a book. Every cupboard and drawer stood open, and Sieglinde felt uneasy at the sight of her family's belongings laid bare, even the special and dangerous things, the things she wasn't allowed to touch: the valuables and breakables, the knives and the poisons.

No food simmered on the stovetop or sat cooling on the table, but perhaps Mutti had just arrived home herself; perhaps she had been busy queueing at the market, only to find nothing left by the time it was her turn. Sieglinde could hear Kurt crying from his cot at the other end of the apartment. Jürgen crawled underneath the table and began running his soldiers down with a tank one by one, each little man of lead dying many times over.

'Mutti?' she said. 'Shall I help you make lunch?'

'We must prepare an inventory,' said Mutti. 'Do you see? Each item must be described, then given a code – a number – according to its size and use, and then it must be listed in order of its position in the room.'

Sieglinde said nothing, beginning instead to prepare some bread and paper-thin slices of sausage for the boys. Mutti seemed not to notice, and did not stop to eat – there was too much to do, she said. But how could she not be hungry? Sieglinde was hungry all the time.

Over the following weeks Mutti worked her way through the entire apartment, taking stock of slippers, books, jigsaw puzzles, gramophone records, searching every centimetre of every room as if she had lost something. She counted Jürgen's soldiers and Sieglinde's hair-ribbons. She counted the everyday tablecloths and the white damask ones kept for Tante Hannelore's visits. She counted the green antique coffee cups with their little gold handles that were almost too small to hold. She counted the light bulbs in the lamps, the envelopes in the desk; she counted the scraps of old aprons and shirts torn into dusters. Cakes of soap. Pairs of scissors. Knitting needles. Piano keys. Vases made into hands. Teeth made into brooches. Old razorblades rubbed sharp on the inside of a glass jar. Glass jars. Pins and pens. Stamps and buckets. And when she had finished, she began again, because of course mistakes were possible, she was only human, and besides, things changed, they changed all the time, whether you were watching or not, but especially if you were not. Sieglinde watched as she rechecked the cutlery, the wine glasses and the china, everyday and best, recording the latest figures in the marbled ledger. You had to keep on top of it, she said, asking Sieglinde to unfold pillowcases and sheets and hold them up so she could inspect them for flaws, then getting her to refold them and return them to their proper row on the proper shelf, neat white squares, clean white squares. It was a relief to have everything sorted and accounted for by the end of the day, she said; she could sit down in the evening and relax.

★

Vati has made a Christmas silhouette: a cottage alone in the falling snow, far from anywhere, the smoke from its chimney spelling out a greeting: *Frohes Fest*. For whom are these weightless words? The snow, the moon? On Christmas Eve I see him hanging it in the branches of their tree, a spangled forest in the middle of the city, four floors up. And Sieglinde and Mutti have assembled a gingerbread house, and in the candlelight it looks almost real, almost like the gingerbread houses they have made for other Christmases, with their walls iced together and decorated with sweets, and liquorice slates on the roof. Vati says they have done a marvellous job, and it's only when you look closely that you notice it's cardboard painted brown and pasted with bits of coloured paper.

The Führer is everywhere present this evening, wherever Germans gather; He will your salvation be; children, let me enter, so cold is the winter, doors to me open, lest I am frozen. Wherever we gather he is there, glittering in the frost on the glass and in the candle flames on the green-black wreaths, adding his voice to our carols; a spotless rose is growing, sprung from a tender root; God has left His throne on high. He is falling so gently on the roofs and the sills; still, still, still; gathering on the thresholds and pushing at the doors, changing the colour of the world; he is covering up the ugly and the barren and bare; let us be glad and merry; he is breathing down our chimneys to coax the fires high. And he is touching his wine glass to ours, and he is stealing into silent rooms and hiding gifts; tomorrow, children, you'll get a surprise; and he is bowing his head and giving thanks for what is to come, and he is cutting the dead-eyed head from the fish and warning of the bones.

And is he also in the cold notes of the church bells? And in the church, too, calling through dolorous pipes as thick as a man's trunk and as narrow as a finger? Is he in the stable, is he watching the manger, is he the bringer of good news? Is he the great forged star, hard with hope?

I have seen him in these places; I have seen him take these forms.

April 1941
Near Leipzig

One of Erich's first memories is this: his mother holding him by the wrists and spinning him round and round, the garden blurring into ribbons of green and yellow, and only her white skirt in focus, the bell-shaped centre of the world. He remembers his laugh falling from his mouth, and hers falling from the sky. He remembers the feeling of spinning faster and faster, gaining such momentum that it seemed the very air was pulling him away from her, and he thought he might catapult from her grasp and travel so far and so high that he would land in an unknown place, from which he could not find his way back.

This is how he feels when he wakes in the night with a fever: as if he is spinning. He has had a bad cold and Mama has been keeping her eye on him, refusing to let him outside – you can't be too careful, she says – but now, despite her being so careful, it has turned into pneumonia. I watch her sponging his face with a cool cloth, holding her hand to his forehead, lifting him to sip from a glass of water. (What is fever? What is thirst? If I knew them, I would only long for someone to take them away.)

For two weeks Erich must lie in isolation, all visitors forbidden from entering the room and Papa choosing not to. Tante Uschi and Oma Kröning call to him from the passage, asking whether he feels any better.

'Not even a little bit?' they say. 'Are you sure?'

He cannot make out their faces but he can see the gold cross around Oma Kröning's neck when it catches the light, and Tante Uschi's pale blond hair, which is the same colour as Mama's only much thinner and shorter. Mama brings him meals at all the correct mealtimes, as well as a selection of books he can look at by himself, and games to be played by one person, and she piles four feather quilts on his bed to try to break the fever. Papa even lets him borrow his cigarette card album, which is not just an album but a proper book with stories about the Life of the Führer. Papa has pasted the pictures into the correct gaps – they are numbered so you cannot make a mistake, you cannot mount the picture of the Führer visiting the Schiller House in Weimar alongside him meeting Mussolini in Venice, just as you cannot have him consecrating the flags with the blood banner next to the one of him being light-hearted in the Harz mountains. That would not match the story; it would make no sense.

'I know you'll be careful with it,' Papa calls – but Erich cannot focus on the album; the photographs begin to blur and swim, and he vomits on his sheets.

On Sundays Mama lights a candle on his windowsill because he cannot go to church; from his bed he listens to the bells ringing, and in the double panes the little flame is reflected twice over, the second fainter than the first, its pale memory. And are two doves alighting in two linden trees? Are two Ronjas grazing on the grass in two apple orchards? Are two Papas tapping the ash from their pipes, the briarwood bowls as shiny as chestnuts, and two Mamas making Leipzig larks in two kitchens, their faces bright with the heat of two ovens? Does everything tow its own ghost?

The doctor comes with his black bag that is dark and deep, and he examines him and confers with his parents, who nod at everything he says, because one agrees with such men; that is simply the proper thing to do. They arrange for a girl from the Reich Labour Service to come to the house and bathe him, too: what is she called? Fräulein Else, Fräulein Ilsa? Erich cannot hold on to her name, nor her face, but he knows her hands, strong and thick, wringing the cloth in the steaming bowl and washing every part of him. She lifts his limp arms, cups his heels in her palms, rolls him first one way and then the other. The water is almost too hot to bear, but her touch does not sting, not exactly; she is so quick that his skin, while failing to register pain, still tingles with the relief of it passing. She does not speak as she works, tending to his body as if laying it out for the family's final viewing. And yes, he has heard them talk of his death, Mama and Papa, peering in from the passage as if trying to catch sight of it in the darkened room, and for a time it lies in the bed beside him and does not sleep. And a wolf sits in the fireplace and watches him, and this too is his death, and the birds on his bedside lamp turn their black eyes towards him, and they too are his death. He thinks of the wicked things he has done: skimming the cream from the milk when nobody is there to see; tearing the story about the thumb-snipping tailor from his Struwwelpeter book and stuffing it into the oven in the kitchen.

One morning Oma Kröning marches into Erich's room and says she does not care about catching pneumonia. She helps him to sit up, and he can see the apple orchard, where the blossom is cloudy white. Near the trees stand the beehives in the shape of people, and Oma Kröning settles herself on the edge of Erich's bed and tells him how Opa Kröning carved them himself, decades earlier: he went far into the forest, to where the oaks grew, and marked the dead ones with his axe. He was still a young man then – this was well before the blood cancer took him – and he sawed down the rotten trees and hollowed out their hearts, standing back and studying each of the trunks in turn, deciding where to cut the eyes, where to open the mouths. On a cool autumn day, when the air was rich with the scent of turned earth and burning chaff, he grasped his chisel and recalled the face of his brother, fallen at Saint-Privat, and the wood took on the shape of this remembered boy. Your Opa was very clever with faces, says Oma Kröning. Look at the high forehead, the narrow shoulders: Gustav is home. Nothing is lost. And perhaps when Erich is better, Papa will carve a hive that has his face, Erich's face. Would he like that? Yes, he says – but I can see that he is not at all sure.

'Who are the other hives?' he asks, although he has heard their stories many times before. Oma Kröning enjoys telling them; she says it is important these things are not forgotten, and one day Erich must tell them to his own children.

That one, she says, is the little Frankish butcher who came with his knife when the pigs and calves were ready, and that one is the thin-haired pastor in his black peaked hat. The most slender trunk, she says, carries the image of Luise, Opa Kröning's first love, who married another and died not yet twenty; he was careful when he carved her, aware of how easily his chisel could gouge and pierce. But Saint John the Baptist in his lambskin cloak? asks Erich. And the hook-nosed moneylender? Opa Kröning didn't know them, did he? No, he didn't know them, says Oma Kröning, but even if you have never seen a wolf, all the same, you can describe one. And she tucks him back into bed, and kisses his hot forehead, which is very strange to me; I think she really must not care if she dies.

Later, when she has gone, and Erich's fever is again on the rise, a breeze picks up. It ruffles the apple trees, runs its fingers across the nearby lake and gushes into the hives. And the bees come and go through their open mouths, and the bees fill their breasts with honeycomb hearts and their throats with glassy wings, and black and gold are the thoughts of the dead. The wooden figures begin to speak, their voices breaking into a thousand thrumming parts, and this is what I think I hear but do not understand. And this is what I think Erich hears but does not understand. Forgive me my errors:

I loved your grandfather but my sister loved him also, and she walked with him in the forest and picked wild berries, and he chose her, my sister with the sweet-stained fingers and the hair that smelled of the trees. I wanted my sorrow to sink me beneath the lake and hold me there until I turned first to water and then to ice. I wanted my sorrow to drag my sister under, and Anton too. The man I married was a good man, a kind man, my second love, and he did not walk in the forest with another, nor eat wild berries from her hand. In the slow hours of my death, my newborn son already cold beside me, I thought of Anton, your grandfather, and I thought he was right to have chosen my sister, because he would not lose me now, and I spoke his name as my husband stroked my hair.

For hours we marched in the high heat of August. We could not drink from the wells; it was said the French had poisoned the water. We came in at the battle's end, when our men had taken Gravelotte; they had forced the French across the ravine, but the dead lay so thick to their backs that they could not retreat. At

Saint-Privat the sun was sinking. The air was full of shot and shells and flashes from the French guns that stabbed at the falling night, and above the smoke and fury the terrible grinding roll of the mitrailleuse. We built barricades from the dead. Heralds on horseback would take word to the king: twenty thousand. In the morning we would be buried, and our rifles fired until they too were empty. The road to Verdun reached out to the horizon.

I make the sweetest honey – so much gold in the pockets of my long black coat – but I will bake my bread from the blood of your children.

I grew so weary of them. Week after week they brought me their souls; they thought I could untangle their every sin. Yet the things they confided took root in me: the stolen coins and the whipped dogs, the curses and the covetings. They clogged me up. I wished they would leave me to my own cruelties, which were my familiar and quiet belongings.

As a boy I travelled from house to house, learning from my father the craft of killing, and when my son reached the proper age he learned it from me. Blood was as usual to us as milk to the farmer; it pattered into the pails at our feet, fat with life. The knife, ash-handled, warmed as I worked, a comfort in my palm. I felt a loss when I laid it down; it brought me a calm unknown since the cradle. We took the clotting blood, my father and I, my son and I, and mixed it with the fat of the animal, and pushed it into the unwound guts of the animal, and this was to us a wonder: a rearrangement of flesh, a restoration. Great meaty ropes we made, the boneless limbs of an uncharted beast. I find myself thinking more and more of the knife. Of its heft and shape in my hand. Of its utmost suitability.

Whom think ye that I am? I am not he. But, behold, there cometh one after me, whose shoes of his feet I am not worthy to loose. O generation of vipers, who hath warned you to flee from the wrath to come?

The next day the doctor listens to his chest, and Erich fears he will hear his thoughts about skimmed cream and torn books – and his thoughts about Fräulein Ilsa or Else, too, which flare in the stethoscope's shrewd ear, a peculiar fever he cannot douse.

'Hmm,' says the doctor, and 'Aha,' and 'So so,' and Erich lies as still as he can and watches the clock that Mama has placed on the mantelpiece.

When he feels a little better he plays Black Peter against himself, and always wins, and then he has to be quick about packing the cards away – it is correct to keep one's things tidy and clean – or else Black Peter begins to rise and to sprinkle the room with soot. Fräulein Else or Ilsa comes and goes, and the doctor listens in on his heart, and the wolf watches from the fireplace and the birds from the lamp and the hives from the orchard, and Papa makes his way up and down the passage and does not stop, passing by his door like a spirit.

And when his death has left him, again he hears the doctor outside his room: *His growth will be stunted. He will always be a weakling.* But this cannot be true, thinks Erich: I beat the disease. I did not die.

★

It rained the morning of the parade. Mama kept going to the window to check on the weather, glaring at the clouds as if she could make them vanish.

'He will still come,' said Papa. 'He was at the Somme.'

By afternoon the sky had cleared, and the Krönings put on their church clothes and made their way into Leipzig. There was a hum in the spring air, the first phase of a swarm; people were straightening ties and adjusting collars, smoothing hair and levelling hems, now and then glancing towards the black hands of the clock. Banners and bunting hung from every window, turning all the puddles red, as if something terrible had happened, and all the church bells were ringing, and the sun caught at the pieces of mirror on homemade periscopes and sent signals flashing like code. Papa bought paper flags on sticks, one for each of them, and when the first soldiers marched into view and everybody began to wave at once you could feel the air flex and shift and change. Erich was not tall enough – all he could make out were shoals of red pennants slipping across the blue sky – but Papa lifted him up high and it was both the same and not the same as when Mama had spun him around in the garden. The cheering crashed against the cobblestones, louder than anyone expected (but were there not persons ensuring this din? Were they not mingling with the crowd, dressed in normal clothes?). The Krönings waved until they thought their arms would crack. Girls strewed flowers in front of the advancing soldiers, and when the Führer's car at last appeared it moved slowly through this instant meadow, its occupant looking to the left and the right as if trying to find a particular address.

Erich held his flag so tightly that his hand hurt, and when they were home again he could still see the furrow in his palm: a life line, a love line. Mama and Papa gave him their flags to keep too, and he put them on his windowsill in an empty honey jar that had a chipped rim and therefore could not be used again for honey. Mama turned on the radio and hummed along to 'Friends, Life Is Worth Living', and Erich asked permission to look at Papa's cigarette card album about the Führer. There were still a few blanks on some of the pages, waiting for pictures Papa had not managed to collect, and he never would collect them now, because the current ones were about Baroque Painting and England the Robber State, and you certainly couldn't paste them into the Life of the Führer. For those sections, all Erich had to go on were the captions, and from them he imagined the missing scenes: *Again and again the Führer is seen surrounded by children; A simple stew, even for the Chancellor of the German Reich; Everyone wants to shake the Führer's hand; Hitler has given us tanks again; 'Here, my Führer, is my grandchild'.* In a way these were his favourite pages of all, because he could picture himself in them.

★

I have watched Erich growing taller and older, swimming as fast as a fish in the lake, building dark shelters in the forest and believing Mama cannot find him. I have watched him lying beneath the needles, so still, so still, listening for the beehive voices that tell him their lives in little pieces. *Above the smoke and fury the terrible grinding roll. Whom think ye that I am?* When Papa goes away to Russia to be a soldier, Mama says that Erich must not hide any more. He is too happy with his own company, she says, sees nothing wrong in playing on his own while the other boys in the village take one another prisoner. Now that he has started school, he must make an effort to form allegiances.

'I don't know what that means,' he says.

'Friends,' she says. 'You must make friends. Don't you want to join in?'

But while he was trapped in bed, all the other boys chose their friends. 'I have nobody,' he says, and in that instant I am in his skin and behind his eyes.

He shows Mama a game he has made: a circle of card with a length of string fastened to either edge. He has drawn half a face on the front and the other half on the back, but when he takes the strings and spins the card the halves combine, and the face is whole.

The Wax Woman

The garden   ,
Cool rain sinks into the flowers.
Summer shudders
Quietly towards his   .

Leaf after leaf drops golden
From the high acacia tree.
Summer gives a   , astonished
In his   garden's   .

For a long while he lingers
At the roses,   for   .
Slowly he closes
His great,   eyes.

September 1941
Berlin

'What do you do at work?' Sieglinde asked her father, swinging his hand in hers as they set out along Kantstrasse. They were visiting the zoo, a treat for Jürgen's birthday, and Mutti and the boys had gone on ahead. Sieglinde was wearing the little brooch made from Vati's baby teeth, and every so often it caught on her braid and made Vati laugh.

'Stop biting me!' she said.

'Delicious,' he said.

They turned into Joachimsthalerstrasse and soon they could see Mutti and Jürgen and Kurt waiting at the Lion Gate, which led not to the lions but the elephants. Against the bright sky to the north the flak tower rose like a castle, and it was full of paintings and sculptures and priceless objects – the head of Nefertiti, the altar of Zeus – and it held an entire hospital, and plenty of air, and it could not be bombed.

'But what *is* your job?' she asked again.

'I make things safe,' said Vati.

'What sorts of things?'

'Just things.'

'Buildings? Bomb shelters?'

'Not those sorts of things.'

'Sharp things, then. Razorblades. Broken glass.'

'It's not like that, Siggi.'

'Ropes on pianos, for all the people moving out of their apartments.'

Vati laughed again.

'The water. The sky. Air. Conversations!'

'Don't be silly. It's not like that.'

'What is it like, then?'

'I take dangerous things away, so they won't be dangerous any more.'

'Oh,' said Sieglinde, and she thought: polio, lit windows, neighbours? She didn't ask, though; she supposed this was another question nobody would answer. Vati would not tell her what he did at work, just as Mutti would not tell her why Dr Rosenberg was no longer their doctor, why a different man sat at his desk, tapping Sieglinde's bones and counting her heartbeats. 'What if your building is bombed?' she asked instead.

'Impossible,' said Vati. 'They've covered it up so it looks like a forest, and put up false ones somewhere else. Isn't that clever?'

Sieglinde nodded; yes, it was very clever indeed.

They had caught up to Mutti and the boys now, and Vati bought their tickets and they filed through the gate. First they stopped to watch the elephants in their enclosure, which wasn't enclosed at all, because there were no walls, just a ring of spikes that would hurt the elephants' feet if they tried to walk across them to where the people stood. The tree-trunks were wrapped in spikes too, because otherwise the elephants would eat the bark and the trees would die. There must have been a time for every elephant, though, Sieglinde thought, when it tried to eat the bark, or cross the spikes – mustn't there? Before it learned that it could not? She wanted to ask Vati, but already he and

Mutti and the boys were moving on, because Titine the chimpanzee was riding her bicycle, which was not to be missed. The chimpanzees could smoke cigarettes and sit at tables and eat with spoons, just like human beings, and Jürgen said he would like to have one for a pet, but Vati said that would not be natural.

'You know,' said Mutti, 'when I was a little girl, they used to put Indians on display. Indians, and sometimes Eskimos, and African warriors with bones through their noses.'

'Can we see them?' said Jürgen. 'Do they have spears? And poisonous darts?'

'Oh no, they don't display them any more,' said Mutti.

When they reached the lions Vati said they should have their photo taken, because there were three lion cubs and three children, and so they waited while another family had their turn, and everyone laughed when the French zookeeper put a cub into the other family's pram, right in with the baby, and Sieglinde tugged Mutti's sleeve and said, 'What if they take the baby lion home, and leave the baby boy here?' but Mutti did not answer her, because she was talking to the other Mutti and saying, 'Six children, my goodness, what a busy life you must have.'

Then it was the Heilmanns' turn, and they sat on the bench and the French zookeeper put the cubs on their laps, and Kurt's cub kept trying to bite his nose and even though the French zookeeper said he was just playing, Kurt would not stop crying, and the photo was ruined.

The bear looked bored. It sat behind its bars and stared at nothing, not even caring about all the people who had come to see it, which was quite rude.

'I don't think he likes it here,' said Jürgen.

'He does look gloomy,' said Sieglinde.

The people stood before the enclosure and waited for the bear to do something: to show its teeth, to growl, to stand on its hind legs like the one in the brochure. A man looked at his watch. A young soldier roared at the bear, but still it did not react. Behind a thousand bars, no world.

'I think it's broken,' said the soldier.

'Boken,' said Kurt, trying out the word in his mouth.

'Is he broken?' said Jürgen, looking as if he might cry.

'Of course not, of course not, what a thing to say,' said Mutti, glaring.

'But he does seem unhappy,' said Sieglinde.

'I think he's just tired,' said Mutti. 'Why would he be unhappy? He has everything he could possibly want.'

'No one is kinder to animals than we are,' said Vati. 'In America they experiment on monkeys, and the French boil their lobsters alive —'

'Thank you, Gottlieb,' said Mutti.

'Well. My point is, we look after our animals,' said Vati. 'Even the wolf is protected.'

★

Sieglinde says, 'Mutti, the apartment is bigger.'

I watch through the window, I sit with the crow. Do the dead take the form of birds? We wait and we listen.

Mutti says, 'Nonsense, Siggi. You shouldn't make these things up.' She has her powder compact open and is looking in its secret mirror, dabbing her forehead and her chin with the little pad she keeps in there to cover any blemishes.

Sieglinde says, 'But the living room is longer. Before, if I sat on the sofa and held out my arms, Kurt could walk all the way from the far wall in ten steps.' (And when he reached his sister he would squeal as she swung him onto her knee and kissed his nose, and he knew he had done something good.) 'Now it's fifteen.'

'Children are like that,' says Mutti. 'One day they can buckle their own shoes, the next day their Mutti has to do it for them again. One day they can feed themselves, the next day they're rubbing stewed apple through their hair like a monkey and their Mutti must clean them up.' Dab, dab, goes the little pad; just enough to look natural. The crow pecks at the window, its beak striking the glass like hail.

'Monkeys eat bananas,' says Sieglinde.

'So they do,' says Mutti. 'You're a clever girl, Siggi. No more stories, now.' In her secret mirror the crow tilts its head.

★

The Heilmanns are happy in their marriage. Look at them: they are a suitable match, a good example; no crooked bones, no deficits, no shadows in the blood. Yes, they are happy, people say they are happy, even though Brigitte's nerves are bad whenever there is a raid. It's just leaflet drops, Gottlieb tells her. Nuisance raiding. But she flinches at any loud noise, any sudden movement; around her Gottlieb feels he is walking underwater. Still, when he considers other wives – the bad teeth and double chins, the veins and the moles, the poorly designed torsos – he counts his blessings. Brigitte does not wear trousers or lipstick or heels; she does not curl or starve or dye. She was just eighteen when they met; a respectable girl from a respectable family in Celle; as malleable as wax. She answered his newspaper notice, and there is no shame in that; lots of decent Germans advertise for the right sort of spouse. Besides, nobody remembers it now, and if they do, it is never mentioned.

'England,' he reminds her. 'We are fighting the English. We are not at war with Britain.'

'Of course we are,' she says.

'Still, we say we are at war with the English. That is what we say.'

'But everybody knows we mean Britain.'

'Yes.'

'Then why don't we say it?'

'Because we are fighting an island, not an empire. When we have won we'll say it was an empire, but for now it is an island. You must listen.'

★

Here is Gottlieb Heilmann on a Monday morning, arriving ten minutes early to his job. See how he hangs his hat and coat on the hook that bears his name, how he places his briefcase at the right-hand side of his desk, sits down at his typewriter and removes its cover. The green carapace unclicks, the blank paper and the carbon paper twist into the machine and the letters raise their inky arms. *Choice*, he types. *Opinion. Love.* His office is one of dozens in the Division – perhaps hundreds; he does not know – but his name is painted on the frosted-glass door, and that is how he knows he is in the right place and has not taken a wrong turn, for the building is the sort of building that can make a man lose his bearings. So here he is, sitting behind the frosted-glass door labelled *Heilmann*, and from inside the office the name is backwards and makes no sense and is not his name, and the letters are painted in gold and shadowed in black to give them depth, the illusion of depth, like letters carved into a gravestone. And I say office because everybody says office, but behind the frosted-glass door the walls reach neither the ceiling nor the floor, and they are set with frosted glass too, winter windows that never clear, and above them drift the sighs and whispers of Gottlieb's colleagues, and through them he can make out the hazy shapes of men like himself, but not their faces (never their faces).

Gottlieb finds it curious to think he could not even type when he began working for the Division in 1939. It was his skill with scissors and blades that secured him the job, he discovered; his neighbour Herr Schuttmann, who had seen his silhouettes and who knew an official who knew another official, passed the information on. At the interview Gottlieb had the feeling that decisions had been made already, but when one of the men asked to see his tools he took them from his briefcase along with a sheet of paper and gave a demonstration, fashioning a tiny Siegessäule in a matter of minutes, black Victory wielding her black laurel. The man recognised the monument at once.

'I choose only German subjects,' said Gottlieb, and this was true; he felt no affinity with such distant marvels as the Taj Mahal or the Parthenon, wanting instead to reproduce his homeland, for the shape of a thing told what it truly was. He never invented, and he took pride in getting every detail correct: the raised hooves of the horses on the Brandenburg Gate; the slant of the artificial ruins overlooking Sanssouci; Neuschwanstein's crow-stepped gable; Munich's spiky carillon tower with its knight who died every day.

The man kept the paper Siegessäule, slipping it into a file. Gottlieb did not catch his name, and when the same man showed him the office that would be his on his first day, he hadn't liked to ask. The man was talking and pointing, making sure Gottlieb knew what was expected of him, ending each sentence with questions that did not seem to require an answer. *Do you understand. Is that clear.* Gottlieb was to type all reports and correspondence himself. He was to start each day with a summary of his output from the previous day, listing the number of words in each category and sub-category as well as the total number of corrections made, and then he was to confirm with a signature that the waste material had been disposed of in the proper manner. The man pulled open an endless drawer as he talked, its steel bed reaching clear across the room, the side-rails recalling the guards on cots that keep infants from falling during fretful dreams. Gottlieb ran a hand along its cool and impossible length. Was this not the kind of drawer that held the nameless dead? The hanged and the drowned, the victims of exposure? It would house Gottlieb's daily reports, said the man, filed according to the title of the parent text. If a report included multiple titles, then carbon copies of that report were to be filed according to their respective titles, with an addendum clarifying that multiple texts were included, and listing the names of those other texts in order for cross-referencing if necessary.

Gottlieb had assumed such matters would be seen to by secretaries: smartly groomed young women with neat desks and quick fingers. Perhaps, he had thought, he would even have such a woman assigned to him for his own use – a Silke or a Minna who always followed his instructions and for whom he would purchase small, suitable gifts on her birthday and at Christmas. She would blush when presented with these tokens of gratitude, and would not cast them to the back of a drawer all but untouched. She would not list them in a ledger as if they were soup bowls or pillowcases. She would not keep breaking them and asking him to glue them back together. She would keep the boxes they came in, filling them with love letters or seashells or dead flowers, and she would smooth the wrinkles from the paper that bore the names of elegant department stores: Hertie, KaDeWe, Wertheim; one could not argue with the quality of their wares, and besides, they were in German hands now.

'I think there has been a miscommunication,' Gottlieb said to the man whose name he did not know. 'My position is Senior Retrospective Editor, Publications Division. This was in the letter.' He retrieved the document – stamped and signed – from his briefcase, but the man waved it away.

'Every employee at the Division takes responsibility for his own documents, even the Minister,' said the man. 'Nobody has access to another's papers. It minimises risk. Words are only a means to an end.'

'Nobody has access?'

'Nobody.'

'So my daily reports – who will read them?' said Gottlieb.

'As I said, it minimises risk.' The man removed the cover from the typewriter and set it aside, gesturing to the machine as if introducing a guest of some standing. Gottlieb stared at its rows of black keys, which were not even in alphabetical order, and the man, who seemed to understand, said, 'It is not a difficult instrument to master.' Gottlieb thought of his Onkel Heinrich's accordion with its many clicking buttons, its papery throat; he thought of his uncle's eyes closing as he picked out tunes from memory, and he remembered his own stumbling fingers getting every note wrong as the thing slumped and groaned in his grasp and his mother shook her head and said *there is no music in the boy*. Gottlieb felt short of air, and the man was leaving him now, leaving him to begin his work, and there were so many questions he should have asked and had not.

Is it really two years since that first uncertain day? Why, he hardly gives his reports a second thought any more; they almost type themselves. He is fortunate, he knows, that the Division granted him a position. They saw something in him; some secret seed that took root and spread into his every hidden corner. There is a forest within him now, and it is full of sounds you will hear nowhere else these days, and the sounds perch lightly on the branches, and flit beneath the dark canopy, and sing and sing.

He takes up his scalpel: *In the beginning was the Word, and the Word was with   , and the Word was   .*

★

Each morning at the factory the new Führers wait, lined up on the tables in their dozens, glinting in the early light. They have cooled and hardened and now they are ready, and I see the women go to them, these newborns, cupping them in their palms and looking them over, checking everything is correct. Their production depends on so many people, a whole chain of people, all doing their part, and any number of things can go wrong: deficiencies and distortions, cracks and tears, crazing, contamination; there is no telling what will emerge when the moulds are opened.

FRAU MÜLLER: This one's not right.
FRAU MILLER: It's a bad batch.
FRAU MÜLLER: The tip of the nose, the left ear . . .

FRAU MILLER:	That's the fourth nose this week.
FRAU MÜLLER:	It's not an omen.
FRAU MILLER:	Of course it's not an omen.
FRAU MÜLLER:	Stop staring at it, then.
FRAU MILLER:	If anything were to happen to him . . .
FRAU MÜLLER:	I don't like it when you talk that way. Nothing will happen.
FRAU MILLER:	Do you know that there are women who kiss his cold form every night?
FRAU MÜLLER:	I have heard of such women.
FRAU MILLER:	Can we blame them?
FRAU MÜLLER:	No. We cannot blame them.

The heads are lighter than they appear, cast in base metal and finished to look like solid bronze. They warm beneath the women's hands, coming to life, but if you turn them upside down you will find they are hollow; you will see the backwards mouth, the backwards eyes, the dark dome of the skull. The women touch the flow lines and the voids, the linden-leaf blemishes, deciding what they can correct with their brushes and cloths and what cannot be fixed. There might be a hole in the temple, the suggestion of a wound, a congenital fault: such examples are returned to the furnace and melted back down. I have witnessed this process, the malformed faces distending and collapsing, unmaking themselves.

And here come the children.

'This is a very special factory, boys and girls. You probably have one of their Führers in your house. Show me how many of you have the Führer in your house . . . Good. Good. Hiltrud, what about you? Irmgard? My goodness. That does surprise me. Well, perhaps your parents do have the Führer but have simply placed him on a shelf that is too high for you to see, yes, up on high in an honoured position. My own parents have done this with their Führer. These parents are the best sort of parents. And those few of you who really do not have the Führer can go home and tell your Mutti and Vati that they need to fix this, and the sooner the better.'

★

Brigitte Heilmann had always admired her sister-in-law's samovar. Whenever she went to visit Hannelore in Dahlem it sat on the sabre-legged table between them like a trophy, hissing during the gaps in conversation.

'It holds forty cups,' Hannelore told her. Of course she meant the tea-glasses the Russians used, not proper German cups, but Brigitte had been taught the importance of good manners, and never corrected her sister-in-law on this point.

The samovar – so Hannelore said – had belonged to the Russian royal family before her parents bought it, and indeed it was very grand, wrought from the heaviest silver, with feet in the shape of lion's paws and rosewood handles to guard against burns.

'Hannelore's samovar is the most beautiful thing. I would love to own such a piece,' Brigitte had said to her husband several times over the years, but he was not a perceptive man.

She had never attended an auction before, although she had passed the salerooms around the Ku'damm often enough. She had seen the people picking over goods from deceased estates, scrutinising hallmarks, questioning provenance, testing the strength of chairs, the softness of sofas, inspecting crystal for chips and linen for stains. There was something distasteful to Brigitte about buying used wares – you never could be sure exactly who had used them – but lately there had been more and more sale notices in the newspaper, and one in particular caught her eye. *General household effects: walnut dining suite, assorted feather beds, upright piano, fine Persian carpets, sewing machine, clocks, silverware, table lamps, costume jewellery, antique samovar, gas stove, typewriter, etc.* She lingered over the word *antique*. Antiques were not the same as used goods; they were pieces of history, and one had a duty to preserve them. And besides, what with the shortages – which were quite necessary, of course they were, she was not arguing with that – it was becoming more and more difficult to find the things one wanted in the shops.

On her way to the sale she fidgeted and worried, jiggling Kurt on her lap and willing the tram to go faster. Sieglinde had begged to come too, and had rushed home from her half-day at school rather than dawdling with her friends as she usually did, swapping pieces of shrapnel and feeding the squirrels in the Tiergarten and who knew what else. All the same, there was no time to spare, no time for Siggi to say a proper hello to Gottlieb and tell him what she had learned that day. Perhaps somebody else wanted the samovar. Perhaps it was not, in fact, antique. It could be dented, damaged in some way, or of inferior quality. Sometimes the newspapers stretched the truth . . . but no, she told herself. No; it was a beautiful early autumn Saturday, hardly a cloud in the sky, if you didn't look for clouds, and the leaves were the colour of the sun and had not yet fallen, and there had been no real raids for weeks.

She was surprised when they reached the right street to

see that it was a residential part of the city, with no auction houses to be found.

'Mutti?' said Sieglinde. 'Are we in the right place?'

Brigitte took the notice from her pocket and checked: yes, this was the right place – but had there been a misprint? Had the sale already started somewhere else, and was some other woman buying her samovar?

'Quickly, Siggi,' she said, and she rushed along the pavement, Kurt's pushchair jolting and jumping. He did not wake. They passed a newspaper display – *Who Is the Enemy?* – and a butcher shop, a single pig strung up by its trotters in the window. Ahead of her she could see a mass of people gathered in a front garden where asters bloomed in the flower beds. Such a crowd, and everyone trying to get inside at once; but still, they did not look like the sort who would appreciate an antique samovar. She and Sieglinde made their way to the fourth floor, dragging Kurt's pushchair up every step and resting on the landings, ignoring the complaints of those impatient to get past. Woe to the nation that neglects its women and mothers, she thought. It condemns itself. The stairwell smelled of potatoes, and her stomach rumbled; they were missing their midday meal to come to the auction, but sometimes sacrifices were necessary. She could hear fragments of music and conversation as she moved past closed doors, and radios interrupting themselves with trumpets and drums to announce the latest victories. When she reached the fourth floor she caught her breath for a moment and straightened her hat and smoothed Sieglinde's hair, even letting two or three other people go ahead of them. It would not do to appear too eager. Kurt had woken, and was struggling out of his pushchair.

'Good day,' Brigitte nodded to the woman at the

entrance, then began moving towards the living room, where she could see a table stacked with neat piles of bed linen. 'Come along, darling,' she said to Kurt, who had sat down on the hall carpet and was playing with its fringe. Sieglinde, she realised, was already in the kitchen, looking at a marble-topped cabinet.

'One moment,' called the woman. 'You need to register. You need a number.' She tapped a pile of forms with a bitten fingernail.

'Of course, yes,' said Brigitte, and filled in her details. She smiled at the woman, because although she was anxious to get inside, she understood the importance of paperwork. 'There's a big crowd today,' she said.

The woman shrugged. 'I've seen bigger. At the one in Delbrückstrasse last week – in Grunewald, you know – there was no room to breathe. Top-quality goods – a whole villa, three storeys. Chandeliers, everything. But who needs a chandelier?'

'Who indeed?' murmured Brigitte. 'Siggi!' she called. 'This way.'

In the living room she picked her way through the crowd, holding Kurt's hand all the while, because it would be so easy to lose him. She paused to consider a piano stool, a pair of bookends, a beaten-pewter clock . . . and yes, there was the samovar, waiting on an armchair like a courteous host.

'Oh!' said Sieglinde, for she had seen it too. 'It's just as nice as Tante Hannelore's!'

'Don't you think? If not nicer,' said Brigitte. Perhaps it too had belonged to royalty; clearly its provenance was sound. The silver possessed that soft bloom seen only on antique pieces, and the handles were of ebony so smooth it might have been black bone.

'Mutti, look at the little tap!' said Sieglinde – and indeed, it was a fine feature. It took the form of a fish, its body curling serpent-like back on itself before flaring out into a graceful tail, its open mouth the point from which the boiling water would gush. There was even a matching tray in the shape of a silver keyhole.

'Tante Hannelore's samovar doesn't have a matching tray,' said Sieglinde.

'No, Schatz, it doesn't,' said Brigitte.

A little time remained before the auction started, so they explored the rest of the apartment, Kurt trailing behind. The kitchen was very well appointed, with two separate sinks, which she had never seen before.

'One for the pots and pans, and one for the plates and glasses,' said Sieglinde.

'Perhaps that's it,' said Brigitte. Siggi was such a logical child; she took after her father.

Breadcrumbs sprinkled the table – a miniature trail through the trees stitched on the pretty cloth – and without thinking she cupped her hand and swept them up. That was better. Next to the oven stood a large cabinet with a marble top – the one Sieglinde had seen when they arrived. She pressed her palm to it, feeling the stony coolness that she knew was the secret to the best pastry. She could make perfect Apfeltaschen – Gottlieb's favourite – if she owned a cabinet like this. Sieglinde was opening the little china drawers, each bearing the name of its fragrant contents: *Cloves, Cinnamon, Nutmeg, Ginger.* They smelled like Christmas.

'Careful, Siggi,' she said. 'Don't spill anything.' Her own spice rack was a small wooden affair that always made her think of a doll's chest of drawers, as if she were just playing house. She had never cared for it. She searched the cabinet for a catalogue number but could find none, and when she tried dragging it away from the wall to check its back she discovered it was fixed in place.

'Isn't it for sale too?' said Sieglinde.

'I don't think so,' said Brigitte.

'But it would be so nice in our kitchen. And look, it still has lots of cinnamon. We don't have any left.'

In the bathroom a showerhead as broad as a sunflower jutted from the ceiling. Brigitte imagined herself standing beneath it, the water surging over her hair and down her body, her own private storm. A facecloth hung over the edge of the bath, and she nudged it with the tip of her shoe. It had dried into a stiff curve and it made a gentle thunk as it fell to the floor, like a book dropped from a sleepy hand late at night. Kurt picked it up and began to chew on it, but Sieglinde took it from him and said, 'Dirty,' and led him away before he could register he had lost something.

They slipped into a bedroom where two women were circling a bassinet. One made a tutting sound as she identified areas of chipped paint on the wicker, while the other, ignoring her, thumped the bare mattress and the pillow.

'Mutti, look!' said Sieglinde, pointing to a vase on the dressing table – a white china vase in the shape of a hand, exactly the same as the one on Brigitte's dressing table at home. She picked it up – no damage, no repairs, just a single dead fly rattling around inside. Sieglinde was tugging at the front of her blouse, saying, 'You've done it wrong. Mutti, that's wrong,' and she caught sight of herself in the wardrobe's mirrored door and realised that her blouse buttons were in the wrong buttonholes. Well, really – could the woman who had taken her details at the door not have spoken up? Did people no longer look out for their neighbours? At least, she told herself, fixing her error, those of good breeding would recognise that the blouse, although incorrectly buttoned, was of the best quality – none of this rubbish made from wood pulp. She was careful with her clothes; she made them last. Inside the wardrobe she found two dozen or more empty coat hangers, each padded with satin in the palest shades of peach, yellow, mint, powder blue, the wire hooks adorned with tiny bows in contrasting shades. She ran a finger along them, setting them swinging.

When she returned to the living room she saw a man examining the samovar; he turned it upside down and its lid fell off, clattering back against the tray. Brigitte winced, but it was not her place to say anything. She busied herself with a pile of children's books, trying to distract Kurt. How curious, she thought: at the moment the samovar belonged to nobody, but within the next hour or so it would be hers, and she would be quite within her rights to report anybody who treated it so roughly. *I write to inform you that today an item that has been in my family for many generations was mishandled and possibly damaged by an individual who obviously has no idea of the value of such artefacts and who is exactly the sort of person we as a nation can do without.*

The auctioneer took his place at a small lectern, as if intending to read from a holy text – and the auction was under way. Hands shot into the air as the woman with the bitten fingernails held item after item aloft. Everything was for sale: the potted plants, the gramophone records, the carpets on the floor, the blinds at the windows. Up and down went the arms of the buyers, saluting the acquisition of these new possessions, and Brigitte, too, found herself bidding on things she had not even known she wanted –

things she had not even inspected to make sure they were sound. Her hand seemed to fly up of its own accord.

As she and the children left the house she saw a woman in the garden frowning at the trampled asters.

'Look at this!' said the woman. 'I shall be making a complaint to the authorities.'

During the tram ride home, Brigitte cradled the samovar on her lap. She could see herself in the silver, the curved surface warming to the temperature of her blood, pulling her face into expressions she could not name.

★

The days are shrinking; the field-grey sky descends over the city, and the war keeps on rolling in like bad weather, and the troop trains keep on leaving. Things are wearing thin; even the books are full of holes. Some pages are missing so many words that those remaining cannot support themselves, and they collapse and tear. Slipshod, faulty, it's all coming apart. In the east they are kicking at Moscow's door, waiting for the whole rotten structure to come crashing down. And in Berlin the Führer is visiting the cemetery, he is inspecting the graves, and they are clean, they are spotless, as tidy as a German hearth, and the people have made their contributions, the living urged to keep the dust from the dead, and this shows pride and national spirit; yes, the living have paid, and the Führer inspects the dead, watching from behind his postage-stamp moustache, a black square sent from a dark country, and the trees hold their leaves in check, the grass orders its blades, the stones keep to their ranks, in their thousands they are still, the wind itself holds its breath, and beneath the earth the dead make their dirty salute.

★

For the first time in his life he found himself face to face with a
*   not to be appeased or fobbed off by a   or a   , not*
to be placated by   or song or impressed by clink of spurs
and arms, not to be wooed or wheedled with charming ways
and light   . For once the boy of twenty-four felt   ,
*   ,   . It was not the clear, tangible   of*
the situation – that his child lay   , that tomorrow he had to
rejoin his regiment, abandon Cornelie to almost certain
and the   of   .

'Look at this,' Brigitte said, holding up a page. 'You can see right through it.'

Gottlieb did not reply, but the book was one of his; he recognised the clean, assured cuts. Brigitte did not grasp the danger of an uncorrected text. He once heard of a bible in Stockholm, written with the help of the Devil and containing his red-clawed image, and that page, the Devil's page, was the most consulted in the entire volume, the most thumbed and soiled. People were drawn to such things. He could see fragments of his wife through the corrections; a small green eye, half a lip, a strand of curly dark-blond hair. Yes, that was definitely one of his. He took pride in making his excisions as neat and as small as possible, placing a thick sheet of card beneath the pages so he did not slice through more than one layer, positioning the blade at the exact beginning and the exact end of each word, taking no more paper than was necessary. He had a feeling for how to manipulate the scalpel so that it skimmed the precise point at which white became black and black became white.

Complaints about the books had been noted, however; they had been collated and typed up and filed.

'Could we not ink out the words in question?' Gottlieb had asked, demonstrating, he believed, exactly the kind of strategic thinking that would win the war. His suggestion was considered; it was expanded into a three-stage report; it was analysed and edited and reviewed.

But no. Then the words would still be there, crouched beneath their inky disguise. And besides, it had also become clear that it was not as straightforward as cutting them out, because underneath those words were more words, and they simply took the place of the missing ones, and although they might function perfectly well in their original context, the meaning shifted and changed when they slipped into the holes. And there were other complaints: removing a word on one side of a page interfered too much with the text on the other side. There had even been reports of people pasting in their own words. All sorts of stories were taking shape. Why had nobody thought of this?

As soon as the Division realised how many altered texts were circulating they established a new procedure, instructing Gottlieb and his colleagues to take only the top layer of the page, and equipping them with blades fashioned from the best surgical steel, blades so thin and so fine they all but vanished when viewed along their cutting edge. It took a little patience to perfect this new procedure, but nobody could say it was not sensible, and after one or two false starts – a torn page, a sliced thumb – it was hailed a great success. Bibles still presented one of the most difficult challenges, of course; their pages refused to behave and often disintegrated entirely, and so a special sub-procedure was established for these cases, and a special blade developed that could scrape away only the ink from a page, leaving it fit to be written on again, and by this means *God* was replaced with *Hitler*.

Was Gottlieb ever tempted to take some of the deleted words home with him? To slip them into his pocket, to fan them out on his dining table, to plant them in other books, perhaps, or toss them to the sky like confetti, like wishes for a prosperous future? No. He was not that sort of man. At the end of each day he carried the material to the cellar and emptied it into the trapdoor that led to the furnace, and on his way home, as he walked to the U-Bahn, he could see the smoke rising from the outstretched chimney. The words were meaningless now; unrecognisable. Tiny specks, lighter than air, dissolving into the clouds. By the time he reached the station they had disappeared.

Sometimes he disembarked one stop early and strolled along Tauentzienstrasse and the Ku'damm, pausing to look at the window displays. They appealed to him, these little scenes, arranged along the shops' glassy façades like postcards propped on a mantelpiece: women in Japanese kimonos sitting in flower-covered boats; bolts of cloth caught into starbursts and waterfalls and sails; shoes without feet and gloves without hands and hats without heads. Most of the goods were not for sale, naturally, due to the shortages, but the shops still had to display them as if they were. Today a woman was assembling a man; he lay in pieces before her, open-eyed, and she fastened him together limb by limb and dressed him for autumn. Already she had fixed dead leaves to the glass – she had an eye for these things – and she nailed piano wire to the sky and drew it down length by length, holding it to the floor, considering its slant, fine-tuning the rain. The weather was turning, and whoever was homeless now would never build a home.

On the corner of Bleibtreustrasse a man was playing 'No Lovelier Land', and Gottlieb dropped a coin into his accordion case to pay for the memory the song revived.

When Onkel Heinrich returned home from the Somme he had lost his voice, and although no doctor could locate any wounds, any damage, he never found it again. Instead, he played his accordion: 'All Men Are Criminals' when his sister's heart was broken, and 'Five Wild Swans Once Went A-Roaming' on Totensonntag; 'The Moon Has Risen' when he wanted guests to leave, and 'Bring Me the Blood of Noble Vines' when he was thirsty. Sometimes on Sundays he took Gottlieb to Luna Park and let him have a sip of his beer in the Bavarian village, and held his hand as they careened down the water slide and into the lake. They lost their footing on the shimmy-steps that never stopped moving, and watched the Somali villagers drumming and stamping, and the swivel-house threatened to topple right over and so did the high-wire walkers, and afterwards Gottlieb tried to explain it all to his mother and father, who did not care for such places, and Onkel Heinrich just smiled and played 'Not Every Day Is Sunday'.

The accordion fell from his hands when his heart failed, letting out a rattle as it hit the floor, the bellows splitting open, the buttons coming loose and skittering away like knocked-out teeth. Gottlieb did not know what happened to it after that. Perhaps they buried it with Onkel Heinrich, two broken things shut in a box. Perhaps, by now, it was threaded through with roots, stopped with dirt. Rise up, rise up, brave comrades.

But times were better now. This war was nothing like the last. And despite the people Gottlieb passed on the street – the women dressed in mourning and the men with their missing arms and bandaged eyes – he felt a great lightening; a bubble of something like happiness expanding in his chest and buoying him homewards along the pavement. Yes, why not happiness? It could be generated if you tried hard enough. When the Olympics were coming people were happy. The Labour Front declared a Week of Jollity – scheduled to last eight days – and Berlin obeyed and was cheerful. What did the source of happiness matter?

★

One Sunday afternoon there was a knock at the door. Brigitte was halfway through counting the cutlery and waited for her husband to answer it, but he called, 'I'll lose my place.' She knew there were times when he could not leave a silhouette; she thought of him shut in those dark structures, no windows and no doors until he cut them himself. There was another knock, and she put down her pen. Eleven, she said to herself. Eleven. It was probably the Hitler Youth boys collecting rags and paper and bottles and fat and razorblades and bones and goodness knows what else, they were always asking for something, those polite boys with their Blood and Honour and their lists of names – but there at the door stood her neighbour from across the landing.

'Frau Loewenthal. How are you?'

'Very well, thank you – I just have a question, if you've a moment to spare.'

Brigitte wondered if she would have to invite her inside or if the matter could be handled on the threshold, away from the disarrayed china, the piles of knives – quite apart from the mess, it wouldn't do for her to be seen asking such a person into her home. *They Are Our Ruin! They Incited the War! The War Is Their Fault!* She could see the Loewenthals' hallway from where she stood, and it was the mirror image of their own: the same shape and size, but everything reversed. The whole apartment was like that – or so

Brigitte assumed, since she had only ever caught glimpses of it when the door was open. Except: there were the overcoats hanging dark and slack from their hooks, breasts freshly stitched with the yellow star. Well, that was only sensible, because it was the law now, and the Loewenthals were sensible people; they had sent their children away even before the bombing began – although Brigitte did not quite approve of the sending away of children. But they put their rubbish into the bins in the courtyard without dropping cores and peelings and crusts that would attract vermin, unlike other residents she could name, and they always made sure the buckets of sand and water on their landing were full, and they never beat their carpets outside the permitted times. And they stayed in their apartment when the sirens sounded, and did not go down to the cellar with everyone else, because that also was the law.

'What is it, Frau Loewenthal?' she said.

'Well . . . you'll think I'm mad, but I keep hearing noises in the night.'

'Noises?'

'They seem to be coming from your apartment. I'm not accusing you of anything,' she added in a rush.

'What sort of noises?' said Brigitte.

'It's hard to say. A kind of dragging – or a heavy creaking. And our apartment, our living room – I can't explain it, but I keep feeling that it's . . . smaller.'

'What an odd thing to suggest,' said Brigitte. 'Smaller? A very strange thing to say. Perhaps it's the darker days – the loss of light. At any rate, I haven't heard any noises. I haven't heard a thing.'

She returned to her ledger. Now, where was she? Where was she? Quite lost. The knives were all a jumble. Nine? Twelve? It was no good. She sighed and started counting again, slipping each knife into its felt-lined slot as she went, trying not to think about what Frau Loewenthal had said. Really, it was too much – neighbours calling on other neighbours on a Sunday, unannounced, and making strange suggestions. There was nothing going on, nothing at all. And even if there were – even if certain realignments and corrections were under way – they were certainly not in her control, nor indeed in Frau Loewenthal's, and there was nothing to be done about it. Nine, she said to herself, a clock chiming the hours. Ten. Eleven. Twelve.

When she had finished she went into the living room and sat in her usual chair. She stared at the closed piano, which she had not played in months; she could not think of any songs. Gottlieb was still busy cutting his new silhouette – a bombed-out chapel, made whole in his hands – but where would they put all these shadows? She did not know how to enter them into her ledger; she could not describe them. Sometimes she thought she might take up the scissors herself and cut out a different skyline, broken and falling, every day less of it intact. She considered the Führer's portrait that hung above the sofa. If the house were bombed, that wall would not be destroyed – so she had heard. To her eye it did seem more distant, as if the wall had moved, as if the room held more and more space in which shadows could fall – but maybe it was just the season, the darker days, as she had said to Frau Loewenthal. That was logical, wasn't it? That made sense. The samovar sat on the Heilmann sideboard, freshly polished. She had displayed it there so that Hannelore would be sure to see it, but her sister-in-law had not remarked on it once. Perhaps, Brigitte thought, she should actually use it when Hannelore visited, but it was in such perfect order, and she did not want to risk spoiling it. A collision with a teaspoon, a knock against the kitchen sink . . . these things happened; they happened. Last time Hannelore came she paused when she entered the living room, and Brigitte thought she had finally noticed it, but all she said was, 'Have you shifted something?' She turned and turned, trying to get her bearings.

'We did make some rearrangements,' said Brigitte.

'How clever you are!' said Hannelore. 'It's so much bigger.'

Brigitte knew this could not be true, not really. If she were asked to turn away and sketch the room from memory, she reasoned, she would make mistakes. She might place the sofa too far from the door to the dining room, or draw the radio too big in relation to the end table. She would be sure to get the perspective wrong, because even when dealing with the most familiar, the best loved, memory is imperfect. No, the room was not bigger, and the Führer's portrait was just where it always had been.

Gottlieb looked up from his black chapel. 'It's an excellent likeness,' he said, nodding to the portrait. 'Very close to the real person.'

'Have you met him?' said Brigitte. It was quite possible, and she did not know why this had never occurred to her before. The work Gottlieb did at the Division was of national importance, whatever it was, so why wouldn't the Führer visit? Had they shaken hands? Exchanged words?

'No,' said Gottlieb. 'I have not met him. But even if I had, I couldn't tell you about it.'

'So you have met him, then,' said Brigitte. 'Imagine Hannelore's face!' Hannelore, with her Mother's Cross pinned to every outfit. Hannelore, with her spacious Dahlem apartment, and her four Wehrmacht sons who sent her coffee from Belgium and furs from Norway.

Hannelore, who had never even remarked on Brigitte's samovar, when clearly it was a finer example than her own – and now she had volunteered to work at a first-aid station at night. Brigitte could never compete with that.

'Hannelore is not to be told that I have met him. Nor that I have not met him. Which I haven't.'

'So . . . you haven't not met him.'

Gottlieb returned to his chapel.

I know that Gottlieb Heilmann has never met him. It is true – or it is said, which amounts to the same thing – that the Reichskanzler visits the Division now and then, and that he has been introduced to several colleagues, including Gottlieb's immediate neighbour. Gottlieb believes he witnessed this through the frosted glass: a flurry of straight-armed salutes, an exchange of pleasantries he could not quite make out. It was just as difficult to make out the figures; the glass blurred them to ghosts, and before Gottlieb could decide who they were the footsteps were retreating down the spotless corridor. Still, he feels quite justified in withholding this information from his wife. It is safer if the Führer's movements are kept secret, so that – in theory – it is possible he is everywhere at once, like the Lord God Almighty, like gas in a sealed box.

The German Face

O bird, are you   now?
    I delivered you into
         sister-hands
Perhaps they might still   you from your   ;
Was there no   to be found?
I saw two eyes, as black as your own,
Meet your gaze, and then
Its   went out.
Did they   to you of   ?
Come now, if they proved   to you,
Then your   was not so   .

July 1942
Near Leipzig

In the honey jar on his windowsill, Erich keeps his precious things: an empty snail shell, an acorn, a dead and perfect bee, even the wings untorn – do bees turn to dust when they die? This one is still whole, but why then is the world not carpeted with bees? – and the paper flags from the parade, which have faded to pink and grey, like an evening sky that promises good weather. There's a banknote in there too, worth ten thousand marks – or it was, at one time, when the people who lived in the cities carried their money around in laundry baskets. Erich's father had given it to him before he went to be a soldier.

'Look,' Papa had said, pointing to the illustration on the note. 'What do you see?'

'A man,' said Erich.

'Look closely.'

Erich peered at the figure. The man was wearing old clothes and an old hat and was looking out of the picture and towards the middle of the note, where its value was printed, and he seemed to be frowning, unable to believe what he read.

'Turn it sideways,' said Papa. 'Now do you see?'

'A . . . sideways man?'

'Look at the farmer's neck.'

'Is he a farmer?'

'Doesn't he look like a farmer?'

'I suppose so.'

'Look at his neck. Here. And his collar. See?'

'Yes,' said Erich. 'Yes, I see.' But he saw nothing, just the farmer lying on his side, as if he had fallen and could not get up, and all the zeroes piled one on top of another like a stack of stones.

Later that afternoon, when Papa was talking to the inspector from the Reich Food Estate, who had come to measure their fields and count their hens and weigh their cows, Erich examined the note again, turning it to one side and looking and looking. He looked until his eyes hurt. He held the note at arm's length and squinted; he brought it close to his face and felt the soft, wrinkled paper brushing his lashes. It smelled like autumn. He saw nothing.

It was the second summer that Papa was away, but the wheat and the barley still rose from the ground without him, and the ears of corn swelled in their husks, and Ronja pulled the wagon and the cows let down their milk and Mama chopped the heads off the hens, all without Papa.

'The Führer will provide for us,' said Mama, and when the foreign workers came to help on the farm, she said, 'You see?'

They slept in the barn, the foreign workers, one section of which they converted into basic living quarters; that was their first job. Erich was not to go there by himself and not to talk to them, no matter how friendly they seemed, because they came from other places and could not be trusted. They spoke almost no German, and who could tell what they had in mind? If they saw him listening to them they stopped talking, but sometimes, if his bedroom window was open, he could hear them. Their language was softer than German, looser, and Erich repeated to himself a few of the words he could catch. They shushed and buzzed in his mouth, and he thought he might know what they meant – he could almost understand them, if he shut out everything else – but it was like trying to remember a dream after you have opened your eyes and risen from your bed.

Mama had to mime to the foreign workers the jobs she needed them to do, and every now and then – when they knew they were out of her line of sight – Erich saw them smiling to one another as she milked invisible cows, plucked invisible hens, dug invisible holes with invisible shovels.

He lay in the long grass and spun his circle of card back and forth, rolling the strings between his thumb and forefinger, watching the two halves of the face merge and separate, merge and separate. The hives were murmuring and bees floated above him, their wings and bodies backlit and black. *I turned first to water and then to ice*, said the hive of Luise. *We could not drink from the wells*, said the hive of Great-Onkel Gustav. Erich could not tell how close or how far away the bees were; perhaps they were just specks of dust in his eyes; perhaps they were great distant birds. At school his teacher had pinned a chart to the classroom wall: German planes and enemy planes seen from below, so that everyone could learn the shapes and know when to be afraid. Erich was aware that some people feared bees, freezing if they saw a single one, or thrashing their arms about and gasping for breath, drowning in air. Lina, one of the girls from the Reich Labour Service, was like that. She'd been sent to help on the farm, as well as the foreign workers, because all Germans had to do their duty and it was an honour to serve. Erich had hoped they might host a refugee family from one of the big cities that was being bombed; some of his classmates were hosting such families, and were already firm friends with the children. It would be like having brothers and sisters, he thought – but Mama said they must make do with the foreign workers and with Lina, even though she didn't know one end of a cow from another, and refused to go near the hives.

'Now then,' said Mama when she found her shaking in the stable. 'There's no reason to be afraid.'

'Yes,' said Lina, crushing straw in her hands, turning it to dust. 'I'm sorry.'

'Shall I tell you something about bees?'

Lina nodded.

'Well, it's true they can attack if they feel threatened, and it's true they are wild creatures, and cannot think the way that you and I can think. But it's also true that we can train them to do as we wish. We can correct nature – stop up a stream to alter its flow. Yes?'

Lina nodded again; Mama was good at explaining away frightening things. Erich had heard her talking to Tante Uschi once: a child who has been frightened in his early years by stories of the bogey man, she said, will often retain a fear of dark rooms, cellars and the like. On the other hand, threats that are never brought to his attention will be ignored.

'But of course,' Mama went on, 'although the bees cannot think the way that you and I can think, still we must win them over.'

'Yes,' said Lina.

'And so we let them sting us now and then, for our own safety, and it does not hurt, or only as much as a pinch from a spiteful sister, so quick that it's over before you notice.'

'It's true,' said Erich, 'it doesn't hurt, and anyway, you get used to it.'

I knew what the girl was thinking, even as she nodded and agreed. *Where am I? What is this place, and what is this safety?* And perhaps it was not just the bees that frightened her but the hives themselves; the carved faces that watched through the trees when she looked for windfalls in the grass. She kept her distance from them, sitting at the other end of the orchard or in the garden when she took a break, picking buttercups and white hemlock flowers. She pushed off her shoes and socks and hitched her dress up above her knees, and the hair on her legs was fine and pale, and the light fell over her face and shoulders and she looked like one of the ladies in the book Tante Uschi had lent Mama, with the pictures of people doing nude gymnastics in forests and fields, and bringing in the harvest with no clothes on.

Erich showed her how to put on Papa's bee-keeping suit, how to make sure not a single patch of skin was exposed – like Siegfried and the linden leaf, he said, but she did not understand – and when she had tucked the trousers into her boots and pulled on the gloves and lowered the veil she might have been Papa, back from the war. She might have reached for Erich's hand and said, 'Shall we have a look at *Pictures from the Life of the Führer*?' and taken the album from the shelf and leafed through it with him, pointing out favourite pictures and wondering if they would ever find the missing ones to fill the gaps. But she coughed when Mama lit the smoker, and stumbled on a root, and pushed the veil away from her mouth even though Mama told her that bees are attracted to breath – and she was not Papa, and Papa was still not there.

'We must keep writing to him,' said Mama. 'We must

keep telling him all the happy things in our lives, and only the happy things.'

On Sunday afternoons, when they sat together at the kitchen table and composed their letters, Mama looked over Erich's shoulder to check what he wrote – not for spelling mistakes but for traces of sadness, which were also a kind of mistake. Erich told Papa about the foreign workers (no, said Mama), and about Lina (yes, said Mama), and about the Hitler Youth boys who came to help with the harvest and who showed him their belt buckles and their daggers (yes, said Mama). He told him how tall his copse of larches had grown (yes, said Mama), and how he hoped Papa would be back to see them change colour in autumn (no, said Mama). He told him that he could trim Ronja's hooves by himself now (yes, said Mama), and that they were lucky she was old and the army didn't want her (no, said Mama). He told him how Frau Ingwer had compared all the boys and girls in his class to her chart of The German Face, asking them to come up one at a time and stand next to it while she measured their skulls and noses and jaws and pointed out certain features with her stick. Erich was the perfect German, she announced, which was to say, he was Nordic, and as a prize she let him sit in her chair at the front of the classroom while all the other children made drawings of him and his German Face. ('You didn't tell me about that,' said Mama, and Erich said, 'Is it a happy thing?' For he could not be sure.)

I see the teacher congratulating Erich, shaking him by the hand and showing him to her chair beneath the Führer's face, and every eye in the room is watching, and he shifts and fidgets as his classmates begin to draw him, to copy his correct forehead and approved ears. One or two frown at their books, look up at him and frown again.

They cross him out; they cannot get him right. Erich still feels the touch of the callipers at his temples, the hands at his mouth and neck, and he stares at the map of the world on the far wall with its rows of swastika flags pinned to mark the advancement of the German troops. They leave little marks each time the children shift them – tiny punctured lines, an army of holes. One day there will be more holes than land.

'What's this?' says Frau Ingwer, bending over Heinz Kuppel's drawing, but before Heinz can answer she has torn it from his book, crumpled it in her fist and thrown it away. 'Monstrous,' she says, though Heinz had not meant to make a monster. Still, a punishment is in order, even for an accidental monster; the Führer does not tolerate art that warps and degrades the thing depicted. Frau Ingwer goes to her desk and takes out a booklet and finds a suitable page. I see the other things she keeps inside the drawer: a broken comb, a glass marble, a photograph of a man holding a white cat, and Erich sees them too, though he should not be looking, it is rude to look. Is Frau Ingwer about to cry? I find it difficult to make such predictions – I had so little time to cry myself – but she cried when she spoke of the Führer losing his sight in the Great War, and she cried when she showed the children a postcard of the cell that was his home for nine long months, and again when she repeated Reichsminister Goebbels's words on the occasion of the Führer's birthday – *We felt as if we had to see him, be it only in a photograph, to gain the strength we need* – and she finds no pleasure in punishing the children, and only does so because it is right. As she closes the drawer we hear the marble rolling around and around in the dark. 'Start here,' she says to Heinz Kuppel, placing the booklet in front of him, and he begins to write:

Courage is a characteristic of people of German blood. In the past, one understood the concept of Germany as the territory that belonged to the German Reich. It was the Führer who taught the German people that Germany is the community of those with German blood. State borders are not created by nature, as are races and peoples, but rather are the work of men. With this knowledge, we realise that the German people extends far beyond Germany's state borders.

After the children have finished their drawings, Frau Ingwer says that it is time for everyone (except Heinz Kuppel) to go outside and pick their herbs: yarrow to staunch bleeding, chamomile for pain, foxglove for the heart, linden flowers to sedate. They are dried in the school's airless attic and the weight is recorded, reported, and each child must pick two kilos per year to help heal the wounded soldiers and to show that they are good children who love their country and want to win the war. And it would be a very fine thing if their school were to exceed the required weight and to pick the most per head in their region, because the Reich Association for Medicinal Plant Science and the Provision of Medicinal Plants publishes the results, and everyone can see at a glance which schools are lazy and disloyal and which are filled with the right sort of children.

Erich has not seen the attic with all the leaves and flowers spread out to dry; each week Frau Ingwer selects two boys to take the bags of herbs up there, but he is still too young to be chosen. He imagines it as a meadow – this is how he describes it to Papa in his letter, before Mama tells him he cannot write about gathering plants to make into medicine for wounded soldiers – but of course, it is not like that at all.

★

Tante Uschi also wrote letters. Her fiancé Gerhard was somewhere in the desert, just as Papa was somewhere in Russia. Uschi and Gerhard had never met: his train had passed through Leipzig one day when she happened to be at the station, and it slowed down but did not stop, for the men were on their way to the steppe, to the desert, to the ocean, to all the places where borders were shifting. The young women on the platform waved to the men, and the men opened the windows and let the scraps of paper fly, and the scraps read *Joachim Kalb, 09589B,* and *Peter Eckstein, 18608A,* and *Ulrich Portner, M13039,* and that is how Ursula obtained her Gerhard, by snatching at his name as it blew towards her in the slipstream of a train, and what a story to tell their children, because there would be children, one day. Ursula did not see Gerhard, and Gerhard did not see Ursula, but the warm gust as the train passed by ruffled her hair like a lover's fingers, and she wrote to him in the desert, and sent him the photograph of herself in her polka-dot blouse, which made her collarbones look prettier than they were. And Gerhard wrote to Ursula – *call me Uschi,* she told him one month in – and he sent her a handful of sand, which scattered itself across her when she opened the envelope, and although she knew that it was the past ground to dust in her hands, it was also the future: a day at the beach, salt water drying on warm skin, a silky pebble slipped into a pocket.

Ursula said to her sister, 'Do you think it's possible to fall in love with letters?' and Emilie said certainly, because what else could she say now that all the men were paper? They were nothing but letters, photographs, certificates; they were little notes cast from a moving train; they were telegrams.

In the evenings Emilie removes her headscarf and brushes out her hair. There is so much of it; it hangs down past her waist, as golden and bright as Erich's. Unpinned and unbraided, she is a girl again. This is how she looked when she first met Christoph, back when she believed her future held many children, when she thought of names and held them inside her: Marco, Annegret, Gustav, Lotte. She pulls these remains from the silt, remembers checking the calendar, counting the days. For months she wondered what was wrong, held her hands to the void of her pelvis and thought: why does nothing take? Here where the new calves raise themselves up on trembling legs, where the glossy hens settle in their nests, where the queen bee lays her thousand eggs, why am I empty? Her sister brewed chasteberry for her to drink and sat with her as she sipped it, steam rising like hope, gone in a breath. And each morning she prayed to the bronze head that Christoph had bought in a shop in Leipzig, asking him to grant her this one wish, and at night he came to her in dreams, not just a head but a complete man, touching her with his bronze fingers, pinning her beneath his cool glinting bulk and sliding inside her until she shivered. She lay on the grass and listened to the lapping of the lake as he moved on top of her, her bronze lover, and daisies and dandelions dug their pollen fists into her back. And when her husband entered her she felt a weightiness forming within, a thick metallic cargo, and she thought of a little bronze child taking hold and beginning to grow, a honey-coloured child buzzing in her, brimming with sweetness.

Later, at the clinic, they laid her on the white-wrapped bed and parted her legs. This is for the best, they said.

You're right to have agreed to the procedure. They told her not to be afraid of the mask but to breathe normally, to count backwards and to breathe in the gas. And she was not afraid, never had been afraid, and had not only agreed to the procedure but requested it, and she wanted this because it was her duty, and she was proud to do her duty. Ten. Nine. Eight.

★

By the end of autumn, the hives are quiet – all the drones have been expelled; all the old and the weak pushed out into the cold. Erich peers inside at the clustering bees. He tells them, 'Don't worry. Papa will come home soon.' Yes, when the windows frost over they will heat pfennigs together on the oven and hold them to the glass so they can see little circles of the garden; they will look at *The Life of the Führer in Pictures*. But it's been months since Papa last had leave, and nobody knows when he will be back again. (And what has he buried, what has he burned?)

'Will the war be finished in time for Christmas?' Erich asks.

And Mama says, 'Wouldn't that be nice?' – which is not an answer but a question.

The following week she and Tante Uschi take Erich to church even though it is not Sunday. When they arrive it is already brimming with people, and Erich says, 'Did somebody die?'

Tante Uschi says no, nobody died, but time is up – today is the day they have to decide which bell to keep.

'Why do we have to decide?' says Erich.

'We're only allowed one,' says Tante Uschi. 'The Führer needs the rest, for the war.'

'Oh,' says Erich. He wants to ask what the Führer will do with all the bells, and whether he needs them for a victory parade to celebrate the end of the war, but the mayor has made his way to the front of the church and is starting to speak.

'The Hosanna is the oldest and therefore the most precious,' he says. 'This is the bell we must keep.'

'But the Saint Paul is the most beautifully cast,' says Herr Kuppel. 'Consider its border of vine leaves, its elegant inscription.'

'The Luther is the most technically perfect,' says Frau Ingwer. 'A noted campanologist mentions it in a book.'

'The Saint Gabriel has the sweetest voice,' says the pastor. 'I first rang it when I was six years old, and I remember the rope lifting me into the air, taking me up inside the belfry, up and up until I thought I might touch heaven, and the bird-like voice of the bell was falling down around me.'

'The Luther is the heaviest.'

'The Hosanna can be heard as far as Leipzig.'

'The Saint Gabriel saved the village from fire.'

Nobody can decide.

'Can we not refuse to give up our bells?' says a voice from the back of the church.

Everybody turns to look at the person who has uttered this extraordinary statement: Oma Kröning. Other villages and towns have hidden their bells, she says; covered them over with piles of timber, buried them in the ground. The people there are aware of the penalties if caught, but have decided they cannot choose just one bell to keep at the expense of the other bells.

Erich's village is not such a village, however.

And when they come to take the bells, they take them all.

In January they watch the lake as it freezes, Erich and Mama, each day checking the depth of the ice, each day creeping a little further across its thickening skin. When Mama says it is safe they will strap blades to their feet and glide across the frozen water, and she will teach him how to spin without falling. Choose a fixed point, she will say. Keep your eye on it as you turn. And if he feels himself losing his balance, if he sees the world tilting on its side and the ice rushing towards him, he might for a moment make out dark shapes moving beneath the surface – but she will take his hand and steady him, her face bright with cold, queen of the ice. This pains me more than I care to say. I have no fixed point. I am nowhere, I am nothing. I have never taken my mother's hand and walked across the water; I have never heard the crack and hush as a branch gives way to snow; I have never seen my breath in winter.

★

When spring arrives and the meadows begin to shine with buttercups and cowslips and violets, Erich watches the orchard for swarms. Mama trusts him to go there on his own, but she reminds him not to speak to the foreign workers if he sees them there, or anywhere else, for that matter. I almost wish we had Lina back, she says – but Lina has finished her six months' service, and now they must make do with these other workers, even though they are not German.

Erich sits amongst the hives, the sun hot on his upturned face, and if he looks at it even for a moment – though Mama says he must not – it is still there when he closes his eyes, a ghost star in a ghost sky, a backwards day. He can hear the bees bursting back into life after the winter. He knows how to catch them if they swarm, how to guide them to one of the empty hives. Perhaps, he thinks, he could shut them in a box and send them to Papa in Russia, and Papa could release them, a wonder weapon, an army too small to be hit by any bullet, and they would sting the enemy in the throat and the temples and the heart and then sink to their own splendid deaths.

He glances around – did someone speak? Are the foreign workers hiding in the orchard, whispering in their own language, making secret plans? But no, they are nowhere to be seen; it is only the beehives, talking softly of the lives they used to have. They rest their blank eyes on him: Great-Onkel Gustav, who fell at Saint-Privat, and beautiful Luise, Opa Kröning's first love, and the Frankish butcher and the black-hatted pastor, and the moneylender, and Saint John the Baptist. *In the slow hours of my death we marched in the high heat of August*, they say, their stories jumbling together. *We came in at the battle's end, they brought me their souls.* He remembers Oma Kröning sitting on his bed when he had pneumonia and telling him about the hives. And he remembers that she asked him if he would like Papa to carve one that had his face, and that he said yes when he meant no, no, no.

You Too Belong to the Führer

No   of   from
And no   of the   ones
Who are still guarding   ,
Which, taking leave, seeks its   .

No   of   ,
And no   of the
Who could never rouse youth to   ,
Who   , whilst all around   is   .

April 1943
Berlin

Sprint 60 metres in 14 seconds. Jump a distance of two metres.
Throw a ball 12 metres. Perform two forward rolls; stand up
without using your hands. Perform two backward rolls. Run
beneath a swinging rope. There will be a test of courage.

On the eve of the twentieth of April, Sieglinde
Heilmann dresses in her new uniform. It is still far too
early to leave for the celebration, but she cannot wait any
longer knowing that the brown jacket and dark-blue skirt
are hanging in her wardrobe. They are a perfect fit, and
she looks just as she should: clean and tidy, hair combed
and braided, face scrubbed, no evidence of unsuitable
ancestors. See, here is her white blouse with its oak-
leaf buttons, and here on her jacket's sleeve is her cloth
badge, sewn on above the left elbow, with the white edges
turned under so only the black border shows. Here are her
brown lace-up shoes fitted with the proper metal plates
on the heels and toes so they make the right sound when
marching. Here is her certificate of health. And here is her
handbook, and it is intact, it is perfect, every page; leaf
through it and check for yourself – there are no holes, no
deletions, not a single cut. So many rules, says Mutti, but
Sieglinde loves the book and loves the rules; they tell her
what to do, how to live, and she learns them by heart.

You must take pride in obeying your leader, and in doing your duty without fail and as a matter of course. Girls aged 10 and 11 must take part in a one-day excursion once a month, walking 10 kilometres at a rate of three kilometres per hour whilst carrying a haversack. After each hour of walking, a break of at least 15 minutes is to be taken. If for any reason you cannot attend a social evening, sports afternoon or excursion, you must apply to your group leader in advance for leave. If an unforeseen event prevents you from attending, you must provide your leader with a note of explanation at the next available opportunity. In the case of absence due to illness, as in the previous situation you must provide a note as soon as you are well. If you are sick for more than a week, you must notify your leader during that time. When you are better, you must report to your leader. If you wish to go away on holiday with your parents or stay with relatives, you must apply to your leader for leave one week in advance. If you cannot participate in a particular area of service (for example swimming, due to an ear condition), you must report to your League of German Girls doctor for a physical examination and obtain written confirmation from her. There is no such thing as an unexcused absence.

That night Sieglinde and the other new girls promise themselves to the flag and the Führer, a birthday present to him, and from then on they are allowed to attend the weekly sessions at their local meeting house, which are compulsory. They learn about the brave Germans of the past who fought for their country – Arminius, whose proper name is Hermann, who united Germania and slaughtered three Roman legions in the Teutoburg Forest; Heinrich von Plauen, who defended Marienburg against the murderous Poles; Queen Luise, who met with Napoleon to plead for Prussia; Andreas Hofer, freedom fighter and martyr, who refused the blindfold at his execution and himself gave the order to fire. And you do

117

not have to be a grown-up to die for Germany – think of Herbert Norkus, just fifteen when the Communists murdered him over in Zwinglistrasse, which isn't far away at all. He came from a family of very modest means, but was he out looking for trouble? Was he picking fights? No, he was delivering leaflets, doing his duty for the Party so that their words might reach the people in those troubled days, and for this he was stabbed six times, and his bloody handprints stained the wall where he fell, and he died for the words, and for the flag that means more than death.

The girls learn songs, too – folk songs and war songs and lullabies – and Julia, their leader, reads them fairy tales from a big red book with golden edges that she keeps in the cupboard along with the paints and paintbrushes, the scissors, the spools of thread, the pieces of fabric, the tail ends of balls of wool and string, the bottle tops, the scraps of wood, and from these raw materials the girls make smiling families, sturdy houses, clean bright trains with clean bright passengers painted in every window. Why, they could make a whole village, a whole city. Is it true, asks Edda Knopf, that there is a false Berlin on the outskirts of town? A decoy built to confuse the enemy? Julia says it could be true; it certainly could be. Didn't we cover the Lietzensee with floating planks to make it look like a suburb when seen from the air? Didn't we strip the Siegessäule of her shining layers of gold? We are a resourceful people, she says, and the girls nod. And the stories she reads them are stories of disguise and change, too, of one thing becoming another: seven sons wished into ravens; a little tailor crowned a king; a severed finger the key to unlock the glass mountain; a bone that works its way free of the earth and sings the name of its killer. And Julia speaks to them of the Führer, who has freed Germany from the fraudulent treaty signed in the hall of mirrors, and who does not ask of us anything he has not asked of himself. Six million were starving, without work – can you imagine such a number? says Julia, and no, we cannot, it is an unthinkable number – and the Führer gave jobs and bread to the six million just as he had promised, and there was no need for begging and stealing, and the streets were safe once more. And girls, you too belong to the Führer! And because you belong to him, you must make your payments each month, even if it is difficult for you and your parents and means you must make a sacrifice, and you must always remember that the Hitler Youth has prospered only because of sacrifice. But the war? The dead? The father who cuts off his daughter's hands? The sun and moon who eat children? Everyone falls silent and uncertain. Sometimes, Julia says after a moment or two, we need to accept things we don't fully understand. What matters is not so much what we believe, only that we believe. The Führer knows exactly what he is doing; we can follow him with our eyes closed. And we must trust him, and we do trust him, all of us, we trust him and we belong to him. We will march on, even if everything shatters. And if our elders scold us, let them bluster and shout. Forwards! Forwards! Youth knows no fear! And we tell ourselves that Barbarossa is not dead, cannot be dead; deep in the mountain he sleeps, his red beard piercing stone, and when the ravens leave the Kyffhäuser he will wake, he will hang his shield on the pear tree's withered branch and it will flower again.

★

'Remember the rules as we move through the factory, children. We are very lucky to be visiting it, unlike some other schools who have been sent away to the country, where there are no factories to visit. And remember to greet our guide Frau Müller with the proper German greeting. Some of you, I've noticed, have reverted to a simple hello. That is unacceptable. And some of you are not keeping your arms straight. Also unacceptable. It is true that there have been train crashes when Reichsbahn officials have mistaken the German greeting used by other Reichsbahn officials for signals – but that is not our concern. Your arms are swords, they are bayonets, they are unbending branches of oak. Yes, Gerd? Stop laughing, boys and girls – it is a good question, a useful question. If your right arm is wounded or missing you may use your left. Was there something else? Well, then I expect you would use your leg – but that's quite enough now. Nobody would lose both arms and legs. Yes, there is the man on Alexanderplatz with his little trolley, but he fought in the Great War and therefore is entitled to certain privileges, and besides, he is very polite and speaks flawless German when begging for food. Some of you would do well to follow his example; for all we know, our Gauleiter Dr Goebbels might be planning another competition to find the politest Berliner. I myself entered the last one – I was unsuccessful, and did not receive a prize presented by the Gauleiter at a special ceremony – but that does not mean I have abandoned my good manners.

'Now children, look at all the different medals and badges you can earn when you are older. Don't touch them. The pins are very sharp – but secondly and more importantly you will dull their shine. You will ruin the crucial work done by all the ladies who sit here day after day, polishing them with their rags so they gleam like gold and silver even though they are not. Aren't they beautiful?

Beautiful rewards for ugly acts. Perhaps ugly is the wrong word. I take it back. I did not say it.

'Here are the Assault Badges – turned out by the thousand every week, children, did you hear that? Isn't that wonderful? Some of you will have seen such a badge before, on your Vati's breast, perhaps, or perhaps he hides it away with his special things to keep it safe. And here is the medal for strengthening our West Wall, with its tunnels and bunkers to hinder the enemy, and its dragon's teeth to stop their tanks, and it cannot be breached. And this one is for battle against the partisans who keep springing up many-headed from their nests as we keep cutting them down. See their forked tongues, their serpent eyes. And if you had fought in the east in that bitter winter you might have earned the Eastern Front Medal, its ribbon woven in red and white and black for the blood, the snow, the death, but this one is just an example, children, because that winter is past, that battle is over, and the factory does not make them any more, and alas, you can never earn one. But here is the Tank Destruction Badge – you must destroy the tank on your own and unaided, so bear that in mind – and see, children, the Sniper's Badge, the sharp-eyed eagle considering its prey. You need at least twenty kills for this one, and forty if you want the silver trim, and sixty if you want the gold, and you must have witnesses to your kills, and each kill must be recorded and confirmed.

'I have been saying children, children, but of course I mean boys. It is important to say what we mean. Our generals call their men children when they speak to them informally, which I have always found very moving. However, man's universe is vast compared to woman's, and I should not have implied that a girl can be a sniper, a destroyer of tanks and partisans – but a girl can be mother to a sniper, et cetera, so do not lose heart. Perhaps our guide Frau Müller might show us the Mother's Cross? It comes in bronze, silver and gold – yes, like the Olympics – and you must bear at least four children to qualify, and none can be born dead. It's not sufficient, though, simply to produce these children – anyone can do that; look at the gypsies. No, girls, you must be judged worthy of the medal – your conduct as well as your blood – and not only the number but also the quality of the children is considered. And once you possess the Mother's Cross you will never have to queue, and you will always have a seat on the bus or the tram – even the elderly will give theirs up – and the butcher will reserve for you the choicest cuts of meat.

'We'll end with the Wound Badges – what a mountain! Hostile action, children. That's what you need to remember. Hostile action? It means you don't have to be a soldier. You can be wounded from hostile action in your very own house – if a bomb takes an eye or a hand, for instance. Facial disfigurement, brain damage, blindness – they all count, but not if they are present from birth, for then they are the fault of the blood and not the result of hostile action, do you see?'

★

From her bed Sieglinde could hear the ticking of the grandfather clock, and beyond that the voices of her parents mingling with the voices on the Volksempfänger; impossible to tell which was which. Her jumper scratched at her neck, but Vati said they must sleep in their clothes, they must be ready, always ready. She thought of the bombed-out people who were sleeping at her school until new homes could be found for them. Some had nothing more than the clothes they wore, and they all but snatched at the soup the Hitler Youth girls served. They had not been ready. She raised the blinds and opened the windows just a crack, and she watched the searchlights weaving the sky into a bright net. Nothing. Nothing. Down below in the courtyard stood Jürgen's sandcastle, splitting as it dried. She thought: here is my left hand, here is my right hand, here is my left eye, here is my right eye. Forwards. Forwards. Youth knows no fear.

The Shadowman

The house is   ,
The   is
In   -   rooms.
Who is an   man?
A father, who cannot   ,
When his chidren   .

November 1943
Berlin

One morning in winter, as Gottlieb was arriving at work, he noticed that the door to the neighbouring office was open. In the four years he had been at the Division he had never seen inside the other booths; he knew the names of the men who occupied them only because they were painted on the frosted glass. He paused and glanced inside and realised that the space mirrored his own. And the man who sat with his back to the door, typing his report – surely he wore the same suit as Gottlieb? And surely his hair was the same shade of brown, with the same slight wave in it? The man opened his filing cabinet, and Gottlieb saw that it was the same clever design as his own, extending from the wall an impossible distance. The Division was an example, he thought, of the shape the new Germany would take: innovative structures that offered solutions to age-old problems; man-made miracles. There was to be a triumphal arch, ten times bigger than the one in Paris, carved with the names of the two million dead from the Great War, and there was to be a great domed hall, built on granite to counter Berlin's sand, so vast it could swallow Saint Peter's, so vast it would have its own climate, the breaths of tens of thousands rising into the vault as clouds and falling again as dew and rain, a world unto itself, the word in stone. He stood at the door a moment or two longer, and then, before the man turned and saw him, pulled it to without a word.

At his desk he typed his report of the previous day's work, but when he looked it over he found he could hardly read the carbon copy. He was frugal with his materials – yes, wars could be won with paper, with ink – and each month he had to account for all supplies used, typing a summary that he then filed along with his daily reports in the cabinet to which nobody else had access. He scrutinised the used sheet of carbon paper, tilting it towards the window, the pale winter light falling on the piled-up letters, the dark impressions. Here were all his excised words, days and days of them, their meaning lost in the layers. Too changed, too buried.

That day Gottlieb made unprecedented progress, his magpie blade flying across the pages of his text and picking out all the shining things: *loss, mercy, remembrance, hope.* As a rule he did not dwell on these removals, putting them out of his mind as soon as he shut them in the furnace, which was the recommended practice. They were just scraps. Today, though, they would not leave him, flickering through his thoughts, following him home. At this time of year it was already dark when he finished work, and he made his way along the pavement to the U-Bahn station as slowly as an old man, trying not to bump into the other pedestrians. No light came from the houses or the restaurants, the cinemas or the theatres – there was only the moon and the hard-edged stars pinned to the sky's black breast, as useless, in the end, as medals of tin.

I watch him squinting at the road ahead. Who knows what waits in the dark? When the zoo was bombed, the newspaper said all the escaped animals were shot – but what is that rustling beside the canal? What is that growling in the vegetable plots? This is a time of imitation. Bakers fill the bread with potato starch and women paint seams down their legs. There are paste jewels, substitute eggs, mock oysters; we treat the wounded with dried herbs; we tell them that coconut water is plasma and they offer their veins to the needle. The walls between cellars are not walls; if you find yourself buried, just unstack the bricks. This coffee isn't coffee and that silk isn't silk; this courage isn't courage and this love isn't love and that honey didn't come from bees. Where is our usual doctor, our usual tailor? Things change when we turn our backs. Christmas trees bloom in the sky to light the enemy's way; they fill the clouds with branching ghosts. We eat thistles and nettles, udders and hearts, smear our bread with Hitler-butter. Everyone is pretending. The bombs have blown open the cages and jaguars walk the streets.

★

'Now children, in a line, please! We are not animals, we are good children, we have nice manners and we do as we are told. Here is the lady to let us in, look, here is Frau Müller, she is a controller at the factory and she will count us to make sure she knows how many we are. Say thank you as you pass her, please, because we are nice polite children and we are not animals. Thank you, thank you, I should not have to tell you this. Other children – non-German children – do not say thank you, they are rude and dirty and have no manners, they are animals, animals and also mushrooms, yes, they are mushrooms, not the kind of mushroom that you might find on a nature ramble through our fine forests, the kind that you can eat, that Mutti might put in a delicious soup, but the deadly kind that poison our soil and are dangerous and must be eradicated. So we are not poisonous mushrooms, no, we are well-bred children who obey and follow and walk in nice straight lines and say thank you.

'Now here we are in this lovely clean factory, and look, it is full of hard-working ladies who are helping us to victory, see, children. These are ladies who probably have children of their own, and plenty of work to do at home to keep their children safe and not hungry, but at the moment these children will be at school, learning about important things the way that you are learning about our factories. Or perhaps the children of these industrious ladies – who can tell me what industrious means? Yes, thank you, Anna, that is correct, now everybody remember that word, it is an important word and it is something we must all be – perhaps the children of these industrious ladies have gone to the countryside and are having a lovely time, as our Gauleiter has commanded them to do. A number of our classmates have already gone, haven't they, but we are fortunate and are allowed to stay even though the city is under attack – even though our winter coal supplies are burning in our yards, impossible to put out, and the firestorms make sunsets at midday – because our Vatis have important jobs. Of course the children who have gone to the countryside must miss their Muttis, it would not be normal if they did not miss their Muttis, but they have gone to the countryside where it is safe, not that we are unsafe in Berlin, and since we have planted vegetables in all of our parks and morphine poppies in the churchyards it even looks a bit like the countryside, doesn't it, but in the real countryside it is very safe and these children have gone

131

there, and soon we will go too, probably, as a class, everyone together, everyone safe together. And then the bombed-out people who have moved into our classrooms will have more space, and so will the wounded soldiers who arrive on trains in the night and are carried into our gymnasium, and whose arms and legs the caretaker spirits away to the incinerator. But we won't talk about that today, today we will enjoy our visit to this wonderful and interesting factory where we will see the very useful items that these good ladies produce. Look at them, children, how hard they work, making these items for us all so that we will be safe and not overrun by poison. Look how they crank the fabric from the shining machines, out it rolls, so well-made and bright, a cheerful yellow, the colour of buttercups, isn't it, children, the buttercups we will be able to see and to smell and to pick when we go to the countryside without our Muttis. See the pattern the ladies print on the fabric now, see how they roll it through another machine, such a clever machine, and see how it comes out the other side of this ingenious machine – who can tell me what ingenious means? Yes, Jürgen, thank you, that is just what it means. Now everybody remember this word because it is what we all must be. See how the buttercup fabric slides from the ingenious machine, printed with its pattern of stars, each one the same size and shape, and this fabric is a tool that is helping us to victory. It is like a big quilt, isn't it, with its pattern of stars repeated over and over, so neat, such neat rows, a beautiful warm quilt that will keep us warm and safe. Now there is the door out, children, and there is Frau Müller opening the door for us, showing us the way out and counting us again, and we will say thank you as we pass Frau Müller, we will all thank her for showing us her lovely and interesting factory.'

★

Gottlieb had not touched his wife for quite some time; hardly at all in the last year. It was not that motherhood had changed her the way it changed some women – thickening their waists and slackening their breasts, turning clear eyes dull and bright cheeks sallow. On the contrary, as far as appearances went, Brigitte Heilmann was still the same woman: a small-boned, pretty creature with dark-blond hair and green eyes, slender hands that were always manicured, slim arms and legs that turned golden in the summer. She maintained her looks with a determination Gottlieb could only admire. He saw the way other men glanced at her, and the way other women did, too, and felt proud at the choice he had made, and this pride satisfied in him a need that some might call love. For a while now, though – perhaps six months, perhaps a little longer – Brigitte had been turning to him at night, the length of her body close at his back, her feet brushing against his thin-skinned arches, a hand alighting on the corrugations of his chest. And although Sieglinde was almost eleven and the boys were past their most difficult stage, it seemed to Gottlieb that his wife was always stopping on the street to admire infants and to compliment mothers. She had devoted a page of her ledger to the baby clothes she had never given away, washing and airing them every few months, because wool could yellow and cotton could rust if they were not cared for, and it would be wasteful to let them spoil when they still had so much wear in them. She drew Gottlieb's attention to articles about the latest findings on the inadequacies of children with too few siblings, and she mentioned certain women of their acquaintance who, having produced the required number of babies, were to be presented with the Mother's Cross. Hannelore, she said, wore hers all the time, pinning it to every outfit, even the more delicate fabrics, with never a thought for the damage.

Gottlieb had tried to explain to her how draining his job was; how he needed to be as well-rested as possible, despite the worsening night raids, so that he did not make any costly mistakes – but he could speak only in general terms about his work, and could tell she did not understand. When she reached for him at night, he murmured that he was too tired – or he did not respond at all, remaining mute to the body and the feet, sensing the hand no more than he might sense the alighting of a silent bird as he slept. And if he were to be honest, the problem was not just his work: why have more children, only to be told to evacuate them? They were leaving Berlin by the train-load. Eventually Brigitte retreated to her side of the bed, waiting, he suspected, for him to advance, when all the while he too was retreating.

His parents had slept in adjoining chambers, the door between them papered to look like part of the wall; at first glance one did not notice it. It could be locked from either side, this private entry, and he remembered rushing to his mother's bed when some monster inhabited his own, and hearing the door-handle turning and rattling as she explained to him that he was mistaken.

'How odd,' Brigitte said when he told her of this arrangement. 'Did you not find it odd?'

'I thought nothing of it when I was a child.'

'And now?'

'And now spouses sleep in the same room and in the same bed, and each knows the other's every habit and private routine.'

'Yes,' said Brigitte. 'Yes, that's the way it is now.'

When Gottlieb was nine years old his parents locked him in his bedroom because he cut the pages from one of his schoolbooks. At the time he hadn't thought of it as damage; his class had already covered those chapters, which concerned the Franco-Prussian War, and he wanted to make snowflakes from the paper to hang on the Christmas tree.

'You have brought shame on the entire family,' said his father. 'And besides, it's only May.'

'What possessed you?' said his mother.

They cancelled his outing to Luna Park with Onkel Heinrich that weekend, and when his uncle visited they would not let him see him. Gottlieb knew he was there, though, because he could hear him playing his accordion, *for verdant green my heart does long in bleakest winter time*, and then the music changed and grew louder and he knew it was for him, a crazy stumbling tune that had no name and no words but brought the fun fair to his room: the muddle of the crowd, and the shimmy-steps that made you trip and stagger, and the swivel-house that took from you all sense of up and down.

Outside his window he could see the tops of the plane trees that shaded the driveway, their cool knuckles meeting and locking overhead, and in the ice house buried in the garden there were blocks of winter packed in straw; they would not thaw all summer. Gottlieb heard the telephones ringing in the rooms below; people talking to people they could not see. Mama could ring from the salon to talk to Papa in the living room, or Frau Kruckel could ring from the kitchen to talk to Mama in the salon. Papa sat in his wing chair, which hid both sides of his face, and Mama listened to her music and wrote letters to friends and important people, inviting them to one of her luncheons or soirées. *We look forward to your visit on Sunday the 25th. The roses will be blooming by then, and I shall ask Frau Kruckel to make her rose-petal sorbet . . .*

And in the entrance hall downstairs, which led to all the other rooms, bears danced along the back of the vast oak bench, and they danced up its legs, they were its legs, they held it aloft with broad paws, dancing upright just as people did, and their eyes shone in the gloom, and they were strong, these bears, they had held up the bench forever, but Gottlieb must never sit on it, because it was not for sitting on.

When the maid brought him his dinner – bread and cheese, and a quartered apple – she produced a pair of scissors and some sheets of black paper and whispered, 'From Fräulein Hannelore.' And he cut silhouettes from the paper, his very first silhouettes, and they were the faces of his family produced from memory, for of course he was alone. But when the maid came with his next meal she said they were a good likeness, and he had a gift, and she brought him more paper from Hannelore and he cut out more faces: his mother from the right, his father from the left, his sister from the left, his father from the right . . .

He wanted to explain to his parents that when he sliced the pages from the schoolbook he was not destroying but creating, and as proof of this he gathered all the silhouettes he had cut in his bedroom – and his parents looked at them and looked at each other and had to admit that yes, he had a gift. And even when he was allowed back into the bright downstairs rooms, with their French doors that led to dragonflies and mimosa, he kept his scissors and his pages of black paper close by, and he was always snipping away, seeing the shapes that lay in nothingness, and after a time he finished with people and moved to buildings and landscapes, which were easier to get right.

A few days after they released him, he smuggled a pair of scissors into his mother's dressing room and cut a hole in one of her gowns. He could not say what prompted it. The clothes surrounded him on their quilted hangers, absorbing all sound, satins as waxy as leaves, velvets that shimmered like half-hidden pollen hearts, shoes waiting primly on their racks, mouths crammed with tissue, and the floor seemed to move beneath him like the shimmy-steps at Luna Park, like the swivel-house always about to fall, and in the tilting mirrors he could see himself from two different angles: two different Gottliebs cutting a hole so small it would not be noticed, not for several months, and even then his mother would decide she must have done it herself, with one of her sharp-heeled shoes.

★

'Look at the piles of clothing, boys and girls! See how ready we are to help those in need? See how carefully the ladies are checking it over, making sure it is all in good order? Frau Miller has asked us not to touch anything, and she is the supervisor and so we must obey her, even though we might long to run our hands over such fine apparel. We Germans take care of our less fortunate; we do not give them rags to wear. Silk dresses, smart shoes, crocodile handbags, lace underwear – one might think one had taken a wrong turn and wandered into KaDeWe! If KaDeWe had not been bombed, that is; if KaDeWe were not a skeleton now. All the items are inspected and cleaned and then they are given to victims of the terror attacks, provided they can prove they have lost equivalent items. What does equivalent mean? Equivalent? Nobody?

'I think you'll agree with Frau Miller that this is the most interesting room in the factory, children. What are the ladies doing? Why are they feeling their way along hems and seams and stopping when they find a lump? They don't seem to speak any German so perhaps they cannot explain – but why are they easing open the stitches, the undone threads kinking and buckling like shaky writing, like anxious messages scrawled in haste? Look at the exposed fabric: unfaded, unworn; I cannot remember when the world was so bright. I cannot remember such colour. But see what the ladies untuck from the holes: diamond earrings that drop to their palms like hailstones; pearl chokers and shell cameos; lockets that hold the faces of the dead. And one brooch can buy fifty bullets, and one diamond bracelet five pistols, so you see, children, nothing goes to waste, not even lost property.'

November 1943
Near Leipzig

'What was I like when I was little?' says Erich. He and Mama are walking home from church; he swings his hand in hers.

'You still are little, Schatz,' says Mama.

'I thought I was eight and a bit.'

'You are eight and a bit.'

'That's not little. Oma Kröning said I'm old enough to read Papa's books from when he was a boy. I meant, what was I like when I was a baby?'

'So she did, you're right,' says Mama. And before Erich can ask another question, she says, 'Tell me about Papa's books. Which one is your favourite?'

Erich says he likes *The Legacy of the Incas* and *Through the Desert* and *The Empire of the Silver Lion*, but it's the Winnetou stories he loves best – and the Führer loves those ones too. He tells Mama about Old Shatterhand, the German hero of the Wild West who can kill a grizzly bear with a single punch, and Winnetou, his brave Apache friend.

'They're blood brothers,' he says. 'They only have to look at each other to know what the other is thinking.'

'Well well,' says Mama. 'Now that would be a useful trick.' She laughs, and her breath clouds ahead of them in the cold air.

'But what was I like when I was a baby?' says Erich. 'Before I could walk.'

'Oh,' says Mama, and looks to the icy sky, as if it holds her memory. 'Well, you were a good boy. You never cried. Sometimes we had to check that you were still in your cradle – that the devils hadn't snatched you away. Papa carved it himself, the cradle, from one of our own pines. Little acorns at the head and foot.'

'Tell me something that happened to me, though.'

I see Mama pause, and again she looks to the sky. This is what she tells him, and the more she tells him the better they both remember it:

When Erich was a baby Mama placed his cradle outside on fine days, under the shade of the silver linden. Its branches curved down around him, muffling the sound of everything beyond the three-note call of the dove and the shifting of the linden leaves, which was also the sound Mama's hand made when she stroked his ear. Erich remembers that, doesn't he? He does. And the acorns carved into the pine cradle? Yes, he remembers them, or thinks he does, because Mama still has the cradle and so perhaps the acorns in the pine are not a proper memory but simply a familiar sight. And Erich remembers watching the hives, their black mouths crawling with bees, although it is difficult to see them from beneath the linden tree – but that is of no consequence. One day a swarm of bees poured from the mouth of a hive – was it Luise's hive? We'll say it was Luise's hive – and hung above his cradle, looking for a place to settle, and yes, Erich remembers the dark shapes overhead, and he remembers that they alighted on him, on the carved cradle, on his little blankets and on his hands, his cheeks, his wispy hair, his eyelids. He remembers that he did not cry – you did not cry, says Mama. You were

140

not afraid. What is it, then, that clusters about him like bad thoughts? Where is this place? And why does Mama snatch him away?

I find that she is often incomplete to me. Sometimes I wish that this were not so, and that I could possess more of her – and sometimes I am thankful that I do not. When I can make out her memories, they are dead days surfacing from silt. I see her as a little girl, stroking dark garnets on her grandmother's wrist and neck; I see her sitting on a hearth, arranging and rearranging the skull-bones of a fish, her father watching her firelight face, watching as the bones charm her and perplex her until she looks up at him, lost, and he tells her the answer to their spiny riddle. There she is out on the ice, walking on knives, spinning and spinning on the water until she thinks she will break and shatter and scatter herself like stars.

I see her waiting on cold Christmas Eves for the blossom trees to bear fruit, the rivers to become wine, gemstones to spill from the mountains, church bells to ring from beneath the sea and the Christ child to shed a white feather, and I see her sister pinching her arm to punish her childishness. I see her as a new bride, acquainting herself with the rooms of the white-walled house that will hold her now, and the whispering goosedown bed that will hold her now, and the man's rope-hard arms that will hold her now, and I see her learning the shapes of the shadows dropped by the linden tree behind the house, and the call of the turtle dove settled in its branches, and the windows that jam and the floorboards that bow, and the names of horses, names to replace the names she has left behind, as every bride must, and I see her exploring the farm, standing in the stable and looking up at the high-pitched roof as steep as a chapel's, and counting the glossy cooing hens, and measuring her height against the hives carved from oak trunks into human form: wooden men and a wooden woman filled with bees. I see new thoughts lapping at her, thoughts absorbed from her husband, from the wives of other farmers, from the air: lake-water climbing, taking her in its cool arms and holding her high: yes, the hungry years are on the wane; yes, Germany will renew herself; yes, that renewal has its source in German soil nourished by German farmers; yes, we must cut out the infection that is spreading; and yes, the solution is this man, this guardian we have hung on the wall, an ancestor we never knew we had, proof we are the bloodspring of the people.

I see her on delirious streets, red banners caught beneath every window, the ground lush with branches cut from firs and still sticky with sap. At a rally she considers the words of a song: *If all become untrue, we remain true*, and they seem to make no sense: if all are untrue, surely none remains true, but the more she listens and sings the more sense the words make, and the more possible they become, and now look, the curtain is rising and there are the actors in black coats and black hats, black curls hanging from their temples and gold spilling from their pockets, and they are robbing the farmers of their homes and their crops and their God-given rights, and there are the farmers, suffering, searching, looking to a light on the painted horizon. And now the stage fills with dance, whirling peasant girls and strong peasant boys, all in neat rows, an orderly crop, their hair as fair as cornsilk, and look, they are tilling the stage, they are swinging their scythes, the blades keen against the risen sun, each dark hook swinging in time, and the audience claps, and she cannot hear her own hands amid the wash of applause, but she can feel the sting in her palms.

Every morning Emilie made an offering to the bronze head, laying bright-skinned apples before it, or fresh hazelnuts, or little dishes of honey.

'But he can't eat them,' said Erich, and Emilie said when he was older he would understand.

'But isn't it a waste?' he said. 'The Führer doesn't like people who waste food.'

'This is different,' said Emilie. 'It's not wasted.'

'But –' he began again.

'That's enough now, Erich,' she said, more sharply than she meant to – but really, he had to learn when to stop asking questions.

She dusted the head with soft cloths, always returning it to its correct position, and if she had a special wish she wrote it on a slip of paper and pushed it up inside the hollow metal form, then knelt before it and closed her eyes, staying perfectly silent, so silent she could hear the heat rising in her, could hear the pelt of blood and the flaring of bones, long white candles. This was something like the restlessness she had felt as a child on Christmas Eve, when from the locked room her parents rang the bell, then made her cover her eyes as they led her to the tree, and she could smell the sap of the newly cut fir and the hot smoke from the candles that dotted the branches like fallen stars. She could feel the lightest of breezes from the carved figures that turned and turned on their little wooden carousel, scattering the walls with twisted shadows in the shape of twisted men, and she knew that something splendid was coming. *Look*, her father would say, *the Christ child has been*, and there on the floor, shining like a clean thought, lay the white feather.

One still day in December, when the bees huddled in their hives and the cows huddled in their stalls and the geese hung by their necks, Mama and Erich went to the market.

'Which one?' asked the fishmonger, his long black apron as slick as an eel.

Erich peered into the barrel and tried to choose a fish. It was hard to tell one from another; they twisted in the water, feeling their way along the smooth wet wood over and over, looking for a way out. Their scales caught the light like falling coins, and he thought of the time his mother had given him a pfennig at the lake and told him to make a wish: he did not know what to ask for, what shimmering future to imagine for himself, and yet Mama was watching, waiting for him to open his fist and let the coin go.

'Well, young man?' said the fishmonger, his net poised.

'That one's nice and fat,' said Mama. 'What about him?'

Already the fishmonger was dipping his net into the barrel and saying that Erich had made a fine choice, and the carp was shivering in the icy air, watching Erich with its white-rimmed eye, its mouth opening and closing as if it could not remember what it wanted to say.

At home Mama filled the bathtub, and the carp all but leapt from the bucket and into the cold water. 'It will be your job to look after him,' she told Erich.

'What does he eat?'

'Nothing,' she said. 'You mustn't feed him – we want him to be nice and clean.'

'He's already clean. He lives in the water.'

'We need him to be clean on the inside,' said Mama. 'That's a very important thing to be, for fish as well as for boys.'

Erich knelt and watched the carp. It kept its distance to begin with, staying at the far end of the tub, but Erich could understand that. Sometimes he felt uneasy in this bare room himself, with its glinting tiles, each one a milky mirror that warped his faint reflection, changing him into someone he was not. (This is what he does not remember: the bare wooden stool, the women in white, the glittering callipers about his skull.) He dabbled his fingers in the bath, and after a time the fish came to him, passing beneath his outstretched hand like the shadow of a cloud, impossible to catch or keep. It did not touch him but he could feel the water shifting against his palm, rearranging itself. Erich knew what the world looked like from beneath the water; how everything wavered and blurred. He could hold his breath for over a minute, lying quite motionless, eyes open, tiny bubbles catching on his arms and legs, his ears, his lashes. One day his mother had come in when he was submerged, but she did not look like his mother, and although he could see her mouth moving, all he could hear were distant notes; a bird trapped in the eaves.

Mama had been saving sugar and flour for weeks, putting it aside into special tins that Erich was not allowed to touch. It was their duty, she said, to have a normal Christmas, even without Papa, even though when the wind blew in the right direction they could smell the smoke from the bombs that had fallen on Leipzig. The house filled with the aroma of hazelnuts and cinnamon, cloves and almonds, and Mama tucked her hair under her headscarf and hurried about the kitchen as if there were an emergency, kneading sweet brown dough and cutting it into fir trees and stars, pinching pieces of sugary white mixture into crescent moons. The shapes were the shapes of a still night in the forest, and Erich wished he could slip through his bedroom window when Mama was asleep and go to the forest beyond the farm and stand in the fragrant dark, looking up through the black branches – but it was not safe there any more. It hid runaways and traitors, all manner of enemies, bad shadows waiting in every hollow.

In the tub the carp was growing. When they needed to bathe Erich caught it in a bucket and set it aside and it waited, curled like a question mark, until he poured it back. At night he could hear it splashing, leaping from the water, and each morning he had to dry the bathroom floor so that nobody would slip and break their neck. The fish was calm then, barely moving, but it came to him when he beckoned it, nudging at his fingers as they fluttered beneath the water. And in the mornings, too, Erich saw Mama saying her prayers to the bronze head with the blank eyes. It glinted just as the carp glinted, although it was not a living thing; no, it was not alive, not alive, but its eyes watched without iris or pupil, and you could not tell where they were looking.

On Christmas Eve Mama killed the carp. She took a hammer, the hammer Papa used for fixing things, and she killed it, and then she cut it open, and it was not clean on the inside, even though it had been in the bath for days, and Mama was wrong. Erich wept for the fish, lying on the sofa and burying his face in the tasselled green cushions where everything was soft and cool and dark, and he could not hear Mama saying that German boys should be brave; that German boys should know some things had to die. He could feel his grandmother stroking his back, and where she stroked, fins appeared, and he swam into the soft darkness, the tasselled weeds parting for a moment to let him through, then closing behind him.

That night at dinner Mama lit the candles and sat in Papa's chair. She placed the fish at the centre of the table, its fins and tail as brittle as sycamore wings. Erich could see the slit along its belly, and the filling of onions and parsley leaking onto the dish that had belonged to Mama's mama, who was dead. The little wooden angels hung on the tree; angels in sleighs, angels playing trumpets, angels doing things that people do, and this was not at all strange, because angels were dead people, after all, and why should they not remember how to play trumpets and ride in sleighs? Erich wanted to ask Oma if angels had memories, but Mama was peeling back the skin and cutting up the fish, cutting a slice for Oma and for Tante Uschi and for Erich and for herself, and telling him to say grace. He did not want to thank God or anybody else for the thing that lay before him, and so he said the words with his eyes open and his head unbowed, and when he had finished Mama said amen, just as she did when she finished her prayers to the head, and then she began to eat, plucking the fine bones from the flesh so that she would not choke. Erich pushed his fork into a piece of the carp and raised it to his mouth, and his mother smiled and the candle-flames shook and the shadows climbed the walls and the snow fell, and the hollow head watched like a father, and Erich knew then that the hand holding the fork was not his own, and nor was the mouth receiving the food; it was a different boy who placed the warm morsel on his tongue, a different boy who chewed and swallowed, chewed and swallowed, and asked for more.

★

In the kitchen I watch Emilie take the carp's head from the dirty plate, its cooked eyes as white as church-glove buttons. She scrapes the flesh from the skull-bones and examines them, turning them this way and that. She remembers her father showing her how to make them into a dove – a charm against witches, a charm to protect the house. When he held it to the light, the bone bird glowed as if lit from within, and Emilie believed she would be safe – but that was a long time ago now, and she can no longer recall how to fit the pieces together. A fish is a fish; it can never be a bird.

I lie on her heart that night, as heavy as I can make myself. And look, the dead soldiers are leaving their watch; they are coming home, silently they enter, you hardly hear the tread of their hobnail boots. They sense they are expected. On the young skin of each child they place their earth-encrusted hands.

December 1943
Berlin

'I don't know if we will be able to visit any more factories after today, because most of us are moving to the countryside, aren't we, where there are no factories in danger of being bombed, so let us enjoy our last special outing today, let us think of it as a special Christmas treat. This is where they make the hair, children, although we cannot see where the hair comes from, but we might like to imagine it is similar to the angel hair we will be hanging on our Christmas trees very soon, and although we cannot see where it comes from, we can see where Frau Müller's ladies make it into other things: stuffing for mattresses so that we will sleep well, and warm socks for the soldiers so that they will not be cold and their feet will not hurt, and thick cloth for uniforms because it is cold on the eastern front, much colder than here in Berlin, and even roofing material and carpet for our houses. How clever these ladies are, to make such useful things from hair, which is not a useful thing when you think about it, not a tool that will help us to victory unless it is changed into something else. It is like magic, children! Just like magic, the way the hair is transformed, until it is not hair at all.'

★

When the shadowman posters appeared in Berlin, nobody knew what to think. He loomed from the advertising columns and the bridges and the blank walls of the apartment blocks, inking them with his strange silhouette. To begin with there were no words, no explanations, just a white question mark floating against his dark form. Was he a secret signal to partisans? A warning to black-frocked clerics who stood in their broken pulpits and spoke of forgiveness and surrender? In the early morning, before the day was certain, he seemed a remnant of the blacked-out night. In other lights he appeared to spring from the walls themselves; a stain leaching from the homes of ordinary people going about their business. Later the word came, pasted over the figure like a correction: *Pst!* People said it to one another although they were not quite sure why: *Pst! Pst!* You could hear it on the trams and at the markets, in the cafés and the stairwells, in the parks and in the cinemas. *Pst!* wherever you went, as if the city were deflating. And still there was no telling who the shadowman was supposed to be. That was the problem with shadows: they could be anybody.

One Sunday morning Brigitte saw two boys putting up posters on the façade of a bombed-out building. She watched them working, Blood and Honour glinting at their waists. The posters showed ordinary people: men drinking at a bar or talking in the corridor of a crowded train; builders working on a house, the mortar drying as they chatted; a woman seated at a switchboard and speaking to someone beyond the poster's edge, the criss-crossing cables flexing like tendons as she spoke; a barber pausing to listen to a customer, the razor suspended above the man's soaped throat. Across them all fell the shadowman. *Pst!* the posters read. *The enemy is listening.*

'Mutti,' said Sieglinde, peering at one of the posters, 'who is that?'

'It's hard to tell,' said Brigitte. 'Excuse me,' she said to the boys. 'Excuse me . . . ? Who is that?'

The boys did not reply. The sky was darkening overhead; it looked like rain. It was all the anti-aircraft guns, Brigitte had heard, messing up the weather, tearing open the clouds.

'It could be anybody, I suppose,' she went on, and still the boys said nothing. One unrolled another poster while the other dipped his brush into the pail of paste. She thought she recognised their faces; they had come to the apartment, hadn't they, collecting bones? 'What does it mean?' she asked, but the boys were already walking away, finding another façade.

Such unanswered questions were usual now. People began to take note of every remark made by friends, neighbours and family, storing them away for leaner times. Children paid attention to their teachers as never before, eager to report problematic points of view, regrettable lapses from the syllabus. Trust no fox on the green heath, they reminded one another. Words were analysed for hidden meanings, conversations taken apart and examined piece by piece like faulty radios.

FRAU MÜLLER:	Have you heard from Hans-Georg?
FRAU MILLER:	Why do you ask?
FRAU MÜLLER:	I haven't heard from Dieter for weeks. I was wondering if you had any news.
FRAU MILLER:	That's not for me to say. But if I were to receive some news from Hans-Georg, it would not be real news.
FRAU MÜLLER:	Yes. They cut things out. Dieter's last letter was almost all holes. An emptiness.
FRAU MILLER:	Where is he?

FRAU MÜLLER:	Why do you ask?
FRAU MILLER:	I cannot say.
FRAU MÜLLER:	Quite correct. I had a tooth pulled without sedation last month in case I let anything slip.
FRAU MILLER:	I often think: they have just gone out, and soon they'll be coming back home.
FRAU MÜLLER:	Yes indeed, they have just gone out, and now they'll return home.
FRAU MILLER:	Frau Ehrlich's neighbour stopped her in the stairwell and whispered that Johann – Frau Ehrlich's youngest – was safe. She heard it on enemy radio.
FRAU MÜLLER:	Frau Ehrlich reported her, I trust?
FRAU MILLER:	She did.
FRAU MÜLLER:	Quite right.
FRAU MILLER:	I don't mind the holes in the letters. It's the official notice I fear, that comes in the black-bordered envelope: when and where and how. Missing or dead. Location of grave.
FRAU MÜLLER:	*(whispering)* I think we don't know just how many have died. Why don't they publish the casualty lists?
FRAU MILLER:	That is a bold remark. I read something similar on a leaflet that fell from the sky. I must remember what you have said.
FRAU MÜLLER:	There's no need. I meant nothing. It means nothing.
FRAU MILLER:	Everything means something.
FRAU MÜLLER:	The lies that fall from the sky – they are not suitable reading. You should not be reading them. They should be burned.

FRAU MILLER:	Quite right. Quite right. And I do. But sometimes one notices a sentence here and there as one is gathering them to burn.
FRAU MÜLLER:	One should stop noticing.
FRAU MILLER:	*(whispering)* What of the other scraps that fall from the sky? The strips of silver that disguise the enemy's planes?
FRAU MÜLLER:	I hear they're radioactive.
FRAU MILLER:	I hear they're smeared with disease.
FRAU MÜLLER:	I hear botulism.
FRAU MILLER:	I hear anthrax.

I hear these words too, but there is no weight to them; they are mirages, false echoes, artificial clouds designed to blind the radar.

February 1944
Near Leipzig

Oma Kröning always had a lot to say. When she visited, Emilie took care not to bring up any matters she wanted kept private – and there were many such matters – but somehow her mother-in-law always knew about these things, or made a point of finding them out. On this particular day she had been following Emilie around the kitchen, too close, far too close, telling her how to cook potatoes and exactly when to take the Apfelkuchen from the oven. Several times Emilie had burnt herself.

'Perhaps you'd like to talk to Erich,' she said. 'He always looks forward to your visits.'

And so Oma Kröning sat on the edge of the sofa, watching while Erich played on the floor, and after a few moments she leaned down to him, and her face puckered out of shape so that she looked a little unlike herself, and she said, 'Shall I tell you a story?'

This is what I heard, so this is what I can relay:

A long time ago, in the region of Saxony, on a hill above a lake, stood a castle. Its walls were as thick as three men and had never been breached. Should an enemy approach this fortress, arrows flew to his heart from the notch-wide windows, and should he reach the gate, then oil rained down on him from the murder hole, so hot it peeled the skin from his flesh and the flesh from his bones, and should he reach the spiralling steps that led to the place where the children hid with their mother, then he would trip and split his head on the uneven treads known only to those who lived there. And these sly defences afforded the castle's inhabitants a peaceful sleep, and no enemy ever so much as cast his shadow on the broad stone walls. Still, all these safeguards – the arrow notches, the murder hole, the stumbling steps – all these were not the secret to the castle's strength. No, that sprang from altogether a different source. Before the building of the great structure had started, when the castle existed only on vellum skinned from unborn calves, a search began for the thing that would make it impregnable: a living child to be set into its foundations. A local woman agreed to sell her son for the purpose, and as the wall went up the boy was heard to cry *Mama, I can still see you, Mama*. And then, as the wall grew higher, *Mama, I cannot see you.*

And Emilie comes into the room and says, 'What are you telling him? You'll give the child nightmares!'

And Oma Kröning says, 'Nonsense – not a word of it's true. And I'm sure you loved hearing it when you were little. Didn't your mama tell it to you?'

And Emilie does not deny this, and clouds pass over me and through me, and I do not know if it is now or then or some time still to come.

In March a man came to stay with the Krönings, and that man was Papa – so Mama said, but Erich couldn't be sure. This man was quieter than Papa, and he wore a beard, and his clothes did not seem to fit him any more – they were neither too small nor too big; they were simply the clothes of a different man. Mama set him to work churning the butter, but he didn't know when to stop and ruined the whole batch. It was the same when she asked him to beat the carpets; he kept on hitting them long after they were clean. Erich studied his face, watching him first from one side and then from the other. At certain angles, at certain in-between times of day, when the light was low, when the sky glimmered like the belly of a fish, he thought he could make out a shadow at his throat. The man who said he was Papa brought presents with him: a brooch for Mama, carved from amber into the shape of a flower, with a stone at the centre that looked just like a diamond, and for Erich a wristwatch with a thick leather strap and initials on the back that were not proper letters – a backwards N, a backwards R, as if seen in a mirror. When Erich brought him *Pictures from the Life of the Führer* to look at he stared at the cover for a moment as if he did not recognise it, and as they leafed through the album together he kept running his fingernail under the edges of the pasted-in photographs as if he might tear them out, undo all his careful work.

One day Erich saw the man crouching before the bronze head – let us call him Papa, this man, because Mama says we must – and bite by bite he ate the piece of bread and honey Mama had placed there, licking his finger to pick up every last crumb. Erich thought Mama would be angry, but when she found the empty plate all she did was take it away and wash it and set it back down with a fresh slice of bread and honey, which Erich knew was the last slice, and which he had been wanting for himself. Then Mama wrote something on a slip of paper and pushed it up inside the head, and then she returned to her sewing, because torn shirts don't mend themselves.

At lunchtime Mama said, 'Is it terribly cold there?'

And Papa said, 'No, it's quite comfortable.'

And Mama said, 'Is there enough to eat?'

And Papa said, 'Yes, there is plenty to eat.'

And Mama said, 'Do you go to church?'

And Papa said, 'Yes, every Sunday.'

You-you, you, called the turtle dove, and the bees sang a long and rising note, a question that had no end.

★

Mama has been saving eggshells; whenever she needs an egg she pierces it at the top and the bottom with a needle and blows out the contents, then rinses it and puts it aside. Now, a week before Easter, Erich and Papa sit at the kitchen table with paints and brushes and decorate the empty shells. Erich is so careful with them, so aware of the weight of his fingers, the pressure of the brush. He paints violets and bluebells and bees, and Papa paints snowflakes, little black sprays that look like spiders, but he presses too hard and the shell shatters in his hands.

'I'm sorry, I'm sorry,' he says, and Erich says it doesn't matter, there are other shells to paint, but Papa says he does not trust himself.

Outside the bees return heavy to their hives, drawn in through the whittled mouths as if by a hungry breath. *We took the clotting blood, my father and I, my son and I. Whom think ye that I am?*

Two weeks later Papa returns to Russia, and that is all Mama will say, that he is in Russia, which is big enough to hold Germany many times over. Erich thinks she must mean the Soviet Union, but he does not correct her, and Papa's letters are sent from nowhere and give nothing away: they do not mention strategy and they do not mention wonder weapons, and he might be in Moscow after all, sipping tea from a little glass cup with a silver handle, and he might be at the Winter Palace, where the statues and the chandeliers and even the throne are made of ice, and he might be riding the steppe in a sleigh pulled by wolves, whipping through frozen air, the snow turning to stars around him. Mama still writes every week, and Erich writes too, telling Papa that the hens are working hard to lay the required number of eggs and that the inspector from the Reich Food Estate wants Mama to plant beets and sunflowers in place of wheat. When he can't think of anything to say he draws pictures: borders of bees marching in single file around the edges of the page, and Mama in the bee-keeping hat and veil, smoke fanning its wings at her back, and the hives in the apple orchard: Saint John and the pastor, Luise and Gustav, the moneylender and the butcher, bearded with bees. They have things to say, sad things that belong to the Krönings' past. *I wanted my sorrow to sink me beneath the lake, it was said the French had poisoned the water, I will bake my bread from the blood the stolen coins the whipped dogs the clotting ropes of vipers.* But Mama still checks his letters for traces of sadness, and so Erich keeps these sad things to himself.

And where is Papa when Ronja falls lame and cannot pull the harvester for a time? Where is he to explain why the milk is turning? And why the hens are laying soft-shelled eggs, and why the lake is sinking? Where is he when the foreign workers talk to one another in their own seditious tongues? Everything starts to go wrong without him. Cankers pit the apple trees and the bees pour from the hives, erupting from their wooden mouths like curses. When the wagon needs mending, where is Papa? And when the slates fall from the roof, and when the weather-vane works its way loose in high winds? The steel bird hurtles across the fields, and it could kill someone, it could pierce a throat, a heart, and Papa is not there to stop it. And where is he when the last of the wheat needs cutting? No Ronja and no Papa, and the Hitler Youth boys have all gone, and the foreign workers are not to be trusted, and Erich is still too small for the job and can only watch his mother swinging the scythe back and forth, the sighs filling the absent air.

'Will Papa be back to dig the potatoes?' he says.

But no, Papa is gathering a different harvest, says Mama – *ah, ah* says the scythe – and Erich knows that this harvest is men, that Papa is cutting down men. And the milk sours in the sun, and the lake sinks into its bed, and the hemlock heads wither, black hooks in the dirt, and there is no telling which way the wind blows.

April 1944
Berlin

Julia held up the book and the girls peered at it, tilting
their heads first to one side and then the other, trying to
make sense of the photographs and drawings. Was it a boy?
Was it even a person? They saw a trampled, empty thing,
the feet and hands torn away, the head pushed into the
deflated chest.

'I agree,' said Julia, though nobody had spoken, 'he
doesn't look very important. Just an ordinary boy. He
doesn't look like the other Notable Germans we've met.'
And certainly, this empty skin was no Horst Wessel, no Karl
May, no Hitlerjunge Quex, who still counted as a Notable
German even though he was in a film and therefore not
quite real. And besides, weren't there plenty of bodies to
be found? Hadn't Sieglinde seen three on the way to the
meeting? But the special thing about Kayhausen Boy, said
Julia, was his age: two thousand years old. Imagine if he
could speak – imagine what he could tell us about the
past. Some of the girls looked a little queasy; they did
not want to imagine him speaking, not at all; the suck of
the leather lungs, the distorted jaw working to form the
words. Not one of them took her eyes off the pictures,
though, because somebody might notice this and mention
it, and questions might be asked, and what sort of girl felt
sick over pictures of a Notable German?

It was our own rich earth that kept him intact, Julia said. He lay buried for centuries, his body preserved by the juices of the bog, until one day a man was cutting peat at the very spot that was the boy's grave. Look at his skin, as soft as our mothers' best winter gloves. How miraculous that he did not decay, because as human beings we all decay and vanish, and that is just the way of things, and we must accept it is so. The man who found him realised he had stumbled across something extraordinary, and he could not keep the news to himself. We know how important it is not to spread stories, how dangerous it is to speak freely; we know that the enemy is always listening and we must hold our tongues no matter how much we want to talk. The man told a man from the museum, which was the right thing to do – to report his find to the correct authorities – but he also told other people, ordinary people, and before the boy could be taken away and the proper experiments conducted on him, these ordinary people had stolen fingernails, bones, and carried them off as souvenirs. Of course we can understand the wish for a keepsake, wc can appreciate the temptation, let me show you something you have never seen before, here in my possession is the thumb of an Iron Age boy, you may touch it, you may hold it, he is ten years old, he is two thousand years old – but it is a shame, a tragedy that the doctors could not examine the unassaulted remains. Nowadays we cut the heads off pickpockets.

Julia tapped the pictures with her finger: look at the knife wounds in his neck. Look at the cords around his wrists, the woollen noose, the bound feet. What do these things tell us, these cuts and knots and bindings? That he was a criminal; that he did something wrong. (Or: that if we tether the dead, perhaps they will not return.) And what was his crime? He was crippled by a limp – the doctors found a defect in his hip – and therefore he would have been costly to keep and feed, and therefore he was eliminated, and so you see, even two thousand years ago we knew that it was better not to let such beings grow up and marry and have their own deformed children. Even then, when in most parts of the world people were eating one another, we put in place civilised laws for the good of all, and we observed them, and Kayhausen Boy is our proof of this.

Julia passed the book around the table and each girl studied the illustrations for an acceptable period in order to demonstrate interest. When it reached Sieglinde, she bent in close to the pages. They smelled of dust and damp and mildew, of rotting leaves and of dark crumbling wood, of shut rooms. She took in the way the boy lay on his back, and she thought: that is the way I lie in my bed when I am going to sleep.

'Would you like to borrow the book?' said Julia, who noticed how Sieglinde lingered over it; she noticed everything.

All the way home along Kantstrasse Sieglinde could feel the weight of it in her satchel, pulling at her shoulders as she crunched across drifts of broken glass and leapt over puddles from broken pipes. Back in her bedroom she sat on the edge of her bed and propped the book open on her chest of drawers, and every night the boy's wilted skin was the last thing she saw, and every morning it was the first. She knew how to look at him now, how to see the shape of the body within the tangle. 'It's gruesome,' she heard Mutti saying to Vati, but Mutti was wrong. The bodies lined up in the streets were gruesome, the corpses cloaked and labelled by the Hitler Youth girls who reached beneath the blankets and tied names to wrists, if there still were wrists to be named; Kayhausen Boy was a worn slipper, a hot-water bottle. And when Sieglinde descended to the cellar and the planes and the guns shook the house, the boy slipped from the book as supple as kelp and walked through the Heilmanns' rooms on his ragged legs, looking at their belongings, wondering at their mirrors, taking a sip from an unfinished cup of tea, a bite from an abandoned slice of bread. He washed his face in the bucket of water that had to last the rest of the day. He touched the pieces of shrapnel that hung from Sieglinde's ceiling; he lay on her bed and watched them spin and flicker, threads of rain blown by the wind. We weight the dead, we bury them deep, bind them and pin them in place so they will not return. This is never enough.

June 1944
Berlin

'How many shirts do you possess?' asked the woman, placing a piece of carbon paper beneath a form.

'Four,' said Gottlieb, 'but two are very worn around the neck.'

'Your wife has already turned the collars, of course?'

'Some months ago,' said Gottlieb.

'You would be surprised to know how many shirt applications we see where this is not the case.'

'I can assure you that these collars were turned in February, Frau . . .'

She tapped her nameplate with her pen.

'Frau Miller.'

'Well, we will return to the matter of the shirts presently,' she said. 'Winter coats.'

'One.'

The woman made a note on her form. 'Suits.'

'Two,' said Gottlieb.

'Casual jackets.'

'Also two.'

The woman continued filling in the form without looking up. 'Pairs of shoes.'

'Three.'

'Any trousers that cannot be classified as belonging to a suit.'

'One,' said Gottlieb.

'Cloth?'

'Yes, they are cloth trousers.'

'No, Herr Heilmann – of which type of cloth do the above trousers consist? Twill, herringbone, gabardine . . .'

'They're gabardine trousers. I find – '

'Socks?'

'Pairs?'

'Yes, Herr Heilmann, pairs.'

'I believe the figure is six, and I believe my wife is currently engaged in knitting me a further pair.'

For the first time, the woman looked up. 'She has not told you she is currently engaged in knitting a pair of socks for your personal usage?'

'No, Frau Miller. It's my birthday in two weeks.'

'And it's your belief the socks are to be presented to you on this future date?'

'It is. I do believe so. Yes.'

'All the same . . .'

'If it clarifies matters, I'm happy to bring the items in for checking once they've been presented to me.'

'I think that would be wise, Herr Heilmann. I shall make an appointment for you at the end of your current appointment.'

'Thank you, Frau Miller.'

'You are welcome.' She returned to the form. 'Now, undershirts. You possess how many?'

'Four.'

'Any mending, holes or fraying?'

'One has been mended at the shoulder seam.'

'Underpants.'

'Also four.'

'It is prudent to have the same number. Mending, holes, fraying?'

'Two pairs show fraying at the waist.'

Frau Miller looked up again, chewed a fingernail for a moment. 'And yet you are making a shirt application only?'

'I'm very aware of the Reich's need for textiles. For the production of uniforms. And bandages.'

'Hmm.'

Gottlieb waited.

'Well, your patriotism is to be applauded. But we will expect you in three months for an underwear application.'

'Thank you, Frau Miller.'

'You are welcome. I shall make an appointment for you when the current appointment is concluded, after I have made the appointment for your following appointment.'

'Thank you, Frau Miller.'

'Now, the shirt application. You have requested two new shirts, correct?'

'Correct.'

'And you have on your person the buttons from the two expired shirts that the new shirts will replace?'

'I do.' Gottlieb placed them on the counter.

'You may keep the expired shirts and your wife may use them for cleaning, which is necessary for national morale.'

'I understand, Frau Miller. Thank you.'

'You are welcome.' She turned the form around to Gottlieb and motioned for him to sign it, then stamped all four copies. 'You may collect your shirts in Hohenschönhauser Strasse, on the other side of town.'

If his mother could see him in his mended shirts, his turned collars. His mother, always so mindful of appearance, always so perfectly turned out and made up. Sieglinde often asked about her, wanting to know what her favourite flower was and what stories she liked, what time she made Gottlieb go to bed and whether she drank hot chocolate with sugar, and how exactly she died. Most of all, though, she wanted to know about her clothes. She pored over the few photographs Gottlieb possessed – studio portraits showing her leaning against pillars or the backs of chairs, hair pushed into flawless finger-waves, the little brooch made from his baby teeth pinned just so to her lapel, or strings of pearls wound about her throat.

'What colour was this dress?' she asked. 'Was it silk? Is that embroidery?'

And so Gottlieb described for her the contents of his mother's cupboards and armoires, the scented chests packed as carefully as a trousseau.

'But where are all her things now?' asked Sieglinde.

And yes, where were the stoles of silk and fur, the stab-stitched purses, the filmy gowns? Where were the kidskin shoes with their cut-steel buckles, the velvet dancing slippers, the cloche hats, the hobble skirts?

'Were they sold, Vati? Were they unpicked? And cut down?'

'I don't know,' said Gottlieb. (Probably. Yes.)

He remembered looking for his mother at one of her parties when he was very small. He passed through clusters of women, brushing against dresses that rustled and shook like flowers, misty chiffon rubbing at his cheeks and hair, and everywhere the tiny beads, glass seeds that glittered in the chandelier light, turning cloth to rain. The gowns were drenched with them: thousands of droplets stitched into peacock feathers, lotus blooms, pointillist sun-rays that burst across the body, so heavy the dresses could not be hung without tearing and had to be laid flat and wrapped like the dead in lengths of linen. His mother's voice glittered when she wore these costumes, and her laugh, too, and sometimes Gottlieb wondered if she might not be little glass beads all the way through. (Is this a mother? Is this, is this? I know nothing of such things.) High above him the women caught the light, perched in their airy and fabulous canopy, and he was not sure which one was his mother, and they all seemed so far away.

And then her hands came to him, white wings fluttering at his back and propelling him towards the fireplace, positioning him there in front of the mottled marble and the darkening mirror. And she bent and whispered in his ear, and reminded him what was expected, the diamonds at her neck tapping him on the shoulder, cold and hard and belonging to the night. When the room fell silent he was word-perfect, and he said:

Over all the hill-tops
Is peace,
In all the tree-tops
You sense
Hardly a breath;
In the forest the little birds fall still.
Wait,
Soon you too shall rest.

And all the hands in the room clapped, and touched his hair, and he left that shining place to climb the stairs and go to sleep, having recited his own lullaby.

This was the mother he recalled for Sieglinde: the one in the jewels and the gowns. He did not tell her what happened when the crisis came – the crash, in which his family lost almost everything. That was how people like the Heilmanns talked about their former lives, when they talked about them at all: in terms of *loss*. They did not mention *ruin* – ruin was for people in cold-water tenements, in one-room flats lit by bare bulbs; women of ill repute were ruined, and so were cakes left too long in the oven, and picnics in October, and woollens wrung too tightly. No, people like the Heilmanns simply lost their money; they lost their silverware and their Meissen porcelain, their telephones and their motor cars – lost them, as if they had been swept under a carpet or stored in the cellar and forgotten, and would turn up again quite by chance, caught between two drawers or submerged beneath a dust sheet lifted only in spring, at which point their owners could resume their tea-dances and their cocktail parties, their visits to the dress-maker and their purchasing of supple Italian shoes and pale French soaps, soon forgetting they had ever lost these things in the first place. This was what the Heilmanns hoped, at least for a time, before the truth of their losses settled and hardened about them. They could not keep their chandeliers and their parties. They could not keep their maids. They could not even keep their friends. They could not keep their villa, of course (of course), and they could not keep the furniture that filled it; they chose a few special pieces, family pieces – a cherrywood sideboard, a grandfather clock, an oak settle carved with bears – and lost the rest. They moved to a succession of smaller and smaller houses, in which the pieces did not comfortably fit, and finally to a flat in Kreuzberg, and Frau Heilmann said *I cannot breathe, there is no space, the walls are too close, this is not a real house.* She did not last; they lost her too. Gottlieb remembered looking at her laid out, her elbows pushing at the coffin's satin walls. *She is in a better place now*, he told Sieglinde, but she was just in a smaller box.

★

FRAU MÜLLER: Could a son denounce his mother, do you think, for cooking the wrong sort of fish?

FRAU MILLER: Fish? For cooking fish?

FRAU MÜLLER: The wrong sort.

FRAU MILLER: Has something happened? What are you asking me? Your meaning is unclear.

FRAU MÜLLER: Yesterday I served Dieter herring for his dinner. It's his favourite. He gets that from his father, rest his soul.

FRAU MILLER: Everybody likes herring.

FRAU MÜLLER: He said to me, Are you certain this is a German herring? And I said, Of course, Liebling. Because I was. I am. And he prodded it with his knife and he said, The nose seems larger than you would find on a German herring.

FRAU MILLER: I don't think herrings have noses, Frau Müller.

FRAU MÜLLER: I told him that. I said, I don't think herrings have noses. And he prodded it again and then he said, I suppose it could be a German-Italian mix. But he was far from happy. Far from happy.

FRAU MILLER: We want our children to be happy. That's why we're at war. Did he eat it?

FRAU MÜLLER: It was his tone, Frau Miller. And the way he looked at it. And at me.

FRAU MILLER: He should be pleased to have any herring at all, with the sea so full of mines.

FRAU MÜLLER: Precisely.

170

FRAU MILLER:	At any rate, we should not coddle children. We must always bear in mind that Nature shows no such consideration. Did he eat it?
FRAU MÜLLER:	Oh yes, he ate it.
FRAU MILLER:	And did not denounce you.
FRAU MÜLLER:	And did not denounce me.
FRAU MILLER:	There you are, then.
FRAU MÜLLER:	It's just that Richard Graeber's daughter denounced her father only last week, for making a joke about the Führer, which I wouldn't repeat, even if I knew it, which I don't.
FRAU MILLER:	I heard that too.
FRAU MÜLLER:	The joke? About the Führer?
FRAU MILLER:	No, about Sophie Graeber denouncing her father.
FRAU MÜLLER:	Why would anybody joke about a child denouncing her parent?
FRAU MILLER:	What I *heard* was that they were giving him twenty-five blows – you know, down there –
FRAU MÜLLER:	Prinz-Albrecht-Strasse?
FRAU MILLER:	– but they had to stop after five because they weren't using the nationally standardised cane. He noticed, Herr Graeber noticed, and he said, I don't believe that's a nationally standardised cane, and so they had to stop the interrogation, and they never did find out who told him the joke in the first place.

171

*

I watch as the bombs continue to fall, as the citizens of Berlin – those strollers and bathers, those bicyclists, those deep-breathers of fair weather, of Führer weather – learn to fear clear skies. Young lovers long no more for the moon, taking comfort instead under low cloud and in soft and starless fog. Few people remember how to sleep. They mourn pre-emptively, fixing black to their windows and keeping a close eye on anyone who flouts the rules of gloom, noting and reporting their neighbours' infringements: an open door, a crooked blind. Death comes squatting on metal wings, pitching his bony bombs at the backlit, a dogged heckler. Cars squint their way along the snuffed-out streets, headlights masked. Blue bulbs cast an underwater light in buses, trains and trams, and pedestrians lose all sense of the ground beneath their feet. Corrections are necessary: adjustments. Stand still for a moment; let the holes in your eyes widen; try to make out the white-painted kerbs that glimmer like a tideline of shells. (That roar is not the ocean.) There are falls and collisions, twists and strains. Layers of skin are lost. Tell me again, where is the ground? And where is home? Some tie white handkerchiefs to their wrists or their bags; you can make them out, these little phantoms, moving along in mid-air as if of their own accord.

And always at your shoulder, the shadowman. People are talking less and listening more, everybody is listening, and this is what I see coming: a silent city, dumb with the weight of listening – for planes, for news, for traitorous remarks – and the shadowman moving through the dead streets, slanting across every exchange, mouthless, anybody. Sometimes I find myself listening with them – for the cuckoo's call, for the siren's rise and fall, which comes in the daylight now as often as it comes at night. And when it comes I follow them underground to brick cellars with ill-fitting doors and cast-off carpets, and I watch them settle on their folding chairs and their camp beds, and the smell is mould and the smell is earth, and I admit that I think: let them moulder. Let them go to ground. And the bombs howl down, packs of wolves, but if you hear them hitting they are hitting someone else and not us, thank God thank God oh thank God, and some bombs are so distant we feel just the slightest pressure on the inner ear, and some bombs we hear as rushing water and some as hail, and you will never hear the bomb that hits you. When the blasts are close enough the ground shakes and the brick dust and plaster dust fall and we know that even though the building still stands above us it is coming apart little by little, the whole city is being undone, turning to dust. The light bulbs pitch and sway, blank suns in crazy orbit, and we hold on, reminding ourselves of the banners we strung up for the Führer's birthday: *Our Walls May Break, But Not Our Hearts.* Even the littlest children know what to do; they have been prepared for this with card games and board games and bright storybooks about fire, injury, damage, and they know exactly what to do, how to crouch, how to cower.

Afterwards, when we have returned to our homes and our own private affairs, men from the camps look for unexploded bombs and muffle them with newspaper and rags and thin-wristed fear, and other men, also from the camps – they are plentiful, such men, they are unrationed – dig up the dead and bury them again. And the children go into the streets and collect the shrapnel that grows like branches of coral, that glitters on the cobblestones and in the grass, in the flowerboxes with their ashy geraniums and beneath the linden trees and the lilac bushes, all mixed up with the brittle fallen leaves, crumpled pieces of sky still hot to the touch but cooling, cooling. I watch the children picking through the ruins and pouncing, unearthing these twisted spoils and assigning them shapes that make a kind of sense, the way one searches for the familiar in shifting clouds, and they say to one another that it feels like New Year's Eve, when you melt lead over a candle and pour it into water to see the shape of the future: a sword, an anchor, a spider, a cross. Sieglinde and Jürgen trade pieces with other children at their new school in Oranienburg, which is a long way from home but has not been evacuated, and these pieces are a sharp and unstable currency, now iridescent, now battleship grey, now as small and light as shells, now as broad as a human heart.

'They are not toys,' said Brigitte when Sieglinde brought them inside and arranged them on her chest of drawers. 'What about your stamps? What about your dolls? Gottlieb, is this even permitted?'

The collection grew, creeping across the windowsills and the dressing table, doubling itself in the mirror. It occupied the doll-house and the little cradle, covered the soft laps of bears and monkeys, swung from the ceiling on lengths of invisible thread, shivering when someone opened the door, caught in a perpetual state of falling. One or two pieces lay like an offering before the propped-open book about the bog boy. Brigitte was uneasy about these jagged and broken things filling her daughter's room, encroaching on her bed; she feared what they signalled. Sieglinde needed to understand that they were dangerous; that they could pierce the skin, embed themselves in a person. Surely it was unlucky to bring them into the house? They were too random and mismatched, too jumbled, glinting like a strange rain, and if she tried counting them she always lost her place – but all the same she began a new page in her ledger and attempted to itemise the pieces, because what else could she do but record every fragment, its particular colours and contours, its identifying marks, its weight, and every day more shrapnel fell, some of it from the enemy and some of it from shooting down the enemy, and every day Sieglinde added to her collection, and Brigitte could not keep up, it was too much, she could not keep up.

'Siggi, we have no room for all this,' she said.

But they did. In the quiet between the air raids, while her family snatched what sleep they could, Brigitte went to the living room and watched the wall behind the sofa. She stood before its whitewashed expanse, face to face with the Führer's portrait, her unslippered feet cold against the parquet. She waited, then brushed a hand across the wall, barely making contact – and no, she was not dreaming: it moved. Just two or three centimetres, but the wall moved, backing away as if recoiling from her touch. She saw it and she heard it, that same dragging noise she'd been hearing for so long, someone shifting heavy and forgotten things about in the attic. Had she done it herself? The Heilmann sideboard and the radio and the armchairs all cast their shadows at her, and the room was so much bigger now – there, she had admitted it. She held her breath, unsure of what to do. Should she wake Gottlieb? Report the matter to Herr Schneck the caretaker in the morning? Still she did not breathe. And then, from the neighbouring apartment, the Loewenthals' apartment, she heard a hand brushing the wall's surface, checking it was solid and stable and real. The hand was just where her own had been moments earlier, she felt sure, and she pictured herself there on the other side of the wall, a silent twin, the hole left in the paper once the silhouette was cut. Should she say something? Should she speak? Ask who was there, ask for a name, give her own? The Führer's portrait had slipped a little, she noticed, and she put it to rights. Ear to the wall now she waited, wordless, but heard nothing more.

The following evening she asked Gottlieb if he noticed anything different about the living room.

He looked around. 'It seems the same as ever,' he said.

'You don't think there's anything wrong with it?'

'Wrong with it?'

'Can't you see? It's bigger. Far bigger than it used to be.'

'Brigitte,' he said, 'the living room is the same size it's always been. Are your nerves bad today? Is it the broken nights? How could it be bigger?'

So, she thought. She had denied it to Sieglinde, and then she had denied it to Frau Loewenthal, and now Gottlieb was denying it to her, and if Frau Loewenthal asked her again she would deny it again, because it would be too late to say anything different. And yes: she knew that if she had more room somebody else had to have less; and yes: she knew that if she bought a samovar that belonged to someone else then that person no longer possessed the samovar; and she knew that these were the laws that spun the world. And yet, she had not moved the wall herself, and she would not have bought the samovar had it not been for sale. And these were also the laws that spun the world. And perhaps somebody else would speak up about the shifting wall. Perhaps, she thought, it had happened in other apartments, even in other buildings. It could be a consequence of the soil in Berlin – poor quality, too sandy, once a swamp. Yes, surely somebody would say something, because although the extra space was all well and good, although it lent a grandeur to the apartment, suggested a certain standing and importance, what of the stability of the building? So yes, someone else would raise the matter, but until then there was nothing to be done. She had tried, hadn't she?

The next time Herr Schneck came to check the buckets of sand and water on their landing she decided to ask him about the apartment opposite – well, was it an apartment? She heard no sound coming from it, had heard nothing in a long while, she was sure, fairly sure.

'Excuse me,' she said. 'That door – where does it lead?'

The caretaker followed the line of her pointing finger. 'That one? It's just a cupboard, Frau Heilmann. For the mops and brooms and so on, to keep them tidied away. It leads nowhere.'

A Puppet Show

You who are from   above,
          all our   and   ,
          him who's doubly
Doubly with your   ;
Ah, I am   of   !
Why all this   and   ?
                    ,

          Come, ah come into my   !

July 1944
Berlin

FRAU MILLER: I don't feel clean. No soap until next week, and I need to wash my hair. You know how thick it is, you can see how much hair I possess, I am fortunate to have my mother's hair, many people admire it.

FRAU MÜLLER: You know, Frau Miller, I have heard that when a woman makes herself look nice, it is often because she takes a secret pleasure in annoying another of her sex.

FRAU MILLER: I don't know what you mean.

FRAU MÜLLER: It's just something I heard. In any case, I have enough soap to see out the month, perhaps a little more. I am careful with my soap. Others may be tempted to use theirs up too quickly, washing their hair more than is necessary at the start of the month and then having to walk around dirty for a week or so at the end, but I am thrifty with my soap and therefore never find myself in this unpleasant state. I rub my face with chestnuts. I boil pine needles for the bath.

FRAU MILLER:	I do all that, and I stew ivy leaves for the laundry. The fact remains, my hair is so plentiful that my soap does not last the full month. I have Gabi's fur to wash too, remember. It's not right.
FRAU MÜLLER:	Well, we all have to make do with what's available, Frau Miller.
FRAU MILLER:	Quite, but it's not just the quantity, it's the quality. Imitation this, replacement that. Clothes made from wood pulp. Tin in our teeth.
FRAU MÜLLER:	Did you hear the one about the would-be suicide? He tried to hang himself, but the imitation rope snapped.
FRAU MILLER:	I thought you didn't repeat jokes.
FRAU MÜLLER:	Did I say it was a joke? Anyway – you've heard the rumours about the soap, of course.
FRAU MILLER:	I don't listen to rumours.
FRAU MÜLLER:	Perhaps you could wear a headscarf during that last difficult week.
FRAU MILLER:	Like a Russian?
FRAU MÜLLER:	I'm sure you could arrange it in a fashionable manner that would distinguish you from a Russian.
FRAU MILLER:	Like a cleaning woman, then.
FRAU MÜLLER:	If you will be frivolous with your soap, Frau Miller . . .
FRAU MILLER:	As outlined above, my hair is so splendidly abundant that the standard soap allowance is insufficient. I am sure there are some people who do not use all their soap within a month – people with

thin and unattractive hair, for example
– but I feel we should be assessed as to
the quantity of our hair, and the soap
allocated accordingly. It would be a
sliding scale, Frau Müller.

FRAU MÜLLER: A slippery slope.

FRAU MILLER: I do not care for your tone.

FRAU MÜLLER: You are saying that you find the system
of soap allocation to be inefficient. You
are saying that the very organisation
governing the distribution of soap is
faulty.

FRAU MILLER: No, I am not.

FRAU MÜLLER: It sounds as if you are.

FRAU MILLER: I am not.

FRAU MÜLLER: This is how it sounds to me. One must
be careful with one's comments and
opinions, Frau Miller.

FRAU MILLER: Naturally.

FRAU MÜLLER: As careful as one is with one's soap.

FRAU MILLER: Yes. Yes, I am of the same mind.

★

Sieglinde woke to Mutti pulling back the covers and telling
her to hurry, and the fox fur that hung from Mutti's neck
was brushing her face, as light as air, not quite real, and
a paw scrabbled at her throat, and she said, 'I was having
a dream,' and Mutti said, 'Leave it, leave it, get out,' as if
the dream were a burning room. It was important to do
everything Mutti asked, because her nerves were suffering.
Sieglinde sat up. How could she have slept through the
siren? It was so loud now that it filled Mutti's mouth, and

the mouth of the fox fur that swung from Mutti's neck, and Sieglinde could not understand a word, and she was so tired. Most parents, she knew, had sent their children away, as the Gauleiter had commanded. They had put them on trains full of other children, whole classrooms of children who leaned laughing from the windows and waved bright paper flags, and the trains took them to distant farms where they could milk cows and feed chickens and ride horses, or to camps where there were no parents with suffering nerves, and they learned how to jump across fire and make bridges of their bodies and tell which plants were poisonous, and there was plenty of food, and they did not have to chew every mouthful thirty times just to make it last, or press their hands to their stomachs just to feel full. Almost her whole class from her old school had gone, and so had the Schuttmann boys, and the younger Glöckners, and more than half of the girls from her Jungmädel group – and the children who used to live opposite the Heilmanns went years ago, well before the bombings started, even before there were any camps to go to. What were their names? And Edda Knopf's cousin, who wasn't right in the head – he was evacuated too, but he died of heart failure and they sent his ashes back in a box.

'Mask,' said Mutti. 'Shoes.' Yes, there might be gas, there might be broken glass, every night the same threats, distilled into single words by now but just as lethal, just as sharp.

Sieglinde did not want to go away to the country, despite the horses and the campfires and the food. Who would remind her how to keep safe? She would cut her feet; she would choke. And she did not want to go and stay with Mutti's parents either, as she had heard Mutti suggest; they lived in Celle, and never came to visit, and Vati said they were as good as strangers. Out on the landing Vati was buttoning up Kurt's coat, and Kurt was saying, 'The blacksmith has a horse to shoe. How many nails do you think will do?' Mutti took his hand and Jürgen's and rushed down the stairs, fox paws jumping, pattering against her chest.

In the cellar Herr Schneck was reprimanding the Hauers for letting their dog drink from the bucket of water on the third-floor landing. 'If there is a fire,' he was saying, 'if you are trapped in your beds and the flames are reaching for you from the blown-out windows, will Fritzi save you?'

'Please, Herr Schneck,' said Vati. 'The children.'

But the time for shielding children was past, said Schneck. He nominated Herr Hauer to go up to the roof and check for incendiaries, which could start a fire that jumped from house to house so fast you hardly saw it happening, until entire streets blazed. In his notebook he wrote down the names of absentees – those grown lazy with their lives, those who stayed under the covers and waited for the windows to shatter, the shock waves to bring down the walls. This was illegal, he reminded everyone. This was selfish and un-German, and furthermore – he held up his pencil – you had to be killed *in* the cellar to qualify for compensation. The English, who did not have the foresight to build their houses with cellars, shut themselves in cages in their living rooms during air raids. He had seen pictures in the *Berliner Illustrierte*: the cheerful enemy, jammed into wire enclosures like the animals they were. By day they used them as ping-pong tables. See how much use a ping-pong table was when Germany unleashed her wonder weapons!

Sieglinde said, 'Vati, are you going to evacuate us now?' and Vati said no, of course not, and what a thing to ask, and anyway there were no evacuations, there were transfers and relocations and holidays, but no, they would not be sent away, and besides, the war was almost won. (Which was true.) Sieglinde felt her hair lifting from her head; the suck of a nearby bomb.

After the all-clear she tucked the boys back into bed, which was her job now, because of Mutti's nerves. The night was quiet again and the sheets had turned cold and outside the rain had started. It spattered down on Jürgen's sandcastle, dissolving the ramparts grain by grain, exposing the chipped and dented men buried in its walls. From the hallway the grandfather clock chimed *no, no, no,* the sound deep and distant. Inside its case the iron weights were making time behave, lowering themselves slowly, slowly, taking a full week to fall.

In the morning, because of Mutti's nerves, Sieglinde gets up and prepares breakfast for everyone, then helps Jürgen to find his schoolbooks and Kurt to brush his teeth and get dressed, and then she starts on the laundry. She separates the washing into dark and light, checking pockets and turning socks back through the right way. There's nowhere Vati can have his two suits dry-cleaned any more – all the dry-cleaners have gone to be soldiers – so Sieglinde brushes and presses them for him, running a little soap along the creases in order to keep them sharp. When she shakes out a pair of his trousers a scrap of paper flutters from the cuff, and she bends to pick it up and sees that it is printed with a word, and that word is *pity.* She turns it over but there is nothing on the back. It is very thin, this piece of paper, as fine as a feather, and so she cups it inside her hands so that it cannot tear or crumble or drift away from her, and then she transfers it to the cake tin with the picture of Frederick the Great on the lid, and it will be safe here, because there is no cake.

Over the following weeks she finds more words caught in Vati's trouser-cuffs – not every time she does the laundry, but now and then – and each one she places in the tin. *Promise, evacuate, exterminate, Versailles, God.* Little scraps, little crumbs. Are these the dangerous things that Vati takes away? Frederick the Great watches her from his rearing horse, its flanks pocked with spots of rust. The tin is so light that when Mutti shakes it to see if it contains anything she should be counting, it feels as empty as air.

★

Mutti would prefer it if Sieglinde stopped attending her Jungmädel meetings. 'I need you at home, to help me,' she says, but she means *I am afraid.*

'It's the law,' says Sieglinde, 'and when Jürgen is ten he will go, and when Kurt is ten he will go too.' (But why is it the law, to teach children songs and customs? To lead them on walks through the forest? To measure how far they can leap, how fast they can run?) I see Mutti start to cry, and Kurt comes and sits on her lap and offers her a piece of his half-eaten Zwieback, and nuzzles his soft little head into her neck.

'You could miss a week here and there,' says Mutti. 'You could just not go.' And again she means *I am afraid.*

'You mustn't say that,' says Sieglinde. 'You mustn't let anyone hear you say that.' She buttons up her jacket, gives her mother and her brother a kiss goodbye and sets out for the tram stop. She knows where all the shelters are along the way, in case of an attack, so she is quite safe. There are more holes in the houses, more craters in the streets, and the air smells of gas. She sees a pair of shoes poking out from beneath a striped bedsheet, and a Hitler Youth girl only a few years older than herself reaching beneath the sheet and attaching a label to a hand. Hitler Youth boys are clearing the rubble, pulling people from it, people so caked with mortar dust they have turned to stone. On the corner another girl in uniform collects money for the Winter Relief, and at the tram stop another clips Sieglinde's ticket. Yes, we are the storm of youth; we are victory.

That afternoon she and her friends tear newspapers into strips while Julia, their leader, mixes the paste in a bowl. They are wearing aprons to protect their uniforms, which their parents have worked hard to buy; the aprons they have sewn themselves, for they will be mothers one day, and mothers must know how to sew, and they are neat and tidy girls who will make good mothers, nice girls with clean hair and correct thoughts, and they shred the daylight terror attacks, the strategic retreats, the losses, and they shred the notices that say *I am a soldier 22 years old, blond and of good health. Before I give my life to the Führer I should like to meet a German woman through whom I can leave a child for the German Reich.*

'This one has a picture of the Führer,' says Edda Knopf. 'We can't tear him up, can we?'

'Quite right. Put him aside,' says Julia, and Sieglinde and all the other girls begin to search for pictures of the Führer they can put aside, but Edda is Julia's favourite for today, Sieglinde can tell. And anyway, co-operation as a group is what matters, and not the work Sieglinde might do on her own or the helpful suggestions she might make; the group is everything and she is nothing, nothing, even though it is also and at the same time true that a single girl or boy can make a difference, like Herbert Norkus, who was stabbed

189

six times and died for their freedom. Julia shows them how to scrunch a page of newspaper into a ball and wrap it with paste-soaked strips, smoothing them flat, building up layer after layer until the torn words and pictures are so dark and wet that you cannot recognise them any more, which is a relief for Jutta Schönbrunn, who had already ripped up the Führer before Edda Knopf asked what to do in such a situation. Slowly the lumps of wet paper turn into heads – witch, policeman, robber, crocodile, grandmother, Devil – and here is Kasperle himself, with his hooked nose and his long chin. Everybody wants to play Kasperle because he is allowed to misbehave, to think up pranks and to say rude things even though at heart he is good, but Julia chooses Margarete Braun because she has the best voice and sounds the funniest, and Kasperle must make the audience laugh.

Before they leave for home that evening the girls set the paper heads to dry on the windowsill. All week Sieglinde worries about them, wondering if they will be hit in a raid – they are so soft, so flimsy – but there they wait the following week, lined up like the shrunken trophies of some savage tribe, and the girls paint faces on them and give them wool for hair and rags for bodies, and make up words for them to say. And when they perform the puppet show their families know what to say too, cheering Kasperle and shouting warnings to him when he is in danger and does not realise it. *Look out! Look out!* All Kasperle wants is to sleep, but visitors keep arriving to interrupt him. The policeman comes to tell him there is a robber in the area who has been stealing coal, and Kasperle should keep his cellar locked and watch out for anybody who has black hands and dirty clothes. His grandmother brings him a hat she has knitted for him, but it is too big and covers his eyes and he cannot see properly, and he stubs his toe when he is making her a cup of tea, and spills boiling water on himself, and everybody laughs. He goes back to bed, falling asleep straight away he is so tired, but the crocodile and the witch knock on his door and embrace him and say they are his parents, and they weep with joy to have found their little boy at last.

Kasperle says, 'Parents? I have no parents. I am made of paste and paper through and through.'

'But so are we,' says the witch. 'And look, my hair is wool just like yours. You are clearly our son.'

'No, no!' calls the audience. 'Be careful!'

'Can't you see how handsome I am?' says Kasperle. 'You're too ugly to be my parents. If I had a mother she'd be prettier than Kristina Söderbaum, and if I had a father he'd look like Carl Raddatz.'

'What a rude boy you are,' says the crocodile. 'I've a mind to eat you whole just to teach you some manners.'

But as the crocodile is opening his jaws the policeman returns and asks Kasperle if he has seen the robber, and Kasperle points to the false parents and says, 'I caught these two breaking into my cellar, Herr Offizier.'

'How could you?' the witch and the crocodile shout as the policeman leads them away. 'Your own parents!'

The audience laughs and laughs.

Kasperle returns to bed and begins to snore. The robber peers in through the window, then goes to the cellar and helps himself to Kasperle's coal, and no matter how loudly the audience shouts, Kasperle does not stir. And as he sleeps on and on another visitor appears at his door, and this visitor does not knock; he lets himself in and makes his way to Kasperle's bed and sits down beside him. And when Kasperle feels his hot breath on his face he wakes, and it is the Devil come to claim his soul, but Kasperle tells him to go back to hell, and that he has no soul, that the little girl who made him forgot to give him one, and he is made of paper and paste and nothing more.

'A boy made of paper?' says the Devil. 'I've never heard of such a thing.'

'It's perfectly true,' says Kasperle. 'And not just any paper, but the *Völkischer Beobachter.*'

'That is a very fine paper,' says the Devil. 'I read it myself. May I?'

He is reaching out a hand to touch Kasperle's face, but quick as a flash Kasperle jumps out of bed and pulls his grandmother's hat down over the Devil's head, and the Devil cannot see a thing, and Kasperle pushes him out of his house, locks the door, climbs back into bed and sleeps and sleeps, and he remains sleeping as the little curtain falls, and for all we know he is sleeping still.

Mutti and Vati and Sieglinde and the boys walk down Charlottenburger Chaussee on their way home, beneath the camouflage netting that turns the street into a dappled forest floor. Mutti asks, 'Which one were you? We couldn't tell. It was the strangest thing.'

And yes, it is a very strange thing, not to know one's own child.

'She was the robber,' says Jürgen.

'The policeman!' says Kurt.

'I was the crocodile,' says Sieglinde, and Vati says, 'You see?' and Sieglinde puts her hand in his and wishes that he did not have to work so hard.

★

FRAU MÜLLER: I thought we'd lost him. When the radio said there'd been an attempt on his life –

FRAU MILLER:	Let's not panic, Frau Müller. Let's remain calm. It was only cuts and grazes. And his trousers torn to shreds. And his underpants.
FRAU MÜLLER :	His trousers? And underpants? In shreds?
FRAU MILLER:	So I hear.
FRAU MÜLLER:	My goodness.
FRAU MILLER:	Naked, I imagine. From the waist down.
FRAU MÜLLER:	Do you know, Frau Miller, that some women write to the Führer and offer themselves to him?
FRAU MILLER:	What do you mean?
FRAU MÜLLER:	They offer him their bodies to enjoy as he wishes. They ask him to give them a child.
FRAU MILLER:	Which child?
FRAU MÜLLER:	His child.
FRAU MILLER:	The Führer does love little ones. He shares a special bond with them.
FRAU MÜLLER:	But can you imagine writing such a letter? What would you say?
FRAU MILLER:	I cannot. I would not. Why? Can you?
FRAU MÜLLER:	*(silent)*
FRAU MILLER:	Frau Müller?

Oh, the women. They were all in love with him, their blue-eyed god, and sent him pieces of their hair and the imprints of their mouths, and when they opened their legs they opened them for him.

August 1944
Near Leipzig

Mama spent weeks thinking about the blanket, sketching different designs like a girl trying out a married name, spreading the square of cloth on the floor and considering it from every position. She counted the rows in its weave with the tip of a needle, murmuring figures under her breath and marking off sections with blue chalk, her mouth full of pins. Each evening she practised her stitches until they were as tiny as possible; little red seeds, little black seeds.

'What's it going to be?' said Erich.

'A present,' said Mama.

'What sort of present?'

'A special one.'

Slowly her design took shape. She unpicked her work if it was not perfect; some mornings I saw her uprooting every stitch from the previous day and starting again. She passed the crinkled lengths of thread to Erich and he dipped them in water and wound them around his hand. Up close it was difficult to make out the pattern; the red and black dashes were stalks of grass, rain on a lake, endless and repeating so that the eye became quite lost, but if you stood back and looked, truly looked, they resolved into Mama's angular intention: a swastika that stretched the length and width of the piece. And then, after a time, you noticed that this held smaller swastikas, and that they held smaller ones still, all locked together as tightly as honeycomb. Even Mama did not know how many it contained.

'Is it for Papa?' said Erich, and she said, 'Papa? For Papa?' and he knew that he had asked a foolish question. Where would they send the blanket? To the snow? To the mud? They had not heard from Papa for months.

'It's for the Führer,' she said, 'to show him we love him.' Erich thought then that he might start to cry, because how many boys could say they had helped their mama make a special blanket for the Führer? The traitors' bomb did not kill him; the Führer could not die. A matter of hours after the explosion he had spoken on the radio, and Erich had closed his eyes and pictured him right there in the room: *It is the duty of every German without exception to ruthlessly oppose these elements, and either to arrest them immediately or, if they should resist arrest, to shoot them without further ado.* Erich imagined presenting the blanket to him in person, the Führer smiling and shaking his hand as the cameras flashed. *Boy in Saxony Presents Adolf Hitler with Magnificent Blanket.* He swallowed the lump in his throat. As Mama kept reminding him, he was the man of the house now.

Word came the following week: Papa was missing.

'What does that mean?' Erich asked, and Mama said, 'They don't know where he is. They have lost him.'

Like a single mitten? Like a favourite book? Erich had lost his favourite Winnetou book for quite some time, and only found it when Lina moved his shelves away from the wall to clean behind them. Had Papa slipped away somewhere too?

'We must tell the bees,' said Mama, and she led him through the withered garden.

'Herr Kröning is dead,' she said, moving from hive to hive and repeating the news, and that was when Erich understood what missing meant. 'Herr Kröning is dead. Herr Kröning is dead. Herr Kröning is dead,' over and over until it stopped making sense and became just a sound, a hum that merged with the humming of the hives. 'Dead, dead, dead,' he whispered in her wake.

A letter arrived from Papa two weeks later, dotted with holes:

We came to a field of watermelon in   and could not believe they were real. We split them open with our bayonets and ate every last one, and we spat out the seeds like black teeth. Home seems unreal to me too. I am forgetting the shape of your mouth. I have no   left.   is lost.

Mama said she did not want to keep the letter and asked Erich to burn it, but he took it to his bedroom to store in his honey jar with his other precious things. He upended them onto his pillow and arranged them in a line: an empty snail shell, an acorn, a dead and perfect bee, the ten-thousand-mark note, the paper flags from the parade. The snail shell was still empty, the acorn unsprouted; the bee was still dead and the money still worthless and the flags were so faded they were almost blank. Erich unrolled the banknote, turned it sideways and studied the little picture of the farmer. He had not taken it from the jar in a very long time, and it kept rolling shut, and he sighed. The bee fluttered its wings in the draught. He held the note down with both hands and lay very still . . . and then he saw it: a pale figure, a monstrous face, there at the farmer's throat, hidden in the light and shadow of his skin, feeding on him. Suddenly Erich could see only the ghoul, the vampire, and he could not fathom how he had failed to see it before; it was so plain to him now. It was there all along.

I watch Erich at night, after Mama has switched on his bedside lamp and kissed his forehead – a guardian of sorts, I tell myself, though at times I wish that I could replace him: that I could creep between his lips as he sleeps and take up residence within his skin, seeing what he sees, touching what he touches. Does this sound like love? I envy him his little room with the window that faces the apple orchard, his bag of glass marbles with their trapped and twisting flames, his books about Apache chiefs and silver lions. Sometimes I fear what I might do to him. I watch the bird lamp as it spins in his sleep. I breathe on it and it quickens, the birds swooping across his bed, flickering on his cheeks like moths.

★

It is autumn when the airman falls, the season of falling, and I see him thrown from his droning machine and out into the night, and then, when the great silk canopy blooms above us, I see him drifting, a spore cast from its burning pod. I drift with him; I take his hand and speak to him of the sky, the birds, the way a turning wing can catch the light. In the darkness – and in his condition – he cannot make out the copse of larches beneath us, soft and gold, planted in the form of a swastika, but I tell him of their bright presence among the evergreens, how they show themselves year after year. He dies on the way down, somewhere between heaven and earth, and I know where he will land.

Erich and Mama leap from their beds and run through the garden and on through the orchard, the bees roaring in their ears, the carved hives staring after them, mouths wide open. *I turned first to water and then to ice the dead lay so thick to their backs I could untangle their every sin a rearrangement of flesh.* By the light of the moon they see the airman lying in the burnt-off barley field, a charred body come to rest on charred ground, and even though they know he must have perished still they run to him, the black earth thudding, marking their feet with ashes. He is a mess of a man, hardly a man at all, already turning to dust, white silk spilling from him, and they peer at him as if to identify the meaning held in his jumbled shape, as if to tell their own future. No eagle on the breast: not one of theirs. They begin to wrap him in his parachute, spinning a white chrysalis about him, but as Mama pleats and tucks the skin-soft cloth she thinks of Uschi, her sister, soon to be married in crêpe, and Gerhard away fighting in France. He cannot attend his own wedding, but that is no barrier: all over Germany young brides are marrying men who are not there.

'Bring shovels and a knife,' she says to Erich, unrolling the silk once more, and I run with him back through the orchard, and the hives call after us, full of caution, and they say:

Blood pattered into the pails at our feet, dark honey in the dusk, and I felt the blood between us, my blood in him, and I knew that someday the blood would fill his own son, there was no end to it, this great rope.

Do not walk in the forest with another. Do not eat wild berries. God is able of these stones to raise up children unto Abraham. Do not drink from the wells. Hide behind the dead.

We do not listen to the hives. We bring the knife to Mama and she cuts the parachute lines, and then we help her dig a hole for the airman, right there in the burnt field, and before we roll him into it she holds her hand to his chest for just a moment, and touches his blackened head. She does not check him for a name, because even though he wears no eagle she has already decided who he was and who he will be: our own missing man, returned home. We bury him where he landed; there are no men left to carry him anywhere else, and he is another man dead, there are so many dead men that they fall from the sky as common as rain. Mama rolls the parachute up into a bundle and carries it home like clean washing, and says it was meant to be. And by still fires would I lie in fields in darkest night.

When Erich woke the next day he thought he had dreamt it all, the moonlit silk, Mama's knife slashing the lines, but when he looked at his hands he saw dirt under his nails, and his arms ached from digging, and there at the back door stood the shovels still clotted with fresh earth. He and Mama found the aeroplane in the forest, its black wings bitten from its body, a drone pushed from the hive at the end of autumn. It was cold to the touch and they nudged at its jagged flanks, its many riveted parts: this was the machine that held men in the air, the miracle that kept them from falling. If this could break, so could anything.

'But where are the guns?' said Mama. 'Where are the bombs?'

'It's a Spitfire,' said Erich. 'He was just taking photos.'

'Photos? Of us? At night-time?'

'Perhaps he was lost,' said Erich.

They both stared at the wreckage.

'At any rate,' said Mama, 'let's be thankful that it didn't burn Papa's larches.'

And yes, there they were, four right angles, butter-yellow and unharmed, yet to lose their needles though it could not be long now. Inside the hollow of the cockpit Erich found another piece of silk; it looked like a dropped handkerchief, and he wondered if this was how death came: a poorly timed sneeze. (Not for most. Luminal in tea; a needle to the heart: this is how death comes.) When he picked it up he saw that it was not a handkerchief but a map of Germany, hardly singed, with all her rivers and railways, canals and roads printed in black. They radiated out from Berlin, Posen, Vienna, Danzig like cracks in glass, each city a point of impact. He crushed the map into his fist – it reduced to almost nothing, the entire country, and made no sound. And the turtle dove sang *You-you, you*, and from the orchard a black line of bees was flying to the house and in through the open door, a river of bees, a black canal, and they were taking up residence in the bronze head, building their combs around Mama's paper wishes. They hummed inside the hollow skull, their newest hive, and it seemed that at any moment the head might begin to speak too, asking for Papa's safety, for Papa's return, for Papa's whereabouts, for another child. And where would Mama find this child? Next to the brook, beneath the Adder Queen's red stone? Waiting on the hillside, whistling the songs of the birds? Combing the snails and the eel-grass from the water sprite's hair? Or dropped by the cuckoo into the wren's strange nest?

★

Tante Uschi stood on a stool in her tacked wedding dress, the silk falling well past her feet. *I know one day there will be a miracle*, she sang as Mama pinned up the hem. Erich had never seen her so happy.

'Unbelievable,' she kept saying, running her hands over the luminous cloth. 'Just like Emmy Göring's.' She felt the side seam for the little hidden pocket that would hold the bread and the salt. She would never go hungry.

'Stop moving,' said Mama.

'I haven't told Gerhard about it. I want it to be a surprise when he gets the photograph.'

Mama looked up at her sister. 'You can't tell Gerhard. Not in a letter.'

'Well, I haven't told him, have I?' said Tante Uschi.

'If word got out . . .'

'How do we explain it, then?'

'It's a family dress,' said Mama. 'We've simply altered it for you.'

'Yes,' said Tante Uschi. 'A family dress.'

When the news came three weeks later that Gerhard, having survived years in the desert, had fallen in eastern France, Uschi said, 'But what about the wedding? What about my dress?' Nobody scolded her, because the freshly bereaved are entitled to say such things without thinking how they will sound, and even though Uschi had never met Gerhard, anybody could see they were in love, and why shouldn't she have her wedding day? And just as Gerhard's absence had not prevented the marriage plans, neither would his death: thanks to the Führer, German women could marry dead men, provided those dead men were also German and of clean blood.

Erich was sorry he would never meet Onkel Gerhard, but Mama said he should not be sad, because Onkel Gerhard was a hero, and not every boy had an uncle who had fallen for Germany. Erich considered the manner of his death, his falling: Onkel Gerhard standing his ground until the last, and when he fell he came to rest quite intact, his rifle still raised, aimed at nothing.

Mama and Tante Uschi went to the town hall the day before the ceremony, sweeping the stone steps at the entrance and polishing the windows in the registrar's office, dusting the long dark table and hanging fragrant fir branches from the walls. The next morning Mama braided her sister's hair and pinned it into place beneath a veil so fine you could hardly see it. She gave her their grandmother's garnets to wear, the earrings and bracelet and choker so dark they were almost black, and then she buttoned her into the wedding dress, which drifted and billowed with Uschi's every step, filled with the memory of sky.

'Have you polished your shoes?' Mama asked Erich, but she did not wait for an answer; it was already time to leave. Ronja was waiting in her bridle and Erich harnessed her to the wagon and they were on their way, Erich driving, which was only proper in Papa's absence. The day was overcast, the colour of stone, and the town hall's stucco façade seemed to vanish against the white air as they approached, its leaden clock tower hanging disembodied above them, ticking away the minutes. On the front steps a mother calmed her baby, duping him with the tip of her milkless finger – a small deception soon learned by mothers, for no good comes from bowing to a child's every demand.

The registrar welcomed them and told them how pleased he was to be conducting a wedding in such times. The groom's parents, who had travelled from Dresden, sat in the front row and did not speak, glancing around them as if unsure they had come to the right place. But look – there on the long dark table, set between lit candles, a photograph of their son; no one could deny the resemblance. The bride and her witnesses took their seats at the front of the room, the chair next to Ursula occupied only by a steel helmet. She held her bouquet on her lap – artificial lilies bound with ivy, the dark leaves disappearing in the fall of her dress. She had wanted a song at her wedding, and so everybody stood and sang *Two stand before you, Lord, to be joined together as one*, and the fir branches filled the small space with their resinous scent, and the candle flames fluttered beside the groom's photograph, wings of bright birds, and the guests stood in this makeshift forest and sang for the living bride glimmering in her silk as fine as the skeletons of leaves, and they sang for the soul of the groom, his grave at the western front but his spirit surely here. Nobody wept. Gerhard's likeness watched from the table, smooth-cheeked and smooth-haired, silent in his pressed-tin frame, the hooked cross stamped above him, a tin star, his face catching the guests' reflections so that the bride saw not her groom but his wordless father, breast pinned with medals, and she wanted to turn the photograph away, but it was too late to change anything now, much too late. And nobody wept, because this was no funeral; nobody wept, because only the defeated may weep, and we are not defeated, and to say that we are is to ask for the noose.

Alchemy

Who   to   his   ,
Who   spent the   hours
Of   in   upon his bed,
He knows you not, you   !

You lead us to into   below,
You   the   in   to   ,
Then you   him to   −
Since all   does for   call.

October 1944
Berlin

FRAU MÜLLER:	They took our fence yesterday. Uprooted it just like that.
FRAU MILLER:	They took ours two weeks ago. It'll be bullets and bombs by now.
FRAU MÜLLER:	There's nothing to stop anybody from simply walking into our yard. And into yours.
FRAU MILLER:	I'd rather have no fence and more bullets and bombs for the British.
FRAU MÜLLER:	The English.
FRAU MILLER:	The English.
FRAU MÜLLER:	The bells are gone too. We no longer note the passing of time. And who will warn us now? And how will we mourn the dead? And repel the lightning?
FRAU MILLER:	Red as blood are the skies. That is not the daylight's flood.

★

Whenever the siren sounded, we took our cases and our masks and began the descent to the windowless hole where the ceiling hung too close and the weight of the building pressed down and down; we went to our graves where the coal dust and brick dust caught at our throats and the cobwebs at our hair, and the damp ground held us and would not let us go. More often than not there was no electricity, and the shelter grew smaller and smaller in the dark. Elbows poked ribs; hips struck hips; coat-cuffs grazed cheeks and dislodged hats. And we gave our attention to these small nuisances rather than to the juddering earth: *Be careful you don't . . . Would you mind not . . . ? Please refrain from . . .* And more often than not − even if Herr Schneck had to mediate − a sour truce could be reached, if only until the next attack. At least we had our own cellar. At least we did not have to crush ourselves into one of the public shelters, hold our children aloft so they could still breathe when the oxygen level began to fall and the candle on the floor went out.

Brigitte lay down on the thin camp bed and rested her head on the thin pillow. Things need not have come to this, she thought. Things might have worked out so differently. If the Heilmanns had not lost their fortune she might be living in the Grunewald villa, with its tree-lined driveway and its lily pond and its telephones that linked every room − but it had been sold long before she met Gottlieb, and she had never even visited it; she was familiar only with her husband's occasional descriptions and his meticulous silhouette cuttings of the house, none of which, he said, were ever quite right.

'We could go back and check,' she suggested, but he said it was some sort of administrative building now, and would not be the same.

She held up her hand to the lantern and saw the blood inside her skin, thick against the cellar's dark horizon, and she closed her eyes. She walked through the lost villa, pulling the sheets from carved Venetian mirrors, uncovering the potted palms, the Bechstein grand piano, the tinkling chandeliers. (Was there a Bechstein? Did Gottlieb ever mention a Bechstein?) In the entranceway the carved bears danced along the back of Hannelore's oak settle and the face of the grandfather clock glowed like a winter moon, so much smaller here than in the apartment. Brigitte reached inside its walnut case and raised the weights, but what was the time? Early morning, early evening? She did not know, she could not tell, she had no sense of where north lay. Out in the garden the crows gathered about the frozen fountain and the oak trees dropped their dead leaves. She opened the door to the ice house and descended the stone steps, and she could see her breath before her, and it was only breath, not smoke, and it did not reach for her lungs and make her cough and gasp, for it was only breath. Beneath the ground the slabs of ice lay packed in straw; cut from the frozen pond, they will last well into summer, when there will be rose-petal sorbet and dishes of ice cream and long pale drinks floating with bruised mint. There will be parties, too: a stylish band playing in the Japanese pagoda, *the whole world is sky-blue when I look into your eyes, I'll dance into heaven with you*, and coloured lanterns strung in the trees, and lilies adrift on the lily pond, and about her shoulders not her little fox fur but wolf, white wolf. Berlin's wealthy and high-ranking will be in attendance, and they will admire the splendid Persian carpets and the samovar and the topiary, and her four shining children in their white sailor suits. 'We always wanted four,' she will say, ringing for their nurse to come and put them to bed. After dinner a man glittering with medals will take her arm and say, 'You must come to the Pfaueninsel. I will show you the birds with their feathers full of eyes, and the place where the king's alchemist made ruby glass.'

But the garden begins to buck beneath her, and the white wolf slides from her shoulders and the lanterns fall from the trees, and the water that pours from the samovar is bitter, bitter, there must be something in the pipes, some sort of disturbance, and the slabs of ice are cracking, the great floes splintering as easily as glass. The crows take flight, they cover up the sky, ragged voices, ragged wings.

'Mutti,' said Jürgen, shaking her shoulder. 'I'm thirsty.' He was holding his bear by the foot, the stuffing oozing from a hole on the side of its head. It had lost its eyes and its claws and he was too old for it now, but she said nothing; she knew he wouldn't allow her even to stitch up the seam, and anyway, it was too far gone. In the corner Sieglinde was singing the little sailor song to Kurt and teaching him the actions: a naval salute, a circle as the ship circled the world. Siggi pressed her hands to her heart, curved them in and out over the girl's figure, rubbed a finger and thumb together for money. She made a noose around her neck, and a hooked question mark drawn in the air, descending with the descending melody, a jabbed finger marking the dot at the bottom – and who was guilty of *this*?

In the apartment two more panes of glass are missing, and Brigitte sweeps up the pieces and tacks cardboard over the gaps. She takes out her ledger, notes the number of windows remaining. They are scarce these days; soon there will be none at all. Views covered up, light lost. The smoke is so thick we cannot make out the stars; they are only memories. We are too acquainted with absence. There are holes in our houses and we carry on around them, skirting

211

the edge of the pit. We receive packages to make up for what is missing: a wristwatch, a winter coat, a manicure set. Whose initials are these? Do I see the shadow of a star? Those arrows won't take you to Wolkowysk or Bialystok, there is no road to heaven, the clock is wooden through and through, it has no ticking heart. Still we trim our nails, wrap up against the cold, keep an eye on the time. There are patterns in the forests, a copse of larches planted in the pines, a note to the gods. Every autumn a swastika blazing in the canopy.

★

Mutti is counting the knives.

'Brigitte,' says Vati, touching her hand. 'Brigitte.'

'Nearly finished,' she says, not looking up in case she loses her place.

Sieglinde wants to talk to Vati, but he is taking Mutti's arm and she is saying, 'You're hurting me,' though he is hardly touching her, Sieglinde can see, I can see, anybody can see.

Mutti checks her ledger. 'Six dinner knives, two paring, two bread, one carving, three vegetable, four miscellaneous, one letter opener.'

'And my dagger,' says Jürgen, though it is only wood and can't cut a thing.

'And Jürgen's dagger,' says Mutti, making a note.

'I suppose you're aware of my spare scalpel blades?' says Vati.

'Blades? Spare blades?' says Mutti.

'I keep them in my briefcase, in case I need them at work. I'm sure you've seen them.'

'I never look in your briefcase, Gottlieb. If I saw something in there, something official, how could I convince myself I had seen nothing? That would be very difficult, perhaps impossible.'

And this is true, we cannot make ourselves forget, and Sieglinde thinks of the words she has found in the cuffs of Vati's trousers and stored in the cake tin.

'All the same, the blades are in my briefcase, and my briefcase is in the apartment.' Vati is smiling; is he joking with Mutti? Should Sieglinde and the boys also smile?

'I must think about this,' says Mutti. 'I must give this my careful consideration.' She begins to jot figures down on a piece of paper, asking herself questions and answering them too. How long is the briefcase in the house each week? Do waking hours count for more than sleeping hours, and if not, should they? Yes, she decides, they should. Therefore, the blades are in the house more often than they are not in the house, and therefore they belong in the ledger.

'Brigitte,' says Vati again, 'it's time for supper.' He reaches across her to shut the ledger but she grabs it and holds it and will not let it go, and the knives topple from the dining table, and one of them – the smaller paring knife – lands tip-down in the parquet. For a moment nobody speaks, and Mutti gazes at her splayed ledger, which has slipped from her grasp and is lying open in her lap, and then she stands and begins setting the table, and the knives remain where they have fallen, and nobody mentions them all through supper, which is only potatoes and bread, and afterwards Sieglinde leads Kurt by the hand around the very edges of the room. Later, when Vati is busy with his silhouettes, Sieglinde retrieves them, handing them to Mutti one by one. You can hardly see the nick in the floor. Six dinner, two paring, two bread . . .

There is nothing Mutti will not count: segments of wood in the parquet; upholstery tacks on the sofa; Kurt's breaths as he sleeps. And Sieglinde's shrapnel, too, though she has never reached the same total twice. She lies with Sieglinde on her bed and says, 'Perhaps if I started in that corner today . . .' and Sieglinde says yes, that would be a good place to start.

She tells her mother where she found her favourite pieces: Barbarossastrasse, Hardenbergstrasse, Winterfeldtplatz, their own courtyard. 'Look,' she says. 'That one's a flower, and that one's a ship, and that one's a bit like a cat – see, it's arching its back.' Mutti turns out the light and raises the blinds for a moment, peering through the glass, checking, checking. The S-Bahn carriages slow as they approach Savignyplatz, sending a blue flash inside, where it flutters across the hanging shrapnel. Sieglinde thinks she and Mutti could make a story with the fragments, but Mutti is back on the bed now and is stabbing the air, counting under her breath, the numbers piling up and up, ninetyoneninetytwoninetythree, and there is no room left in which to speak. Sieglinde can't recall much about the time before the war, but she knows Mutti was different then, knows she has been changed into something else. Who is this new mother? Who is this faint substitute, this shadow?

'All is well,' says Vati. 'We have nothing to fear. We are happy and secure – the radio tells us so.'

And it is true that it still sputters into our living room, assuring us that victory is at hand, that the damage to our cities is slight; the enemy's sights are inexact, their bombs fall wide of the mark, into open fields and cemeteries, they hardly touch us – or at least, we think that's what it says, because the reception comes and goes, and if Vati has to

214

scratch his nose while he is holding the wire we miss a few words. But yes, we are happy and secure, even as flares shaped like Christmas trees fall from the sky in the wrong season, even as housewives scrub flights of stairs that lead to holes in the ground, even as the shrapnel flies like hot hail and boys come collecting our bones. The enemy eats raw potatoes and rotten turnips but we have plenty of everything, rules and procedures and wonder weapons, substitutes and shadows, we are strong and our strength brings us joy, our work makes us free, our strategic retreats buy us time, our reverses lure the enemy to their doom, the newspaper and the radio and the loudspeaker on the corner tell us so, we are winning the war and we're glad for the war, we have no need to think otherwise, no need to dwell on our losses and no cause to mourn the dead.

But if we are so secure, why does Mutti flinch at every noise? And if we are so happy, why does she never laugh? Or only at the newsreel stories, at least, with their footage of warehouses brimming with food, barrels of butter, great dunes of wheat.

'Shh,' Sieglinde whispers in her ear, because nobody else in the cinema is laughing, this is not the main feature, this is not make-believe, and anybody could be listening to Mutti laughing in the wrong place. And at our backs the projector hums like a swarm of flies, the beam emerging from a high and secret room, and if you could see memory it would look like that, dust motes caught in a streak of light like silt in mussed water, thousands of them, all scattered and strange.

I am not sure about any of this. Did I lie in the peat, my hands and feet bound? Did I call to my mother from the castle foundations? Did I sit on the stool pigeon-chested, my heart waiting for the needle? Or hang on a windy tree nine long nights? As I said – smudges and traces, breaths in and out. The evidence is unclear. Over the years you have tried to name me, pin me down, but I change my shape and slip away, a phantom, a rumour. And we have a talent for transformation: straw to gold, gold to iron, books to ashes, ashes to wonders. Where am I now? On the crease of the map; the place rubbed blank by years of folding and unfolding, turning to see where you are. You cannot get your bearings. If you look for me, I am not there.

I am the wish child, the future cast in water. I am the thrown coin, the blown candle; I am the fallen star.

November 1944
Near Leipzig

Sometimes, just now and then, things were not where Erich expected them to be. A window was on the wrong wall, looked out to the wrong view; a cupboard changed size; chairs bumped at his knees, footstools at his shins. His teacher said he was the most forgetful child she'd ever known.

'You've always been like that,' said Mama. 'Think nothing of it.'

The bees buzzed inside the bronze head.

And it was true, he had always been that way, forgetful for as long as he could remember. He wondered if his parents had been too careful with him when he was little – if they had stopped him from running about and learning the shape of the world in case he hurt himself – but that could not be true, because hadn't Papa hoisted him up on his shoulders at the Führer's parade? Hadn't Mama whirled him through the air in the garden, spinning him faster and faster until he thought she might lose hold of him?

'Is it because I was in the sanatorium?' Erich asked one day. 'Because I was sick?'

'The sanatorium?' said Mama. 'What do you mean?'

'That place I stayed at when I was little. I slept in a ward with other sick children.'

'Can you remember that?' said Mama. 'You were barely four.'

In truth Erich didn't recall much, but sometimes certain images returned to him as he was falling asleep or waking: a woman in brown offering him a slice of bread and taking his hand; cool instruments against his skin; white-headed nurses serving cups of milk and tea, pulling curtains around a bed. 'What was wrong with me?' he asked. 'Was I sick?' and Mama said, 'They just wanted to be careful.'

At the end of autumn Erich watched the drones being driven from the hives, their legs and wings torn off by the worker bees. They did not survive long, and eventually he stopped trying to catch them in jars to revive them with their own honey; they died all the same.

That winter was the coldest in many decades. Erich stayed inside by the fire and read all of his Winnetou books again from start to finish, and when Mama found him crying and asked him what was wrong he told her that Winnetou was shot in the chest and died in Old Shatterhand's arms. *The air was full of shot and shells. Who hath warned you to flee?*

'It's just a story, Schatz,' she said, wiping his eyes with her handkerchief.

'And they shot his horse Iltschi, too, so they could be buried together.'

'They shot his horse?'

'It's an Apache custom.'

'What a savage practice.' She stroked his hair.

In December Tante Uschi's cat had a litter of kittens, and Mama said Erich could keep one as a Christmas present. He chose a black-and-white girl – the tiniest of the six.

'Are you sure?' said Mama. 'She doesn't look very

strong. We need one who can look after itself. Catch the rats in the barn.'

'I'll call her Anka,' said Erich. 'She reminds me of the other Anka.'

'Anka?'

'The cat we had when I was little. She was black and white too, remember?'

'So she was,' said Mama, but she was looking at Tante Uschi and Tante Uschi was looking back at her and something unspoken passed between them. 'Yes, she's a bit like her, like Anka,' said Mama at last. 'Very well then.'

When the kittens were weaned, though, and the time came for Erich and Mama to collect Anka, Tante Uschi told them that she had died. 'She was just too weak,' she said. 'I'm sorry, Erich.'

She offered him one of the others but he didn't want a different cat; they were the wrong colour; they were all wrong, just as windows and cupboards and chairs and footstools were sometimes and without warning wrong. In his bedroom he took Papa's letter from the honey jar and unfolded it, smoothing the thin paper flat. *Home seems unreal to me too. I am forgetting the shape of your mouth.* When Mama came to tell him supper was ready she found him reading it and she took it from him. He should not be looking to the past, she said, because nobody could change the past. Think instead how lucky he was to be born a German boy, how beautiful Germany would be when the war was over and the Führer could build his pavilions and palaces, and turn the cannons back into bells.

'Will the fighting reach us?' said Erich.

'Perhaps.'

'Are you scared?'

'We've done nothing wrong,' said Mama.

'Heinz Kuppel says the phosphorus bombs can turn you into a human torch.'

'Does he,' said Mama.

'And it keeps burning even if you put water on it. In Hamburg the people jumped into the Alster, but when they came out the phosphorus on their skin just started burning again.'

'Well, we don't live in Hamburg,' said Mama.

'The police hunted them down and shot them. To grant them a merciful release.'

'There you are, you see,' said Mama. She was still holding the letter; now she folded it up without looking at it.

'Heinz says the Führer has invented a plane so fast it has to shoot backwards,' said Erich. 'So it doesn't hit its own missiles.'

'Come and wash your hands,' said Mama.

In the distance I hear a thunderstorm starting to roar, or the hiss of bees against hollowed wood, or planes approaching Leipzig. I am unsure which; I make mistakes. The letter has given Mama ideas, and I watch as she packs up Papa's things – his hairbrush and shaving brush, his church hat, his shoes and braces. She keeps one pair of trousers to cut down for Erich, as well as a shirt or two, but everything else disappears into the boxes for the Winter Relief, and this is the decent and correct thing to do, because there are people in sore need, bombs blowing apart their homes, firestorms sucking the clothes from their backs, and it is our duty to help them (and if we do not, then our names will appear on the board in the main street).

And Erich wants to do his duty, he has learned about it at school, and he knows there is a knife he can own when he is older that he can wear at his waist as a sign of his duty, and although he is not sure of the purpose of the knife, owning one is the important thing; after that a knife's owner discovers its purpose as a matter of course. And are there not needy people on his doorstep? Mama seems to have overlooked the foreign workers, even though they are doing the jobs that Papa used to do, and sleeping right there in the barn, but once she realises there is a need for Papa's things on the farm she will wonder why she did not think of it herself, and she will say how clever Erich is to come up with such an efficient solution.

Later that evening, when Mama is washing the dishes, Erich takes some of the clothes from the Winter Relief boxes and goes to the barn. When he pushes open the door he sees shapes in the hay, and at first he cannot tell which shapes are animal and which are human, but one of the shapes stands and comes towards him.

'These are for you,' says Erich, and the shape lifts up the trousers and jumpers and socks and says, 'Dziękuję.'

'Dobranoc,' says Erich, and even as he says it, even as the shape in the barn smiles at him and ruffles his hair and repeats *dobranoc*, he knows he must never let Mama hear him speak this word, nor any words like it.

Erich wonders what Papa would say if he returned home and found the foreign workers wearing his clothes – and then he reminds himself that missing means more than missing, and lost means more than lost, and fallen more than fallen, and he remembers Mama taking him to the hives and telling the bees about Papa. Dead. Dead. Dead. A hammerhead driving in nails. The bronze man stands in for Papa now, watching over the house day and night, the bees humming inside his head, creeping through the notes Mama tucks up inside him. Sometimes Erich imagines this hollow father putting on Papa's clothes and doing Papa's work, fixing all the things that are broken, brushing Ronja's coat until she shines, a bronze horse for a bronze rider, baling up hay for winter and choosing the seed potatoes for the coming year, his cool hands checking for rot, counting the eyes.

Early the next morning Mama winds the wedding clock, and the little husband emerges from its insides to signal a fine day. She scrapes some butter onto Erich's rolls – how fortunate we are, how removed from all danger – and she is standing at the kitchen window drinking her cup of chicory coffee and looking out into the yard, where the puddles have turned to ice and the hens are pecking at the frozen ground, and all of a sudden she catches her breath. She blinks, and blinks again, and Erich looks out the window too and sees Papa walking past, and Mama is still not breathing – except this Papa is too young to be Papa, and a little too tall, and it is not Papa but only his clothes. And Mama has understood this now, and she turns away from the window and places her cup down on the table and says, 'Erich, what have you done?'

He tells her about giving the clothes to the people in the barn, but she does not praise his clever solution, and she does not wonder why she failed to think of it herself. Instead she says that Erich must take the clothes back again, and he must wash them and return them to the boxes, because we have to consider our own people first, the people without homes or butter or clothes, and besides, the foreign workers are used to a lower standard, and the barn must seem a palace to them.

'We won't mention this again,' says Mama, and she pats Erich's hand.

There are so many things Mama does not mention: the foreign workers, Anka the cat, Papa, Tante Uschi's dead groom. More and more Erich senses Mama is keeping things from him.

'Look at him,' she once said to Tante Uschi. 'My beautiful boy.'

'More German than we Germans,' said Tante Uschi, and Erich did not know what she meant, and he wanted to ask, but he saw how Mama looked at her, and it was the same look she gave her when Anka died.

And Erich cannot stop repeating the phrase to himself now: more German than we Germans. He writes it down to see if it makes more sense that way, but it is a phrase that holds its tail in its teeth and will not let him in. There are others: the secret that is not a secret; life unworthy of life. Just as with certain words, even your own name, the meaning drains away the longer you look.

In January the army visits the village and hands out anti-tank grenades, and all the mothers line up for their turn. See how easy they are to use, see how effective? The recoil is so slight you will hardly feel it. A brief talk, a hasty demonstration: hold at shoulder height, take aim at enemy, fire. Heinz Kuppel is allowed a turn because he is already ten, and when Erich is ten he will be allowed to join the Jungvolk and fire a Panzerfaust at the enemy too.

'Do you want a try?' one of the soldiers asks him, but Mama says, 'He's only nine.'

'Go on,' says Heinz Kuppel. 'Are you a coward? You know what they do to cowards.' He tightens an imaginary rope round his neck, lolls his head to one side.

At school Frau Ingwer says they must be prepared, because the war is coming closer all the time, and there is no telling when it might arrive. She reads to them: *Emergencies in daily life, in war as well as in peace, can confront you at any moment. Only those who know what to do and who are alert and quick in the face of danger will survive. If your house is on fire, if you are threatened by flooding, if you enter a room filled with gas, if you are caught in a mass panic, if enemy planes are approaching, you won't have time to check this book for the most sensible thing to do!*

The children make themselves very small on the classroom floor, pretending the bombs have found them at last, and when Frau Ingwer gives word they curl up even smaller, mouths open wide to release the pressure, arms crossed tight over their chests to hold themselves together. They no longer mark the movement of German troops on the map; in fact, there is no map on the wall at all any more, and sometimes Erich looks at the blank space where it used to hang and finds himself thinking: where am I? What is this place? At home he still has the silk map from the wrecked Spitfire, and he has identified where he thinks his village is – he knows where it lies in relation to Leipzig and Dresden, although it is far too small to be named. And that is a lucky thing, because the silk map is an enemy map, a map of escape and evasion, which is why it is so quiet when Erich crushes it into his fist, and if the enemy does not know about his village then perhaps the war will miss them. And if the scale is one to one million then his house must be less than a millimetre wide – less than a stalk of grass, less than a piece of string, and he himself less than a hair's breadth. (And yet, and yet, there is always another home hanging in the shadows of the places we inhabit, hidden in the crease of the map; always another mouth, another cat, another window.) He folds the map up as small as it will go, the silk cities collapsing silently in on themselves, and he thinks: I am nowhere, I am nothing.

'What do you have there?' says Mama, and Erich has to show her the map, because keeping secrets is wrong, although talking is also wrong if you talk to the wrong person or mention the wrong things.

'I found it,' says Erich, and he knows that Mama knows where it came from, but the airman is another thing she never mentions: to do so would be to raise him, a black-winged curse, and who can say what he might demand? And so Erich does not mention him either, even though he is buried on their land, so close to their house, as close as the foreign workers in the barn.

February 1945
Berlin

When the Heilmanns visit Tante Hannelore in Dahlem to wish her a happy birthday, the top floor of her building is gone. Through the smoke – which is part of the weather these days – Sieglinde can make out the remains of the figures that flanked the windows: stone children reaching skyward, fingers missing, heads missing, holding up the air. Two of the bombed-out neighbours have been moved into Tante Hannelore's apartment – Frau Hummel, and the elderly Herr Fromm.

'I'm happy for the company,' she says, but when Herr Fromm is out of the room she mouths, 'Not very clean.'

Each day she goes to the chestnuts and oaks in the courtyard and chops off another branch for the stove. A terrible shame, but what's to be done? It's trees or furniture. Sit down, she tells the Heilmanns, sit down, and tell me how you are. She is sorry she does not have any Spekulatius biscuits for Jürgen, but she cuts some bread into oblongs and serves it on the blue china plate; they can pretend, can't they? 'I think this one's a windmill,' she says, examining a piece before biting it in half. 'Yes, it definitely tastes like windmill. What do you think?'

Sieglinde does not want to pretend that a slice of bread

is a biscuit; everyone can see it's bread, and not very nice bread at that. She longs for the soft warm rolls they used to have for breakfast, and every night she dreams of food: meatballs with capers, potato pancakes, stewed berries with vanilla sauce.

'Mine's definitely a windmill,' says Jürgen, nibbling around the edges. 'See, Siggi?'

'Looks like bread to me,' she says. 'I heard they're putting sawdust in it now.'

'Is that true?' says Jürgen, examining his piece.

'Of course not,' says Mutti. 'Sieglinde, apologise to your brother.'

'It's just what I heard,' says Sieglinde.

'Well, you shouldn't be listening to rumours.'

And she is right, Mutti is right, she shouldn't be listening to rumours, but how to ignore their glint? They make the best stories: bread from sawdust, bread from bones, soap from fat, books from skin.

Jürgen slides his piece of bread back onto the blue plate, which is very bad manners, but Mutti does not notice; she is looking around the room and frowning. 'Where is your samovar?' she says.

'Oh, I hadn't used it in so long,' says Tante Hannelore.

'But where is it? And where's the bamboo screen, and the Persian carpets? And your Mother's Cross?'

Sieglinde notices it now too: Tante Hannelore's apartment is emptier, even with the extra people living there, which is a strange thing.

'The Russians will take it all anyway,' says her aunt. 'They're cutting glass from windows and leather from chairs and sending it home.'

'Hanne,' warns Vati. 'There are still possibilities.'

She laughs. 'Did you know, children,' she says, 'that

227

den-tists have to start pulling people's teeth through their noses?'

'Hannelore. Don't,' says Vati.

'Because nobody dares open their mouths.' She takes a small embossed case from a drawer and hands it to Sieglinde. 'An early birthday present for you. It's a long time until you're eighteen.'

Inside the case are the iron bracelets, black against the sky-blue silk, and Sieglinde lifts them out and fastens them about her wrists, and they are bands of dark forest, a night full of holes, as fine as Vati's best silhouettes. 'Look,' she says, 'they fit me.' She shakes her hands, and the bracelets do not slip off; yes, she has grown into them.

'And this,' says Tante Hannelore, removing the iron ring from her wedding finger. It is warm and smooth and Sieglinde traces the message scored into its surface: *Gold I Gave For Iron*. Round and round she turns it, and the end is the beginning, iron and gold side by side, one slipping into the next.

'It's too much,' says Mutti, but Tante Hannelore insists.

'She might as well enjoy them now. Just keep it to yourself, or Adolf will want them for bullets.'

What a thing to say out loud! But this time Vati lets it go. She is over-tired, that's all, just like everyone; she is not herself. The long hours working at the first-aid station are taking their toll.

Sieglinde is allowed to wear the bracelets underneath her sleeves on the way home, and she is unafraid as she passes the broken buildings, the men digging for bodies, the Hitler Youth boys pumping water from people's cellars so they do not drown. She is made of iron, and nothing can hurt her. She is not even tired. Fire, stand on this earth like a raised sword. When the siren sounds, she does not flinch.

'Quickly, children,' says Vati, and they make their way to the great flak tower next to the zoo; it is too late to return home. Towards the bunker they file, remaining calm, hurrying but not jostling, not shoving, even though there are so many of us, many more than the tower was built to hold.

'Siggi,' says Jürgen, 'are we losing? Have we lost?'

'Of course not,' she says. 'There are still possibilities.'

'What kinds of possibilities?'

'Well,' she says, 'the cold. That's a possibility. It's been so cold this year that it'll freeze the Russians in their tracks. Stop them from reaching Berlin.'

'Can't you read?' says a woman, jabbing Vati with her umbrella and pointing to the sign above the entrance: *Men Aged 16 to 70 Belong in Service, Not in the Bunker!* But she knows nothing of Vati's important work, this jabbing woman, and now is not the time to explain it, and anyway, it is a secret and cannot be explained.

Inside there is no room to sit down, no room even to kneel to tie Kurt's shoe though he is tugging at the hem of Sieglinde's skirt, telling her his laces are undone. The flak guns pound and pummel the sky above us and something is pressing at the walls and forcing the doors; something is sweeping in from the steppe, hackles raised, teeth bared, it is the season of the wolf but we are safe here, the walls are thicker than Vati is tall, and if they are strong enough to shield the altar of Zeus, the head of Nefertiti, all our priceless treasures, all the things that cannot be replaced, then they are strong enough to shield us, and so we are safe, we could not be safer, and even if we cannot move, even if we have to empty our bladders where we stand, we have nothing to fear. We are made of iron. Look, there are signs telling us what to do, there are procedures and rules and warnings, and radium arrows that glow in the dark like the hands on Vati's watch. And what time is it? How late is it? Impossible to say.

★

The next day Edda Knopf comes to tell Sieglinde the news – Julia is dead, killed in an air raid as she was walking to her grandmother's house.

'But how did she die?' says Sieglinde.

'I told you, an air raid,' says Edda.

'Oh,' says Sieglinde, but she thinks: did a mine hit her directly? Or was it shrapnel, falling masonry, shells from their own anti-aircraft guns? Did she suffocate? Bleed out? Did the pressure burst her lungs? Was she decapitated? Shrunk by the heat to the size of a child? Is she all mixed up with other people's bodies? Or flattened like Kayhausen Boy, an empty skin, a person-shaped bag? There won't be a funeral, says Edda; there's no wood for coffins, and no cardboard either. After she has gone Sieglinde takes the Frederick the Great tin to her room and shakes the words out, turning them face up and whispering them to herself: *mercy, promise, love, surrender*. Kurt and Jürgen are chasing each other round the apartment, firing imaginary guns and launching imaginary grenades, dying imaginary deaths.

'Please, boys,' calls Mutti. Her nerves are bad, and she needs some peace and quiet. She lies on her bed and asks Sieglinde to bring her the ledger. She leafs through it for a moment or two, brushing her hands over the pages of neat figures, everything accounted for, and then she enters the iron bracelets and ring, ruling up perfect columns and rows, writing the date where the date should go and the description where the description should go. She stops, frowns.

'Is a pair of boxed bracelets one item or two?' She does not know and cannot decide. She looks around for the bracelets so she can solve the matter once and for all. A crow is on the window ledge, black and grey. 'How much meat is on a crow, do you think? People are trapping and eating them, Siggi. Crow schnitzel. Crow roulade.'

'I'm sure that's just a rumour, Mutti.' Sieglinde has slept in the bracelets; she can feel them through her jumper and does not want to take them off, but she must not aggravate Mutti's nerves and so she pushes up her sleeves.

'They keep rabbits on their balconies, don't they?' says Mutti. 'Kitchen rabbits. Everybody knows what that means. Why not kitchen crows?' She takes Sieglinde's hands and studies the bracelets, unhooking them and holding them up to the light. 'They torpedoed our cruise ship, Siggi, did you know? Thousands lost. All the poor refugees.' She shakes her head. 'Two separate items, I think. We'll put them away for you until you're older.'

And she is shutting them in their case and shutting the case in her dressing table, and the hand-shaped vase that sits on top is trembling on its crocheted mat, but it does not fall over, which is just as well, because Vati doubts he can repair it again, and what then? Sieglinde remembers the story he told her when she was little, about the lady trapped inside the dressing table, waving her white hand for help – she had believed him, even though the drawers were far too small to hold a person. She had believed him for months, despite the evidence in front of her, and then when she no longer believed him, she still pretended that she did.

'And the ring,' says Mutti, holding out her hand, and

it is not fair that Sieglinde should have to surrender the jewellery, because hadn't Tante Hannelore given it to her? Hadn't she wanted her to enjoy it now, right now, before there was nothing left?

'Frau Metzger wears her jewellery all the time, even to the cellar,' she says. 'I'll be careful with it.'

'And if Frau Metzger is buried in a blast when she's wearing all her jewellery? If her body's never found? It's too risky.'

Sieglinde says nothing; she must not make things worse. She thinks of a story she has heard: that the Führer is keeping a gentle gas in reserve, specially for the German people, so that they can be put to sleep if the torturing Asiatic hordes arrive. But she does not mention this either.

Mutti unlocks her jewellery box – why does she keep the key in the lock? – and clears a space for the iron wedding ring, taking out the brooch made from Vati's baby teeth.

'Can I see?' says Sieglinde, and Mutti passes it to her. It is slight between her fingers, the teeth impossibly small. 'Why don't you ever wear it?'

'They've fallen out of fashion,' says Mutti.

'Can I wear it?' says Sieglinde. 'Just for today?' She can still make out the shape of the bracelets pressed into her wrists, red lines looping like brambles, but they are fading fast.

'Just for today, then,' says Mutti, and she pins the brooch to Sieglinde's collar.

If Vati notices it he does not say anything. It nibbles at Sieglinde's braid when her hair falls over her shoulder, which used to make him laugh – but she knows his work is hard on his eyes, even though he never says how, exactly, and perhaps he has not noticed the brooch.

'What are the possibilities, Vati?' she asks him.

'What?' he says.

'You told Tante Hannelore that there are still possibilities. What are they?'

'Oh,' he says. He doesn't answer her question, but it's clear that he knows about the possibilities, and it is just his job that prevents him from explaining them.

And then later that day, as if by magic, Sieglinde finds a leaflet; she is tidying the kitchen and there it is, slotted into the letter rack, and even before she picks it up she can see that it is about the possibilities.

'Look, Jürgen,' she calls. 'I told you so.'

There Are Two Possibilities . . .

We are Germans!
There are two possibilities:
Either we are good Germans or we are bad ones.
If we are good Germans, then all is well. But if we are bad Germans,
Then there are two possibilities:
Either we believe in victory, or we do not believe in victory.
If we believe in victory, then all is well. If we do not believe in victory,
There are again two possibilities:
Either we take a rope and promptly hang ourselves, or we do not hang ourselves. If we take a rope and promptly hang ourselves, all is well. But if we do not hang ourselves,
Then there are two possibilities:
Either we give up the fight, or we do not give it up. If we do not give it up, all is well. But if we do give it up,
Then there are again two possibilities:
Either the motley criminals of the Red mob following hard on

the heels of the Anglo-Americans liquidate us immediately,
or according to Stalin's wishes deport us to work in the icy
wastes of Siberia.
If they liquidate us immediately, that is still relatively speaking
good. If they deport us to Siberia or somewhere else,
Then there are again two possibilities:
Either one succumbs on the way there due to the unaccustomed
stresses and hardships, or one does not die so quickly.
If one dies quickly, one has deserved it, but is still lucky. If one
does not die quickly, that is unfortunate.
Then there are still two final possibilities:
Either one slaves away for foreigners until the end of one's life,
without ever seeing one's homeland and family again, or when
the opportunity arises one gets shot in the back of the neck.
Since both of these possibilities lead to the grave, there are no
further possibilities.
Therefore:
There are not two possibilities!
There is only one!
We must win the war, and we can win it! Each man and each
woman, the entire German people, must summon their utmost
in courage, discipline and readiness for action.
Then our future and the future of our children will be secured,
and the German people will be saved from a descent into
Bolshevist chaos!

'What is it?' says Jürgen.

'Nothing,' says Sieglinde.

In the living room she opens the door of the tiled stove
and throws the leaflet inside. She thinks of the words she
has stored in the cake tin: *defeat, mercy, sorrow, Versailles,*
forgive, the scraps of paper as tiny as lost teeth. All day she
can taste blood in her mouth.

That evening I watch as Sieglinde goes down to the cellar, where the walls are not real walls but stacks of loose bricks; should a bomb hit the building, should rubble block the door, should a fire above suck out all the air, she can simply step through to the neighbouring cellar, and if their door is blocked she can try the next one, and the next. The whole street is like this; the whole city: false walls, trick exits (and there are other ways to leave: the rope, the revolver, the glass ampoule bitten open). She listens for a moment, but everything is silent. One by one she lifts the bricks away, then steals through to next door. She examines their board games, their small shelf of books, the bucket behind the curtain, the ticking clock. She lies down on one of their camp beds and closes her eyes, and she belongs to a different family, and lives a different life. Mutti plays the piano and buys her sky-blue ribbons for her hair, and Vati is in the Wartheland, helping the new settlers and winning medals for mercy, and Kurt is a little sister and Jürgen is a dog. Julia is not dead, and she is training Sieglinde to be a youth leader herself, because she has noted how well Sieglinde knows her songs and her rules and her German history, and how much she loves the Führer, would do anything for the Führer. I lie beside her on the narrow bed. I have a mother and a father and I jump on icy puddles in my winter boots, I build sandcastles and help with the harvest and swap marbles for shrapnel and shrapnel for marbles. I attend the meetings, sing the songs. I leap the fire. I earn the knife. We could just keep going, she and I, passing through walls, changing our names, until we find a way out.

March 1945
Near Leipzig

'I'm going to apply for a child,' said Tante Uschi.

'Yes. Good,' said Mama, nodding. 'There are so many of them.'

'Will you help me with the letter? The forms?'

'Of course. Boy or girl? You can specify.'

'A boy. I'll name him Gerhard.'

'Yes,' said Mama. 'Yes!' She clapped her hands. 'This is just what we need!'

'But what about the real mother?' said Erich. 'Won't she mind?'

'Oh,' said Tante Uschi, stroking his hair. 'Oh, Schatz. They're dead, all the real mothers. That's why the children are in the children's homes.'

Erich could not sleep that night; he kept seeing Anka the cat running through rooms he thought he knew, chasing leaves in a blurred garden. Mama was holding him by the wrists, whirling him round and round, but the sun was too bright and he could not see her face, and the bees were too loud and he could not hear her voice, *I will bake my bread from the blood of your children, who say ye that I am? I am not he*, and look, someone is taking his hand, a woman in brown is offering him a piece of bread and taking his hand and leading him away. The shadow birds slip across the walls, over his bed, his face. They retreat to the corners of the room, and then they come back.

In the end it is Heinz Kuppel who tells him. He and Erich are in the school attic, sweeping up the remains of last year's medicinal herbs so that everything is clean and ready for the new crop when spring comes, and although the March day is cool outside, the space beneath the roof is warm and close and sends their voices echoing back at them. Heinz says there's no point in collecting herbs for the soldiers any more, not now, not since the Americans have crossed the Rhine and the Russians have crossed the Oder, and he does not know why Frau Ingwer still wants them to do it, and perhaps it is just to make everyone feel they are helping. He eats a foxglove leaf – he says it is a foxglove leaf – to prove it cannot harm him, to prove he will not die, and then he says that in the cities they are handing out cyanide, you can get it from the chemist, and then he says that Erich is not Erich, that Mama and Papa are not Mama and Papa.

'They got you from a children's home. They went there and they picked you out. You're Polish. My brother told me.'

'You're lying,' says Erich. 'Your brother's dead.'

'He told me ages ago. He remembered you arriving here. You weren't even a baby.'

'You're lying,' repeats Erich, but we both know this is untrue. 'Mama still has my cradle, I've seen it. Papa carved the acorns on it himself.'

'There's always been something different about you,' says Heinz Kuppel. 'Don't you think? I bet you wouldn't eat a foxglove leaf if I told you to.'

'They're for the soldiers. We're not allowed to eat them.'

'These? They're just scraps. Leftovers.'

'We're not allowed to.'

'Coward. Polish dog.'

When Erich tells Mama the story Heinz Kuppel told him, she says the Kuppels are not the most honest of Germans. She happens to know that they lie to the Reich Food Estate about their crop yields and then sell the difference on the black market. 'He's always been trouble, that boy,' she says.

'He told me they're giving people cyanide in the cities,' says Erich.

'Well there you are!' says Mama. 'What nonsense.'

The next day, when Oma Kröning comes for lunch, Erich says, 'I remember the sanatorium, the home. I remember sleeping there with all the other children.'

Oma Kröning turns pale and puts down her knife and fork. She says, 'Emilie . . . ?'

And Erich knows that it is true.

Mama says it makes no difference, none at all. 'You are the child we were meant to have,' she tells him.

'But where did I come from? Am I Polish?'

'You're German. Anyone can tell that. What other things did Heinz say?'

'Nothing.'

She nods. She offers little else on the subject; the more Erich asks her about it the shorter her replies grow.

'What have I done?' he asks. 'Why are you angry with me?'

'I'm not angry,' she says, but she no longer tucks him into bed or kisses him good morning, and her voice is the same voice she uses when she speaks to the foreign workers. *Sweep the floor. Count the eggs. Clean out the ashes.* It is the same voice she uses, too, when people from the cities come to the farm wanting to exchange carpets and gold rings and oil paintings for eggs, meat, schmaltz. *Such bartering is illegal. You should know better.* The only time Erich hears her soften is when she whispers her prayers to the bronze head.

★

And finally the war came to them: a flurry of bombs meant for someone else but dumped on the nearby countryside in those final imprecise weeks, impossible to divert by prayer or fear or charm. There were no factories here, no bridges or railway lines of any significance – but weren't we loyal Romans destroying those ourselves? – and for the most part the bombs landed on potato fields and turnip fields, in the forest, in the lake. Mama and Erich were inside when it happened, eating lunch; they heard the noise of the engine in the distance and thought it was the bees, and although the noise came closer and closer they did not move, because nothing could happen here, because here was nowhere, strategically speaking, a place too small for the map – and then they looked out the window and the dirt was spraying skywards in front of the barn, and the house was shaking, and the foreign workers were shouting and running. Erich rushed to the door and pulled on his boots, and Mama leapt up as well, and Erich thought she was coming to help him, to help the foreign workers, but she took him by the shoulders and he felt the hunger in her hands – holding him back, pushing him away? – and then she said, 'No. They're not our people. We cannot risk ourselves for their sake.'

He ran from her, as fast as a greyhound, past the stable where Ronja whinnied and stamped – Ronja, who flinched at neither thunder nor fire – and on to the barn.

The yard and the buildings and even the sky seemed not quite real through the smoke, and he headed towards the voices rather than trusting his eyes.

'Here!' cried one of the workers, signalling to Erich, who could hardly make out the brown-clad figure against the dirt. He could see now, though, that the side wall of the barn had collapsed, and that a man lay trapped; two others were struggling to lift the wall away from him. Erich crawled underneath it, squeezing himself into the tight, low space, then pushing up with his back and shoulders, and finally the men were able to lift it free, and then he was dragging himself to his feet, as brown as the men now. The air had cleared enough to make out the crater in front of the barn: a great hole in the soil, as if something had been uprooted.

At first Mama refused to allow the injured man to recuperate in the house. 'He'll steal from us,' she said, 'or worse.'

'He can have my bed,' said Erich. 'I'll sleep on the floor.'

'Your bed!' said Mama. 'Do you know what the Polish did to our people?'

O generation of vipers.

'I'm Polish,' said Erich.

'No,' said Mama. 'You're an orphan, you were a German orphan born in Poland, which is now Germany.'

The sound of hammering reached them; the two unhurt workers were repairing the barn.

'What happened to my parents?' said Erich. 'Is my name even my name?'

'You are Erich Kröning,' said Mama. 'I am your mother.'

No, Erich thought.

No, I thought.

She finally allowed the injured man inside when Erich pointed out that he would recover more quickly that way, and be able to return to his work; the fences needed mending and the ditches clearing, and the bomb crater had to be filled in and smoothed over. The man slept in Erich's bed and Erich slept in Mama's, occupying the hollow left by Papa. It was strange to lie down in a different room, with the sound of Mama's breathing so close by and the darkness coming at him from unfamiliar directions. He could not fall asleep. He began counting the months until his tenth birthday, and then the weeks, and then the days. It occurred to him that he might be ten already; that his birthday might not be his birthday, just as his mother was not his mother. If he were ten he could join the Jungvolk, and then he could learn how to launch a Panzerfaust, how to operate searchlights and flak guns, how to blow up a tank, how to slit a throat. And perhaps if he did well at these things – if he showed what Frau Ingwer called *a natural ability* – he might be chosen to meet the Führer, who thought of all children as his own. For you are flesh of our flesh and blood of our blood, and in your young minds burns the same spirit that possesses us. Erich had even heard of children invited to stay in the Führer's bunker for a week or two, and they were fed marzipan and vitamins and hot chocolate. He had seen photographs of them in the newspaper, these children, shaking the Führer's hand and asking him questions they must have rehearsed a hundred times, questions approved by the officials, because you couldn't ask the Führer just anything.

When Mama had fallen asleep Erich crept back to his own room and switched on the bird lamp for the foreign worker. For a moment the two of them watched the shapes circling the room, round and round, round and round, and then the foreign worker made his hands into the shape of a bird, swooping them across the quilt towards Erich and alighting on his wrist for just a moment.

'Czesław,' he said.

I see the enemy surging into Germany from all sides, pouring through the many holes in the map: Cologne, Frankfurt, Dresden, Hamburg. I hear Mama and Tante Uschi speaking in hushed voices about *falling*, about *taking*. They cut off each other's hair, sew their grandmother's garnets into their hems and seams. Where are the wonder weapons to save us all? What of the limitless foodstores, the vast shelters hidden in the mountains? And who will lead us there now? Look: is that not Anka in Tante Uschi's garden, Anka the black-and-white cat who was too weak to survive? Is she not sunning herself on the path, drinking from puddles, stalking the sparrows? We have called up the spirits, and can no longer get rid of them.

Kindertotenlieder

O   ,   each of us our own   .
A   that proceeds from a
In which we knew   ,   and   .

April 1945
Berlin

It is hard to keep a steady hand these days. I watch Gottlieb in his office at the Division; the books are piled so high on his desk that he cannot see over them, cannot even see the blurred outline of his neighbour, also walled in by books, and the faster he works, the less precise his cuts. There is so little time. With every line, he breaks off a piece of the world.

He has never been a careless man, but quotas must be met, and the list of prohibited words is growing longer and longer. Soon, he thinks, there will be no language left – only margins. And questions are being asked about the disposal of the excised material; a routine weighing of the ashes from the furnace has suggested that not everything is being destroyed. Where, then, are the survivors? There are reports of stolen words, smuggled words, turning up in people's cellars and attics, hiding in their allotment sheds, making their way onto the black market – does Herr Heilmann know anything about this? Is it possible he has been taking the waste home with him, to burn as fuel, perhaps, given the scarcity of wood and coal? (We must not speak of scarcity.) Or might he have suspicions about one of his colleagues . . . ? There are two possibilities, Herr Heilmann. You can tell us what you know, without fear of reprisals (we must not speak of reprisals), or you can remain silent. If you choose to remain silent and later it comes to light that you do know where the missing words have gone, there will be serious reprisals.

Gottlieb has no idea what to say. It might be simpler, he thinks, for the Division to start from scratch; to write books that need no correcting. How would such a book begin? With a family? Yes, with a family who live in Berlin – a good, decent, German family. A song his uncle used to play on his accordion drifts into his head: *Five wild swans once went a-roaming, swans that shone so softly white. Sing, sing; what came to pass? None was seen again.* He considers the qualities of paper: the peach-skin edges of old books, the slip and sheen of playing cards. Membranous bibles, dead-leaf postage stamps, newsprint that tears along certain grains. 'Perhaps the furnace is hotter than calculated,' he says. 'I read of a church bell reduced to a handful of ashes.'

He begins to take very careful note of his actions, monitoring himself for any lapses. He cuts out a word, moves it to one side of his desk, cuts out another, moves it to one side, and when he has amassed a reasonable pile he sweeps them into the bin at his feet. True, his briefcase sits nearby, but he never leaves it open, he is certain, fairly certain, and besides, if any words fell into it by accident he would find them when he unpacked his things at home. He watches the little slips of paper tumbling through the air: snowflakes, leaves, white-winged birds. If he chose he could still read them, but he has trained himself to recognise only their shape, not their meaning. He can work more efficiently that way.

'You haven't found anything unusual in my briefcase, have you?' he asks Brigitte.

'Like what?' she says. 'What's unusual?'

'Small pieces of paper. So small you'd hardly notice them.'

'You know I don't look in your briefcase.'

'I just thought you might have noticed something.'

'Noticed something that's almost too small to notice?'

He does not like the direction the conversation is taking; soon she will be asking him again if he notices anything different about the living room. He examines his latest silhouette – the Dom in Cologne. Is it accurate? True? He compares it to his book of photographs. He knows that a silhouette cannot show every detail – the saints in their sooty niches, the jutting gargoyles – but the outline is what matters, the suggestion of complexity, of dark and light. He snips at the black paper, removing a splinter here, a splinter there, each as fine as an eyelash. He understands the perils of cutting away too much at once. Patience, precision: he had hoped to pass these qualities on to Jürgen, and tried giving him a pair of scissors and the outline of a house, but the boy cut smoke and flames rising from ruins, a dirty mess, not a straight line in sight.

Gottlieb imagines entering the paper cathedral, the air close and cool, and he lies down on the paper flagstones and looks into nothing, nothing, a relentless black that rolls over him and about him. Here there are no saints and no gargoyles, no great fanned ribs of stone, no spires that strain to pierce the sky and open heaven, just his own dark solitude, the darkness inhabited before birth, the still dream before we wake into blood to face the knot and the knife.

The evening is quiet, for now: the children are in bed and Brigitte is making notes in her ledger, the nib of her pen gasping across the page. And if he is honest, if he stops what he is doing and looks around, then yes, he can see that the living room is bigger, just as Brigitte has said so many times, although he has not noticed it happening, has not noticed a thing – or at least, nothing worth mentioning. And perhaps he should have listened to her, and perhaps, for a time, there were two possibilities: speech or silence, yes or no, white or black – but now that time has passed.

And then one day, as Gottlieb is sweeping his deletions from the clifftop of his desk, he sees a word separate itself from the rest and lodge in his trouser-cuff. And when he retrieves it, he sees that two other words have settled there also, and he might have been carrying them around for weeks.

That night he asks Sieglinde if she has found anything in his pockets or cuffs, anything unexpected, though there's nothing to worry about, no reason to be afraid. Why then does he start when she says yes and fetches the cake tin with Frederick the Great on it? The rearing horse, the stone king, he stood with his four million Prussians against forty million enemies, but they were not able to defeat him even in the most hopeless situations. She shakes out the words, every last one – there must be a dozen or more – and holds them in her cupped hands as if she has found a fledgling too weak to survive on its own. There are not enough of them to explain the discrepancy in the weight of the ashes, it's true – but there are enough to cause problems.

'We'll burn them,' he begins to say – but all of a sudden the siren is sounding and Schneck is at the door shouting at them to hurry, the warning system did not activate and the raid is starting and they must hurry.

Gottlieb turns off the gas and opens the windows; already the planes are overhead and the flak guns are booming. Kurt and Jürgen are blinking, barely awake, and Sieglinde is ushering them out to the landing while Brigitte pauses to wrap her fox fur about her neck. They leave their door open, as they must, and as they make their way down to the cellar the stairwell shakes beneath them, and Gottlieb thinks of his visits to Luna Park when he was a boy, and the shimmy-steps that would not keep still, and the swivel-house that tilted to one side, forever on the brink of falling.

★

In the cellar Sieglinde notices that Kurt's jumper is on inside-out and back-to-front, and she wants to fix it, to tell him to raise his arms and let her pull it over his head, but he is leaning his soft body into her side and asking her to sing the song about the little sailor and the girl who dies for love of him. Together they do the actions to go with the words – the salute, the ocean, love, death – and each time they start the song again they drop another word and another until they are hardly singing at all, and only their hands are telling the story: And who was guilty of *this*? I can hear the shrapnel clattering above them, filling up the world, and it is the future falling all at once and in shapes nobody can decipher, and Sieglinde imagines opening the blinds in the morning to find every window blocked with it as high as the fourth floor. And we can hear bundles of stick bombs rustling like flocks of doves, and canister bombs slapping down like wet sacks. And she does not hear the bomb that hits them, but she feels it pick her up and shake her and shake her until all she can see is dust.

April 1945
Near Leipzig

One day Erich finds Mama removing the candles and flowers and little plates of food she has placed about the bronze head.

'They're almost at Berlin,' she says. 'We cannot win.' Out with the dish of honey. Out with the quartered apple.

'You're not allowed to say that, Mama.'

She laughs. 'If they come, we must hang a white sheet from the window.' She hands him a vase of dead crocuses to empty, and when he tips the green water away the rotten stems collapse in his hands and leave behind their rotten smell on his skin.

And yes, Mama has stripped the altar bare. And yes, she tells Erich to surrender, but she also gives him a knife and tells him to aim for the heart. Like *this*, like *this*; the Russian is a savage and will butcher us in our beds. She empties the head of its bees, shaking them out like coins, but they do not fall; they hang humming in the air around her, spinning their wings, mumbling amongst themselves: will they swarm, will they sting? She opens the window and away they fly, disappearing into the orchard, into the wooden mouths of the hives, where, after all, they belong. She cannot dislodge the honeycomb from inside the head, though – or she does not care to; it holds fast, a tumour clogging the cranium, and within it lie her many wishes, all the little notes she has pushed into the dark since before the war began, their paper wings caught in the wax. There are too many to remember. *You-you, you*, calls the turtle dove.

'Take this,' she says, handing Erich the head, and she moves through the house gathering up his toy soldiers, the flags from the parade, their volume of *Mein Kampf*, the framed portrait of Papa in his uniform, the Führer's blanket, which she has never finished because she could never get her stitches perfect, and *Pictures from the Life of the Führer*, with all its pasted-in photographs that took Papa so long to collect and mount.

'What are you doing? Mama?'

Before he can stop her she has fed the paper flags to the oven, and they are flaring and roaring, a crowd welcoming their king, and then they are withering away. She slams the door shut on them and piles everything else into a box. Papa's photograph lies on top, his face cut out of his uniform.

'Follow me,' says Mama, putting on her shoes.

'But where are we going? And where is Papa's face?'

'Are you a German boy?' she says. 'Are you a true German boy?'

He no longer trusts her, this woman who says she is his mother. The head is cool in his hands, lighter than expected, and out in the bright white day he can see the tiny blemishes in its surface. He hugs it to himself. Of course he is a true German boy, and he is ready to defend Germany, and the Führer is Germany and Germany is the Führer. He wants to fight, to run away to the front. He could run away to Leipzig easily enough, or even Dresden – but Leipzig is too close to home, and there is no Dresden any more. One last note flutters from the head: *A child for Ursula.*

'Leave it,' says Mama.

At the shore of the thawing lake she puts down the box. I know she is going to throw everything into the water; Erich knows this too, and so do you.

'Help me,' she says, weighting down the Führer's blanket with a rock, and I want him to say no, to stop her, but he takes up a little lead soldier and hurls it as far as he can, and then another, and another, and I feel myself sinking – for despite everything I am a German boy, a true German boy. Papa's album of the Führer's life is next; it lies open on the surface for a moment, walking on water, until its pages steep and swell and can no longer bear their own weight: Goebbels at the opening of the Autobahn; Himmler with the Führer, inspecting his personal guard; Göring applauding the Philharmonic; the Führer sailing on the Rhine – down they go, the demigods, the demagogues. Erich is crying now, but is she sorry, is Mama sorry? I cannot tell, I cannot read her, even when she throws the framed photograph of Papa, though Papa's face is missing and so it is just a uniform she throws and not Papa, not Papa, and perhaps at the bottom of the lake, in the secret movement of the currents, a picture from the album will float free and position itself in the hole left by Papa's missing face.

The last thing to go is the bronze head. When it leaves Erich's hands his body seems to want to follow its trajectory, to plunge with it into the water, but he stops himself and watches as it hurtles through the air, its eyes turning to the sky, a single bee escaping from its neck. Now it is time that gods stepped out of lived-in things; time they ripped down every wall in my house.

On the way back home they pass the bomb crater, which the foreign workers still have not fixed. It is starting to fill with water, and when Erich peers inside he sees the shape of himself, his double caught beneath the surface. He raises a hand, and so does the boy in the hole. He shakes his head, and so does the boy in the hole.

He cannot stay here.

In his bedroom he packs the things he will need: his bag of marbles, the silk map, the ten-thousand-mark note that may still be worth something, the wristwatch that Papa sent him with the backwards N and the backwards R engraved on the reverse. He is no coward, no Polish dog. He thinks of the Führer, who has chosen to stay in Berlin to defend Germany to the last, and the Führer is Germany and Germany is the Führer. There is only one way to save ourselves, and that is through bravery at all times. That will in the end result not only in laurel wreaths, but also in victory. We wipe the blood from our eyes and look directly and without fear at the enemy. Their seductive phrases find only deaf ears with us. Our salvation is in weapons.

If Erich were in Berlin instead of here, which is nowhere and nothing, he would be issued a weapon and ordered to fight, no matter his real age, and when the enemy came Erich would push him back street by street, and he would take on tanks single-handed and blast them to pieces no bigger than coins, and bring down aeroplanes too, snatching them clean out of the sky, and the Führer would decorate him and call him his Winnetou, his Indian brave, his blood brother.

He waits until Mama has left for the market and then he packs some apples, a piece of sausage and a small jar of milk in his bag. He goes to the stable and says a quiet goodbye to Ronja, who pushes her head into his neck and sighs a warm sigh. And then, on Mama's pillow, which still smells like her, he leaves a piece of paper. I think it must be a letter, but I don't know what it says; I don't know what a boy who is leaving his mother would write to her.

April 1945
Berlin

Someone who looks like Herr Metzger is standing over her, saying her name, helping her to her feet and leading her away from the crumpled building. You're all right, he keeps repeating, you're all right, but Sieglinde does not know whether to believe him, this man in the shape of their neighbour: he is white from head to foot, even his hair, even his mouth. And then she glances down at herself, at her own arms and legs, and they are white too, and there is a row of white figures laid out on the pavement, though it's not a pavement any more, and other figures are being pulled from the rubble. The fork will prick, the broom will scratch, the child will choke, the mother crack. Don't look, Herr Metzger is saying, don't look, but she has looked already, she has seen them already lying broken beside the broken building – Mutti, Vati, Jürgen and Kurt, she has seen them laid out and she knows they are dead, all four of them. Herr Metzger holds her tight against the black woollen coat that he keeps in camphor to repel the moths, though it is white now too, and again he says that Sieglinde mustn't look, and Sieglinde agrees she will not look, because Herr Metzger has told her not to and it is wrong to disobey.

'Come and sit over here for a moment,' he says, leading

her to the kerb that is painted white so people will not trip and hurt themselves. 'We'll try to find you a blanket. Wait here like a good girl. Everything is fine.'

So Sieglinde sits where she is told, her back to the broken building, and she spies a book lying open on its spine, its pages turning and turning as if the smoke is thumbing through them, looking for a place it has lost, and she knows that it is Mutti's ledger, and she tucks it into her jumper and looks for other things she might recognise. She sees shoes without tongues, lamps without shades, clocks without hands; she sees ripped-open sofas, their stuffing burst from gashed velour, and patterned stove tiles scattered like one of her jigsaws tipped from the box before she has picked out the corner pieces and the edge pieces, when it seems impossible it will ever look like the picture, and she sees part of a fox fur that might be Mutti's, its satin belly torn, its mouth stopped with brick dust, the rest of it buried in the rubble, and she sees a broken Volksempfänger with a smashed dial and a bent needle, and it looks like their Volksempfänger, but everybody has one, after all, so that the Führer can be in everybody's living room at once, and therefore Sieglinde is not sure if this Volksempfänger is theirs, and she does not think it would have the Führer's voice inside it now anyway, which is terrible and makes her want to cry, because he would know what to do, and when she turns it over she is right: it's quite empty. And amongst the disorder she does see things she knows – parts of things, from other apartments in the building, although when she looks again she sees that they are not things, or rather, until the bomb hit the building they were not things but people, neighbours, and Sieglinde looks away from these things just as Herr Metzger told her to do.

The smoke hurts her eyes and she spits out gritty fragments of brick. A burning curtain drifts past like a bird. She sits down again, and at her feet she finds some of her shrapnel collection.

'Sieglinde!' calls Herr Metzger. 'Just stay where you are, I'm still looking for a blanket but I'll be back soon.'

And all of a sudden Sieglinde does not want to stay where she is, not at all; she wants to get away from the broken things, the things she is not supposed to look at but has looked at, away from Herr Metzger and his blanket, which, she knows, will not be her own blanket from her own bed. She pulls the fox free from its burrow of brick and wraps it about her neck, and then she sorts through the pieces of shrapnel, recognising some, picking out the best ones and putting them aside: a flower, a tree-trunk, a snowflake, a star. And then, before Herr Metzger returns and wraps her up, she creeps back to Mutti and lays the flower at her head, and for Vati the tree, and for Jürgen the snow. And Kurt – at his head she lays the star, which was one of her favourites; it hung above her bed and she watched it every night as it spun on its thread. Yes, she places a star at his head, and then she slips into the smoke that is already in her throat and in her eyes, already part of Sieglinde Heilmann, and the ashes rise and flurry about her, black sycamore wings, black feathers, and she disappears.

Goodbye, calls the fox. *Goodbye, goodbye.*

April 1945
Leipzig

FRAU MILLER:	Shall we get out and stretch our legs?
FRAU MÜLLER:	Why not. A bit of a walk, some fresh air – how long do we have?
FRAU MILLER:	Seventeen minutes and forty seconds.
FRAU MÜLLER:	All right, but we'll need to keep an eye on the time. Heads must roll for victory.
FRAU MILLER:	Wheels, Frau Müller. Wheels must roll.
FRAU MÜLLER:	What did I say? Never mind, you know what I mean.
FRAU MILLER:	I do.
FRAU MÜLLER:	When Dieter was little he always said he wanted to be a train driver.
FRAU MILLER:	So did Hans–Georg, for a while. But all little boys say that, don't they?
FRAU MÜLLER:	How can we know what all little boys say? Do we listen in on all little boys?
FRAU MILLER:	Be careful, Frau Müller.
FRAU MÜLLER:	I am careful. I'm always careful. I'm merely pointing out that it is not possible to know what all little boys say. Is that not true?
FRAU MILLER:	What's true is this: our boys will never be train drivers.

FRAU MÜLLER: Imagine what they'd say if they saw us now. How much time is left?

FRAU MILLER: Sixteen minutes and thirty-eight seconds.

A train is waiting at the station; it has so many cars that Erich cannot make out its end. Among the crowds of Red Cross nurses and soldiers and refugees he sees two women in Reichsbahn uniforms on the platform.

'Are there any seats?' he asks.

'Seats!' says one of the women. 'He wants to know if there are any seats, Frau Miller!'

'Seats!' says the second woman. 'Does it look like the Orient Express?' She gestures to the string of freight cars, iron-walled, windowless.

The first woman says, 'May I interest sir in our dinner menu? The roast goose is especially fine today.'

The second woman says, 'Allow me to show sir to the sleeping wagon. In the evening the guard will turn down your bed.'

'. . . and bring you a cup of hot chocolate.'

The women laugh, shake their heads. Above them the clock says six o'clock, but that cannot be right, and the hands do not move.

'But can I buy a ticket?' Erich asks.

'A ticket!'

'That's a first, Frau Müller! A ticket!'

'I don't mind sitting on the floor,' says Erich. 'Is there any room?'

'There's plenty of room,' says the first woman.

'It's completely empty,' says the second.

'Room is not the issue,' says the first, 'but they've left it in a terrible state.'

'Which just goes to show.'

'Precisely.'

The first woman taps her colleague's wrist. 'How long do we have?'

'Four minutes and seventeen seconds.'

'Will there be any more trains?' says Erich.

'I shouldn't think so,' says the second woman. 'Not passenger trains.'

'Oh,' says Erich. 'Only I need to get to Berlin, to fight for the Führer.'

'Do you indeed,' says the first woman.

'The Führer,' says the second.

'Are you going to Berlin?'

'Where's our next load, Frau Müller?'

The first woman consults a clipboard. 'Sachsenhausen. So yes, we'll be passing nearby.'

'Sachsenhausen?' says the second woman. 'Sachsen-hausen?'

'Sachsenhausen,' says the first.

'That can't be right. Word was sent – they don't need the train any more. I thought I told you . . . ? I know I meant to.'

'That is not the same thing, Frau Miller,' says the first woman.

'I'm tired. I must have forgotten,' says the second.

'Everyone is tired, Frau Miller. I am tired. This boy looks tired. I imagine the Führer is exhausted. At any rate, Sachsenhausen is next on the list. Do you see? Right here.'

'I do see. I do see the list. However, I believe I am correct that word was sent.'

'You are saying that I – that we – are to deviate from the list?'

'Yes. The list is superseded by the word that was sent.'

'And where is this word? Do you have it?'

'I did have it. I'm sure I can find it again, if you give me a minute.'

'We don't have a minute.'

'It's an expression.'

'All the same,' says the first woman, 'the list is the list. It says Sachsenhausen. Therefore we are to proceed to Sachsenhausen.'

The second woman is silent for a moment. She checks her watch. Then she says, 'Very well, Frau Müller.' She glances at Erich. 'And the boy . . . ?'

They lower their voices.

'He could travel up the front, with us . . .'

'It's against the rules. He might be anyone.'

'He's just an ordinary German boy. Think of Hans-Georg.'

'You know, he's a little like him. Around the mouth.'

'Don't you find? With Dieter's eyes.'

They regard him for a moment, which lasts six seconds, leaving them fifty-six seconds in total, and then they say that Erich can travel up the front with them, but he must not touch anything and he must not tell anyone.

'Do you have somewhere to go once you're there?' the second woman asks him.

'Oh yes,' says Erich, because anybody in Berlin will be able to point him to where the Führer lives. And when Erich does meet him he will ask him which book he loves best, because he knows that the Führer loves books, and that he loves Karl May books in particular, which Erich also loves, and perhaps his favourite book will be Erich's favourite too. *The soul lives in the blood*, the Führer will say, exposing his forearm and cutting himself with a knife. He will let a few drops of blood fall into a bowl of water and then Erich will do the same, cutting his own forearm and letting his own blood fall into a bowl. *We two warriors wish our souls to merge to form a single soul*, the Führer will say. *Then my thoughts will be yours, and yours mine. Drink!* And each will drain the other's bowl, and they will be blood brothers for life, just like Winnetou and Old Shatterhand.

The women ask Erich if he would like a sandwich. Or perhaps a blanket? It can get cold in the trains. They'll drop him off at Schlesischer Bahnhof, if it's still there by the time they reach it.

April 1945
Berlin

And am I to enjoy the spectacle? The flash of flak, the radiant clouds? Shall I delight in the bubbling asphalt, the rubble rain, the fuses that play dead? The firestorm gusts that bend trees four storeys high? The haphazard blockbusters, the incendiaries that drop into chimneys and gutterings, fierce stars deaf to any wish? The phosphorus fires that cannot be put out with water, the phosphorus burns that cannot be treated? Feet without legs, hands without arms, eyes without sight: oh, the monsters I could make. Hasn't Herr Mammon lit his palace splendidly for the party? Everything is wrong: the living are buried, the dead exhumed. We sleep outside for warmth and offer diamonds for bread, chalk our names on the places we used to live in case anyone comes to find us. I can't unsmash the glass, re-pin the grenade, and it's far too late to leave: two-and-a-half million men are gathering at the edges of the city, two-and-a-half million beasts who will nail us to doors, cut out our tongues, cut off our breasts, two-and-a-half million savages waiting to pick our bones. They are selling the skin of the bear before it has been shot. As they draw closer our pictures fall from the walls and our telephones start ringing by themselves with nobody but ghosts on the line. At the concert hall the orchestra plays

Twilight of the Gods and boys distribute ampoules of poison, glass semibreves that sound their long, low notes in the private thoughts of those who tuck them into pockets and handkerchiefs and fists for when the time comes. We've been swallowing it for years; what's one more taste? Enjoy the war; the peace will be terrible.

It is fine and mild on the Führer's birthday; the women queue for water, the traitors and the suicides rock in the early spring breeze, and from beneath the earth the Reichsminister speaks to us: *Führer, command! We will follow.* He is in us and around us. See, he has not deserted us. See, he is emerging from the ground, blinking in the daylight and touching the children's faces, feeling for something vital. But why does his left arm tremble as he makes his way along the line? Why does he hold it behind his back as if hiding a surprise? The day is mild but his greatcoat is belted, his collar turned up. Is this really Our Führer, this slumped and slackened creature, as pale as the dead men who sway with their heads at thoughtful angles, reflecting on their transgressions, placards strung about their necks: *I Did Not Believe in the Führer*? Is this who we hung in every wise home, this revenant blinking in the daylight? There must have been a switch; this must be one of the doubles; the real Führer is on his way to South America, and he will be safe there, and he will release the wonder weapons to save us. But as he comes closer and closer we can see that he is Hitler, we know that he is Hitler and nobody else, and we catch the scent of the hole from which he has emerged; the grey woollen coat drenched with the smell of earth, of rotting leaves, of dark and buried things: when the victim is dead, the vampire dies too. And yes, here he is, the shadowman, the Nachzehrer risen from his grave to consume his winding sheet, to make the church bells ring so that all who hear them perish, to kill any his shadow touches. To devour his own. A fly drifts around his head and settles on his hair but he does not notice. He stands before the youngest boy and offers him a listless hand, a bloated smile.

'How old are you, my child?'

'Twelve, my Führer.'

'Were you afraid when you helped the wounded soldiers?'

'No, my Führer.'

'And would you like to go home or would you like to go to the front?'

'To the front, my Führer.'

He strokes the boy's cheek the way a parent might, and the boy wishes him a happy birthday, but already he is eyeing the next child.

★

There has been a mistake, Erich thinks. They have taken a wrong turn, they have brought him to some primitive place – but look, the train is stopping and the women are handing him his knapsack and a blanket and an extra sandwich and wishing him luck.

'Where do I go?' he asks them, because it is clear that his map from the airman will not help him.

'Anywhere,' they say. 'Take your pick.'

I see him passing streams of people fleeing to the untouched heart of the country, their possessions piled high on handcarts and sledges, on dented prams, on wagons pulled by dark-eyed oxen: pots and brooms and dining chairs; ladders, bedsteads, buckets; tables lying on their backs like dying animals; children packed in tight around bulging suitcases and feather beds; and everything tied down with rope so that it is not lost, because so much has been lost already, and this is what remains. We have slaughtered our animals, set fire to our homes, destroyed our bridges so the enemy cannot follow us. There is no going back; the country grows smaller every day. And should we move troops from the west to fight the hordes devouring the east? And what then of the undefended west? What possibilities remain? We are emptying the camps, covering our tracks, bringing back into Germany all the criminals we sent away: the gypsies and the Jews, the homosexuals, the asocials, the defeatists and the degenerates. The many heads of Hitler lie buried in our gardens and sunk in our lakes. Beneath arches of thorns, o my brother, we blind clock-hands climb towards midnight.

'Are you lost?' a man asks Erich. 'Where is your mother?'

No, says Erich, he is not lost, even though he does not know where he is. (How long has he been walking? Two hours? Three?) 'I'm older than I look,' he says, and this is quite possible; rationing has stunted us, and we are a smaller people than we were, and shrinking all the time. Some of the refugees eye him as if he might pick their pockets.

'Where are you going?' asks the man.

'To fight for the Führer.'

'You'd better hurry then.'

But this cannot be right. This cannot be Berlin. The buildings are crumbling and collapsed, sliced open, insides hanging out, windows missing, chimneys toppled, roofs gone; here and there Erich can see right into abandoned rooms where mirrors and clocks hang crooked on waterstained walls. S-Bahn cars barricade streets littered with baths and couches and tables and radiators and beds, and boys on bicycles wind their way through the mounds of rubble with Panzerfausts clipped to their handlebars. Ashes are falling like dead leaves, like dirty snow, catching in Erich's hair, settling on his shoulders. In the ruins mothers squat before campfires stoked with books, cooking for their children, and crosses made from chair legs mark hasty graves in front yards. The trees are charred, the lamp posts bent double, and a great yellow haze hangs over it all, blocking out the sky, stinking of sulphur and gas and things that need burying deep. No, this cannot be right.

When the noise starts up it cracks him open and rushes inside, filling his skull with iron bees battering themselves against bone. He cannot breathe. The sound tears through the smoke and he does not know which way to run. He can tell that people are shouting because he can see their mouths moving but he cannot make out a word. He thinks of Frau Ingwer reading to the class from her little book: *Panic is always more dangerous than the danger itself. Where can panic arise? In any place where people are together in large numbers, and not just in an enclosed space, but also outside. What do I do if panic erupts? I remain calm and keep my wits about me. I assess the situation quickly and accurately. I call with a calm and firm voice, 'There is no danger at all!'*

And then a girl is grabbing his sleeve and dragging him through the maze of rubble, and he is stumbling behind her, half tripping over a dented sign saying *Nollendorfplatz*. He tries to watch his feet, tries to keep his wits about him and assess the situation. She runs ahead of him, weaving through the smoke, a fox-fur stole hanging over her shoulder. Its paws jump and dance, as if it too is running, and it watches Erich with bead-black eyes. The girl gestures to him to follow her down a flight of steps; the door at the bottom is blocked with rubble, but she climbs through a smashed window and then helps Erich in.

To begin with he can't see much, but the girl takes his hand and they make their way through a set of swinging double doors and down another flight of stairs, carpeted this time, to a subterranean room. He can feel broken glass cracking beneath his feet, and he remembers one winter when he walked out on the frozen lake before the ice was thick enough, and Mama calling him back.

'Wait here,' says the girl, and he stands alone in the blackness with the noise still thundering above, and when he pushes his knuckles into his eyes to stop the tears he sees black honeycomb, and he wonders why on earth he came to this place. His stomach growls and twists; he has already finished the sandwich the women gave him on the train, as well as the sausage he brought from home, and all but one of the apples. He hears footsteps, and then the girl is setting a torch on a ledge and swinging herself up next to it, and he sees that it is not a ledge but a stage: they are in a theatre.

'What were you doing out there?' she says. 'Where are your parents?'

'I lost them,' he says, 'Mama on the farm and Papa somewhere in Russia.'

'A farm? In Berlin?'

'Oh, no – I came here to fight for the Führer.'

'Are you in the Volkssturm?'

'I don't think so.'

'You'd have an armband if you were.'

'I don't have an armband.'

'We could try to get you one.'

'It's all right. I don't mind not having one.'

'I thought you wanted to fight for the Führer.'

269

Erich looks away, shakes his head.

The girl nods. 'Well, just say if you change your mind.'

As his eyes adjust to the low light he sees a large mass to her left, crouched at the end of the stage.

'Don't panic,' he whispers, 'but I think there's a wolf in here.' He points to the animal; its flanks gleam in the glow of the torch and he begins to back away. But can't wolves see in the dark? Can't they scent their prey?

The girl laughs and shines the torch on the beast: a golden sphinx gazing out to the rows of empty seats, and a second identical one at the other end of the stage. Columns decorated with Egyptian hieroglyphs soar up behind the sphinxes, as thick as oaks, and Erich can make out desert scenes painted on the walls: pyramids and camels and sand dunes, Bedouin tribes dressed all in white, oases ringed with slender palms. Directly above the stage a great gold half-sun sends its rays as high as the ceiling, and behind the girl the red velvet curtains ripple and shake with the force of the firing overhead, and they are dark trees in the wind, and Erich thinks of the forest behind the farm, the soft rippling pines. The girl takes the torch and runs down the aisle and up the carpeted stairs again, sliding a broomstick through the handles of the double doors. When she returns to the stage she steps into the wings and Erich hears a rolling sound. Slowly the curtains part, and in the shadows to the rear of the stage he sees a makeshift bed.

'Do you live here?' he says.

'Just for now.'

'Can I stay here too?'

'If you like.'

'Do you want an apple?'

'Yes please.'

'What's your name?'

'Erich.'

'I'm Sieglinde.'

She takes him to a room filled with mirrors. The only source of light is a row of high, narrow windows set at pavement level; most of the glass is missing, and Erich can see soldiers' boots walking past out of step, and women's legs wearing men's shoes. A jumble of music-stands takes up one corner, and a large wardrobe occupies another, its door hanging open to reveal lamé, sequins, feathers; the lair of some strange and glittering bird.

'Do you have any more food?' she asks.

'I'm sorry,' he says. 'I didn't know Berlin would be so, so . . .' He looks away for a moment, then searches through his knapsack. 'I have this,' he says, handing her the jar of milk, and she does not wait to be invited; she unscrews the lid and drinks, and he watches almost half of the milk disappear. He has never seen such a hungry girl.

'You finish it,' she says, but he shakes his head. She pushes aside the clothes in the wardrobe and stores the jar at the very back, where Erich can see a box of sprouted potatoes and half a cabbage, a few jars of vegetables, a stump of bread. Every now and then a draught from the street pushes the smell of smoke inside and riffles through the racks of costumes and the piles of old programmes. Posters droop from the walls: Renée Debauga the Kaleidoscope Dancer, Mario Tombarell the Incredible Ape Man, Helly the World's Youngest Equilibrist.

'What do you think?' says Sieglinde, holding up a shawl that tinkles with dozens of thin gold coins. 'It's not real money.' She wraps it about her head, turban-style, and looks at her dim reflection for a moment.

'Where are we?' says Erich.

'We are crossing the desert,' she says. 'We are on our way home. Our slaves are making the palace ready, unrolling the carpets, polishing the bells, filling the fountains with wine.'

'Picking the dates from the date palms,' he says.

'Cooking the larks and the peacocks.'

'How far away are we?'

'It's hard to tell in the desert.' She hands him a cloak stitched with birds and eyes, and he ties it around his shoulders, and he is a pharaoh, a blue-eyed king, and he will live forever.

On the stage she makes him a bed next to her own, fashioning a mattress from a pile of costumes. He spreads the embroidered cloak over the top, and his blanket from the train, and she draws the curtains closed and stands the torch on its end like a little lamp while they get into bed. From beneath her mattress she retrieves a large, marbled ledger and tucks it under her covers. The guns have stopped firing and in the quiet of the enclosed stage their voices come and go, as if their words are taking form in the dark air and gliding about them, looking for a place to roost. High above like a vast book hang a dozen different backdrops, a dozen different possibilities: ballrooms lit by chandeliers, castles overlooking snowy ravines, exotic marketplaces filled with spices and silks, bare washes of white and blue to suggest the shimmering distance. And beneath their beds are trapdoors; you can run your fingers along the cracks in the boards, feel the faint musty breeze from below – but they are latched shut, these secret doors, they are solid, they will not fall away without warning. Here in the ground Erich thinks of the bees, who are of the air, touching the earth only to gather water or to die.

Sieglinde is shining the torch against the stage curtains

and making shapes with her fingers: foxes and bears that tremble against the folds of cloth and do not hold.

'We should save the batteries,' says Erich.

'There are others backstage. I hid them in a bag of lentils,' she says. 'And I don't like the dark.' But she switches the torch off.

Erich can hear her turning over on her mattress of costumes, sighing, trying to get comfortable. Somewhere in the distance a clock strikes; he counts off the hours and can sense Sieglinde doing the same. Eleven. Forever until dawn.

'Do you have brothers and sisters?' she says.

'No,' he says. 'My parents couldn't have children.'

'But they had you.'

'They adopted me, from an orphanage in the Wartheland.'

'Are you Polish? Can you say something in Polish?'

'I'm German.'

'What happened to your parents?'

'I lost them,' he says. 'Mama on the farm, and Papa in Russia. They're gone.'

'No, your real parents.'

'Oh. I suppose they're dead.'

'Do you know their names?'

'No.'

Her voice is becoming slow, drowsy. 'Do you know your name?'

'Erich Kröning, of course.'

'But your other name,' she says, yawning. 'You would have had a different name before.'

'I don't know it,' he says. 'I don't know any other name.' He stares into the dark, up to the unseen backdrops. A river, a snowdrift, a mirrored hall – who is calling him? What is she saying? Yes, there is another name, a different name; he can feel the flicker of its wings, but it will not settle.

'How many in your family?' he asks.

Sieglinde is silent for a moment. 'I'm the eldest, and then there are two boys – Jürgen's ten and Kurt's five. Jürgen looks like me but with curly hair, and Tante Hannelore thinks Kurt looks just like Vati.'

'Were they evacuated?' says Erich.

'No,' says Sieglinde.

'Oh.'

She is silent again, and Erich wonders if she has fallen asleep. 'Did you lose your family too?' he whispers.

She does not reply, but after a moment she says, 'Do you know any stories?'

He closes his eyes and thinks of his grandmother, of her soft lap, her mottled hands, her voice in his ear. 'A long time ago, there was a castle in Saxony,' he says. 'A fortress. It had a murder hole and stumbling steps and marksmen who could fire arrows straight to the heart of any attacker – but it had another defence too. A secret inside its walls.'

'Like a secret passage?'

'No, a different sort of secret. When it was built, people thought that setting a child into the foundations would protect them, and so a boy was bought from a local mother. As the wall went up everyone heard him cry out *I can still see you, Mama –*'

'Everyone heard him?' says Sieglinde.

'Yes, and then when the wall was finished and he was trapped inside he cried out again – *I can't see you now, Mama*. The mother went mad and threw herself off a cliff, but they say her ghost came back, scratching at the castle walls, trying to find her son.'

'It wasn't a very secret secret,' says Sieglinde. 'Is the castle still standing?'

'I don't think so,' says Erich.

'Hmm.'

Some time later a noise wakes him. For a moment he does not know where he is, and the darkness is so total it makes no difference if his eyes are open or shut. The noise comes closer, a low drone, and he thinks he hears the voice of Luise's hive speaking to him through her wooden mouth, and she is saying his name, *Erich, Erich*, wanting him to follow her into the forest where the wild berries grow – but no, it is not Luise, Opa Kröning's first love; it is the girl from Berlin, the girl who saved him.

'Are we safe here?' he says.

'As safe as anywhere,' she says. 'I always put the broomstick through the door handles.'

That is not what he meant, but the noise is not the engine of a plane and it is not flak guns and bombs. It is pebbles at the bottom of a rushing river; it is glass marbles; it is beads in a baby's rattle; it is bees humming in their hives.

When Erich wakes again Sieglinde is making her bed.

'What time is it?' he says.

'I don't know, but it must be early. No fighting yet.' She slides the ledger underneath her mattress. 'Come on,' she says, pulling back his blankets. 'We need to have breakfast, and then I need to find some shoes. Mine are worn through.'

In the dressing room she breaks the last of the bread in half and spreads it with sauerkraut – more juice than sauerkraut, in truth, but it softens the bread enough that they can chew it. They share the remaining milk, and then they search the cupboards and shelves, rummaging through programmes, wigs, parasols, sheet music, boxes of makeup.

'What about these?' says Erich, holding up a pair of black patent-leather pumps.

'Oh yes! They're just like Tante Hannelore's dancing shoes,' says Sieglinde. 'I'll have to grow into them, though.' She finds a pair of scissors in a sewing basket and trims a skein of hair from one of the wigs, packing it into the toes, adding a little more and a little more until the shoes fit.

Erich is sitting at the long table that runs in front of the mirrors, cutting a circle of paper from a programme.

'What's that for?' says Sieglinde.

'You'll see.' He takes a pencil from his pocket and draws a pair of wings on the front of the circle, then a bee's body, wingless, on the back. With a needle he pierces a hole on either side of the drawing and feeds a length of cotton through. 'Watch,' he says. He rolls the threads back and forth between his thumb and forefinger, and the picture flutters and flips, and the wings join to the wingless bee.

'Like magic,' says Sieglinde, clapping her hands.

He draws more pictures for her, and when the fighting starts again they keep on playing, cutting out more circles, thinking of more pictures, forgetting they are hungry, until the table is covered with riderless horses and riders suspended in mid-air, empty cages and cageless birds, fishbowls and fish, beetles and jars.

'Wait, I have an idea.' Sieglinde cuts out a new disc of paper and writes ER on one side and ICH on the other. 'Look,' she says as the two words spin and combine.

Er and ich, he and I; we turn and turn and for a moment we merge.

★

One afternoon, about a week later I think, though I cannot be sure, I follow them up the carpeted stairs to the swinging double doors. I wait as they pull the broomstick out of the door handles and then I go with them into the streets. We can hear the rifle fire and the thudding of the shells a few blocks away. We keep to the walls whenever we can, stealing along them like shadows, until we come to a long line of women. That's where the food will be, says Sieglinde, and we join the end of the queue even though we cannot see its head. We do not remark on the bruise-coloured bodies piled like a barricade on the street corner. We look no further than the person in front of us. The air is gritty on our teeth and tongues and we cannot see the sky.

'He's gone to Argentina,' a woman just in front of us is saying. 'They smuggled him out in a U-boat.'

'No, he's in Bavaria, in the alpine fortress,' says another.

'I heard he's on his way to the South Pole,' says a third.

'I heard Spain.'

When the shelling reaches us we run for a burnt-out tram. Five or six of the queuing women are hit, perhaps seven, but we do not care, we do not look at them, we regroup in the correct order, we make sure we hold our place in the queue.

Hitler Youth boys arrive and hand out pamphlets: *Berliners! Hold fast. Wenck's army is on the march. Just a few more days and Berlin will be free again.* We know there is no army to speak of, just as there is no meat, no school, no water, no news, no power, no milk, no home, no hope, no sun, no sky. The Americans have not turned against the Russians and are not coming to our rescue, there are no wonder weapons, the ghost army will not save us, these boys will not save us, those ditches and these barricades and that Panzerfaust will not save us.

'We'll be lucky if there's anything left,' says the woman ahead of us, checking her watch. She turns and looks Sieglinde up and down. 'How old are you?'

'Twelve.'

'Rub your face with ashes,' she says. 'Tie a shawl over your hair. Tell them you have a disease. Paint sores on your skin.'

When the woman reaches the head of the queue she is asked for her ration card.

'I lost it in a raid,' she says.

'I can't give you anything if you don't have your card.'

'But I lost it in a terror raid. It's gone.'

'Without the card there's nothing I can do.'

'Quite right,' calls a voice from further back in the queue. 'You should have brought your card. She should have brought her card.'

'I don't have a card,' whispers Erich.

'Neither do I,' says Sieglinde.

★

We are lying on our beds in the dark theatre. Is it day or night? How long have we slept, and how much time is left? Listen: the tanks are crossing our flimsy barricades; the rockets are shooting by like comets, setting the sky on fire. I feel it haunting all my limbs: magnificent Walpurgis Night. Will the world break apart, will it bury us, will the castles and ravines and rivers fall all at once, a ballroom in the marketplace, snow in the mirrored hall? We pull back the stage curtains and the rows of seats crouch in the gloom. Bring on the juggler, the strongman, the conjurer; bring on the dancing bear.

Erich moves the beam of the torch around the walls. 'Is that a new crack?' he says.

'Perhaps it was always there,' says Sieglinde. She is making her bed, tucking the ledger underneath it for safekeeping.

'No, I think it's new.'

'The building's stronger than it looks,' she says, coming and sitting next to Erich on the edge of the stage. 'Did you know, if you hold an egg longways between your thumb and finger, and press down as hard as you can, it won't break?'

'That doesn't sound right,' says Erich.

'I know, but it's true,' says Sieglinde. 'Vati showed me, when we still had eggs. It's because of physics.'

'What are physics?'

'The laws that make the world work.'

'Our hens have to lay sixty-five eggs each per year,' says Erich. 'That's the law.'

'What happens if they don't?'

'They're punished, I suppose.'

'Sent to the camps?'

'Maybe.'

'We're safe here,' says Sieglinde.

'Yes, we're safe here,' says Erich. He switches the torch off. 'Have you ever met him? The Führer?'

'No.'

'He came to Leipzig once, for a parade. I saw him drive past in his black Mercedes. He didn't look like the stamps.'

'It might have been a double.'

'A double?'

'How do you think he does everything he does?'

Erich turns in the direction of Sieglinde's voice; he can

just make out her shape, sitting to the right of him on the edge of the stage. 'So I didn't see him?'

'I don't know. Perhaps not.'

A small amount of light is trickling down the stairwell now, picking out the gold-pawed sphinxes. They are pricking their ears, pressing their wings back against their haunches, waiting for an updraught.

'How many doubles are there?'

A boom sounds overhead, louder than thunder, and pieces of plaster patter down from the ceiling. The stage floor shakes. *Look out! Look out!* Another boom, closer this time. Sieglinde catches her breath.

'I heard that he invites children to come and stay in the Führerbunker,' says Erich. 'He gives them marzipan to eat, and lots of vitamins to make them healthy, and they can hardly hear the fighting. It's like being in a pyramid.'

'How does he choose them, the children who get to eat the marzipan?'

'I don't know. I suppose he takes the ones who are very good, and always obey their parents.'

'What about the bad children? What happens to them?'

'They're sent to the camps,' says Erich. 'They have to concentrate on what they've done and promise not to do it again.'

'And if they don't promise?'

'They're made into glue.'

Sieglinde laughs. 'Yes, glue!'

'They end up holding wallpaper to walls.'

'Sealing letters shut.'

'Sticking stamps to envelopes.'

The noise above grows louder; closer. There is a sudden rushing sound as one of the backdrops falls partway open and hangs high above the stage; a night sky, clear and deep and full of moonlight.

'He's going to fix everything,' says Sieglinde. 'After the war, he's going to put it all back together. New trees in the Tiergarten and new animals in the zoo. He'll mend all the houses, and he'll build the Triumphal Arch, ten times as big as the one in Paris, and the Great Hall, which will have its own clouds.'

For a moment I can see it too, this new place, all the pieces put back together. The Reichstag unburned, the Gedächtniskirche unbombed, all the little lakes in the Grune-wald joined up again and turned back into the ancient river they once were: ships sail through the forest, winding through the beeches and the oaks, their masts as tall as trees.

Somewhere nearby, a wall collapses.

'How long until they're here, do you think?' says Erich.

'Not long.'

'How far away is the Führerbunker?'

'A few blocks.'

Outside on the pavement a dozen people are cutting meat from a dead horse and a dozen more are hovering about it, zooming into any gap that opens in the swarm. With its muddy eye the animal stares up at a buckled air-raid shelter arrow that points nowhere. Volkssturm men and boys are digging trenches in the road; only their heads are visible, and their shovels full of dirt. A woman wanders past pushing a corpse on a wheelbarrow.

'It's not far,' says Sieglinde, though as she looks around and tries to get her bearings she is not quite sure which direction they should take. She and Erich clamber past the piles of broken bricks and the abandoned vehicles with their smashed windows and their bullet-riddled bodies. Flames still flicker in some of the black ruins and every now and then a crash shudders through the air as masonry falls.

They make their way north, to where they can still see the Siegessäule rising up through the haze. On Charlottenburger Chaussee, as they near the Brandenburg Gate, Erich points to a blurry mass a block or two away. 'Is that it?'

'I'm not sure,' says Sieglinde, trying to peer through the wraiths of dust and smoke.

And is that the Reichskanzlei, that grey blur? There is a stench in the air that nobody wishes to name, and Victory's stone horses are gouged and cracked, and Victory is crowning the ruins with laurel though she is no more than a smudge, and all the linden trees are stumps.

An armoured truck slows down as it passes and a Wehrmacht soldier calls out to them. 'What are you doing here? Go home. It isn't safe.' He is dirty and unshaven and his arm is bandaged.

'Is that the Reichskanzlei?' says Sieglinde. 'We wanted to ask if the Führer is inviting any more children. He gives them marzipan to eat.'

'The Führer?' says the soldier. 'Didn't you hear the broadcast?'

But no, we didn't hear; almost nobody heard. Wagner's *Das Rheingold*, Bruckner's Seventh Symphony: music for the dead. Our Führer has fallen, fighting to his last breath for Germany; at the end of his struggle he met a hero's death. I cannot forsake the city that is the capital of this Reich. Thus I salute the fortress, safe from fear and dread.

Hand in hand we return to the theatre and shut

ourselves in, sliding the broomstick through the door handles. The great painted half-sun is rising above the stage, or else it is setting. The night sky hangs at half-mast, too high to correct. Can it be true? Can the Führer really have fallen? That evening we feel the air shifting above us, lifting the corners of our covers, ruffling our hair. We blink and blink again, trying to dispel the after-images of our own eyes – black moons, black suns. Yes, there is something moving back and forth above our beds; a dark wing drifting through the dark air, brushing our cheeks.

'Siggi,' we whisper.

'Erich,' we whisper.

And our eyes adjust and we realise it is not a wing but a palm frond. The camel bows down to us, lowering its gaze, waiting. Erich grasps the skin behind the animal's neck – warm and thick, a picnic blanket at the end of a day at the beach – and he pulls himself up just like Old Shatterhand, just like Kara Ben Nemsi, and then he helps Sieglinde aboard. To our left and our right the hieroglyph birds are shaking themselves free of their pillars and taking flight, and the hieroglyph eyes are blinking, blinking. The camel raises itself up on its beanstalk legs, up and up, until Erich thinks he might touch the stars, and then it begins to move, swaying along the sandy floor, pausing at the date palms so that Sieglinde can reach into their rustling hearts and pick the ripening fruit, and pausing again at a pond so she can choose a white lotus bloom to tuck behind her ear. On it sways, with the rhythm of a cradle, the theatre opening out ahead of us into a rippled desert. Our slaves crouch before us in rows, their foreheads pressed to the sand, awaiting their orders, and all the black birds are dissolving into the black sky. Erich forgets his mother and his father, and his other secret name. There are only the stars and the moon now, and Sieglinde at his back, and the soft dunes rising around us like dreams.

★

FRAU MÜLLER: Is it true?
FRAU MILLER: Can it be true?
FRAU MÜLLER: They say he was leading a charge against the Ivans.
FRAU MILLER: They say he died with his hand on his heart.
FRAU MÜLLER: Where is he now?
FRAU MILLER: Where have they taken him?
FRAU MÜLLER: They have picked his bones.
FRAU MILLER: They have laid out his jaw in a box.

★

Something is emerging from the smoke: a cow heavy with milk, a line of horses and shaggy ponies pulling carts of hay and oats, a rooster that crows at the red sky though it is well past dawn. And then the Russian soldiers come with their grimy faces, their quilted jackets, their disintegrating boots, women as well as men, cocking their rifles as they pass. Up their arms they stack their stolen watches, four apiece, six apiece, on Moscow time and Berlin time. They set up their field kitchens, unload their rockets. They call them their Katyushas, like the sweetheart in the song who walks by the misty river. We make way for them at the water pumps, let them track manure through our homes; we give them our bicycles, our beds, and we hope they will not find the daughters we hide under piles of rags, the daughters we shut in cupboards and conceal inside walls. For whom should we fight now? There is no coming man. We have torn up the photographs of our sons and our husbands in their proud uniforms. We have unpinned our lapels, unhung our portraits; we have burned our books. And I am not sorry.

★

'Vati would enjoy this,' says Sieglinde, twirling a new disc of paper. It shows a bare tree on one side and a cloud of green leaves on the other.

'Does he like trees?' says Erich.

'He likes making things with paper. He cuts out silhouette pictures.'

'Of people?'

'Of places.'

'Where is he?'

'In Berlin, because of his essential job.'

'He's here?'

Sieglinde rolls the threads back and forth; the tree is green and the tree is bare. Outside the rockets are taking wing, sounding their thin, high cries. She opens her ledger and shakes a handful of words into her lap: *defeat, freedom, Mendelssohn, surrender.*

'Where did you find those?' says Erich.

'They're Vati's job.'

'Why do you have them, then?'

'I'm looking after them while he's away.'

'Isn't he in Berlin?'

'He had to go away, for his essential job. He'll be back soon.'

Erich knows this is untrue; he knows that her father is

gone, just as his own father is gone, just as Onkel Gerhard and Great-Onkel Gustav and the airman in the barley field are gone. But he nods and listens as she talks on, as she invents her father the way all children invent their parents, the way the present invents the past, overlays it with visions of the things we have lost. The tree is bare, the tree is green.

I see the news spreading, snaking down the line at the water pump. Erich and Sieglinde don't wait to fill their buckets; like everyone else, they run for the abandoned shop. By the time they get there it is already teeming with people helping themselves to the supplies: tins of meat and fish and condensed milk, packets of rice and barley, cubes of gravy, jars of jam, sauerkraut and pickles. Two women are squabbling over a bag of semolina, digging in their fingernails until it bursts. Erich hesitates at the door but Sieglinde pushes him into the throng and they grab as much as they can, packing it into their water buckets and their stretched-out jumpers. They would like to eat it all on the way home; to sit down in the ruins – anywhere would do – and pour peas and sauerkraut and jam into their mouths, stop the clenching in their stomachs. They wouldn't even need to sit down, they say to each other; they could eat while they were walking, never mind bad manners. They could wolf down half a dozen tins of meat each, suck at rolled oats and condensed milk until it turned to porridge. Dip cabbage stalks in sugar and swallow them whole. Bite into onions as if they were apples.

By the time they have finished talking about how they could eat the food they are back at the theatre, and they store it in the dressing room, hiding it at the bottom of the wardrobe.

'Shouldn't we have paid?' says Erich.

Sieglinde laughs. 'Did you see a shopkeeper? And besides, we don't have any money.'

'I have ten thousand marks,' he says, and shows her the banknote his father gave him, turning it sideways and pointing out the ghoulish figure hidden in the picture, feeding at the farmer's throat.

'Is it real?' she says.

'I don't think so,' says Erich. 'Not any more.'

Sieglinde pulls two chairs up to the table that runs along the wall of mirrors and spreads out the embroidered cloak, smoothing it flat as if it is Mutti's best white damask, as if it is a normal Sunday afternoon and they are preparing for a visit from Tante Hannelore. Mutti always uses a damask tablecloth on these occasions, and the little green demitasse coffee cups edged in gold with the handles you can fit just one finger through. Where are they now? Where is the tablecloth with its white-on-white chrysanthemums, and where is the dining table beneath it, and the carpet beneath the table, and the parquet beneath the carpet? What happens to all the broken things? Are they buried? Burned? Sieglinde thinks of the coffee cups and their special spot in the sideboard. She pictures herself reaching out to unlock the upper door, turning the little key, hearing the click as the snib releases. Then comes the waxy smell of the inside of the cupboard, and the shimmer of the cherrywood, a little deeper in colour than on the outside. The coffee cups are lined up on their shelf, each facing the same way, each sitting on its matching saucer. In a moment she will lift them down for Mutti, in a moment she will place them on the white damask cloth, in a moment Tante Hannelore will knock at the door and hand Mutti a box from the bakery, a white box tied with red ribbon and containing a nicer cake than the one Mutti has made. And Sieglinde must be careful with the cups, they are very old and precious and impossible to replace, and they will be hers one day. Every week Mutti counts them, ticking them off in her ledger, and that is the only place Sieglinde can find them now, unbroken, unlost, and that is the only place she can find the parquet and the carpet and the table and the damask, each one accounted for many times over in Mutti's black ink.

'Here,' says Erich, handing her a can of condensed milk. He has stabbed it open with his pocket knife and they take turns drinking from it; long, sweet sips. He grins at her in the mirror and she loves him then, this boy who came from nowhere, his hair papery pale in the low light, one eye tooth twisted a little sideways, a freckle like a comma on his temple. They do not see me but I am there too, drifting between themselves and their reflections, waiting for my turn.

They sleep soundly that night, and when Erich goes to fetch water the next morning the streets are quiet. He passes a man digging a grave in the blackened front yard of an apartment block; next to him a woman's body lies on a handcart, stiff, livid. The scent of lilacs is in the air, and every now and then Erich can make out birdsong. There are no rockets, no bursts of gunfire, no tanks churning their way through the rubble.

'It's over,' says a woman at the pump. 'We've surrendered.' She heard the news from her neighbour, who heard it from her sister, whose lodger has a crystal set. And is it true, this news? Is it to be trusted? All over the city the queues of women are talking, and so are the hidden daughters, and so are the boys with the helmets that cover their eyes. *Pst*, says the shadowman from the pitted walls, but there are no more secrets to keep. White bedsheets hang from windows.

When Erich returns to the theatre he calls to Sieglinde but she does not answer. It feels even quieter than when he left that morning; different somehow. As he descends the staircase he notices that the double doors are open and the broomstick is snapped, and he can see the golden sphinxes flanking the stage, and the hieroglyphs painted on the thick white columns: birds, eyes, jackals.

'Sieglinde?' he calls. 'Sieglinde?' Something makes him lower his voice to a normal pitch, and when he says her name again he cannot shake the feeling that he is talking to himself. 'Siggi?' The sphinxes watch him, and the sun reaches its painted rays across the ceiling, and why are the doors open? And then he hears it: a whimpering coming from the stage, the kind of noise the farm dogs make when they tread on nettles, and he sees something on the stage and his heart stops ticking and the theatre is so silent; he climbs onto the stage and behind him the doors are open and he hears the whimper; he comes down the stairs and into the theatre and hears something and sees something and everything falls silent except for what he hears coming from the stage, and he can see something there, something that makes his heart stop ticking. You must not enfold the night in you.

He finds her caught up in the folds of the curtain, the fabric half torn from its hooks and crushed about the footlights, red velvet spreading around her. In the curtain he finds her, half torn, red spreading and crushed, her hair stuck to her face, clogged with blood and half torn, her bed mussed and her mouth spreading red, you must not enfold the night in you, fabric ripped from her and crushed about the footlights. She holds her black leather pumps in her lap and skeins of hair spill from them, they are too big for her, the black shoes, but she will grow into them, and when Erich lifts the curtain he sees blood on her thighs, and over her lap she holds the shoes, blood and glass, her bed mussed, and the neck of a bottle jutting from between her legs, from beneath her shoes held over her lap, the blood and the glass on her thighs and the bottle jutting, its edges barbed and keen, the glass teeth of a glass beast, and you must not enfold the night in you.

She recoils at his touch. Tears run from the corners of her eyes and across her temples and mix with the blood in her hair, clotted with red and spreading, and he can think of no words to say to her apart from her name, but his mouth forms sounds he does not know, or does not remember knowing, and they are soothing sounds although they have no meaning, and he speaks these to her, *teraz jesteś bezpieczna, jestem tutaj*, and eventually she stops crying.

'Siggi,' he says. 'It's Erich, your Erich, I'm back.'

She answers him but he does not know what she says – has he lost all his words, can he no longer understand plain German? – *jestem tutaj, jestem tutaj* – and he puts his ear close to her ragged mouth. 'Out,' she says. 'Take it out. Take it out.' The bottle barbed and keen, the glass beast, the glass teeth.

Did I see what happened to Erich's Sieglinde, to our Sieglinde? Did I see who did this? Yes. I watched from the wings. I felt the kicks against the double doors, the tearing of the broomstick as they forced their way inside. I heard the boots descending the stairs – ten men, more? – and I heard their stumbling voices, saw the bottle flashing in the gloom, full when they arrived, drained as it passed from mouth to wet mouth. And I saw the wristwatches buckled about their thick sleeves, a dozen to every man, the radium aglow, sick moonlight, every one of them telling the wrong time. And I felt the kicks against her body, and the tearing of her skin as they forced their way inside. And after they each took their turn with her I admit that for a moment I wished that Erich would never return, that he would just go home to his mother and leave all this behind, unseen, unreal. But the sound of breaking glass jolted me back to Sieglinde: Siggi lying broken on the stage, far too convincing, a drowned Kristina Söderbaum pulled from the water in the final act. They broke the bottle's neck and forced it in, blunt end first, because they were not animals, not like their comrades who were bedding down with grandmothers and invalids, so they'd heard.

Erich takes the hem of the stage curtain and folds it over the bottle's splintered edge, then begins to ease the piece of glass from Sieglinde. On the farm he has witnessed the births of many creatures, including a few who never should have entered the world, nor even drawn breath – a two-headed lamb; a goat with its heart on the outside – and he has seen his father reach into a weakening cow, fasten a rope around the feet of her breech calf and draw the tangled animal from its mother. So this – yes, Erich can do this, he can undo this, he can make it right. He shakes his head to clear his thoughts. Sieglinde is quiet now, and utterly still. How long does it take? Neither child knows. Time is no more than a prize to be plundered, another spoil for the victors to snatch. For a moment Erich stares at the glassy broken thing already cooling in his hands, then flings it as far away as he can: let it smash against the painted pyramids, sink into the sand. He helps Sieglinde to sit up. The costumes on her bed are covered in blood; it looks black in the gloom. He tears off a piece of the velvet curtain and wraps it around her shoulders, then finds her fox fur and drapes it around her neck. She starts to shiver and will not stop. The fox's paws scramble at the air.

'Do you know the way to your aunt's house?' says Erich.

She nods, teeth chattering. 'It's in Dahlem. But the roads are blocked. I tried to go there before, when my house . . . when it . . .'

'It's different now,' says Erich. 'Do you think you can walk?'

'I . . . I . . .'

'All right,' he says. 'Wait here a moment – I'll be back as soon as I can.'

'No,' she says, grabbing his arm.

'We need a way of getting to your aunt's. I'm sorry. I won't be long, I promise.'

He takes three jars of pickled vegetables and a packet of gravy cubes from the hoard in the wardrobe, as well as a bag of lentils; he and Sieglinde tried to eat them uncooked one night when there was nothing else, chewing away at the hard little pellets until they agreed it was like eating stones. He pulls out the two spare torch batteries hidden inside the bag, then sets off for the apartment building where he saw the man digging the grave. The man is still there, shovelling soil back into the hole now, and the cart is empty save for a dirty headscarf.

'Excuse me,' says Erich, but the man keeps shovelling. 'Excuse me,' he says again. 'The cart – is it yours? Can I buy it off you?' He opens his rucksack and takes out a jar of vegetables, the lentils and the gravy cubes.

'One jar?' says the man. 'Are you crazy, or what?'

'And some lentils and gravy cubes,' says Erich.

The man prods Erich's rucksack with his foot. 'What else do we have?' Before Erich can answer he is rummaging inside the bag, pulling out the other jars. 'That's more like it,' he says, twisting off a lid and fishing out a carrot.

Erich bumps the cart down the flight of steps outside the theatre – he can't risk leaving it unattended on the street – and then climbs through the smashed window. Inside, he props the double doors open to let in the light and hurries down the stairs, but even before he reaches the stage he can tell that Sieglinde has gone. She is not in her bed at the rear of the stage, either – and the ledger is missing. He searches the wings and the dressing room, checking inside the wardrobe, between the racks of costumes, calling her name. Back in the theatre he looks behind the columns covered in hieroglyphs and behind the golden sphinxes; one of them has been kicked in around the base, and he can see that it's hollow inside, made only of plaster and wire. He walks down the central aisle, shining the torch along each row of seats – and there he finds her, crouched on the floor beneath the torn piece of curtain, no longer shivering, all too still. She is holding the ledger close. Hooking her arms around his neck, he half-carries, half-drags her up the stairs and then pulls her through the smashed window. Her eyes are flickering open and shut and her cheeks are cool and white, as white as the belly of the fish he once kept in the bathtub at home. He leans her against the building's flayed wall while he heaves the handcart back up the steps and pauses to line it with his overcoat. For a moment the taste of the carp returns to him, and the smell of the beeswax candles burning in the branches of the Christmas tree, and Mama with her shining hair pinned about her head like a crown. He looks up and down the broken street: word of the surrender has spread, and people are emerging from their hiding places, climbing from their tunnels and their tombs, pushing their way to the surface to find out what is left. The dust and the smoke eddy in the dirty air and nobody can see very far ahead. Erich catches sight of a woman who looks like Mama, and he knows he must ask her for help; he is so tired, and he cannot lift Sieglinde on his own, Siggi who is so pale and still, her hair hard with blood. And the woman is turning towards him, and he is lifting his hand to her, waving her over, and now that she is approaching he sees that she is nothing like Mama, even though she wears a dress like Mama's and shoes like Mama's and a headscarf like hers too, and he wonders why for a moment he wanted to run to her and put his arms around her, this wrong mother.

Together they carry Sieglinde up the steps and place her in the handcart. Erich covers her with the piece of velvet curtain and the fox fur.

'Which way is Dahlem?' he asks, and the woman points down the street in the same direction as the plundered shop.

'I don't know how bad it is there,' she says, leaning over Sieglinde and clicking her tongue. 'It's a disgrace, what he's done to us. A disgrace.'

Erich runs back inside the theatre and fills his rucksack with the remaining food. Then he sets off, trying not to jolt the cart too much, every few moments asking, 'Is this right? Is this the way?'

Sieglinde murmurs, gives the smallest of nods.

Now and then a smattering of gunfire can still be heard, but already the neighbourhood is busy with women putting things to rights: look at them shaking the dust

294

from carpets and quilts, sweeping entranceways, clearing paths. How else are they to pass the time? One or two men have emerged too, but they don't seem to know what to do with themselves; they linger in the shadows, awaiting their instructions, silver in their hair, gold in their mouths and lead in their bones. Tell me, who shall play the captain? On the corner a group of Russians is setting up a field kitchen and preparing to dole out soup in tin mugs.

Sieglinde turns onto her side, watching the gutted buildings, the mountains of rubble pass by. Rows of soldiers clutter the kerbs, dirty and unshaven. Where have the streets gone? It's far from clear. But isn't that Mutti and Vati and the boys up ahead in the smoke, making their way along Kantstrasse – is it Kantstrasse? – and heading for the train that will take them to the Wannsee? A swim on a hot afternoon! Mutti will have packed a flask of coffee and a bottle of milk, some pears, buttered bread, some of her Apfeltaschen, and perhaps some boiled eggs, which Sieglinde and Jürgen will crack on each other's heads when Vati isn't looking. What else? The red bucket and spade for Kurt, and the picnic rug, and their swimming things, of course; a comb, so that everyone can be tidied up before they return home, and for Mutti herself the latest issue of *Filmwelt*, and the bottle of sun oil, and the wide-brimmed straw hat that casts forest light on her face. Vati will remind everyone of the dangers of speaking too loudly in open spaces such as the beach, where rumours can take off, skipping across the water, impossible to keep in check. Once he has changed into his swimming costume he will stand on the shoreline for a moment, hands on his hips, then wade out into the water and dive underneath. And look, he has disappeared, and Sieglinde wonders where he has gone; she can see no ripples, no kicks, no bubbles breaking the surface – but a few moments later there he is, quite some distance away, his hair dark and different, a different Vati. It is strange to see so much of him. His arms are bare, and his legs, too, thinner than you would expect, the ankles and knees showing their bones. And on the sand his watch still ticking, flaring in the sun, too bright to look at. Jürgen goes searching for stones that are the right shape and size, and who knows where they go when he flicks them across the water? No telling, no telling. He will ask Sieglinde to bury him in the sand up to his neck, but it will only make him cry, and she will have to dig him out again straight away.

Mutti is wearing her sailboat skirt and sits in a wicker beach chair, flicking through her *Filmwelt*, studying the photographs of Zarah Leander and Marika Rökk. She shakes sand from the spine of her magazine, frowning.

But it's so cool in the water! It makes you forget the heat, the acrid streets, the city caught in your throat. The cut of the fallen glass. Do Jürgen and Vati push her head under the water and hold her down a little too long? Do they call her names? Do they wind her up in a towel and leave her there, knotted and wet? Does the sun beat her until everything hurts?

No. No. She is sitting in a wicker beach chair with Kurt, digging her toes into the sand, pushing hot heaps of it from side to side; she is taking it in her fist and feeling its shifting form. The shape of nothing. You were rock once, she thinks. Her hair is drying in the sun, and when she unbraids it at home it will ripple and curl, but the curl never lasts; it slowly calms and smoothes, and by morning she is Siggi again.

'Sorry,' says Erich each time they hit a bump. 'Sorry, I'm sorry.'

No, they are not on Kantstrasse, never were on Kantstrasse. Just ahead her smoke family rises and darkens, figures of ash that hold their form for a moment, then crumble even as she reaches for them. And on Erich pushes her, through the crumbling ash, and it is nothing after all. Fine sand, falling.

'Where are we now?' says Erich.

It might be Winterfeldtplatz, but Sieglinde cannot be sure; nothing looks quite right. She and Mutti and Tante Hannelore were forced to wait there for quite some time one morning while thieves and murderers were loaded onto the backs of trucks. It was snowing that day, an early winter, and the flakes sprinkled the cobblestones like powdered sugar, gathering about the roots of the dormant trees, clinging to the dark fragrant tips of the potted firs that guarded the grand doorways. Now white ashes cover the ground, this winter's field, and smoke rises from the ruins, warm breaths spreading into the sooty air. All the trees stand raw and limbless. Nothing grows. If I now close heart and mouth, which to the stars do love to cry, still in my heart's depths gently sound the washing waves, low and mild.

'It is like the moon,' she hears a woman say. Who can tell her age? A dirty scarf covers her hair and ashes streak her face, and look, there is another woman with ashes on her face, and there a third, dabbing her face with ashes. Dab, dab. Across the brow, the temples, across the nose and the cheeks, the chin and even the eyelids.

This is nothing like the moon, thinks Sieglinde. The moon would be clean and quiet and empty; a clear place, a new world. She would float in its cool light, clean and quiet and empty, she would be light, as light as nothing, the moon would be nothing at all. But nobody has seen the moon for such a long time, and perhaps, above the ashes and the smoke, it has rolled away from Berlin, a dropped coin, and when the skies clear it will have vanished, and people will wonder what they have done to deserve such darkness, and how they can restore the lost moon.

'This way?' says Erich. 'This way?'

Sieglinde nods, and they pass a sign that might say *Barbarossaplatz*, and a sign that might say *Kaiserplatz*, though she cannot be sure. She rubs her cheek against the fox's sleek head. It warms to her touch, blinking its polished-pebble eyes, and begins to speak. *A long time ago*, it says, *I could feel dew on the pads of my paws and the soft fur of my belly. At night the moon turned the forest to silver, and I watched the trees cast their silver shadows and heard the night birds sound their silver songs. The hens fell silent as I passed their flimsy coops, my shadow vast and spreading, my coat growing lustrous with blood. Now these eyes are not my eyes and I am split open, my heart removed.*

It's all right, she says, everything is all right. Here is Tante Hannelore's house, here are the stone children holding up the sky.

Erich does not need to knock; the front door is wide open. The entranceway smells of urine and faeces, and a woman is kneeling, scrubbing at the tiled floor with a damp rag. She startles when Erich speaks.

'Frau Schirmer?' he says. 'Are you Sieglinde's aunt?'

'Who are you?' she says.

'I'm Erich Kröning – I've brought Sieglinde. She's been hurt.'

The woman peers through the door at the handcart. 'You'd better come in,' she says. 'I'm Frau Hummel.'

But where is Tante Hannelore? Who is this woman, this Frau Hummel, showing us into Tante Hannelore's apartment? Why is she beckoning to Erich to follow her past empty rooms and into the kitchen, where a bundle of nettles sits in the sink, and why is she bending to whisper into his ear?

'Frau Schirmer took cyanide,' she says.

'What do you mean?' says Erich. 'Is she all right?'

The woman straightens, eyes him for a moment. 'Do you know her?'

'No,' he says.

'Well, she poisoned herself,' says the woman. 'It's quite the fashion. We buried her in the yard last week.'

Sieglinde simply nods at the news. 'I lost her jewellery,' she says. 'I don't know how to tell her.'

Frau Hummel unwraps her from the velvet and fur and checks her injuries, sponging her as clean as she can with a handkerchief dipped in water, combing the dried blood from her hair. 'How many were there?' she asks Erich, and then, when he doesn't answer, 'How many men?'

'I didn't see,' he says, looking at the floor. 'I wasn't there.'

The apartment is almost bare; a dining chair lies in pieces next to the tiled stove, and two of the four bedrooms are empty of furniture, their mattresses rolled up and standing on end. Frau Hummel and Erich help Sieglinde to her feet and put her to bed in her cousin's old room, which is now occupied by Herr Fromm.

'And where am I to sleep?' he says. 'What about my bad shoulder?'

'You and your shoulder can sleep on the floor. Honestly,' Frau Hummel says to Erich, 'they're quite useless. Do you live far?'

'Near Leipzig,' he says.

'Leipzig! What are you doing here?'

'I came to fight for the Führer.'

'And what does your mama think about that?'

'I lost her.'

Frau Hummel nods. 'You can have the other room,' she says. She unrolls the mattress for him, raising flurries of dust motes and soot. There is no glass in the windows, and Erich can see out to the treeless courtyard that is filled with rubble.

'There's my apartment,' says Frau Hummel, pointing to a mound of bricks topped with a broken bath. 'Herr Fromm and I were both on the second floor —' She waves an airy hand at the ceiling. 'Well. Nobody owns anything now. And everybody owns everything. Isn't that the way they want it?'

The septicaemia takes hold of Sieglinde the third night, dirtying her blood, running through each part of her before returning to her heart. She asks for Mutti and Vati.

'We're here, we're here,' say Frau Hummel and Herr Fromm.

I sit at her side; I see the glint of glass that lights her dreams, and the vase in the shape of a hand that points with its broken fingers from beneath the rubble. We dig it free, we wipe it clean and we return it to Mutti's dressing table, placing it at the centre of the crocheted mat Mutti made before she was married; a little net hooked in white silk. I take the bone-smooth fingers in my own, as if to introduce myself, but it knows me already: the china hand draws me close, and I feel the cold spreading from its fingers to mine, passing through my wrist-bones and travelling up my arm. This is how you die from a snake-bite or a bee-sting, I think. This is how you die from poison. The hand holds me fast, as fast as Mutti's hand when she and Siggi cross the tramlines or alight from a crowded train, and sometimes Mutti walks too quickly and Sieglinde can hardly keep up, and she feels her feet might leave the ground and then she will not know where she is, and it is the same feeling now; I feel the urgent drag of the hand, there is somewhere we need to go, and we are diving into the tight-knotted centre of the lace mat, following the hand into the white loops that close above us like sea foam. This is how you fall in love, I think.

By morning the sheets are drenched and Sieglinde is clammy to the touch, now hot, now cold. Frau Hummel taps her cheek, her hand, but she does not respond.

'Go next door and ask for Frau Blaschke,' she says. 'Tell her to come quickly.'

'Is she a doctor?' says Erich.

'Her husband was.'

Another substitute, another shadow.

Frau Blaschke says Sieglinde needs penicillin; she gives us her last two ampoules, but there are no more to be had. All we can do is keep her cool when she's feverish and warm when she's cold and hope that the poison works its way out.

'Is she bleeding already?' she asks.

'Well?' says Frau Hummel. 'Is she bleeding already?'

Both women are looking at Erich.

'I . . . she was, she did bleed, but it's stopped now,' he says.

'I mean her monthly blood,' says Frau Blaschke.

'Monthly blood?'

'Never mind.' To Frau Hummel she says, 'Get her checked in a few weeks. Yourself too. There's a woman in Steglitz.'

We sit with her day and night; even Herr Fromm takes his turn. We sponge her face, brush her hair and tell her she must not leave us; so many have left already, and we cannot lose one more. When the Russians come to the flat they peer in at her and we say *typhus* and we say *diphtheria*, which are words we know they know, and we drag our fingers across our throats, and they do not stay.

The first thing Sieglinde asks for is her ledger. She runs her finger down the columns, reminding herself of the items they describe, resurrecting home. She fills the bare bedroom with the ghosts of vases, clocks, scissors, shoes, and when she reaches the empty section at the back, where she has stored her father's excised words, she moves the little scraps of paper around the page, trying to make sense of them, trying to put them into some kind of order. What had Vati said that final night, just before the siren sounded, when she opened the King Frederick cake tin and showed him the words inside? *We'll burn them.* But she had pushed them into her pocket, and they had fallen with her when the building fell, and they were buried with her when she was buried, and dug up again when she was rescued, and she had forgotten all about them until she put her hand into her pocket at the theatre and there they were, deep in the crease of the seam, catching under her nails: *love, sorrow, surrender, promise.* She knows she should have rid herself of them, burnt them, as Vati said – and there have been so many opportunities; so many fires – but here they still are, toppled across her lap like tiny bricks. And she cannot disentangle the memory of the opening of the tin from the memory of the siren, and the look on Vati's face, and the falling of the building, and it is as if she pushed those things deep into her pocket too, and carried them with her: the siren, and Vati's fear, and the great plunge into black. She should not have kept the words; she should have returned them to Vati as soon as she found them lodged in his trouser-cuff, and he would have dealt with them, and everything would have been different. She remembers what he told her that day at the zoo, when she asked him about his work: *I make things safe. I take dangerous things away, so they won't be dangerous any more.* Why had she run away the night the building fell? Why had she not stayed sitting on the whitewashed kerb, waiting for Herr Metzger to come and put a blanket around her shoulders? She can feel Kurt tugging at her hem, trying to get her attention. She shuts her eyes and she is back in the theatre, back on the stage, and the men are reaching for her with their arms full of time, and they are opening the bottle and drinking its colourless contents, and they make her drink it too, and it is fire inside her. And when she sleeps now she dreams glassy dreams that will not hold their shape; they splinter and fall and lie sharp-toothed beside her, taking up too much room.

'We must put these things behind us,' says Frau Hummel, sitting on the edge of the bed. 'We must forget them.' And she presents Sieglinde with a tin of herring she has been saving, mashing the fish with a fork and feeding it to her morsel by morsel. Sit up; dry your eyes. There is nobody waiting in the wings.

★

If Erich knew what the men looked like, he could try to find them. He could track them down like Winnetou, following their traces, stealing closer and closer until he snared them and brought them to justice – but Sieglinde says she does not remember their faces and does not remember what happened, and he knows better than to insist. And when he tries to imagine the scene all he sees is a page of holes, the core of the story gone.

Persilscheine

May 1945
Berlin

And so we turn the clock to zero. The fighting may be over but we're still smothering the fires, stamping on the ashes. Every garden is a grave. We live with the lice and the rats; we are nowhere; we are nothing. There are no linden trees on Unter den Linden. We unpick the eagles and the swastikas, we weave our shoes of straw, stitch our shirts of nettles, sew the victors' flags from the rags of our own. When the water supply is restored the Cossacks and Tatars kneel before our flushing toilets and wash themselves. Our skins are packed with dust that we can't rinse away. We surrender our radios, give up our weapons, obey the curfew. We breathe in the smell of our ruin: wet bricks, rust, sodden plaster, charred wood. When the guns sound again we shudder for a moment, but it is only our conquerors rehearsing their parade. We report for work according to our names and we strip our factories bare of all the clever and marvellous things we have made, loading them piece by piece into wagons to be sent east, down to the very last bolt. Every garden is a grave, and every grave is too shallow.

Slowly our daughters emerge, and the roses and jasmine bloom, and the lizards sun themselves in the wreckage, and songbirds return to the city, and every intact bell rings out, but not for us. I did not vote for him, and nor did they, and nor did you. Nobody speaks his name any more; he is the black sheep, the family disgrace, though we miss him, we miss him, and cannot say that we miss him – but we are discovering relatives we never knew we had: second-cousin Rachel, Great-Onkel Chaim. Glorious unwritten pages in our history, pages that never will be written. The cathedrals were tricks of the light. These days it is hard to keep clean, but out in the streets we begin to tidy up; we make chains of ourselves, passing the pieces of our homes from hand to hand, counting our blessings. We couldn't leave even if we wanted to; there are no passenger trains and no petrol. But look, we say: the people in the rear flats have a view of the Ku'damm. Now that the war is over, let's travel the whole of the German Reich. And what shall we do in the afternoon? We don't know it yet, but the hunger year is coming: we will eat the leaves off the trees and we will eat grass, just like the animals they say we are. Our hands we clasp, our heads we sink.

Erich and Sieglinde try to do their part, knocking the mortar off salvaged bricks alongside all the women; the Americans let them help as long as they don't get in the way. They walk down roads that are ribbons of rubble; on some houses it reaches as high as the first floor and the front doors are buried shut. They launch themselves from rubble mountains, arms spread like wings, and hardly feel the jolt in their bones when they land. I watch them from blackened rooms, this rubble girl, this rubble boy; they have no tools but they pound brick against brick, pulling out the whole ones that can be used again, every so often catching sight of a mangled sleeve or a ripped shoe and looking away. What will happen to all the broken things that cannot be fixed? They will not be wasted; nothing is wasted. In a few years the Teufelsberg will rise up amongst the Grunewald trees. It might be scrap through and through, this devil's mountain – broken bottles and twisted gates, smashed tiles and rusted springs, torn sleeves, torn shoes – but in time it will grow grass and flowers, and in summer people will bring their picnic baskets there, and in winter their skis and sleds.

One day, when he is picking through the ruins, Erich sees something glinting in the ground at his feet. He digs at it with a piece of pipe and out it leaps: a tiny lead soldier, the same as the ones Mama made him throw into the lake. It leaves behind an imprint of its body, a corrugated hollow so detailed he can see the laces on the boots, the hands on the rifle. In a thousand years, he thinks, when dust and ashes have filled the hole, another boy might be digging at the same spot and find a copy of the soldier, a calcified double, and he will prise it from the earth and wonder at the tiny man made of stone.

'I had a whole set of these,' he says.

Sieglinde nods, chipping off slabs of mortar that thud to the ground and raise grey dust. 'So did Jürgen.'

'Mama got rid of them.' His voice is soft as he turns the toy soldier over and over in his palm. 'She should have told me,' he says. 'They should have told me I wasn't theirs.'

'She did tell you,' says Sieglinde.

'Only because Heinz Kuppel told me first.'

'What did she say, exactly?'

'That I was the child they were meant to have.'

They stack their cleaned bricks into piles for the rubble women to load onto wagons. Their faces and hands are grey with dust, as grey as the broken children holding up the façade of Tante Hannelore's building. Sieglinde ignores a group of Russian soldiers when they pass by, keeping her head down, her eyes on her work.

'Hello Fräulein,' they say, but she does not reply, and when they touch her shoulder, tug at her sleeve, she simply turns away and keeps working. The chunks of mortar rain down.

'Leave her alone,' says Erich, his voice high and tremulous, a leaf in the wind. 'Don't touch her.'

And are these the ones? Are these the men who kicked in the theatre doors, broke the bottle off at the neck? They laugh, clap Erich across the back. 'Good little brother,' they say.

On the way home they pass signs nailed to trees advising the private addresses of functioning telephones, in case of emergency – but there is nobody to call. Sieglinde takes Erich's hand and does not let it go.

★

FRAU MILLER:	I dream of bricks, you know. Of piles and piles of bricks that never grow any smaller. One thousand by one thousand by one thousand.
FRAU MÜLLER:	I don't think I dream at all. I can't remember.
FRAU MILLER:	I found a dead horse in the street yesterday. Well, as good as dead. I cut some meat from it and took it home and when I returned only bones remained.
FRAU MÜLLER:	I saw the bones. People were fighting over them for the marrow. I saw a woman take the tibia, I believe it was, and strike another woman with it.

FRAU MILLER:	How dreadful. Did you . . . did you see the face of this woman who struck the other woman with the fibula?
FRAU MÜLLER:	The tibia.
FRAU MILLER:	The tibia.
FRAU MÜLLER:	Yes, I saw her face – as clearly as I see your face now, if you understand what I mean.
FRAU MILLER:	I believe I do, but I'm sure you did not witness the entire incident. I'm sure the woman concerned was only protecting herself and her family.
FRAU MÜLLER:	With the thighbone of a horse? Are we cave people? Are we savages?
FRAU MILLER:	I don't believe cave people kept horses, Frau Müller. They ate them, perhaps, but I think you'll find, if you check the history books, that the horse was not domesticated at that time.
FRAU MÜLLER:	My point, though, is that we cannot go around hitting each other with tibias.
FRAU MILLER:	Fibulas.
FRAU MÜLLER:	Fibulas. We are not savages. We are not monsters. If you must supplement your rations, go to Potsdamer Platz. Sell your mink. Sell your Meissen.

★

At Potsdamer Platz you can buy anything: minks and Meissen, silverware, cognac, chocolate, silk underwear, cigarettes rolled from the ends of other cigarettes. The vendors offer their wares in the latticed shadow of Haus

311

Vaterland, which once held the world. *Who is guilty?* say the posters nailed to the ruins. *You watched in silence. Why no word of protest? These shameful deeds: your fault!*

'What are you looking for?' a man asks Sieglinde and Erich. He has straight dark hair and blue eyes and wears the brim of his hat turned down.

'I want to sell these,' says Sieglinde, taking a handkerchief from her pocket and unwrapping her father's deleted words.

The man sifts through them, shaking his head. 'Not much demand any more,' he says. 'To be honest, they're not worth the paper they're printed on.'

Erich is staring at him and he pulls his hat down a little further.

'Are you sure?' says Sieglinde, lowering her voice. 'Mutti told me she'd give anything to fill the holes in her books.'

The man shrugs. 'You should have come a year ago. It was a different story then.'

Erich is still staring at him, his eyes flicking from his face to his hair to his trembling left hand.

'Is something the matter?' says the man.

'I . . . you remind me of someone,' says Erich.

'I hear that a lot,' says the man.

As they walk away Erich keeps looking back over his shoulder. 'I think it's him,' he says.

'Who?' Sieglinde is folding the handkerchief away, tucking it back into her pocket. 'Careful,' she says as Erich catches his toe on a dislodged cobblestone. 'Watch where you're going.'

'*Him.*'

Sieglinde turns to look back now too, but the man has disappeared into the crowd. 'You think he's alive?'

'Maybe,' says Erich. 'He wouldn't leave us, I know he wouldn't leave us.'

'He'd be in disguise, though,' says Sieglinde. 'A beard, a pair of glasses . . .'

They study the face of each man they pass, but they agree: he would not look like himself any more. He could be anyone.

★

Why can I not leave them? Erich and Sieglinde, Frau Hummel and Herr Fromm: a family of strangers living in someone else's house. Why can I not look away? I sit with them in the evenings when they eat their bread and fat; I cheer with them when the electricity returns, when the water comes stuttering out of the tap. I keep an eye on their tobacco plants growing on the terrace and cross my fingers for a good price. I know I am pretending. I know I am not one of them. Sometimes I want to kick at the walls until they come tumbling down; I want to set their borrowed rooms ablaze . . . and then I see Frau Hummel's swelling waist, and I hear the ticking of the child inside her taking form. I keep waiting for her to rid herself of it – the abortionists are doing a roaring trade – but the months pass and the weather turns and she does nothing, and doing nothing is doing something, after all; doing nothing is making a choice. We could all remain here, couldn't we, our little family? Tante Hannelore is not coming back, and her sons are in prison with the other fathers and sons, and there is no telling when they will come home. Yes, we could stay here forever, mother, father, brother, sister, and in February a baby to rock and wash and wonder at, a little life to love, a blank book. I hold up the broken windows with my broken arms.

She finds us, of course; in the dead of winter Mama

313

finds us. (Why did I think she would not look?) Papa is lost in Russia and the bronze head is at the bottom of the lake and even the foreign workers have left her: Erich is all she has. When the letter arrives from the Red Cross he has to change his story. He was mistaken, he says; he thought she was dead, killed in a raid on Leipzig, but he was wrong, and here is the proof: a note in her handwriting, sent to a son she also thought lost. He should not have given up hope and he should not have left the farm to come to Berlin and fight for the Führer – but Frau Hummel says none of that matters now, all that matters is that Mama is alive, which is a miracle, and we are grateful for miracles, and Erich can go home, and how many can say that? Mama wants him to come back and feed Ronja her favourite apples; she wants him to heat pfennigs on the oven and press them to the windows to make peepholes in the frozen glass. *You are my only child*, she writes. And this is why I cannot leave, and this is why I cannot look away.

'Come with me, Siggi,' says Erich. 'Mama wouldn't mind, I know she wouldn't.' They could go swimming in the lake in summer, and skating in winter, and he could show her where to find the juiciest mushrooms, and let her taste milk straight from the cow and honey straight from the hive.

But Frau Hummel says no; Siggi is her responsibility now, and she cannot allow it.

'I'll come and visit one day, though,' says Sieglinde. 'And you must promise you'll come back to me. Promise.'

★

When Emilie sees him step down from the train she does not run to him; she does not sweep him into her arms and cover his face with kisses. She stands quite still, watching him scan the platform for her. Almost a year has passed since he disappeared, and he is taller and darker, his pale hair deepened to tallow. His eyes alight on her for a moment and then move away, searching for the mother he left behind. Is she really so different? I see her taking off her headscarf and calling to him, and he sees her then, and when they embrace she feels a low, quiet hum in him, something that has survived the winter, and when he whispers, 'Hello, Mama,' his voice thrums against her ear like little wings – but inside her still, the frozen lake and all it holds.

'I told the bees you were dead,' she says.

She forbids him to write to anyone in Berlin as punishment for running away. 'How do I know you won't leave again?' she says.

★

The hives are waiting for Erich when he returns to the orchard; I watch them standing their ground, open-mouthed, their wooden eyes fixed on him. He shakes the apple-tree branches free of their snowy load so they do not break, and for a moment he is caught in a blizzard of his own making, and the figures surrounding him could be his parents and Tante Uschi, Frau Hummel and Herr Fromm – and Sieglinde, his Siggi, a shadow trapped in the shimmer of dust. And then the loosed snow settles, and the hives begin to tell their stories once more, and Erich stands and listens and tries, as always, to follow them: *Of course my mother pleaded with me, sweet-stained fingers already dead beside me. A good man, a kind man, my cousin loved the knife, ash-handled . . .*

'Please!' he says. 'Please! You're making no sense!'

But on they chatter, the words merging into one long chord, filling the white orchard. In his pocket his fingers close around the little scrap of paper Siggi gave him when he left Berlin. He does not need to read it to know what it says, and as the hives babble and hum he repeats the single word to himself, and so do I: *promise, promise, promise.*

★

Even though Erich cannot write to Siggi, Siggi writes to him. One after another the letters arrive; I see Emilie slipping them into her apron pocket and then, when Erich has gone to bed, opening them and reading them. She is a polite girl, this Sieglinde, always signing off by sending her greetings to both Erich and his mother.

But that is not the point.

After Emilie has read the letters she folds them up again, along their original creases, and puts them back in their envelopes. And then she feeds them to the fire.

And in our lakes and rivers the lightning bolts and skulls, and beneath our gardens the pins and medals and heads, and the little lead men in their lead uniforms, and on our bonfires the photographs, and yes, the names, too; the Adolfs and the Adolphs and the Hillers and the Hiedlers curling at the edges, going up in smoke. Our clothes are cut down to size, field grey, marine blue, marked with the ghosts of eagles. We are only living shadows – the remains of a dead era. The Reichsmarschall grows thinner by the day; he bites on poison and slips the noose, but they bring him to the foot of the gallows all the same. We will watch the films, we will visit the camps and we will answer the questions. Did we ever belong to the NSDAP? Did we ever donate to the NSDAP? Were we ever members of the National Socialist Doctors' League? The National Socialist Students' League? The National Socialist Women's League? No, no, no, no and no. Stamp the forms. Sign off on the past. This is our evidence: we saw nothing and we heard nothing, we did not know, how could we have known? Despite the bones in the foundations, the children in the walls, this is our story. We chip away at the bricks, the whole ashen city rings with the sound of our hammers and chisels, we hardly flinch when a buried bomb explodes. And the hunger year comes, and we do eat the leaves off the trees, and we do eat grass, but we are not animals and we did not know.

The Wish Child

1955
West Berlin

For some years, Sieglinde noticed, certain words were no longer spoken – certain words and certain names – in case they flew from the mouth and joined into sentences, rebuilt themselves into something that should remain broken. The days were blue and gold, blue and green, and the city was rising, beating the ash from its wings; how carefully we were putting ourselves back together! Trees were regenerating and houses too, and so were bankers and librarians, mothers and mayors, bus conductors, shop keepers, doctors, none of whom had ever been Nazis. In her history lectures at the new university in Dahlem, Sieglinde learned of the Gutenberg Bible and the Thirty Years' War, the Prussian kings and the Year of the Three Emperors, but nothing about *him*, nothing about *them*; the textbooks stopped at 1913. After she graduated she took up a position at the Dahlem archives, which held antique maps and court proceedings, and letters written by royal hands, but she knew there were newer documents too, locked away, uncatalogued and undiscussed; great cairns of paper that could bury a person if disturbed. Sometimes, if she looked into the faces of children born soon after the war – if she studied, for instance, the face of Melanie, Frau Hummel's daughter – Sieglinde thought she could glimpse that more recent history: high cheekbones, Slavic eyes. She remembered other faces then, and felt the sweat falling from their brows to hers, and the scratch of sour uniforms against her wrists, and she tasted the fermented breath forcing its way into her mouth. She heard the sound of a bottle breaking at the neck, and the ticking of the watches wrapped like tourniquets around rough arms, so much time, so many minutes ticking away while the men took their time with her, the radium faces and radium hands glowing in the dim theatre, and afterwards, her whole life long, she would always be running late because she could not bear the feel of a watch about her wrist. She remembered Erich's face, too, leaning over her after the men had left, and his voice talking to her in a language she did not understand. He pulled the broken bottle from her and wrapped her in the velvet curtain and her mother's fox fur, and the fox watched with its bead-glass eyes and said *This did not happen. This is not real.*

Nothing would ever grow inside her: that was what the doctor who examined her had said. Frau Hummel stood at the side of the bed and wept, but it was not until a few years later that Sieglinde understood why.

'You're lucky,' a friend said. 'You don't have to be careful like other girls.'

Not damaged, then, but free. She supposed she could see it that way – had to see it that way – and when she told Jonathan he said that it didn't matter, that they could be a family of two. She met him at the Ballhaus Resi, where the tinted fountains danced in time to the music: a tall, broad man with toffee-coloured eyes, English skin and thick black hair. The Resi was where Allied men stationed in Berlin came on their free nights; wherever you turned

322

you could hear conversations in broken German and broken English and see people waving their hands about, searching for the right word. Jonathan spoke excellent German, though with a trace of a Bavarian accent – the German master at his boarding school in Kent had fled Munich in 1933. He wore a carefully pressed suit and his hand at the small of Sieglinde's back directed her with the lightest of touches. *When the white lilac blooms again, I'll sing you my prettiest love song.*

'Shouldn't you be sharing yourself around?' she said, aware of glances from the women obliged to dance with each other.

'Probably,' he said, and stayed with her. *In Capri, when the red sun sinks into the sea, and the pale sickle moon gleams in the sky . . .*

At first she had not noticed his slight limp, and when she trod on his foot and he did not react she thought he was simply being polite.

'I'm sorry,' she said. 'I'm out of practice.'

'Didn't feel a thing,' he said.

'I'm sure that's not true.'

'No, honestly. It's artificial.'

'Oh.'

'I left the real one behind in Crete.'

'Oh.' His eyes were on her, waiting. *Turn around once more before we go our separate ways, and tell me why you don't want to see me again.* She said, 'That was careless.'

'It was,' he agreed. 'I don't know what I was thinking.'

★

'You didn't tell me he's English!' Frau Hummel hissed in the kitchen.

'Didn't I?' said Sieglinde. 'I must have forgotten.'

'How can you forget something like that?' Frau Hummel stabbed a knife into a plum Streuselkuchen, dumped a few slices on a platter. 'You can't just forget.'

Sieglinde put the coffee pot on a tray and Melanie went to the cupboard to get the good cake plates.

'Not those,' said Frau Hummel. 'Use the blue ones.'

'But they're all chipped, Mutti.'

'Mm.'

Jonathan jumped up as they brought the tray into the living room. 'Let me help,' he said.

'We can manage,' said Frau Hummel.

'It's no trouble —'

'Stay where you are.'

'Thank you, though,' said Melanie.

'Yes, thank you,' said Sieglinde. He is too handsome for me, she thought – but as he sat back down on the sofa and crossed his legs she caught sight of the strap holding his artificial foot in place, and she saw him tug at the cuff of his trousers to hide it, and she knew she could love him.

'I don't think your aunt likes me very much,' he said later, when they were alone.

'My aunt?'

'I thought you said you lived with your aunt.'

'Oh – no. I live in her apartment. She died in the war.'

'Who's Frau Hummel, then?'

'She looked after me when . . . when my building was hit. There was nobody else left. We just stayed together – I helped her with Melanie – you know.'

He nodded. The coals in the tiled stove hissed and popped. 'Do you have any photographs of them, of your family?'

She shook her head. 'No,' she said, 'but wait a minute.'

In her bedroom she took her mother's ledger from its drawer, lifting it from its cradle of soft jumpers and cardigans. She felt something tugging at the hem of her skirt – had she caught it on a nail? Stepped on an unravelled thread? But there was nothing there.

She sat next to Jonathan and they leafed through the eggshell-white pages together, she describing for him the belongings listed in her mother's hand, and as she spoke the grandfather clock and the cherrywood sideboard and the green coffee cups and the little brooch made from Vati's baby teeth rose from the ink and filled the room.

1957
West Berlin

Each evening before supper, when, she imagined, other young wives were bathing babies or sterilising bottles or reading bedtime stories, Sieglinde worked on her puzzles. She always had a jigsaw in progress on the dining table and she sat and fiddled with it while Jonathan brought bread and cheeses and meats from the kitchen and set them along the periphery of her unfinished scenes. They lay between them as they ate, these scattered places, upside down to him, she knew, like a reflection in a lake.

'Where are we now?' he asked when a new puzzle appeared, gesturing with his fork.

'The eighteenth century,' she said. 'Just in front of the Doge's palace.'

'Tricky,' he said, twisting his head to see. 'The sky's the same colour as the water.'

After supper she laid out her clothes for the following day. It was a habit Jonathan observed without comment now, though in the early months of their marriage he had joked about German efficiency. No, she had told him, not that – it was in case she had to get dressed in the dark in a hurry; in case there was an emergency. When everything was ready – underwear, skirt, blouse, cardigan, shoes, all arranged like a flattened self – she clipped the crossword from the newspaper and stretched out on the sofa with a small dish of peppermints or sugared almonds. Letter by letter she inserted the answers to the clues, each one slotting into its place in the grid. She felt a flurry in her chest when one of her father's deleted words appeared; these were as familiar to her as certain names, and she still had all the little scraps of paper she had found in his trouser-cuffs – all except the one she had slipped into Erich's pocket when he kissed her goodbye at the train station. *Promise you'll come back*, she had said. *Promise*. Rain was pelting the roof and the platform was jammed with people and he stood so close to her that she could smell the damp wool of his overcoat and the clean soapy scent of his hair. He had black lines of boot polish under his fingernails despite Frau Hummel making him scrub them with her nail brush: *We can't have your mama thinking we didn't look after you.* He squeezed Sieglinde's hand and said *I promise*, and then he boarded the train with all the other travellers trying to find their way home and was lost behind the rainy windows. She hadn't heard from him since, even though she had written him dozens of letters. *I am studying history. I think I want to be an archivist. Herr Fromm died this week – they say it was his blood pressure. I'd love to come and see your lake, and look for the giant carp. I am marrying an Englishman.*

Sometimes Jonathan came and joined her on the sofa, lifting up her feet and putting them in his lap and then scanning the newspaper. If part of a story was missing, its remainder on the back of the clipped-out puzzle, he read the first half to her and then added possible endings, inventing lightning strikes and locust plagues until she laughed and held up the corresponding piece for him to see. One night he started to read an article to her about a bog body – the remains of an Iron Age child found in the 1920s.

'Kayhausen Boy,' she said. 'I know him. I used to have a book about him.'

She turned over her puzzle and there he was in her lap, his skin welted by the pressure of her pen. The photograph was the same as one in Julia's book, but they knew more about him now: they had X-rayed him, teased out the traces of old illness, the faults in his bones. Here was the cause of his uneven gait, and here the proof that he died in a cold season: two appleseeds from his last meal.

'The reason for his death remains unclear, however,' read Jonathan. 'Was he a criminal, or the victim of a crime? A sacrifice offered to the gods despite his deformity,' he reached for Sieglinde's piece of paper, 'or because of it?'

The next day they visited their garden allotment. There were more than two hundred plots tucked in next to the S-Bahn tracks, and from the train they looked like a toy village, the paths making neat little shingle streets, each piece of land occupied by a tiny house complete with shutters and window boxes. Jonathan and Sieglinde came here on the weekends to tend their fruit trees and vegetables, and today there was a bag of pears waiting for them on their doorstep; a present from the widow who owned the adjoining garden. They often passed the time of day with her and the other neighbours, chatting over the fence about the hardiest varieties of climbing roses or the best time of year to prune a weeping cherry, but nobody ever asked about missing husbands, missing children. The fact of Jonathan's Englishness was avoided too, for the most part; only one or two of the older neighbours refused to speak to him. Sieglinde tipped the pears into a bowl and arranged it on the dining table – a battered office desk, but it looked pretty covered with a cloth and decorated with a vase of flowers. She had sewn lace curtains for the windows and braided a rug for the floor from scraps of cloth, and Jonathan had painted the walls the same shade of yellow as the chrysanthemums that grew by the gate. A pair of deep armchairs sat in front of the fireplace, and on the wall a calendar showed castles of the Rhine.

Jonathan took the ladder from the back of the house and began picking apples while Sieglinde collected fallen walnuts, their hulls split apart and turning black. She prised them open and picked out the meat, taking care not to crack the shells, which she stacked next to her on the grass.

'You're only going to throw them away,' called Jonathan.

'I know,' she said. He was a dark shape above her in the apple tree, backlit against the pale autumn sky.

'When I was little,' she heard him say, 'my Irish grandmother showed me a tiny pair of gloves from Limerick. They were made from the skin of a stillborn calf and you could only wear them two or three times – the leather was that fine. They came inside a walnut shell.'

'People were smaller then,' said Sieglinde.

Jonathan climbed higher and higher. 'We could stay here forever,' he said.

'We could,' said Sieglinde, squinting up into the branches.

She remembered lying in her bed and listening for the sound of planes, the book about Kayhausen Boy propped open on her chest of drawers. She remembered the peaty smell of the pages, and tracing the boy's shape with one outstretched finger, and listening. The pieces of shrapnel shivered on their threads. *It's gruesome,* said her mother. Jonathan was calling something to her but she felt herself sinking into a swamp, wet earth closing around her, already dissolving her bones, turning her skin to leather.

And who will dig her up? Who will find her and name her and decide: criminal, victim, sacrifice?

Only now and then did she catch herself wondering what her children might have been like. She could almost see them, little figures running on ahead of her, never quite turning back to look her in the face. Did they have Kurt's curls? Would they lace and unlace their fingers as she sang the song about the lovesick sailor, their hands encircling the world, clasping the heart, making the noose? On they ran, Sieglinde's children, into the smoke and the ruins, to where the rest of her family lay. Yes, she thought, they looked like her baby brother – a little like Kurt, and a little like Erich.

Erich. Over a decade later, she still thought about him, though she no longer wrote him letters: a choice is made, and first love fades, and the heart beds down in its basket of bones. At times she wondered whether she had invented him – a friend to wait with as the fighting grew closer and closer. Frau Hummel seemed not to remember him at all.

'The boy who brought me to you,' said Sieglinde. 'Erich Kröning.'

'It was so untidy then,' said Frau Hummel. 'So many people on the move. It's hard to recall what happened.'

'He lived with us, though. He sheltered with me in the theatre, and then he brought me to you. He stayed with us for months.'

'It's best not to think about that time,' said Frau Hummel. 'It's best forgotten.' Burn it, bury it, sink it in the lake.

But Sieglinde did not forget, and even as she lay next to Jonathan, Erich returned to her from the shadowy theatre, his pale yellow hair glinting beneath layers of costumes. He watched her from dreams, slender fingers spinning and spinning the paper discs pencilled with riderless horses and riders suspended in mid-air, bare trees and clouds of green leaves, and when he smiled at her she caught a glimpse of the one tooth that sat a little sideways, and when he turned away she saw on his left temple the freckle shaped like a comma, the suggestion of something still to come. And even as the years passed, in these moments she was not an adult recalling a child – not a woman of twenty-five, thirty, forty remembering a distant playmate – but a girl of twelve, and she could see herself in that twilight too, there on the dusty stage, the curtains hushing as they closed. *Shh, shhhh.*

April 1976
East Berlin

Outside the Palace of the Republic, the women wait. They squint up at the slick façade, the thousand mirrored windows turning the air above the crowd to bronze. The whole building seems to quiver. Nearby the old cathedral hunches beneath its scaffolds and the television tower points to heaven.

When the doors open on this first day, the women cannot believe their eyes: the great glass flower spreads it glass petals, and marble walls and marble floors shimmer beneath countless bubbles of light; they have never seen so much light.

FRAU MILLER:	Is it real?
FRAU MÜLLER:	What do you mean?
FRAU MILLER:	All this polished marble.
FRAU MÜLLER:	Of course it's real. Can't you see yourself in it?
FRAU MILLER:	But we don't have marble here. It must have come from somewhere else.
FRAU MÜLLER:	Somewhere else?
FRAU MILLER:	Over there.
FRAU MÜLLER:	I doubt the Party would approve that.
FRAU MILLER:	Perhaps it's not real, then. They must have made it specially.

All day the women wonder about it – but they do agree, they are lucky to be living in this place, where everything seems so real.

Erich is here too; he has brought his daughters to Berlin for the day, to celebrate the Palace's grand opening. Their mother Bettina has a cold and has stayed at home in Leipzig – 'but I'll send you a postcard, Mama,' said Steffi as she blew her a kiss goodbye. 'I'll find one with the Palace on it.'

'Thank you, Schatz,' said Bettina. 'I'd like that.'

'We'll be home by tonight, stupid,' said Karin.

'It doesn't matter,' said Bettina. 'I'd still love a postcard of the Palace.'

The April morning is cool, and coal dust hangs in the air and smears the sky a dirty orange.

'It doesn't look like a palace,' says Karin as they wait in line.

'Where are the turrets?' says Steffi. 'For the princesses?'

'It's not that kind of palace, Schätzchen,' says Erich.

The first thing the girls want to see is the bowling alley. The lanes are as bright as rivers, and when the balls skim the waxed wood it sounds like a dozen trains approaching at once – and then, like magic, the balls pass beneath the floor and return to the bowlers, a never-ending supply. Karin puts her hand into the hole to find out how it works, to feel for the trick – and before Erich can warn her a ball has squashed her fingers.

'Let me see,' he says. 'Mmm. I think we'll have to amputate at the shoulder. You won't be able to swim in straight lines any more. What do you think, Doctor Steffi?'

'At least the shoulder,' she says. 'Even a bit higher.'

'It's a terrible shame,' says Erich.

'Very very sad,' says Steffi.

'You're both dumb,' says Karin.

The refreshment bar is a perfect circle.

'So nobody's served ahead of anybody else,' says Karin, and Erich says yes, perhaps.

The girls have a Vita Cola each, which makes them burp, which makes them giggle, and then they buy a postcard to send to Mama.

'Tell her about all the lights!' says Karin. 'And the Toilettenfrau!'

They sit in the vast white foyer on one of the sofas that stretches on forever before it turns a corner; there is room for half a dozen families at least, including grandparents. Two women sit to their right, wondering whether something is real or not; Erich can't quite hear.

Before they leave they look at the paintings, Erich and his daughters and Frau Miller and Frau Müller: larger than life, the youth of the world fly red banners, and the ruined Frauenkirche looms against the red sky, and a white sheet covers the fighter's body, and books burn, and Icarus glides higher and higher while a pilot falls from a plane. The way the earth is now is not the way the earth must remain.

Er Ich

1980
Leipzig

At the hospital a girl with light-brown hair and green eyes waits with her father, one arm in a sling. Erich blinks, blinks again – but of course, it cannot be Sieglinde. It still happens from time to time: he catches sight of her on the train, or in a passing car, or reflected in a shop window – and yes, sometimes in the faces of the patients who come to him with their breaks and cuts.

'What have you been up to?' he asks, gently unpinning the sling and checking the girl's swollen wrist.

'I fell off the beam,' she says. 'I wasn't concentrating.'

'The trials are in three weeks,' says her father, gripping her good hand.

'Trials?'

'She's the next Comăneci – that's what everyone's saying. Is it broken?'

'We'll need an X-ray,' says Erich, 'but it looks like a sprain, at this stage, rather than a break.'

'That's good,' says the girl.

'Good?' says the man, who may not be her father after all. 'Good?'

Erich pins up the sling again. 'Let's just wait for the X-ray.'

He sees her on television some months later, competing

at the Moscow Olympics; she flips and coils across the screen, as supple as a fish.

'Papa, Mama, watch us,' cry Karin and Steffi as they dance around the living room, vaulting over chairs and balancing on tiptoes. The girl who looks like Sieglinde is making her final dismount, pausing for a split second to steady herself when she lands, and Erich is back in Berlin: he and Siggi are scaling the rubble piles, daring one another to climb higher, higher, and Frau Hummel is calling *you'll break your necks, you'll kill yourselves* – but when they jump it feels like flying.

He does not tell his wife and daughters that he treated the girl on the television, and as the footage replays she really is Sieglinde, whole and undamaged, leaping through the years to him. She twists in slow motion, a bright souvenir he has never let go. He thinks of his grandfather's wooden hives, the carved likeness of Luise, Opa Kröning's first love. We fashion simulacra of those we have lost and keep them as charms against time; we fill them with swarms of memory, clear-winged and sweet.

Karin and Steffi are bowing now and Bettina is applauding.

'How many points?' they ask. 'Who wins?'

'It's a draw,' says Erich.

'We couldn't possibly decide,' says Bettina.

They have their mother's auburn hair and pale complexion; he sees nothing of himself in them, though every now and then Bettina identifies certain mannerisms that come from the Kröning side: the way Steffi laughs, the way Karin tilts her head.

'You forget,' Erich tells her, 'I'm not really a Kröning.'

'And thank God for that,' says Bettina.

She has met Erich's mother only once, on their wedding

day, and refuses to allow the girls to visit her. *That woman*, she calls her. *That Nazi.* Erich does not argue.

In the evening, when Karin and Steffi are cleaning their teeth and putting on their pyjamas, Bettina says, 'The next Olympics are in Los Angeles.'

'Oh?' says Erich. The news is droning away on the television: this foreign dignitary visited that factory, which has far exceeded its target output; this local dignitary opened that new block of flats, which will offer families in Marzahn a modern and cheerful home.

'That's how we do it, comrade. We train the girls up to Olympic standard and accompany them as their coaches.'

He knows she is joking; it's one of their games, devising ways to escape across the border. All the same, he motions to her to keep her voice down – even in their own home, even in their bed, someone could be listening. Best to speak in code or over rushing water; best to tune the radio to nothing. Once, years ago at a student café, he noticed a woman at the next table making notes while he and Bettina, tipsy on birthday Rotkäppchen, sketched their plans in the air: a giant catapult made from rubber bands, a jetpack powered by pickled onions, a pair of telescopic stilts. And occasionally, too, he has noticed a click on the telephone, a man shadowing him in the street or watching from a doorway: it is hard to be alone here.

When Karin and Steffi are in bed they ask Erich for a story. He recalls for a moment the one his grandmother told him about the castle with the murder hole and the stumbling steps, the narrow notches from which arrows flew like curses, the many ways of keeping people out – but instead he tells them this:

There was once a boy who kept a fish in the bathtub – a carp he bought with his mother at the market. At first it seemed the same as any other fish, but although the boy did not feed it, it grew by the day, and soon it was so big that it could not turn around, and then it was so big that it filled the entire tub. Its scales were great silver coins and its tail jutted from the water like the fan of a Spanish lady. The boy's mother seemed afraid of the fish and stood at the bathroom door and would not enter. Normally nothing could frighten her, neither the lightning that tore through the sky in summer, nor the headless hens that for a few bloody moments survived the fall of her axe, nor even the stories of children bricked up behind walls. But the eyes of the fish were as fat as the candles she lit under the teapot, and in certain lights she said she glimpsed a flame in them also, something wise or something wicked; it was not clear which.

'What are we going to do with this monster?' she asked.

Plainly the fish could not stay; by now its gills rose above the water whenever it tried to move, cuts that would not heal.

'We could take him to the lake,' said the boy.

'Yes,' said his mother. 'Yes, that is what we'll do.'

Already she seemed less afraid, but the boy's father said, 'The lake is frozen.' And the boy and his mother looked at each other – it was December, of course! How had they forgotten the winter?

That night the boy could not sleep. He thought he could hear the fish gasping, but told himself it was just the wind shifting in the pine trees, pouring in and out of the mouths of the wooden hives. He opened the shutters and lay looking at the night, the frost casting its crooked spines across the windowpane. At some dark hour – he did not know when – he awoke and saw yellow lights moving in the distance, and he thought of a story he'd read about a little bird who mistakes a wolf's eyes for friendly lanterns. No, he told himself. No, the lights were not the eyes of something untamed and vicious approaching the house, but simply passing travellers finding their way. He closed the shutters and fell asleep, and his dreams were as light as the mists that ringed the lake on winter mornings, and when dawn came he knew how he could save the carp. He took his father to the lake – it was not far away – and walked out on the ice, carrying candles to the frozen centre, where the water was deepest. He had made them himself from beeswax: stubby little nuggets that would not take long to burn down. He had to go alone, as the ice would not hold his father's weight, and with every step he listened for cracks, for the sound of distant, broken bells that called out cold disaster. When he reached the centre he lit the candles, placed them in a ring, then stepped back and waited.

'Is all well?' cried his father.

'All is well,' cried the boy, the words a jumbled echo. Before him the candles began to tilt and to topple, to sink into the ice like suns until they vanished beneath the white horizon, and he took his chisel and gouged an opening, following the ring made by the flames. He and his father returned home then, and together they lifted the fish onto the back of the hay wagon. His mother watched from a distance, pacing, lacing and unlacing her fingers.

'Don't hurt yourselves,' she warned. 'It's too heavy, you'll injure yourselves. You should kill it instead, kill it and eat it. Yes, that would be for the best. Look at its teeth. It means you harm.'

But the boy and his father readied their horse and jumped into the wagon, and the boy sat on the back of the fish while his father urged the horse to run faster, faster, and beneath the boy the great cold creature opened and closed its mouth and thrashed its tail. When they reached the lake it began to buck and writhe, and the boy and his father lifted it from the wagon and pushed it out across the frozen surface. It seemed to sense the opening in the ice and slid towards it, the boy following behind and giving it a push when it started to slow. A few metres from the hole he gave it one last shove, and it slipped away from him and disappeared into the water with barely a splash.

'Well?' said his mother when they returned home.

'It's gone,' said his father.

And she began to weep.

Over the next few weeks the boy returned to the lake each day, watching as the hole in the ice grew smaller and smaller, a cold fontanelle. In his dreams he dropped beneath it, and the carp caught him on its back and took him down to its silty bed, where things lay buried and forgotten, and when he looked up he saw the ice sky was as thick as winter, and he knew he would never go home.

1994
Berlin

They found the bomb when the river fell one dry summer; little by little it showed its hunched back above the silt. It made headlines, this unfinished business, this rusting grudge, and everyone within its imagined reach had to evacuate. Officials checked the streets fanning out from its dark centre, looking in restaurants and flats, libraries and offices, banks and schools for anybody flouting the order to withdraw: *It's for your own safety, madam, sir. Pack a few things – you may need to sleep elsewhere.*

'They're always digging up something,' said the man sitting next to Sieglinde on the bus. 'It's probably a dud.'

He must have been in his seventies, a little older than Sieglinde, and she found herself thinking the question that everybody thought from time to time around such men: *What did you do?* On her lap she held an overnight bag containing the essentials for this small evacuation fifty years distant but too close to home.

As the bus drove by the great concrete cylinder on Dudenstrasse – twelve thousand tonnes of proof that the ground in Berlin could not hold a triumphal arch – the man said, 'I was here at the end. There was nothing left to fight with, but we would have done anything for him. Ja, ja. We would have died for him.'

The other passengers shifted in their seats, coughed, stared out the windows. Neat trees, green squares, unharmed buildings – or at least, so carefully mended you could not tell. It was a different story in the east of the city, in places, but that was being fixed now too: façades restored, cracks plastered over. When Jonathan's nephews and nieces had visited from England, Sieglinde had taken them on trips to Mitte and Friedrichshain, showing them the shrapnel marks and the bullet holes, the houses that still stood open to the sky. She tried to convey to them the extent of the ruin: hundreds of air raids, tens of thousands dead, a third of all homes destroyed. She should have told them instead of the hands and faces smeared with mortar dust; the men who came with stolen watches glinting like rows of moons on their arms; a boy with yellow hair who helped her to her feet and wrapped her in velvet and fur. I saw them riding on her shoulders for decades, these constant ghosts, testing whether she could bear their weight. How long should we bow to the memory of damage?

'All this nonsense,' said the man. 'It's been in the Spree for fifty years.'

Sieglinde nodded, keeping her eyes on her overnight bag. She had seen the stories about other bombs that had surfaced, ploughed up by farmers, exhumed on building sites, caught in fishing nets. A road worker died when his digger struck a mine; a boy lost his hand to a grenade he found in the forest. Fifty years meant nothing: these things were still live.

'Such a performance,' said the man. 'I'm supposed to be taking my grandson to the zoo. It's his birthday.'

Sieglinde nodded again and listed the contents of her overnight bag to herself: one hairbrush, one toothbrush, one tube of toothpaste, one nightdress, one change of clothes, two crossword puzzle books, two cheese sandwiches, an orange, a chocolate bar, a pencil. I have everything I need, she told herself. Here in my lap, right here. I haven't forgotten anything.

'Things were simpler before the Wall came down,' the man went on. 'I can't get from A to B. All this digging.'

Sieglinde did not look at the news that night. The all-clear had been given; she was back home, and in the two-faced city everything had returned to normal. There was no need to watch the footage of the abandoned streets, the empty schools, the shuttered windows, no need to witness the detonation, fire bursting from water, nor hear the applause of the men who stood back and cheered as if it were New Year's Eve. Instead, she sat and thought about the call that had come from the Federal Commissioner: they were assembling a team to work out of an office down near Nuremberg, reconstructing the torn Stasi files. Sixteen thousand sacks, six hundred million scraps of paper. Sieglinde had not responded at first when they asked for expressions of interest; she would have to move away from Berlin, away from her job at the archives and the life she had built with Jonathan. But now – now she thought: I could do that. I would be good at that. Jonathan used to tease her about her endless crosswords and the way she managed to shut out all distractions when she worked on them. Sometimes he wrote extra clues in the margins when she wasn't looking – five across: *name of man you married (8)* – or underlined certain words in the dictionaries she kept in every room. *Antisocial. Obsessive.* He never interfered with the jigsaws that crept across the dining table, though, and took care not to disrupt the little pieces arranged according to colour around the fragmentary alps, sailing ships, waterfalls. She had a knack for it, he admitted: a peculiar ability to lock the sky together, to build a forest from so many scraps of green and black. Sieglinde had thought she would have a good twenty years of retirement with him, going to the Philharmonic and the Staatsoper, visiting the places on the jigsaw boxes. You need to pack up his things, her friends told her. You'll feel better once you've done it. Then you can move on with your life.

She opened Jonathan's cupboards and drawers and began to sort his belongings into boxes; she had been putting it off for months, but now she cleared the bedside cabinet of his bottles of pills, removed his coat from its hook, threw away his toothbrush and his soap. You have to start somewhere, her friends said. An hour or two and it's over. At least he didn't suffer; at least it was sudden. A heart attack at home: that was the best way to go, wasn't it? At the back of a cupboard she found his old artificial foot – the one he had worn when they met at the Ballhaus Resi some forty years earlier. Almost real, it gleamed in the half-light, cool and silky beneath her fingers. Softly she closed the door.

The next day she applied to join the reconstruction team. Perhaps a change of scene was what she needed; she could sublet her apartment, pack away anything precious – and besides, it would only be for the next couple of years, until she retired. There were puzzles to solve; there was blame to lay. Six hundred million pieces of it.

It must be very exciting, her friends said when they phoned to see how she was getting on. You must be finding out all sorts of things. I can't talk about it, said Sieglinde. We have to sign a gag order. Of course, they said, of course; it's highly sensitive information. There was a pause on the line. It is, Sieglinde agreed. Highly sensitive. Another pause. Well, then.

It was true that some of her colleagues were handling material on foreign espionage or the doping of young athletes or the Baader–Meinhof Group – but Sieglinde's friends would be very disappointed if they could read her files. *M. has long straight hair, greying at the temples, and appears older than her age. She habitually wears a red knitted cap, and her favourite item of jewellery is a short string of yellow beads (probably plastic). W. frequents a public house on the corner of Tieck- and Novalisstrasse, where he typically situates himself at the table nearest the door and plays chess with other regulars. In terms of personality, F. appears reserved, polite, able to be influenced.* Don't you want something a bit racier? her colleagues asked. Not at all, she said. I'm happy with my ordinary people. What she did not say was that every day she looked among the ordinary people for him, for Erich. So many times his name seemed to materialise in her hands – er and ich, ich and er, right there in black and white – but they were common words, of course, he and I, I and he, and the name was a common name. And even though she never could piece him back together, still she found satisfaction in the daily sorting of the scraps; a hypnotic peace. You are doing important work, the director said at their staff meetings, and so did the journalists who wrote stories about the reconstruction project. There was even a picture of Sieglinde in a *Spiegel* article with a caption that said as much: she was sitting at her desk, piles of torn paper surrounding her, a serious look on her face. Don't smile, the photographer had said. And can we add some more paper? It doesn't look authentic enough.

347

1995
Leipzig

It was only after Bettina had gone that Karin and Steffi began to ask Erich about his birth family. There wasn't much he could tell them: he was born in Poland, then brought to Germany as an orphan and adopted by the Krönings. There must be records, though, they said. There must be traces. Can't we ask Oma Kröning?

That woman. That Nazi. Since their mother's death they had met their grandmother Emilie a handful of times, but she did not know who they were; memory was retreating from her, certain details blurring. Even when Erich visited, some days she did not recognise his face and did not know his name.

'Gerhard?' she said. 'Christoph? Gustav? It's on the tip of my tongue.'

'This is Erich,' said Tante Uschi. 'He's your son.'

'No,' said Mama, looking him up and down. 'No, he's Polish – but clearly he's of German stock. That's why he was chosen.'

Erich had read just how the choosing was done: children rounded up in the streets like stray dogs, lured with a bit of food, or snatched in the night from their homes, then transported to institutions to be tested and measured before being placed with German families. Piecemeal memories still returned to him: a woman in brown bending to offer him a slice of bread; the callipers at his skull and jaw and legs; a palette of eyes of different colours; the occasional word: *Tatuś, kotek*. But which mother whirled him around in the garden? And which family owned Anka, the black-and-white cat? He was no longer sure. Each time he visited the farmhouse he wanted to tell Tante Uschi that he wouldn't be visiting again, but from the orchard he heard the hives repeating their jumbled stories and he felt his tongue turning to wood. *You-you, you*, called the turtle dove.

'They've all escaped to the West now, anyway,' said Mama, gazing out the window. 'All the Nazis.'

★

One winter's day I see her sit up in bed and ask Erich to take her to the lake. 'My son and I used to go skating there,' she says. 'Tell the nurse we won't be long.'

'Who's the nurse, Mama?'

'She is, of course,' she says, pointing at Uschi. She grabs Erich's hand, pulls him in close. 'She's stealing from me,' she whispers. 'I used to have an amber brooch – a pretty thing in the shape of a flower, with a real diamond at the centre. She's stolen it. You can't trust them, you know.'

'That's your sister,' says Erich. 'That's Ursula. She's looking after you now.'

'It's all right,' says Uschi. 'It's not her fault.'

I see him take his mother's arm and slowly they make their way along the path behind the house. The air is still and bright and turns their voices to glass, and in the orchard the mouths of the hives glitter with icicles. Erich stops to peer inside them, to listen for the sound of the bees slowly beating their wings to keep warm – but they are empty, have been empty for years.

'Opa Kröning carved those,' says Mama. 'I used to make a lovely bee-sting cake. The doctor from Berlin had two slices and then he said yes.'

Yes, says the breeze that floods the wooden heads, *yes*.

At the shore of the lake Erich brushes the snow from a bench and he and Mama sit and watch the skaters. One boy, dressed in black, flies past the others, leaping and turning, never putting a foot wrong.

'He's very good, isn't he?' says Erich – but Mama is gazing into the distance again.

After a time she says, 'She wanted to come here.'

'Who did?'

'She wanted to look for a giant fish beneath the ice. I didn't like it.'

'A giant fish?' Moving through the weeds, stirring the silt.

A little girl slips and falls and begins to cry, and for a moment nobody goes to her, or even seems to notice her. Erich gets to his feet – 'Is she yours?' says Mama – but now the boy in black is helping her up and she has stopped wailing. Nothing broken.

'What do you mean, a giant fish?' says Erich. 'Mama?'

'Mama?' she echoes.

'Who wanted to come here, Mama?'

'Oh, I don't know. I don't know, it's gone now.'

The boy in black is off again, streaking past the other skaters, and Mama is worrying at the fringe of her scarf, digging her fingers through the tassels.

'There were so many letters,' she says.

'Letters?'

'She must have written him dozens. He's very good-looking, my son. He's perfect. Not like the first one.'

Erich turns away from the skaters and looks at Mama, and she looks right back at him.

'These letters –' he says.

And she says, 'I burned them all.'

The boy in black swoops past them and begins to spin, first holding his arms out straight, then crossing them over his chest to turn faster and faster. Phantom, you are not my equal.

'What was her name?' says Erich, though he already knows; we both already know. Mama doesn't answer, and for a long moment he thinks she has drifted away.

'Sieglinde Heilmann,' she says at last. 'Siggi. That was how she always signed off – *greetings to you and your mother, your Siggi*. And then Sieglinde Thorpe. Oh yes. She kept writing even after she married, if you can believe it. Which just goes to show.'

She falls silent. The temperature has dropped and everyone has left apart from the black skater, who seems to draw closer to them with every circuit. The only sound is blades on ice, knives being sharpened.

'You mustn't blame her,' says Tante Uschi. 'She thought you would run away again. Try to get to West Berlin. It was too dangerous.'

They are changing the sheets on Mama's bed. Erich tucks in the blankets, smoothes the pillows. The sound of the television reaches them: in the living room Mama is watching the Sandman sing his goodnight song. *Children, dear children, I've had a lot of fun . . .*

351

'You don't remember an address, do you?'

'Somewhere in Charlottenburg, I think. But there can't be that many Thorpes in Berlin.'

After Mama is asleep Erich searches the house. He looks in every drawer and cupboard, upends shoeboxes, leafs through piles of receipts that date back twenty years and more. There are no letters from Sieglinde – but hidden in the toe of a slipper, wrapped in a handkerchief, he finds the amber brooch with the diamond at its centre.

'I knew it would turn up,' says Uschi. 'It's not her fault.'

When Erich returns to Leipzig he goes to the post office and looks up the telephone book for Berlin. Tante Uschi is right: there is only one S. Thorpe. That night he begins a letter, then tears it up and throws it away and starts another. For hours he sits at his desk, trying to get the words right, beginning and beginning and beginning.

The Secret That Is Not a Secret

1996
Near Leipzig

All glories of this earth decay, sing the mourners at Mama's funeral. *In smoke and ashes pass away.* Due to the acoustics of the place Erich cannot hear his own voice, only those of the people around him: Karin and Steffi, their husbands and children, Uschi and her son from her second marriage. *Nor rock nor steel can last. What here gives pleasure to our eyes, what we as most enduring prize, is but an airy dream that fadeth fast.* Every now and then Erich thinks he can make out a faint hum, but it must be the echoing of the hymns, the lingering notes of the organ, mustn't it? He wants to get away, to leave this place where he cannot hear himself. Part of his last conversation with Mama keeps returning to him: *He's perfect. Not like the first one.* When he asked Tante Uschi about it she changed the subject, and he was too concerned with finding out about Sieglinde to pursue it. Now, though, the remarks won't leave him, and as he follows the coffin out of the church and watches it sliding into the hearse he asks his aunt again: 'What did she mean? Who was the first one?'

I hold my breath.

'I'm not sure,' says Uschi. She will not look at him. 'You know how she was by that stage.'

The back of the hearse clicks shut; the flowers gaze out

the window with their yellow eyes. Uschi takes Erich's arm and says, 'I'm sorry' – but for what?

'I remember your wedding day,' says Erich. 'Your beautiful dress.' The veil as fine as ashes. The photograph and helmet in place of the groom. The sawn fir branches trickling with sap. The spilled silk in the moonlight, Mama cutting through the parachute lines, Mama pushing the dead man into the hole. 'Uschi, what did she mean? *He's perfect. Not like the first one.*'

His aunt sighs. 'Well,' she begins. 'Well . . .' She leans in close to his ear, pauses again. The hearse's engine starts. Someone is sobbing. 'They had a child, before you,' she whispers. She nods to an acquaintance Erich does not recognise, searches for something in her handbag and does not find it. She clears her throat.

'When?' says Erich. 'Another child?'

'A boy, but it was terribly deformed.'

An elderly man stops to shake Erich's hand and offer his condolences. Uschi waits until he has moved away. Are there tears in her eyes? For whom?

'They wrote a letter,' she says, so quietly Erich hardly hears her. 'They wrote to Adolf Hitler. To request a mercy killing.'

So here I am at last: the false start, the incomplete casting, the secret that is not a secret. There is nothing Erich can say, not now, not with the mourners clasping their hands and sinking their heads. And is it just the organ's final notes hanging in the air, this low hum? Is it the murmuring hearse? *You are the child we were meant to have.* No. No, because now Erich knows that there was another boy, and that there is another story inside his own that is buzzing in its box, wanting out.

Oh Mama, oh Papa. What parents write such a letter? What parents offer cake to the doctor who comes from Berlin to check their child is as damaged as they say, a useless mouth, a life unworthy of life? Look at him sitting on the sofa in his spotless black suit, admiring Mama's needlework. Look at him standing at the window, backlit by fields of wheat. He seems to fill the room.

'I foresee no obstacles,' he says. 'The Führer has already given his permission.'

'We'd like the matter dealt with swiftly,' says Papa. 'To prevent further suffering.'

The doctor nods, accepts another slice of Mama's bee-sting cake.

At the hospital in Leipzig he views me in my little white bed. The future presses in at me from all sides and I buck and writhe, a grub pulled from the earth. *It is blind*, he writes. *Missing a leg and part of an arm. Most likely an idiot.* He consults with the other doctors and they agree this is the right thing to do, the merciful thing. In some maternity wards, they say, when such cases arise, it is quite natural for a doctor to take action. The nurses tuck me in tight. But why do their voices change? And what are they crumbling into my milk? Who rides so late through night and wind?

No one remembers my real name – the records have been lost, as well as the certificate that identified the cause: a weakness of the heart. (Not mine; not mine.) They say, though, that I was the first, a prototype of sorts: that because mercy was shown to me, then mercy should be shown to other infants – the spastics, the epileptics, the half-breeds – and if infants were shown mercy then older children should not go without, and nor, for that matter, should adolescents. The paralysed, the deaf, the delinquent; all must receive their share. And what of the adults? Did they not deserve mercy? The depressive, the senile and insane? Those unable to walk, to speak? And so the mercy grew and spread. At first it came as hunger, as needles and as pills, and then, when we needed more and more of it, as a gas that we piped into sealed vans. Soon, though, the vans could not contain all our mercy, and so we filled rooms with it, rooms big enough to hold hundreds at a time, and it piled up and up, this colourless mercy; there was no stopping it.

And if I had not been chosen he would have chosen someone else, the doctor who visited from Berlin: Mama and Papa were not the only parents to petition the Führer. He would have visited a different home, inspected a different child, and made the same recommendation.

Years later, when he stands in the dock, he says: *For fifteen years I had laboured at the sick-bed and every patient was to me like a brother, every sick child I worried about as if it had been my own.*

And he says: *I am a doctor and I see the law of nature as being the law of reason.*

And he says: *I am deeply conscious that when I said yes to euthanasia I did so with the deepest conviction, just as it is my conviction today, that it was right.*

And he says: *Death can mean relief. Death is life – just as much as birth. It was never meant to be murder.*

And he says: *I bear this burden but it is not the burden of crime. I bear this burden of mine, though, with a heavy heart as my responsibility. Before it, and before my conscience, I prevail, as a man and a doctor.*

And when the day comes, he puts on the red jacket and we walk to the gallows. His son, his only child, has chosen not to visit him one last time, but I climb the thirteen steps with him, count the thirteen coils in the knot. I stand on the platform, I wait for the hood and the noose. He begins to make his final speech but the hood cuts him off mid-sentence. And the trapdoor opens and hangs like a tongue, and I feel the great gulp of space beneath me, and I wait for the snap of the rope, and death can mean relief, and death is life.

The killing of a person is a hard strain on the nerves of the person doing it, say the nurses. *It never occurred to us not to follow the orders given to us. Just as soldiers at the front had to do their duty, so did we.* I peer into their faces but they do not see me. I sit on their shoulders I hang from their ceilings I hunch on their windowsills. *If the patient was extremely restless, which happened quite frequently, then three caregivers were required for the procedure.* I clog the air I am smoke I am shadows, the ghost of the boy I should have become. *The patients were relieved of terrible sufferings. We took them lovingly in our arms and stroked them when we gave them the medicine.*

Mama had herself sterilised after she gave birth to me, so it could not happen again. There she is, lying on the operating table as they lower the mask. There she is, counting backwards, undoing the possibility of me. Ten. Nine. Eight. How proud Papa is of her. What an example she is to her race. And soon she will be a mother again – an orphan is coming from the new Reich. Soon she will get her perfect boy, her reward, and the false start need never be mentioned. I look away.

1997
Berlin

One spring day Erich takes a train to Berlin. First he goes to Normannenstrasse, to the grey concrete Stasi complex he still can't quite believe is open to ordinary people – but there they are, the ordinary people, leafing through piles of buff-coloured folders, finding out about themselves.

For years Karin and Steffi have urged him to request his file – but how could he simply walk into the building on the Dittrichring, right in the centre of Leipzig, where anyone could see him?

'And why would it matter, if someone saw you?' said Steffi.

'Well,' said Erich, 'then they would know what I was doing.'

When he told them he was going on a trip to Berlin, they would hear no more excuses. 'You can ask to read it there,' said Karin. 'We checked.'

Erich's folders stand more than a handspan high. He pulls his chair into the table and looks at them for a moment, not knowing where to start. And then, without thinking, he glances over his shoulder – but of course, nobody is watching him. Nobody is taking notes.

He turns to the last page – the most recent entry, made in 1989 – and begins to read, working his way backwards in

360

time through hundreds of forgotten outings, conversations, purchases. *On 26 April 1975 at 13:07 K r ö n i n g Erich, wearing brown trousers and a blue pullover with brown cuffs and waistband, entered the western hall of the Leipzig Hauptbahnhof on foot. He proceeded through the terminus to the Mitropa kiosk, where at 13:15 he purchased a cup of coffee. The presence or absence of milk could not be ascertained.*

He stares at the flimsy pages, draws them closer until the words turn to dust, but they offer up nothing beyond themselves. Here is his unremarkable life, told by those who shadowed him, who watched from doorways, waited in parked cars, listened on telephone lines. Someone using the codename 'Körner' had sketched a floor plan of his apartment in July 1980 . . . had they passed in the street? Sat next to each other at the bus stop? The dimensions of every room are recorded; the distance from the sofa to the telephone and from his bed to the light switch. He tries to remember back to that summer: was there a day when the apartment felt different? When a picture was crooked, a cupboard left ajar? If Körner had planted something, perhaps it is still in place, even now; perhaps it has kept on transmitting, telling secrets to a country that no longer exists. He turns the pages, skimming the entries, the lines blurring into ribbons of smoke. He thinks of the scraps of paper Sieglinde showed him in the ruined theatre, the little deletions she kept in her pocket like money – *love, mercy, promise, pity, remembrance* – and he wants to pry open all the sentences piled in front of him and splice them in. Backwards he goes, back and back, until he comes to the first page.

MALE: We could build a giant catapult from rubber bands.

FEMALE: They'd have to be big rubber bands.

MALE:	Or hundreds of small ones.
FEMALE:	Thousands.
MALE:	[inaudible]
FEMALE:	A jetpack.
MALE:	Powered by what?
FEMALE:	Compost. Or Rotkäppchen. Or my mother's pickled onions.
MALE:	Would it take both of us?
FEMALE:	Depends on the potency of the pickled onions.
MALE:	[inaudible]
FEMALE:	Telescopic?
MALE:	Yes.

I see him closing the last folder and walking to the front of the room, past all the other people reading their files. 'Thank you,' he says. 'I've finished.' I see him hailing a taxi and asking the driver to take him to Charlottenburg. He stares out the window, looking for something he might recognise. Outside a Kaiser's a young Turkish man is stacking oranges and pineapples, and inside the store, Erich knows, there are ten different kinds of butter, and more than a dozen flavours of yoghurt, and fluorescent lighting hanging from the ceiling like strips of the moon. After the Wall came down, he remembers, he and Bettina would go to the supermarket and stand in front of the rows and rows of different kinds of butter and yoghurt and cereal and jam and have no idea what to choose.

When the taxi drops him off he pauses at the door of the apartment building and puts on his reading glasses, runs his finger down the list of names.

'Erich?' says a voice when he rings the buzzer.

'Yes,' he says. 'Yes, it's me.'

'Come up,' says Sieglinde, and the door opens.

1997
Berlin

On a clear October afternoon a man and a woman take
each other by the hand and make their way towards the
Siegessäule. The sandstone column rises before them, a
great fluted candle, and the figure in gold blazes against
the blue high above, extending her wreath of laurel. The
last time the man and the woman were here they were
children, and the street had a different name, and they
could hardly see for the smoke that stung their eyes and
made them lose their bearings; the golden goddess was a
smudge in the sky, a memory of light. They hesitate for
a moment at the flight of steps that leads underground –
but yes, this is the way, and they pass beneath the buzzing
traffic and surface at the foot of the monument, where they
can see the bullet holes in the granite base. There are holes
in the bronze reliefs, too: in the Prussian soldiers leaving
for battle, and in the flanks of wild-eyed horses, and in
the major general brandishing his sword and the bugler
sounding his horn. A priest with a punctured temple weds
a headless man to a headless bride. The king is without his
foot, the crown prince without his face; old victories drift
apart and fragment. I press myself into these featureless
places, these gaps in the record; I look to the east and the
west. I cast my small shadow, fleeting, imprecise.

Past the glass mosaic we go: past Germania reaching for
her crown, past Barbarossa and his ravens. At the bottom

of the spiral staircase we pause – we are not as young as we used to be – but the doors are open until half past six, and we have time, there is still time. We take it slowly, letting others by, resting and catching our breath. Up and up we climb, all 285 twisting steps, and when we emerge into the bright autumn day Berlin stretches out beneath us in all directions. The roads are rays and we are the heart of the star, and we blink and look up, and there she is, the figure we followed here, larger than we ever thought. She is the past melted down and recast; her gilded wings cup the light.

A young tourist asks Erich to take a picture of him and his girlfriend. 'With the Reichstag in the background, if you can,' he says, and they kiss for the camera.

I watch Erich and Sieglinde: the man I might have been, the woman I might have loved. Yes, we have time, there is still time. Little smudges, traces of light and shadow, breaths in and out. They feel like mine.

The sun is sinking now, and the trees in the Tiergarten are darkening.

Sieglinde says, 'Sometimes it seems like yesterday.'

Erich nods. Beneath us the cars start to switch on their headlights. You and I on a frozen lake, in a swarm of bees. You and I in a buried cellar, in a room full of shrapnel.

She says, 'There's an ice-cream parlour where the theatre used to be. They give you tiny plastic spoons and let you sample the different flavours for free.'

You and I putting the rider on his horse, you and I putting the leaves on the tree.

'I could never find it,' he says. 'The theatre. Nor your aunt's building.'

'That's gone too,' she says.

The shadow of the Soviet memorial lengthens. You and I sleeping and sleeping on an empty stage.

'My daughters want to know who you are,' he says. 'They want to know what happened.'

'Then tell them,' she says. 'Before you start to forget.'

You and I and our stitched-together lives, our haphazard selves. You and I, my rubble girl, my puzzle girl, my love.

I look out at the view. I see a spring, a site of ancient worship filled with the holy bones of birds. I see a warrior leading an army across the city long before the city is there, a man so terrible that no grass grows where his horse has trod. There is nothing to stop him: no mountains, no wide and perilous rivers; nothing but plains. We learn to build our own fortifications. Palisades on our river islands, monasteries on pagan land. With Jewish gravestones we bolster the citadel. We whitewash over the dance of death; white is the usurer, white the burgomaster. The queen hides her children in a field and weaves cornflower wreaths to keep them still. In the royal hunting ground the fox hangs from the hunter's hand and all the trees are firewood. The stone boy and girl hold up the house long after the house has broken. We feel for the jewels in the seams of our clothes. I see searchlights weaving the sky into a bright net; I see werewolves and shadowmen, hanged men and starved men and men wearing twelve watches each; they cut the glass from our windows and the leather from our chairs. The Motherland weeps for her lost sons. We hide microphones in walls and trap human scents in jars and there is no God in the east of the city but that does not mean prayers go unheard. We mark out our death zones, say our goodbyes at the palace of tears. We bury Lenin in the forest, encase the stone sentinels in concrete. We have built on swamp and sand and we will tear down the glass palace, the ballast of the republic, extract its thousand windows.

Out and out I look, out to the Devil's Mountain, out to the alchemist on the island who makes glass instead of gold; out to the dragon's teeth and the foxholes and the wolf's lair, and the camp that rises around the poet's oak. I see blood and earth; I see night and fog. I see two women talking for years, and one is always right and the other never wrong. We tell our children to paint the Wolfsangel on the walls so other children will know whom to kill. The dead bells wait on the dock, nothing lasts, all things earthly fade away. The demon seed gives birth to a magical world. Look: the cathedrals of light reach to heaven. Look: the Führer's face made of fireworks. The quarry I hunt is death.

Beneath the sunken fields, beneath the supermarkets and the car parks and the apartment blocks and the playgrounds, beneath the barley fields and the driveways and the glasshouses and the bus stops, beneath the cinemas and the schools, the bones are moving. They are taking slow shape; they are rearranging themselves into something vast and blind, turning in the rich German earth, rib slotting into socket, clavicle fusing to sacrum, vertebra and metacarpal clipping together like the tracks of toy trains.

Mama, I can still see you, Mama.

She and Papa are lying beneath their feather quilt, the goosedown settling over them as softly as new snow, and they know they have done the right thing, it is a blessing and a relief, and they put themselves to sleep with their tender agreements. And at the clinic the doctor from Berlin is taking my head in his hands. He is hooking his thumb beneath my chin, he is pressing at my throat. He shines a light into my eyes and says I am blind – but I see him, and I see the other doctors leaning in around him, nodding their heads, and I see the nurses making their preparations and doing their duty, over and over again.

Historical Note

The narrator of *The Wish Child* is based on a historical figure, generally referred to in the literature as Child K. The exact details of his short life are unclear; his name, date of birth and death, and even gender are disputed. It is believed, however, that he was a boy who was born blind and with severe disabilities in 1938 or 1939, and that his parents, who most likely lived on a farm near Leipzig, petitioned Adolf Hitler to grant them a mercy killing. Hitler's physician, Karl Brandt, was sent to investigate; after he examined Child K, the infant was put to death, probably at the Leipzig University Children's Clinic.

The murder of Child K marked the very beginning of the Nazis' programme of organised euthanasia, which in turn led to the development of more efficient methods of killing, including the gassing of victims. It is argued, therefore, that the death of Child K was the impetus for the mass murders that were to follow in the camps.

Karl Brandt spoke of the case in his testimony at Nuremberg. He was hanged in 1948.

Note on Sources

The Wish Child is a work of fiction. It is informed by the years I spent living in Berlin during the mid-1990s, as well as by many books and websites that deal with the German experience of the Second World War. The following sources were particularly helpful.

Anonymous. *A Woman in Berlin*. Virago, 2005.

Axis History Forum: forum.axishistory.com

Beck, Earl R. *Under the Bombs: The German Home Front 1942–1945*. The University Press of Kentucky, 1986.

Beevor, Anthony. *Berlin: The Downfall 1945*. Penguin Books, 2003.

Bielenberg, Christabel. *The Past Is Myself*. Ward River Press, 1982.

The German Propaganda Archive (Professor Randall Bytwerk): research.calvin.edu/german-propaganda-archive

Grunberger, Richard. *A Social History of the Third Reich*. Phoenix, 2005.

Kitchen, Martin. *Nazi Germany at War*. Longman, 1995.

Koehn, Ilse. *Mischling, Second Degree: My Childhood in Nazi Germany*. Hamish Hamilton, 1978.

Moorhouse, Roger. *Berlin at War: Life and Death in Hitler's Capital, 1939–45.* The Bodley Head, 2010.

Schmidt, Ulf. *Karl Brandt: The Nazi Doctor.* Hambledon Continuum, 2007.

Schneider, Helga. *The Bonfire of Berlin.* Vintage, 2006.

Shirer, William. *Berlin Diary.* Hamish Hamilton, 1972.

Stargardt, Nicholas. *Witnesses of War.* Pimlico, 2006.

Vassiltchikov, Marie. *The Berlin Diaries 1940–45.* Chatto & Windus, 1985.

Whiting, Charles. *The Home Front: Germany.* Time-Life Books, 1982.

Readers will notice that some aspects of the novel bend the facts: Gottlieb's censorship work, for instance, or Sieglinde's factory trips. I take other smaller liberties with the historical record, too – which is to say, please regard any perceived errors as deliberate.

The novel is threaded through with quotes, some overt, some subliminal. These include German songs and poems, as well as the words of Hitler, Goebbels and Himmler, among others. The book that Brigitte is trying to read on p. 95 is *The Wish Child* by Ina Seidel, a popular 1930s German novel. The 'two possibilities' piece on p. 243 was a real document (published in 1945 in *Rüstzeug für die Propaganda in der Ortsgruppe,* Issue 2); this is my translation.

Excerpts from the following poems open Chapters 2–10, listed here in order. All translations are my own.

'Hands' by Henriette Hardenberg, © 1994 by Arche Verlag, Zürich-Hamburg

'My Songs' by Louise Otto

'September' by Hermann Hesse, *Sämtliche Werke in 20 Bänden*, Herausgegeben von Volker Michels. Band 10: Die Gedichte. © Suhrkamp Verlag Frankfurt am Main 2002. All rights with and controlled through Suhrkamp Verlag Berlin

'On the Death of a Bird' by Eduard Möricke

'Perchance to Dream' by Sophie Hoechstetter

'The House is Bare' by Friedrich Rückert

'The Traveller's Night Song I' by Johann Wolfgang von Goethe

'Who Never Wept to Eat His Bread' by Johann Wolfgang von Goethe

Untitled ['O Lord, grant each of us our own death'], by Rainer Maria Rilke

Acknowledgements

I am grateful for the generous support of the Robert Burns Fellowship at the University of Otago; the Rathcoola Residency in County Cork, Ireland; the University of Waikato/Creative New Zealand Writers' Residency, the University of Otago Wallace Residency at the Pah Homestead, Auckland; the NZSA Peter and Dianne Beatson Fellowship; the DAAD; and Creative New Zealand. Thank you to my publishers Fergus Barrowman and Juliet Brooke; my agent Caroline Dawnay; my Berlin friends Annie and Detlev Brandt, Susan Graunke, Hilary Irving and Kimberley Nelson; and my former German lecturers Hansgerd Delbrück, Peter Russell, Monika Smith and Margaret Sutherland. Thank you also to Tusiata Avia, Kate Camp, Tanya Carlson, Pat Chidgey, the Krumstroh family, Robyn Lynch, Kirsten McDougall, Kirstine Moffat, Keely O'Shannessy, Fiona Pardington, Sophie Scard, Sally-Ann Spencer, Cindy Towns and Ashleigh Young. Particular thanks to Bert Rosenthal (International Outreach, Federal Commissioner for the Stasi Records/BStU) for his patient answering of my many questions; to Tracey Slaughter for her unwavering support and friendship; and especially to my little family, Alan Bekhuis and Alice Chidgey.

I did not want to risk identifying my narrator by including him on the dedication page at the start, so here at the end of the story I make my second dedication: to the memory of Child K.

Author photograph by Helen Mayall

CATHERINE CHIDGEY's debut novel, *In a Fishbone Church*, won the Betty Trask Prize, Best First Book in the Commonwealth Writers' Prize (South East Asia and Pacific Region), and was long-listed for the Orange Prize. Her second novel, *The Strength of the Sun*, was a *New York Times* Notable Book of the Year. *Sunday Express* (UK) called her third novel, *The Transformation*, "a highly original read, as beautiful as it is terrifying." Chidgey is the recipient of the 2017 Janet Frame Fiction Prize, and lives in Ngaruawahia, New Zealand.

Printed in the United States
by Baker & Taylor Publisher Services